THE LAUGHING MAN CHRONICLES

THE LAUGHING MAN

ROBERT J BARLOW

The Laughing Man

A copy of this publication can be found in the National Library of Australia.

ISBN: 978-0-6480613-6-6
Also available as an e-book

Published by Ouroborus Book Services
www.ouroborusbooks.com

Cover by Sabrina RG Raven: www.sabrinargraven.com

The Laughing Man
Robert J Barlow

Allowing space for dedications for everyone involved in writing this book would likely be longer than the book itself. Suffice to say then that if you think you're entitled to some of the credit, you are, if you think you were involved in the process you were, and if you think I should be grateful to you.

I am.

More than I could say

A homeless man wandered the streets of Berlin, his hair was thinning and he wore three threadbare coats over each other, pushing his few possessions in a shopping cart. He shook his head and searched for something, his hands roaming through thin air as he became frustrated. A black sedan pulled up in front of him and four men in suits got out. Without a word, they bundled the struggling man into the car and took off. They were never seen again.

In New York a young woman with a power suit and power hair made her way out of work, cutting a shortcut down an alley and plugging her headphones into her ears. A tall, bald man in a leather jacket approached her from behind, the sound of boots on gravel obscured by the tune. She hit the ground seconds later.

In London, a mohawked musician slung a guitar onto his back and walked out of the bar he'd been playing in. He sung softly to himself and stopped when three beautiful women approached him. He gave them his most charming smile and the most stunning of them approached him. She leaned up to kiss him and broke his neck.

On the Stockholm leg of her tour a popular teen singer was gunned down in broad daylight. Security reports said she was shot by a crazed fan. The police never identified the killer.

A pair of children ran through the Beijing streets, scrambling and stumbling through a crowd. They tried to give away no angle of attack, to vanish into the crowd and hide behind people. They didn't blend well enough.

A building that contained the boardroom of a fortune 500 company was bombed. The explosion took out several floors and cost thousands of innocent lives, including the company's entire board. No clear motive was presented.

Only one thing was found in common on every scene. Two circles, one white with a red dagger inside it and one black with two intersecting triangles.
To those who didn't understand, it seemed random, like a sudden burst of unreasonable violence in a world full of unreasonable violence. Dead men and women in a world of dead men and women. Senseless tragedy in a world of senseless tragedy.

To those who did understand, the answer was clear. The Seraph were falling, the Eldritch were rising, and the Legion and Lost were going to war.

It was harvest time. Magical potential was about to be discovered and for a few of those who would be caught in the crossfire there would be adventures, or tragedies. The rest, would be found by the wrong side and killed before they ever began to understand why.

Forty seconds either way changed everything for one.

CHAPTER ONE

Adam Westbrook made his way home from a house party he'd been at until later than he should have, shaking his head as he walked. He'd probably been too drunk to make this a good idea, and he'd definitely been too drunk to get in without waking his housemates and having to answer some awkward questions.

The late-night bus pulled up at his stop and he got to his feet, carefully putting one foot in front of the other until he made it out the door. Shit, his head was already spinning, this was stupid. He took a shortcut across the street, one foot in front of the other, not more than a few hundred steps from home, right? Shouldn't be a problem.

He could take a break in the park, get his breath back. He made his way across the street to the park and admired the familiar scenery. The swings, did he want to go on the swings? He liked the swings after a couple of drinks. Made him feel like a stupid kid again. No, bad idea, things were spinning, he was too far gone for that to not go bad.

He took a few more steps and found the bench, falling back onto it. That was it, he could wait until his head cleared, then get himself home. Where the keys? He checked his pockets, patting himself down. Everything was spinning, if it could just stop spinning for half a second he could find them.

'Fuck.' *Okay, spare key it was. Where was the spare key? Wouldn't be too hard, couldn't be too hard, he'd find it.*

3

'Excuse me, Sir?'

The guys he was looking at looked too rich to be here. They were both in blue suits with watches and ties. They looked like they were brothers, tall, short slicked back hair and the exact same smile.

'Yeah? Whatcha want?' He blinked to clear his eyes and looked at them.

'Are you lost?' The taller of the two looked at him. The smile was widening. Too many teeth, it looked like he had too many teeth.

'Huh?' He shook his head and yawned.

'Huh?' the other one mimicked him, pulling a comically stupid look on his face. The taller one shook his head and smiled, leaning down to look at Adam.

'I asked if you were lost, Sir,' he repeated.

'No.' He managed to shake his head. Maybe these guys were okay after all. 'I'm good. I live down the street from here. Just clearing my head.'

'Well then,' he shook his head and sighed, 'that is quite disappointing. I was truly hoping you were lost.'

'Look guys.' He shook his head and got to his feet, stumbling a little. 'You're starting to creep me out.' He didn't want to get up, but he really didn't want to be here with these weirdos. It was only when he looked back at them he saw that the shorter brother was pulling a knife out of his coat.

'Yes well,' the taller one said, taking a step in front of the short one so he couldn't see it. 'This is our nature, nothing we can do about it. We are unsettling and it breaks our hearts. Not to worry though, you shouldn't have to endure it long.'

'I'm afraid I can't let you do that gentlemen.' The voice from the other side of the park didn't even look alarmed. Adam's fear was sobering him up and he could see the weirdo for what he was. He was tall, thin and smiling, wearing a bright red suit with a black shirt, a black top hat and no shoes. His smile was too wide and creepy, just like the suited guys. 'After all, killing a boy before he even has a chance to get lost, that's just ungentlemanly. It is the action of a coward, the lowest and most contemptible act and I'm afraid I must step in.'

'Must you?' The two suited men turned to the new voice, the smaller of them was actually laughing a little. Adam got up and walked backwards. He should run, take advantage of this psycho's distraction to get away.

'Yes.' The man in the top hat spun the silver cane in one hand, in the other he was smoking a cigarette in a long, old fashioned style holder. He took a moment to blow smoke and looked across them. 'I'm afraid I must. I have no desire to do so, and I will take no enjoyment in it.' He laughed and shook his head. 'That's a lie, but I have to give you the chance to retreat. So, feel free. Go on.' He flicked one hand. 'Scat.'

'Well since you have such a fanciful parlance then allow me to respond,' the taller one said turning around to face him and advanced. 'We feel disinclined to retreat and since you have chosen to make this business your own we will have no choice but to inhume both you and the young gentleman. Prepare yourself.'

'He means we're gonna kill ya both.' The small man suddenly grew, his skin going dark and thickening, his body twisted and grew bigger, bulkier. He wasn't short anymore, his hands doubled, doubled again, doubled again and grew massive, his claws hooking and twisting.

He looked at Adam and raised his hooked hands. The tall one had become taller and thinner, paler and his arms had extended into long whip like tentacles. He then sprouted more and more of them. He smiled at Adam again as his mouth vanished and his skull contracted into a white skull with two slit-like eyes.

'Slender man,' he whispered, suddenly feeling much sicker than the booze had made him.

'Very good,' the man said softly in a harsh rasp. 'Now you will die, in agony. You have two minutes left to live.' His tentacles began to swing and whip as he advanced on Adam, then turned around as he heard a whistle.

'My apologies,' the man in the top hat said, dropping his cigarette holder in his pocket, then removing his jacket slowly and swinging it over his shoulder. 'But I fear I will not be able to give you that long. Some of us have things to do tonight.'

The guy removed his hat and threw it in the air. As eyes went up toward the hat he made his move. He ran toward the two figures and the cane flashed, a sword slipping out of the dark wood. He slid between the black one's legs and rolled forward to his feet, ignoring the tentacles and simply moving out of their way. He turned and tossed the coat over the shelled creature's head, then spun around, pushing the sword clean through its body. The sword glowed for a moment and the Slender man fell into a puddle of goo. He took a few steps and caught the hat, chuckling a little.

'Kill you!' the big creature roared.

'Ole!' He turned and tossed his hat at the creature's arms and the band cut them clean off. He hurled the sword at the back of the creature's head, landing it between a crack in the armour on the neck. The creature buckled and fell, collapsing into goo, which immediately caught fire around his jacket. He walked over, picked it up and slipped the sword away, fetching his hat and throwing his coat back over his shoulder. The smell of tar and burned plastic filled the park and Adam threw up, his dinner and lunch pouring into a puddle on the floor.

'Sorry.' He burped and slumped back on the bench.

'Think nothing of it.' The hat was back on his head now and he flashed a kind of nice smile. He had a comforting face, kinda, well, if he was a little drunker he would have called the guy pretty. 'Natural reaction to one's first encounter with a Blank,' a hand was on his shoulder. 'Put your head between your legs and breathe deep, focus on that. One, two, three, breathe, one, two, three, breathe, one, two, three, breathe. Do you have the pattern?'

'I do.' He nodded. 'Thanks.' He let himself breathe for a while, then straightened up. 'What the hell just happened?'

'Never mind about that.' The top hat man smiled, putting his jacket gently around Adam's shoulders. 'Where are you?'

'In a park.' He shrugged. 'In Brisbane, near my house. Why?'

'Where are you going?' the voice was calm, but it rang warning bells in Adam's addled brain.

'Home,' he shook his head. 'Why do you wanna know?'

'The suspicion.' He nodded. 'That's good for you, well done.' He slapped a hand on his back. 'I just wanted to know if you were lost.' He said it like it really mattered, like being lost was something important to be. 'But if you know where you are and know where you're going then I suppose that would be about the furthest thing in the world from lost, is it not?'

'Yeah.' He shivered a little and held the coat closer to him. 'Yeah I guess so.' The guy pulled the jacket closed around him and, all of a sudden, he was warm. 'What the hell just happened?'

'You already asked that.' He smiled and started to walk Adam down the street. 'Though I suppose now would be the time for it. 'I killed a pair of monsters who wished to end your life. Who are you?'

'Adam.' He smiled up at the weirdo. 'I'm Adam.' The sober part of his mind tried to tell him he didn't want this guy knowing where he lived, but the bigger drunker part told him it was fine and to stop whining. 'You?'

'You may call me Xavier.' The man chuckled a little. 'Or you may call me the Top Hat Man, or the Red Gentlemen. Any of the names are appropriate, and any would be welcome.'

'Xavier.' So the guy was a little nuts, who wasn't? The world had apparently turned a little nuts lately, a few more days like this and he might take to wearing stupid hats and funny names himself. 'What were those things, the Slender man and the... other one?'

'Slender man.' Xavier nodded and the voice had a chuckle in it again. It seemed like half of what the odd man did was laughing. 'Yes, the things you see on the internet were based on psychological triggers implanted by sightings of those beings. I suppose it is as good a name as any for them. Very well, the things you call the Slender men are inhuman servants of the Legion, the least of these servants. Believe it or not they were men once, men like you and me.' He paused and appeared to be thinking for a moment. 'Well, like you anyway. They lost their faces and destinies. Now they have only what the Legion chooses to give them.' He spat on the ground.

'Oh.' He nodded. 'So, you're insane.'

Xavier appeared to think about that as they walked down the quiet suburban street, a couple of street lights flickering onto them as they walked. It seemed so strange, walking through normal streets and houses, a car in the middle of the night cruising slowly down the street slowed down just a little to look at them. 'Well that is actually distinctly plausible. I may be insane. That is a definite possibility that I have discussed in my very own cranium.' He knocked his skull with his knuckles.

'I may be mad, off my rocker, out of my mind, losing my marbles. I may be going around the bend or up the wall,' he said, poking Adam in the chest, 'but you saw the thing I saw, you watched me kill what I killed. So, either you're as mad as I am, or a great deal madder, to imagine a figure like me.' The man considered for a moment. 'Or I've imagined you, which makes your relative sanity rather unimportant doesn't it?'

'I'm seein' shit,' he decided. 'That's what it must be. Someone slipped something into my drink and now I'm seein' shit. All I gotta do is get home, fall asleep and I'll be fine.'

'Let us hope.' Xavier smiled. 'If we are lucky then when you awaken you have no memory of anything that has just happened and can live your entire life never experiencing anything like it again.' He handed Adam his top has and Adam took it, though the man kept his hand on it. 'But just in case you do remember everything, let me give you something worth remembering.'

With that he turned sharply, spun on his heel and

threw Adam through his own second story window, the hat spinning in his hand, and him spinning as he flew, by some miracle of luck ending up just the shape to get in the window.

Adam fell onto his bed and held his stomach for a moment. He shook a little and tried not to puke, he closed his eyes and took a few deep breaths. He must have walked upstairs, and just thought he was flying through the sky by a strange man's hat. He relaxed against his bed, pulling his shirt and the jacket off. It was time for bed, everything would be better tomorrow. The dark room lit up by streetlights was covered in his familiar posters and he stared at them, letting the familiar figures comfort him.

'Excuse me, Sir?' He was shaken out of his admiration of a movie poster by the voice. The voice was soft, but it carried. 'If you would not mind tossing me down my hat? You may keep the jacket if you should so desire. It is a fine garment, but I have more of its kin. However, I require my hat, as it is unique in all the world.'

Adam looked down at the hat, he hadn't realised he was holding it, but one of his hands was still gripping it so tightly his knuckles were white. He got up, walked to the window and threw it out, making a token attempt to aim for Xavier. Xavier reached up and caught it with ease, smiling widely and waving before he headed off down the street, twirling his cane in one hand as he walked.

'I'll go to sleep,' he said to no one in particular,

laying down and pulling the blanket over him. 'I'll go to sleep, and I'll wake up with a headache, heave my guts and this'll all have been some kinda screwed up dream.' He closed his eyes and quickly enough he was asleep, the warm comfort of the dark, letting him forget for a few hours.

Adam woke up with a smaller hangover than he expected, and no need to throw up. He managed to make it to the bathroom and start brushing his teeth to get the corpse stink that came with a long night of drinking out of it before he remembered the night before.

'Must've been spiked,' he said to himself, spitting toothpaste into the sink, then moved into the shower, remembering that he hadn't showered after, well, afterwards. He took his time getting himself clean, letting the hot water wash off tired body and mind alike, and by the end of it had more or less convinced himself that the whole last night had been a kind of weird, but very interesting dream when he stepped back to his room. That the mysterious Xavier was some weird picture in his mind and things like that simply didn't happen. He headed in with a smile on his face and...

'No.' He looked down. 'No no no, this is not happening!'

But it was, regardless of what he thought and with no regard for his protests a red suit jacket sat on his chair. It was slightly rumpled and messy, but it was still bright red and laying exactly where he'd left it. He bent down and picked it up, and it felt just like the fabric he'd felt, that strange softness that suits didn't usually have. He pulled it on and felt the same strange warmth he'd worn that night.

'What is that?' He heard a voice from the background and turned around, wrapped in a towel and wearing a jacket. He shook his head and closed the door, pulling on some pants and then stepping back out holding the jacket.

Bethany was Adam's roommate, one of them anyway. They lived in a two-bedroom house along with her long-time boyfriend. She was nice enough Adam supposed. She cleaned up after herself, didn't get in his way and neither of them bothered him, but they weren't exactly close.

'Hey.' He held the jacket up. 'You like it? I picked it up last night, someone left it behind.'
She thought about it for a second, one blond eyebrow raising thoughtfully. Bethany always thought about anything before she spoke. 'I mean it's not exactly your usual style.'

'My usual style hasn't done wonders for me lately. Maybe this will be the start of a whole new thing.' He smirked. 'Or maybe I'll leave it in the closet forever.'

'You got any plans for the day?'

He'd have to go back to university soon, the break was over in a couple of days, and he intended to make the most of it.

'I'm gonna eat, game, crash, that's the plan. I might

go outside at some point if I absolutely have to.'

'All right, well, you have fun now.' She smiled, then turned and closed the door behind her. He sat down on the bed and stared at the coat. Had he really seen what he thought he'd seen? Had some kind of red-suited lunatic really cut through two monsters and set things on fire, with this coat no less?

'I'm going nuts.' He shook his head and pulled some clothes on., There was only one sure-fire way to find out. He tucked the coat under his arm and headed out.

'I thought you had no plans?'

'Fresh air and sunlight is good for headaches.' He rolled his shoulders. 'I have one.' He headed out of the door and to the park at the end of the street. There were no kids there, because police tape covered the scene. He didn't hesitate. Normally the idea of stepping over a police cordon would have terrified him but today, for whatever reason he wasn't even shaken. He pushed it away with one hand and walked through the park to the place the fight had been.

There were ash marks, strange footprints and, there it was, a puddle of black goo sitting on the ground, bubbling gently as he looked at it. He looked at it and unfolded the coat. This would prove it, this would prove that none of it was real, he fanned it out and laid it over the goo. After a few seconds of nothing happening, he picked the coat up and turned to leave only to reveal the grass being scorched and blackened away.

'What the fuck?' He looked at the ground. He looked at the coat to reveal only a small scorch mark on the cloth. He folded it up and looked at it for a few long moments, then realised he'd sat down without meaning to.

It didn't make any sense, but he'd never not trusted his own eyes before. He leaned back on the ground and shook his head. What the hell was going on, and what was he going to do about it? There were suited freaks that turned into Slender men, and guys in coats that could make black goo burst into flames and had a magic hat. He had a cane sword and talked all weird and there were monsters in the world.

He lay there for five minutes before he remembered that there was police tape in the park and people were driving by. Not wanting to end up arrested he got to his feet and walked home, trying to talk some sense into himself.

He spent the rest of the day trying to distract himself, playing games, each one given up on within half an hour, drawing and writing. He tried entertaining himself with his roommates but he got bored pretty quickly, and he slept badly that night, dreams of monsters and fire and blades in the dark. He hung the coat on the door of his closet, looking back at it every time he tried to convince himself that something didn't happen.

It was important to face reality no matter how ridiculous it was, no matter how little you liked it you had to face it. His old man had taught him that, it was important to be realistic, even when reality was insane. Of course his dad had been talking about his mum leaving, not the existence of monsters, but it boiled down to the same thing. He had no intention of deluding himself further; this was his reality now. So how was he going to deal with it?

He'd keep his eyes open and wait. He'd have to.

Everything was more or less normal for the next few weeks. He went back to university, hung out with friends, flirted, goofed off in class and lapsed into his usual patterns of drinking, socialising and occasionally studying. Until the day he saw the Top Hat Man again. He was in Queen Street, getting something to eat with his friends when, walking down the middle of the busy mall, was that obvious hat.

'Do you see that guy?' he pointed to him. 'The one with the hat?'

'No.' His friend Shelly shrugged. She was usually the first to notice any man who stood out. As she looked around, apparently unable to see the man who was right in front of her face he dropped his meal and got up, walking away from the group. 'Where are you going?'

'Gotta do something.' It was the best answer he could give, though it wasn't exactly a good one.

He moved quickly across the food court and hid behind a pillar, watching the strange, jacketed man as he moved. The top hatted man moved through the group and Adam followed, trying to keep to the crowd and ducking his head under normal people's sight lines.

He didn't really know anything about tailing people, other than the fact that you should do your best not to look at them too often and try not to be seen, so he ducked in and out of a few shops to keep busy. He had to let himself get ahead of him a couple of times so he could avoid looking two suspicious, only to realise, after one of them, that the guy had taken an unexpected turn and he'd lost him.

He took a lucky guess and found him again. This process repeated itself a few times, losing the man for seconds or even minutes before finding him again. For a tall guy with a top hat and a cane he was surprisingly good at not being followed. Honestly, Adam was starting to wonder if the guy didn't want to be seen, why wasn't he taking his hat off?

'Though if I'm going to be asking that kind of question I might consider asking why I'm spending my afternoon following a complete stranger down alleyways rather than, you know, going to him and asking what the hell is going on,' he muttered angrily to himself. 'Or better yet, letting the hell go and going back to my friends.' But he kept moving, ignoring the few strange glances he was getting for mumbling to himself. The streets of Brisbane weren't exactly crowded, but there were more people than he was used to having to deal with.

In the end, he managed to follow the guy into a tiny

café he'd never seen before, a little hole in the wall place covered in graffiti he only just realised was on purpose. He took a few seconds to gather up his courage; he was supposed to talk to the guy, right? Then he should go talk. He took a couple of breaths and walked inside.

The place kept up the graffiti theme all throughout, every wall painted with imaginative designs. The bar stools, because apparently it was a bar and café, were made of what looked like junk sculptures you sat on. He took a deep breath and sat down at one of them, ordering himself a coffee and looking around, the bartender/barista, a small tattooed man with three piercings in his eyebrows nodded to him as he studied the place.

Since the top hat man hadn't come out, and there wasn't a stage or a private area he could be in, he'd have to go into the staff only areas. He'd have to slip back there one way or the other. He walked over to one of the tables near the back and started to sip from the cup, sitting down at the booth. He waited until no one was watching him and slipped through the "staff only" door.

Behind the staff only door was pretty much what you'd expect, a small hallway and a stockroom. As he pushed his way into the stockroom, stacked high with supplies, coffee, cutlery, cookware and a bunch of cardboard boxes full of god only knew what. He was halfway into the room and headed for the back door when the lights went out.

'Jesus!' He jumped back. 'What the hell is going on?'

'Where are you?' The voice coming from directly behind him was soft and quiet, and he didn't recognise it.

'What's going on here?'

'Where are you?'

'Turn the fucking lights back on!' Adam moved across the room and fumbled for the switch, but he found nothing.

'Where are you?' The voice was different this time, but still male, from the other side of the room. He backed himself against the wall, if someone came at him he at least wanted his back to something solid.

'In a café, somewhere.' His voice was cautious.

'And where is that café?' The voice was calm, infinitely patient, like it could stand there asking one question for the rest of its existence.

'I don't know,' he admitted. 'Now let me out of here!'

'Where are you going?' He jumped. The voice from behind him was a woman, and it was from behind him, in spite of the fact his back was to the wall. He reached up, but there was no vent or hole in the wall. Take a deep breath Adam, be as calm and honest as you can until you can get the hell out.

'I don't know,' he shrugged. 'Wherever the hat guy's going I guess.'

'Doesn't sound like much of a plan.'

'There wasn't exactly a destination in mind.' He headed across the walls, checking the shelves with his hands. He grasped something that felt solid and heavy in one hand and made ready to swing it if anyone touched him.

'Who are you?' The third voice wasn't from behind him, it was from across the room, this voice was deeper and hoarser and from the far corner.

'My name,' he took a couple of deep breaths and held his fear back, don't let them see you're scared, 'is Adam.' But his voice wavered a little. Dammit now they knew he was scared, still, he was blind, surrounded and locked in a room so it was a pretty reasonable time to be afraid.

'Oh?' the woman's voice rang out from over his shoulder again. 'And what does it mean to be Adam?' This time he saw her, a brief movement, a quick flash of long hair over his shoulder. She gave a soft melodious laugh.

'What do you mean what does it mean?' He shook his head and lashed out with one hand to push her away from him, making no contact at all.

'What does it mean to be Adam? What does it mean to be you?' She was in front of him and he saw her for a second, just a flash of pale skin and dark eyes.

'I don't fucking know,' he snapped. 'What does it mean to be anyone?'

'Doesn't know where he is.' The light flashed on, a figure in the corner with a deep hood and a jacket.

'Doesn't know where he's going,' the first voice spoke again, showing a tall man with spiked hair. It revealed thick shoulders, folded arms and a vest.

'Knows who he is,' the girl spoke up again and the light

flicked on, showing a whirl of colour on a female form.

'But doesn't know what it meant to be him.' This last one he could recognise by the red jacket and black top hat. The light began to flicker, showing the different figures one by one. First the hat man, the hooded man, the woman, and the big man, again and again, finer and finer details showing.

Finally, they all appeared around him, moving slowly without ever seeming to take a step. The tall guy wore black gloves and vest, he had a mohawk and a tattoo of the word LOST on his skull. The girl had green and pink hair, a long rainbow skirt and a heavy black jacket. She had about a dozen piercings in her face. The next figure was a small, hooded man, all in black.

'Seems lost to me,' they all said together.

'What's going on?' He swung what turned out to be a coffee maker at the big one's head, who took the hit. The metal crumpled on his skull and he ignored it completely.

'All things will be explained in time,' he said softly. 'But first, we need you to answer a question.'

'Are,' the woman spoke.

'You,' the man in the hood muttered.

'Lost?' the hat man finished. He tried to get out, pushing at the hooded man and then the girl, neither of them moved, standing as solid as if he was pushing solid steel. He heard the question echoed in his head over and over again. Are you lost, are you lost, are you lost?

'Yes!' he screamed. 'Yes, okay I am!' He looked at

them for a few more moments and then the lights went out. In front of him the lights began to flicker faster and faster and the room filled up with bodies. People who looked strange and odd and different and frightening and beautiful in a hundred different ways. He saw a woman naked but for hundreds of tattoos that covered every inch of her skin. He saw a man dressed like a Victorian dandy wearing a metal arm, he saw a tall man in a business suit, hunched and howling like an animal as claws burst from his hands. He saw and he saw and he saw.

The world around him shifted, and he felt like he was spinning and falling plummeting and then standing still on the air, on the air in a giant city he'd never been to; a city he didn't think anyone had ever been to. The skyscrapers went up as far as he could see, massive buildings of glass, concrete and steel, but no colour. As he looked around he saw hundreds of people in suits, women with power hair in grey outfits, men who were bald, or balding, or had over-styled slickness about them, walking down the street looking at one another, chatting about things he couldn't see.

'They know who they are,' the voice rang across the sky. 'They know where they're going, and where they came from. They know that this is their world. They have had the fact that they own it comfortably explained to them ever since they were young, and they continue in that knowledge their entire lives. They do not look around, they do not look inside, they are contented and do not need to. That is their right, burden, and privilege. They have the ability to know what they are and what they do, and, in exchange all they must do is stay on their path.'

Suddenly he was on the street, and walking with this crowd of people who didn't notice him. He saw the path, a simple red line that everyone followed. None of them looked at him or met his eyes. They didn't move to step away from him, they just, didn't seem to be in his path, even when he moved directly into theirs, their path simply changed to not include him. As soon as he did, he saw a large black clad man whose eyes swung to meet his. He moved confidently toward Adam and in spite of the fact he'd seen eyes just a moment before he could swear the man in black had no face.

As he moved they turned to step around him, rather than the unconscious parting for Adam. He reached Adam and seized him gently but forcefully, leading him calmly and silently back onto the clear path. The implication of a smile appeared on the faceless face, and he turned back to the crowd.

'The Legion is what guides them, the Legion is what controls them, the Legion is what keeps them safe in exchange for their freedom, for their will, their right to choose any path other than the one they were born to. Walk the Legions path and you will be safe, as long as you continue to walk it as the path grows ever more narrow.' He had walked off the path without realising it and the faceless creature turned its head. He knew it could see him, it was looking at him, and this time when it reached him it wouldn't be a gentle correction.

It started toward him, and the people moved out of black suit's way; not in the gradual general way they got out of Adam's, or even the neutrality with which they moved before but with deliberate intent. He shifted them, gently but firmly from his path and Adam took off running down an alley shoving without restraint. He pushed a few of the suited people who didn't move fast enough into black suit's path, forcing him to correct them as he moved and giving Adam a little space to manoeuvre. He saw a bridge passing over a river, took a deep breath and dove in, landing with a small splash in the freezing water. It seized up his muscles and knocked the wind out of his lungs, but he managed to swim to underneath the bridge, righting himself to breathe and hanging onto the support pillar.

'What the hell is going on?' he asked the voice that seemed to be everywhere and nowhere.

'The Legion locates the extreme, the strange, the wild and uncatchable. They kettle and control them, and the ones they cannot control they destroy.' Suddenly he could see so much clearer, his eyes zooming in on the man in black, his eyes scanning the area. 'This is the world as it truly is, beyond the world you know, beyond all you see and understand. The place you see here is truer than reality, though it may be only the smallest piece of the puzzle. Until you have seen what you need to see you must not return to the world you know.'

Suddenly he was dry again, standing on the street, the cold slowly leaving his bones. He took a few deep breaths and looked around for the ones in black. He saw four, but none close and none with eyes. This time he kept himself unobtrusive, walking slowly and following the path of the others. He stayed quiet and made sure not to bump into anyone or walk off the path.

And then he saw the others doing the same. People taking too much care to walk with the others, people who flashed with colours and brightness, glitter and shine. As he watched them he saw hair falling long, piercings in their faces, flashes of emblems across their skin. On some it was subtle, a suited man whose hair was a little wild and smiled a little wide. A woman with streaks in her hair and her dress showing a little more than the others, taking care to stay in lockstep with three other women. Then, in a sudden momentary flash of movement she disappeared down an alley, unnoticed by anyone. Anyone but Adam that is.

'These are the Lost,' came the voice. 'They have stepped off their own paths, opened up their own roads, ignored the path that was so deliberately and clearly laid out for them, or refused to compromise themselves to walk it forever. Those who refuse to accept where they are, where they are going and what they must do have no choice but to make their own path. Some are born without a path, others choose not to have one. They will destroy the Legion if they can, and have everyone free, even if it endangers themselves and the world around them. This may not be a wise choice, but it may be the right one.

If you intend to lose yourself, then you must accept this reality. You must endeavour to find a better path than the one you were on. It is fine to break something, but you must have something to replace it with. You may attempt this if you wish.' Adam turned down an alley, following the running girl, picking up his own pace.

She didn't move with panic, but with joy and soon she filled the air with laughter. She kicked out at a panel in the ground and it fell away, allowing her to slip down it. As she reached up to replace it he took it from her gently. She gave him a smile with bright blue eyes as he took the panel and then turned from him and headed off running. He slipped down, popped the panel back in place and dropped onto the ground. He started to walk down a sloping path as the world lit up around him. As the lights went up the faintly glowing figures started to light up like beacons.

The lights on the roof, as well as the ones whirling off the people, lit up the strange architecture, buildings lit up in abstract art styles with no consideration for practicalities and statues that made no sense at all. The colour scheme seemed to be more or less completely random. And the people! They seemed to be playing a series of weird games, jumping and playing, painting the walls and putting on strange performances for each other. They used the architecture as an obstacle course as they ran from building to building. In front of Adams eyes, a large man, lit up with yellow, ran up the slope, waving at him as he ran past, launching himself up and knocking the top of the panel loose in order to climb up and out.

'What is this place?' he whispered. To his surprise the response wasn't a voice that came from nowhere, it came from behind and below him. The man with the LOST tattoo smiled, climbed up a pole and came to rest beside Adam, the tattoo burning bright red on his scalp.

'It's one of the lands of the Lost, the silent hidden places, known only to those who don't know who they are, or where they're going.' He laughed and settled on his feet, wiping his gloved hands on his pants.

'Who are you?'

'Call me Pan,' he smiled.

'A member of the Lost, called Pan?' he stared at the man, who had the decency to look a little embarrassed.

'It's a little on the nose I know.' He nodded. 'But yeah, and now you've found the place, I can show you the way out if you like.'

'Okay, but first,' he looked around, 'what is, all of this?'

'This place is a Lost bolt hole in the Upper City. In any one place we can see, there are always at least three places in reality. The one you know, the upper world, which belongs to the Seraph, and the lower world, which belongs to the Eldritch.'

'What are, those things you just said?'

'The Seraph are the creatures that live above our world. They've been angels, they've been called aliens and they've been called plenty of other things. Everything in their world starts out bright, white, silver, gold, shining and sparkling, eerie and glowing. The Eldritch...' Pan almost seemed possessed as he talked, spreading his arms wide, the light inside him blazing brighter and brighter, a gleaming white and purple spiral.

'The Eldritch are the beings that live below. They've been called demons and boogeymen and a dozen other things too. They live in places that are dark, black, purple and blue, slithering and shadowy, passionate and warm.' With that he turned in three sixty and fell on his back on a ruined looking couch that was sitting there for no good reason. He relaxed into the cushions and Adam sat down beside him. 'Our worlds reflect each other, but they don't affect each other, except during harvest time.'

'Harvest time?' Adam looked away from the other man and stared at his hands for a long moment. 'Well, that's... ominous.'

Pan pulled a pack of cigarettes out of his jeans and tapped one out for himself, then offered one to Adam, who waved it away. 'Oh, it is more than ominous.' He lit up and took a long puff. 'The harvest is what happens when the walls between the worlds start to crack and leak. Powers from the Eldritch and Seraph begin to bleed into our world, and if we are quick and clever we can take that power and use it to strengthen ourselves. It lets us walk between worlds, and use that power to make ourselves stronger.' He shook his head.

'If we are very smart, and very quick, and very lucky. Anyway, some of us show potential to become Legionnaires, and some show potential to get Lost. While we're busy recruiting, those of us who are a little less than scrupulous,' he grabbed Adam's head and forced him to look the bigger man in the eye, 'attempt to track down the other side's potential recruits and remove them before they can access any power.' He released his head.

'As I'm certain you remember,' the familiar voice came from his other side, as Xavier jumped over the couch to land on Adam's other side, 'from when the Blanks were trying to do that to you before I strode onto the scene.' He gave a strange little bow from the waist from his seated position. 'You are welcome, by the way.'

'Well if it aint the Top Hat Man.' Pan held up the spare cigarette, sounding more annoyed than pleased. 'How ya doin'?'

'Well enough.' He snagged the cigarette and put it behind his ear before looking at Adam. 'So you managed to find your way here after all? I can't say I'm surprised. I do hope you managed to get some use out of my old coat?' He ran his hands down his new one, which was exactly the same. 'As you can see I crafted a new one, so you are welcome to retain the last.'

'Thanks man.' He didn't know what else to say. 'So what, this was an entrance exam? I get to be one of you now?'

'Well,' the Top Hat Man made a show of being uncomfortable, though Adam didn't buy it, 'less get to and more, must be one of us now.' He sighed and shook his head. 'I am explaining this poorly. You are one of us. You have been one of us ever since the Blanks first identified you as a threat. You will need our help until you have something to defend yourself with.'

'So what?' He got up off the couch and turned to them. 'I'm supposed to just go by some weird new world's rules all of a sudden?' He spread his arms. 'I'm supposed to just accept all this?' He dropped his arms and shook his head. 'Fuck that I'm going home. I'm not dealing with this. Pan, take me home now.'

'That is of course your choice,' Xavier said with a smile. 'Well, good luck.'

'Really?' Pan snapped. 'That's it, you're not going to warn him or anything?'

'Well he's obviously a clever lad.' Xavier's patronising tone dripped from his lips. 'I wouldn't want to put any undue duress on him. He might feel forced, and that's bad.'

'Worse than him feeling dead?' Pan folded his arms.

'I don't know.' Xavier was smiling now. 'Perhaps he truly values his freedom of choice.'

'Okay.' He shook his head, feeling a little ridiculous and sat back down. 'Why don't you tell me what's going on?'

'The Legion know where you go, they know what's in your home. They know how to find you, and if you can't defend yourself against them...' He gritted his teeth and looked awkward.

'You'll die.' Xavier didn't seem at all awkward about it.

'So what?' He looked around. 'I'm supposed to stay here?'

'Oh, gods no,' Xavier laughed. 'If you stay here you'll go insane!'

'You're supposed,' Pan cut across the conversation, 'to go and gather some Eldritch or Seraph Presence with which to defend yourself. If you can gather them and you make it clear that you're willing to leave them alone, they will decide you're problem enough and leave you alone.'

'So,' Adam got up again and this time the others got up with him, he looked at them as he walked over to a nearby railing, 'I suppose you both have these, Presences?'

'Two.' Xavier smiled and spun in place. 'Eldritch here.' He tipped his hat. 'Seraph here.' He spun the cane. 'You've met them of course.'

'Three.' Pan raised both hands. 'Eldritch.' He then reached up and tapped the side of his skull. 'And that one's special.'

'So what?' He looked at them. 'I go on some grand quest to find some hidden power? I'll die before I get twenty steps.'

'Worry not, kitten.' Xavier patted his shoulder. 'It may be dangerous for you to go, but we have a vested interest in watching you return. You see, there is a value in allowing any agent to take on a Presence, and a far greater one in allowing a new agent to take on a Presence. This places another piece on the board and the Lost,' he rubbed his hands together, 'we love new pieces. So you won't be all on your lonesome.'

'You two are coming in with me?' He looked at them. Well that was a little hope, he supposed.

'Not just us.' Pan smiled and wrapped one big meaty arm around Adams shoulder, leading him off in the right direction. Xavier fell into step behind them. 'Now keep up, we've got a concert to get to.'

'We're going to a concert?'

'That's what I said.' Pan's voice was gentle and amused. 'Concerts are one of our best spots, and one of theirs too. We gather around bands that draw our kind of people. You'll find the Legion around teeny boppers and hip hoppers, you'll find us around punk bands, rappers and metal heads. The band we're going to see is one of ours. We'll also meet the rest of our team there.' They picked up speed, climbing down gangways and across rooftops before they finally came to their way out.

'It's a slide.' Adam looked at the two of them.

'It is a slide.' Xavier nodded.

'Why is it a slide?'

'Why wouldn't it be?' Pan shrugged and climbed onto it, pushing off.

'It is as good a question as any.' Xavier put his hat under his arm. 'I don't have a better answer I'm afraid. Whoever made the way down into our world liked the idea of it being a slide, so we made it one. Don't worry, you'll be fine.' He grinned and started to slide. 'You know, probably, if you're lucky!' The voice died away, fading into a laugh. Adam took a deep breath and looked down, then started to slide.

As he began to move he decided that he didn't mind the ride. It was a little childish, but actually kind of fun. As they cleared the dark area they went into the light, and he saw the skyscraper city again. He started to see obstructions and rails riding up around him, coming to a sharp turn and he started to struggle, scramble and try to slow himself down. His scrambling only seemed to serve to bring the walls closer to him, so he just relaxed and tried to let what would be, be. A half dozen times he swore that the guard rails and walls were going to turn him into salsa; he just hugged his arms close to his chest, feeling his heart pounding and his gut twisting, but they never seemed to hit him.

He hadn't noticed he was picking up speed, how fast was he moving now? Faster than he could believe you could move on a slide. As he got faster and faster the colour of the sky began to change, from white to black to red to gold, purple to blue to silver, over and over again and again, spiralling patterns of clouds and lightning and swirling until he could barely place one single colour and he began to feel sick. As he started to get dizzy things blurred and something started to appear in front of his eyes. A giant white winged creature that shone like a diamond. Its face was cold, its eyes were black, but its wings lit up with golden fire. It swooped down at him with an eagle cry, and then pulled up suddenly, chased away by a set of black tendrils.

The creature, unnoticed beneath him, began to rise and unfurl, slowly but surely. He couldn't describe what was going on, what this creature was. Its body extended at all the wrong angles, sometimes it seemed inside out. It twisted and deformed and collapsed on itself again and again. It wasn't ugly, wasn't grotesque or deformed like he thought it might be, but it was so impossibly strange that he couldn't describe it with anything other than its lack of description.

He watched the two creatures fight, fierce swoops and swipes from the white monster undone by a reforming, striking, shifting attack from the creature below. The angel moved rigidly, swooping and diving in sudden movements, by comparison the creature from the bottom struck with a strange flowing pattern he couldn't understand.

He saw a giant man in a black suit with a white metal mask locked over his face, he saw a flash of white and red striking at an ocean of black figures. He saw a figure wreathed in pure blackness advancing indomitably toward a crowd of bright figures, undaunted by the fire and light they hurled at it. He saw himself crawling across pavement, bleeding red as black and white sludge oozed out of his body.

He struggled to his feet while a crowd of monsters laughed and jeered around him. He saw himself wielding white weapons in black armour that swirled and changed shapes, unable to stick to one for more than a second. He saw himself at the centre of a crossroads with dozens of roads running in dozens of directions.

And suddenly the slide was over, and he landed quite simply in some kind of strange fabric. It slowly ripped and tore and he fell through it, letting out a scream. He lashed out with both hands, trying to catch hold of something. He reached out and caught a pair of hands, he slipped and caught hold, then slipped and caught hold, then slipped and caught hold. In the end, the final set of hands caught him and placed him on the ground. The grip hurt his arms, pain running down from his hand to his shoulder and jarring up his chest. He let out a wail of pain and took a seat on the ground.

'Did you have fun?' Pan was laying on the ground where he'd apparently fallen. He had apparently lit himself another cigarette and decided to finish it before he got up. As Adam looked around he saw that he was in a completely normal stockroom. 'I didn't like the slide the first time. But now it's a kinda fun little journey for me.'

'I always enjoyed it.' Xavier spun his cane in his hands, smiling to himself.

'I don't know how I feel,' he admitted. 'I mean it

was, kind of fun, but also kinda, I don't know. I mean all that stuff I saw; will it actually happen?'

'It may.' He shrugged. 'It may be prophecy, it may be possible prophecy, it may be a lunatic dream you had due to vertigo and dizziness and because you're a loon?' He approached Adam, and he did limp when he wasn't using his stick to walk. He reached out the walking stick, tapping him gently on the head. 'Or it is distinctly possible that even after all this time this may just be one very long dream. Perhaps you're in a coma, perhaps you were never born and you're just an alien consciousness making up stories so it will feel less alone in the void. All of these things are relatively plausible and a I hope you possess enough wisdom to give each and every one of them their due consideration.'

'The Red Gentleman is good at spinning stories.' Pan flicked his ashed cigarette. 'If you're smart, you'll listen to what he says, examine every detail and choose to disregard it all. He is a fucking lunatic after all.'

'I may in fact be a fucking lunatic,' Xavier allowed. 'But I am eminently useful and occasionally insightful. You will be relying upon me for your survival.'

'So, what's the band we're going to see?' He chose to ignore the ranting of the Top Hat Man and let Pan speak.

'They're a punk band called Lash Out in Anger. They have a small, loyal following.'

'And they're you guys, I mean,' he swallowed, 'they're us?'

'Just the drummer.' He shrugged. 'For the band itself I mean, but a few of the tech guys and road crew are

36

among our number. We use the band as cover, so we can walk the paths we need to walk without too much suspicion or scrutiny. No one asks where the truck loaded down with speakers manned by serious looking guys in black go. Of course they're setting up the sound system, what else would they be doing?' He laughed. 'Now come on.'

CHAPTER TWO

They made their way in a black van to a bar with a concert space in the back room. There were a few people lounging around in leather backed chairs and nursing drinks as a tech crew of black clothed people moved equipment. As he walked in and moved up to the bar Adam noticed something weird, the tech crew were completely silent. Adam had been roped into setting up for his friend's performances a few times and the one thing crews had in common were that they were always bitching and whining, bantering and correcting one another, desperately solving one new problem or another. He would have expected at least grunts of effort as the crew lugged heavy things across the stage, but these guys were all completely silent, like someone had switched them onto mute.

'There's something weird here,' he noted.

'Very observant.' Pan stopped him with one hand. 'What is it?'

'The tech crew.' He narrowed his eyes. 'There's something weird about them.'

'I'm impressed.' Pan looked up. 'Hey, Raven! The new kid caught you already.'

He had a Long Island iced tea in one hand and a pair of scars like vertical slits across his eyes. He reminded Adam of a scarecrow. 'Well done.' His voice was soft. 'What tipped you off?'

'What tipped me off to what?' He shook his head. 'The crew aren't bitching or whining, they're not asking questions, it just seems a little off is all. I'm not sure what's off about them, but it's something weird.'

Raven looked around, looking over the sparsely decorated space with critical eyes and making sure everything was in its right place before he answered. 'I have them under my power.' He didn't speak loudly, an understated mumble. 'Whenever I defeat one of the Blank Faced I can gain their obedience. It is as good a life as any other, though perhaps not entirely justifiable.' He smiled and shook his head. 'Still it is the gift I was given and I am willing to use my enemies against them. I am no fool.' He looked like he was about to keep talking, but Pan wrapped his arm around Adam and pulled him away.

'Come on, we need to talk to Annabelle, and that guy creeps the shit out of me.'

'I like him,' Xavier opined cheerfully.

'Of course you do.' Pan glared at him. 'Because you're a freak too.'

'And of course you are the paragon of normality.' Xavier smirked. 'Because everyone working nine to five has skull tattoos and goes by the name of a fertility god. If we were normal we wouldn't be here now would we Peter?' He tapped Pan on the head and Pan shoved him away with one hand.

'There's a difference between being a little off and making people into brain slaves,' Pan protested. 'I mean yeah he's useful, and yeah they're Legionnaires, but him and those dead eyed,' he shook his head, 'things, are creepy. Now where is she? Hey Annabelle! Annabelle!'

'Just a minute.' The girl from the visions, currently in an outrageous mixture of yellows and blues was bent over a switchboard, playing with the switches and dials, one hand extended to the rest of them in a "give me a second" gesture. Apparently after a moment she had tinkered to her satisfaction, so she turned and jumped off the platform towards the others. 'All right then.' Sure enough, other than the colours, she was just like he'd seen her in the light. She had piercings in her eyebrows, nose, lips, ears and from the look he snuck when her top rode up her belly button as well. 'And I've got three more you can't see.' She clicked her fingers in his face and pointed at her own eyes. 'Did your mother never teach you its impolite to stare?'

'No,' he blurted. 'I mean sorry, I mean I wasn't staring at your...' His words stumbled and she smiled, waving away his apology.

'You were counting my piercings. I know, I've seen that before, and for the record the number is somewhere between eleven and twenty-five depending on how many I have in each ear at any given time. Now that we've addressed that, I'm Annabelle. Known to the Eldritch as the Spinning Sister and to the Seraph as the Queen of the Carnival.'

'Yes, we all have titles,' Xavier answered the unanswered question. 'Annabelle will be taking us to find the leaked sources of power, for you to use.'

'Provided he can handle them of course,' she smirked. 'If not, I'm here to take it off you.'

'We are aware of your contract.' Pan was glaring and his voice was cold.

'So, where's the fourth guy?' Adam breezed over the awkwardness. 'The one in the hoodie?'

'He'll make himself known when the time is right.' Annabelle nodded. 'He knows the time and place to be, and he'll be there.'

'All right,' Adam accepted the not really explanation. 'So, what do we do?'

'We wait until the show is over, and then we go walking the ways.'

'What ways?'

'The secret ways.'

'What secret ways?'

'The ones that are secret,' she laughed at him.

'And you know these secret ways?' He was on the back foot now and he knew it.

'No.' She shook her head, a yellow lock falling over one eye. 'My sisters do. Now go on out, enjoy the show and I'll see you afterwards.' She blew the three of them a kiss and jumped back up to the equipment, seemingly forgetting they were even there.

'Come along.' Xavier dragged him back and Adam made his way into the mosh pit with the others. The truth was Adam didn't like to be in a crowd of writhing bodies, and he preferred to hear music recorded to be sure of the best possible performance. So he wasn't exactly entirely thrilled about being in the middle of a pack of bodies he didn't know.

Then they started to play. In hindsight, he would

have admitted that what they were playing wasn't exactly great, the singer was pitchy, the guitarist was out of time with the drums and the whole band seemed more interested in playing around than they were in playing well, but as people started to dance and have fun Adam couldn't help but notice his spirits lifting a little.

He noticed that people were going a little wilder, dancing a little harder and acting a little freer than he'd ever seen at anything but the wildest concerts before. Everyone was letting go, cutting loose. This only increased as the set went on and the songs got louder and faster, more and more aggressive. People began to speed up, move faster and Adam felt himself getting caught up in the whole affair. He felt a fire lighting in his gut and he started to move without any idea why or how he was moving. His limbs danced in to the flailing and wildness of the crowd. He felt bodies pressing and bumping and slamming against his. A couple of girls he'd never met in his life before ground back and forth against him for a couple of minutes before everyone moved into the crowd again.

And then he noticed something, someone else. A single face in the crowd who wasn't moving like everyone else. He was moving, sure enough, but something about how he was moving seemed off. It was like he was seeing everyone else around him moving and trying to copy them but couldn't hear the music himself. Had no idea what the beat was.

As he watched the crowd he saw Raven advancing

on the man from behind, his tall, scarred frame impassive. He saw the man's eyes open wide as Raven stepped up close and did something to him from behind. Seconds later the surprise in his eyes was gone, his expression disappeared and the man went quietly toward one of the service entrances, joined by a few members of the road crew.

As the dancing went on Adam tried not to focus on what had happened, but his eyes kept slipping back to the spot the man had been in. He watched the crowd for more people like that but he couldn't see anyone dancing strangely. Well that wasn't true, he could see plenty of people dancing strangely but no one with that particular alienated, tuneless imitation. Eventually he managed to get lost in the music again, dancing with whoever was around and trying to avoid the big ones who looked like they were seeking out a fight. After about half the set, and dodging a flailing arm that went a little too close to his nose, he pushed and slipped his way out of the place. He took a deep breath and leaned against the wall, taking in the fresh air and trying to ignore the smell of cigarettes and cheap perfume.

'Not your ideal setting I take it?' The man who asked him that couldn't have looked more out of place if he'd tried. He wore a pristine white suit and gloves, along with a mask over his face. Behind him was a man in brown and red, short and sallow faced. The small one looked like he was halfway between man and the thing that came before, and the other looked like a mix between the bourgeoisie dream and some horror movie villain.

'Not really.' Adam shrugged. 'I mean it's not a bad place and the music's good, but the atmosphere gets a little heated for me. Gotta take a break now and again.'

'I understand all too well,' the man said softly. 'Not fitting in is a trial I am not altogether unfamiliar with.' He placed one hand on his masked face. 'I had similar troubles at one point, but I adjusted to the world, or rather, the world adjusted to me.' He leaned against the wall beside Adam. 'My name is Legate, and this is my associate Ursas.'

'Those are–'

'Strange names?' Legate said softly, shaking his head a little. 'I am aware. But unless I am much mistaken you yourself arrived in the company of two beings known as the Red Gentleman, and the Lost Soldier.'

'Not sure what you mean exactly.' It wasn't a total lie; he had no real idea what the hell was going on, so he couldn't exactly be sure of anything.

'Then you didn't make the acquaintance of the Spinning Sister? Or the Slavebreaker?' Somehow, despite the faceless mask, Adam could tell the expression was sceptical and looking into Legate's eyes he couldn't help but notice that they were pure white, like a blind man's.

'No idea what you're talking about. I don't know what's going on. Now leave me alone.'

'Bull shite.' Ursas's voice was harsh as the small

thick man stared at his hands.

'Now, now, Ursas, there is no call for rudeness.' Legate's face snapped to Ursas for a moment before he looked back at Adam. 'You must accept Mr… Adam, is it? I'm afraid I don't know your last name, that I do not find that particularly easy to believe.'

'Why wouldn't you?' He looked at him. 'I mean you don't know me at all. I've never met either of you, you haven't…' He paused. 'Wait how do you know my name?'

'That is not your first concern,' Legate sighed. 'And far from you most immediate. You see you find yourself in an unenviable position. You find yourself vulnerable to attack from any and all angles, regardless of the agents accompanying you. The Legion will have agents up and down every road, we have weapons, we have power and we have numbers.'

'So what?' He raised an eyebrow at the blind man, dumb as that felt. 'You're one of the Legion here to recruit me or something?'

'You cannot be recruited to my side,' Legate sighed. 'The few people inclined enough to be able to be either Legion or Lost at will are few and far between. What I am offering you is the opportunity to go about your business unhindered and unmolested.' Legate spread his arms helplessly. 'This is the best I can do.'

'So what?' Adam looked around. 'I just go home and you let me?'

'Hell no.,' Ursas snarled.

'Please do not mind Ursas, he is just hungry.' Legate's voice was calm. Adam looked at Ursas and the sallow man smiled and showed his teeth. The big jagged yellow teeth and dark look in his eyes said that Adam shouldn't find the fact his hunger was influencing his mood reassuring.

'Now regrettably I cannot offer you a simple amnesty. You cannot simply go home, that door is no longer open to you. Not without completing the road you are currently on.' He put a hand reassuringly on Adam's shoulder and stepped away, wiping a smudge of grey stuff off his shoulder with disdain.

'We all embark on journeys whether we want to or not, and once we have begun we must see it through to the end, and if not to the end then at least to an end. This is one such journey for you. You must go with your little rabble of Lost, and you must retrieve whatever Eldritch or Seraph Presence you can find. But if you are willing to take the items with that Presence to me, rather than keeping them for yourself I will be able to convince my people to allow you to be left alone. You may continue unharmed and live your life as you did before this entire mess started.' He sighed and shook his head.

'I truly despise the idea of fighting. Were it up to me you would be allowed to simply leave, but I have masters to serve and partners to sate. One of those partners being the hirsute individual behind me. If I ask him to let you go he will likely attempt to kill us both.'

'No likely about it, and no attempt neither,' he growled. 'And what did you just call me?'

'Hirsute,' Legate replied calmly. 'It means covered in hair.'

'Oh.' Ursas took a moment to think. 'Then yeah, I'll kill ya both, it'll be fun.' He smiled broadly, as if unreservedly proud of himself.

'You see?' He gave Adam that helpless gesture again. 'There is only so much even one such as me can do. However, if you can deliver me the item, I will be willing to keep them at bay. My word goes a good distance toward pacification.'

'So what? I just finish this one job, I bring to you this, whatever it ends up being, and I'm out for good?'
'Those are the terms of the arrangement I wish to enter into yes,' he nodded. 'However, I will be unable to protect you until this is complete. I will present you with any and all assistance and advice I can give you but I will not be able to hold back other members of my side from action.' Legate turned on his heel and began to walk away, then turned and looked back. 'Best of luck in all of your endeavours Adam. I shall watch you closely.'

'Me too.' Ursas fixed him with a glare and licked his lips languidly over his cracked and broken yellow teeth, then wiped his nose on one hand and walked away. Adam looked at them for a few seconds as they walked away and took a couple more breaths of the suddenly not so comforting air before he headed back in. At least inside he had the others to protect him. He slipped back among the dancers and tried to act as if he'd been there the whole time. These people may have been willing to help him, but they didn't seem exactly stable and they probably wouldn't take it well to hear that he'd spoken to this Legate, whoever that was.

It was the end of the show when Xavier and Pan found him again. He was tired, his arms and legs sore and sweat running down his back. Pan's hair had mostly fallen down and he was giving an exhausted grin. Xavier for his part gave him a smile and a wave, apparently untarnished.

'Did you have fun?' he asked.

'It was weird.' He shook his head. 'I mean it wasn't my usual thing, but I still felt myself kind of losing it you know? I kind of, got all swept up.'

'That happens when one of our people plays.' Pan clapped his hands and grinned. 'It can be fun, and can even teach you a little about yourself if you let it.'

'Yeah well, I'm not sure what I think about it yet.' He turned away. 'I'll decide when I'm ready, and try again then.'

'Then you are well placed among the Lost, possessing a virtue that so many of our people lack.'

'Huh?'

'Moderation.' Xavier tipped the brim of his hat. 'It is wise to take matters at one's own pace. But if you allow your mind to be free and cease holding back, you will do better.'

'All right,' he snapped. 'Now can we get going? Or

do you have more rhetoric I'm probably going to ignore first?'

'Oh.' Xavier quirked an eyebrow. 'He has a level of impertinence! A certain fire! Well, very well then, feel free to ignore or heed my guidance as your no doubt considerable wisdom guides you,' he huffed. 'I've only been Lost longer than you've been alive.'

'Don't be whiny Red.' Pan smiled and rolled his eyes. He started to load things with the faceless people who answered to Raven. Adam didn't go looking for the one he'd seen converted in front of his eyes, but whenever he saw one he couldn't help but wonder.

'Hey!' Annabelle was sitting on top of the equipment truck. 'Come here.' He walked up to the truck and she patted the spot beside her.

'I can't.' He looked around the area, laying one hand on the truck. 'How am I supposed to get up there?'

'Climb the equipment.' She flashed him a sudden smile. 'That should get you to the back, and I'll help you up the rest of the way.' She tossed her bright hair and leaned back to catch him. He started to climb the cold equipment, feeling a slight burn up his arms and chest as he mounted up.

'You know,' he grunted. 'This would be a lot easier if you just came down here.'

'Probably,' she agreed cheerfully, kicking her crossed legs on the truck like a child. 'But if you have any interest in conversing with me, you will have to climb this truck. Until then,' she yawned. He scrambled up the back of the truck and managed to get one hand on the lip, she reached down and settled her hands on his wrists. With surprising ease, she took a tight hold and pulled him up, leaving him at the top of the truck with her. 'So,' she adjusted her skirt, 'how ya doin'?'

'You brought me up here to make small talk?' He couldn't keep the incredulity out of his voice, and she let out a little titter.

'How are you on a normal day, is small talk,' she conceded. 'But how are you on the strangest day of your entire existence to date. That's the question that defines you, your situation and your actions here on out. Which makes it about the biggest question there is, now doesn't it?'

'Assuming that I'm as important as you think I am,' he looked around and chuckled a little, 'which seems pretty weird to me, since we're sitting on the top of an equipment truck in an alleyway.' He looked at her, then down at himself. 'Honestly, I'm still kind of waiting for someone to shake me awake so I can start my day and get back to doing normal stuff again.' He put his head in his hands and ran his fingers down his own face. 'I'm not sure what to think of all of this. I mean yesterday people tried to kill me so that's frightening, and there's no indication that that's going to let up any time soon.'

'It will not,' Annabelle agreed, sounding a little too cheerful about it for Adam's liking.

'All right,' he scowled. 'But on the other hand, I

mean, it's sort of exciting. I mean it's the kind of thing I've never even heard of before. Something I couldn't have even imagined before today. All of a sudden there are monsters under and above the earth and groups running the world and people fighting them and everything I know is bullshit and everything I thought was made up is true.' He realised he was rambling and stopped himself. 'So, in answer to your question, I have absolutely no freakin' idea how I am. Thanks for asking.'

'Welcome.' She nodded and patted him on the shoulder. 'Well I don't know how you are and you don't know me either, but until you fuck everything up and something goes wrong I've got you okay? I'll protect you from everything but your own bullshit.'

'Seems fair,' he nodded, 'and thanks. So where are we actually going?'

'We'll head down the coast.' She pointed into the sky over the crowd of people taking care of menial tasks, with her other hand she reached into a cooler and tossed him a beer, which he cracked and started. 'And where there's a bleed in the dimensions,' she shoved her fingers forward and split them, 'my sisters and I will force our way through and we'll get to the roads to the other planes. When we get onto the road, we'll have to ditch the convoy and head through the hard way,' she sighed and dropped her hand, grabbing out her own drink.

'The hard way?'

'The way where I don't have a clue what we're

doing. We'll have to walk until we catch the scent of Eldritch or Seraph, or rely on Pan for help. Things will get a little confusing at that point and we'll have to help you find your trail. There'll probably be some tests we'll have to pass and some battles we'll have to fight but Pan always knows the way.' She scowled. 'The problem is once we've crossed that line everyone in the entire area will be perfectly aware of what we've done and where we are. We'll have a lead on the enemy, but everything we break open will be open, every path we've beaten will be beaten and they'll be able to get in after us.' She tossed the can off the roof of the top of the truck, aiming at the bin and missing horribly.

'All right,' Adam said looking at her. 'And that's where you guys protect me right?'

'That'll be largely Pan and the Top Hat Man,' she corrected, saying their names like it was a poem. 'I'll be the one pushing the lead out and making sure you don't fail the trails, as best I can. Pan and I know some short cuts through the worlds.'

'So you're my Sherpa?'

'A little more pleasant than some grizzled old bastard in a parka wouldn't you say?' She flashed him what seemed like a genuine smile.

'Much.' He looked at her for a second. She was cute, in a weird way. Not his usual thing but then nothing in his life had been usual lately. She was all attitude, colour, metal and trouble, nothing he'd ever for a second consider wanting. Kind of like this entire new life he was apparently being offered.

'Hey.' She clicked her fingers at him again. 'If you get lost in thought looking at me again I'll have to decide whether to be insulted, flattered and creeped out.'

'Sorry.' He shook his head. 'I'm just, a little overwhelmed you know? I wasn't, you know, actually staring at you specifically. I was just staring into an area that you were in.'

'Staring off into space and drawn to my head huh?' She shook her head. 'Don't fuck this up and I've got you.'

'Yeah but that's exactly what you'd say if you didn't isn't it?'

'Fair.' She glared at him. 'Well then let's put it another way. If you can't count on me you're going to die way before you realise it. And if you fuck up I'll leave you behind and forget about you completely.'

'That,' he paused for a few seconds, 'is possibly the least reassuring thing anyone has ever said to me.'

'Did you know that if I cut your femoral artery right now you would have bled out before anyone could even make it to the top of the truck much less help you?' They stared at each other for a few long seconds and then she laughed. 'Sorry, I had to beat the record.'

'You,' he looked at her for a long moment, 'are a deeply disturbing woman.' She laughed a little too long and too loud.

'Baby you aint seen nothin' yet.' She jumped off

the truck and landed on her feet like it was the simplest thing in the world. 'I gotta go load my things before we head out. So is there anything else you want to talk about?'

'Raven,' he looked at her, 'the rest of you, I can just about accept. Aggressive, angry, weird and all, but he's taking slaves. Actual slaves, and I have absolutely every kind of problem with that.'

'All right,' she sighed. 'Climb down and we'll settle this.' He managed to scramble down after a few moments. As they made it he followed her over to Raven, who she waved to with a smile. 'Hey Raven, the new guys a little upset with what you do. So come on, Slaver's Blade out.' The tall man rolled his damaged eyes, got up off the car hood he was leaning on and pulled out the knife, slamming it into Annabelle's stomach.

CHAPTER THREE

Adam lunged at Raven and tried to push him away, and the larger man shoved him back. Holding him at bay Raven pulled the knife out, and when he stepped back Annabelle stepped back too and showed her stomach. The wound didn't even exist, only a light white patch on her belly which was fading away.

'Come here.' Raven pulled him close with a sudden furtive friendliness. 'I need to explain something to you, because you seem pleasant enough. I can't trust anyone else not to fuck it up and I have an entire script for this and everything. Now what was that metaphor?' He jumped back up onto the hood of the car and pulled Adam up with him.

'It wasn't a highway or a bus or, right, it was a train. Imagine destiny as a train system. You get on one and you have to take the journey. You have to go to at least one stop, but after every stop you have a choice. You can stay on your train, or get off and take a different one. The further out on one line you go, the fewer chances you have to change lines. Even until right up to the end you always have the choice though; at any stop, you can change. That's what makes you a person. What the Blank Legionnaires are is people who have traded the power of an Eldritch or Seraph for every path but the one available to them. They have agreed to stay on that one train forever.'

'That did not clarify things as much as you seemed to think it would.'

'As you go longer and longer in the world you can make choices that expand your options or limit them. As a member of the Legion you can take some power into your body, granting you instant and complete mastery of your abilities, in exchange for cutting off all of your paths, in exchange for sacrificing your destiny. Each one of the Blank Legionnaires, the transforming ones, has a mere portion of a single Presence within them. Yet they are almost as powerful as one of us is with an entire complete Presence. All you need to give up in exchange, is the right to make any of your own choices.' Raven spun his knife on his hand and held it up, pointing it at Adam.

'The slaver's blade can only take your destiny if you only have one. If you have no choices, no options of your own it can steal your destiny, rendering you only capable of obeying me. If you have even a single choice of your own left,' he drew back his blade arm, 'I could stick you right in the throat right now and it wouldn't even tickle.'

'I'll pass,' Adam said with a nod.

'Probably the sane option.' The knife vanished up his sleeve.

'Thanks.' He looked at him.

'You're welcome.' Raven smiled. 'The Blank Legionnaires are shock troops, basic units, no individuality. They aren't really people at all.' He looked at the roadie and jerked his head. The man turned, grabbed his face in his hands, and calmly peeled it off in one quick movement, revealing a black empty mask with only a wide gaping mouth. Raven waved one hand and the guy put the skin back on his face. 'I hope this has comforted you slightly.'

'Very slightly. I mean don't get me wrong, all of this still disturbs me, but at least you've made me kind of okay with Xavier killing the ones he killed.'

'Wonderful,' Raven sighed. 'Because of course I live entirely to make Xavier's life easier rather than my own.' He waved his hand dismissively at the world in general and climbed down off the car, muttering to himself.

CHAPTER FOUR

Once the group had finished packing they started out on their journey. Music blared in the van in which Xavier, Pan, Adam and Annabelle were sitting, the four of them taking it in turns to pick the music. They managed to make more or less cordial small talk as they worked, but in the end Adam ended up falling asleep against the side of the van.

'Hey,' Annabelle demanded his attention as soon as he woke up. They'd pulled over outside a more or less decent looking hotel. 'We'll sleep here for the night, it's friendly, well, ish, and it'll give us all a chance to prepare.'

'What do you mean prepare?' He looked across the armed and hardened looking group.

'Not everything we do is as simple as pull blade from sheathe and drive into enemy face meathead,' she smirked. 'Some of what we do is much deeper and subtler than the day to day confrontation. If we take a little prep time we'll be able to do a few things over the journey that we otherwise won't be able to do. Things you likely won't notice, but will come into play. You should use the time eat, change, we've got some clothes about your size, shower and sleep. If you have anything you like to do to prepare yourself for trials and difficult times I would advise you to do it.'

'I'm not the praying type.' He shrugged and headed for the shower.

'Oh and stay out of everyone else's room.' Pan

looked at him. 'We're going to be doing some fairly delicate work, and I would prefer you not get yourself hurt interrupting something you don't understand.'

Washed and wearing new clothes that barely fit, he knocked on Pan's door. The big man emerged, his skin covered in some kind of oil. Past him Adam could see spiralling patterns all over the floor. 'What's up?'

'I wondered if anyone wants food. I was gonna go get something from down the street.'

'Good plan.' Pan nodded and wrote a few things down on a piece of paper and handed it to him. Annabelle and Raven added a few more items each and Adam begrudgingly knocked on Xavier's door. The strangely dressed, goofy man gave him the creeps and he really didn't want to snub him.

'I don't need to prepare as long as the others.' Xavier pulled himself to his feet and set his cane. 'I will come with you.'

'It's fine,' Adam sighed. 'Frankly I'd prefer to pick it up on my own. Give myself a little peace and quiet.'

'Do you really think you can carry all of this alone?' Xavier held up the paper. 'Pan has a most prodigious appetite.' He wasn't wrong, Pan's order was about the same amount as everyone else's combined.

'All right,' he sighed. 'I guess we'll go together then.' The two of them headed across the street and Adam decided to try to make small talk.

'Do fast food joints have any territorial things I

should know about? Do they belong to anyone?'

'Not exactly.' Xavier shrugged. 'The Legion likes the uniformity of them, but by and large the people who frequent them are more likely to be from our crop than theirs. Their scenery, our company. The result is something of a neutral territory, neither of us use it because neither of us want it. Truth be told they make us all uncomfortable.'

'But not you?'

'Me most of all.' Xavier was indeed fidgeting, scratching his sleeves. 'Many of us enjoy being Lost, and many of us feel obliged to do so because of our enemies and our work. Very few of us pride ourselves on it like I do. If I were to find a destiny of my own, it would likely cost me a great deal of who I am.'

'Well if it makes you uncomfortable why did you insist on coming with me?'

'My reasons were threefold.' Xavier counted them on his fingers as they entered the place. 'Firstly, I do not like the idea of there being places I cannot go. Secondly, we need to eat; the others want this and they need to prepare. One cannot let one's own impulses override necessity.'

'And the third?'

'I enjoy challenging myself,' he chuckled. They walked up to the counter and ordered. When they turned to carry the things out they found themselves blocked by a pair of men in suits.

'You stand out here,' Xavier said softly, like he was noting a rather boring fact.

'You stand out everywhere,' the suited man replied. 'We are here to warn you that we are coming and we do not hold back. We are watching you, we are everyone, we are everywhere.'

'Well yes,' Xavier said like he was more bored than anything. 'You can file that under things I already know.' Xavier took an uncomfortably close step to them and they ignored him completely, their eyes fixed on Adam.

'We speak to you Adam,' their voices were together. 'You have no title, no name worth having, no power and nothing to hide behind. You could look around any corner and see one of us. Your brother, your best friend, your father, we are everywhere.'

'We are everyone,' came the voice from the counter. 'Around every corner, and you will learn to fear us.'

'My father's dead.' Adam tried to keep the fear out of his voice. 'Guess you don't know as much as you thought you did.'

'That's quite enough of this.' Xavier looked at them and unsheathed the sword from his cane about an inch. The suited men stepped one to either side and Xavier put one hand on Adam's back and pushed him forward.

'Do not sleep,' came the voice from one.

'Do not drop your guard,' said the other.

'Trust no one, for we are everywhere.'

'You may surrender to the inevitable at any time.'

Adam pushed the door open and made his way

across the almost abandoned street, an ice cold feeling in his gut. He looked around, his eyes scanning the few people who were walking the street. He saw a tired looking old man talking on a phone and steered away from him, just in case he should pull some kind of weapon, or pull his face off to show one of those blank masks. He sped up a little, making his way across the street.

He heard the beep of a horn and the sound of breaks screaming and jumped as a car only just stopped in time to avoid hitting him. He felt Xavier's hand on his collar, as if he was going to haul him back just in time if the car hadn't already stopped.

'Keep your head about you. They cannot do anything to you while I am here. Nothing that you do not allow.' Xavier pushed him forward, moving him forcefully over to the hotel and pushing him inside. Adam went to his room, letting Xavier make food drops to all the others, ate and tried to relax.

He may have managed to get two or three hours of sleep that night. He wasn't sure.

To say that the Blank Faced Legate viewed Ursas as a necessary evil was false on several levels. First and foremost a belief in good and evil would have been required and he was far too evolved for that. Legate fancied himself a being above a number of things, good and evil being one of them. Things as base as brute force and unthinking violence were, of course, another. Because of this he regarded Ursas as a necessary indignity. Ursas did not regard violence as beneath him. In fact he regarded most forms of violence as above his acceptable threshold. He seemed to regard things such as punching or one to one combat as an unnecessary extravagance, living in a world of elbows, knees and claws. Most men, no matter how hardened, will pause before the initiation of violence. Ursas, in such an event, tended to speed up.

Legate knew full well that Ursas regarded him much in the same way a showman's tiger regards its master: a thing you listen to because it feeds you when you do and can punish you if you don't. Something you watch and wait until the barest second where one of these facts isn't true, until he lowers the whip or skips a meal so you can finally kill him.

'You should have let me kill 'im,' Ursas complained, looking at his white-faced ally. Legate's expression twisted into distaste, knowing full well that his mask covered it well enough.

'And then the Spinning Sister would find her way to the Presence and keep it herself, or give it to one of her family. They gain more power and lose a potential, a trade we both know they would take and be glad.' He shook his head. 'My way is better.'

'Oh? And you reckon he'll give that power over to us and just go home?' Ursas spat on the ground. 'Nay fuckin' likely.'

'First of all I wholly believe that this strategy has at least a moderate chance of success. This is not a warrior. This is a normal man, afraid of us, afraid of

63

the choices he will have to make. He is waiting, hoping, praying for someone to wake him up and have it all just be a dream. This is what I will do for him.' He smiled to himself. 'And even if our plan should happen to fail, no great loss, there are other advantages to having him there. He will slow down his people, they will be forced to drag him with them like an anchor around their necks, adding nothing and taking time and effort. With any luck he will even get one of them killed. And should they succeed in spite of him? Well,' the smile widened beneath his mask, 'that plays into my hands just as well.'

'So what?' Ursas growled. 'I can't kill 'im at all?'

'No.' He was costing Legate his good mood. 'Scare him, kill his friends, drive him low but do not kill him until he has had a chance to surrender his Presence to me.'

'Then I can kill 'im.'

'If he handles the situation poorly, then you may kill him. However if he should play the part I wish him to play then no, you will not lay so much as a finger upon him.' Ursas snarled and moved at him and the pairs' eyes met, the beast man's red eyes meeting his commander's white. Legate folded his arms and they stared at each other for a long moment. Ursas broke the gaze first, picking his teeth with a blackened fingernail and spitting on the ground.

'All right then,' he nodded. 'I'll kill that slut instead. It'll be good to feel her skin ripping under my hands.'

'Capital idea.' Legate patted Ursas on the shoulder. 'Good man.' It had been a long-held theory of Legate's that any man could be controlled, could be talked down and reasoned with given the right impetus.

'I'm not either of those things,' Ursas sulked. Well, if Legate was wrong that would be when he let his pet off the leash. After all there was no need to dirty his own hands.

Adam woke up, helped the others load the gear and said goodbye to the band. Raven announced that he would be accompanying them with some of his crew until they opened the door to the next world. Apparently he couldn't go with them, something to do with the way they were going.

'What way are we going?' Adam asked about a dozen times throughout the day and received the same non-answer every time.

'My sisters will be taking us,' was all Annabelle would say. They drove down the coast another half dozen hours before they managed to find their destination. Which was, apparently, a condemned building. There were danger signs hung up around it, beams and roof tiles falling away, a vaguely rotten smell permeated from the walls, the paint peeling, graffiti or burned away.

'Wow.' He looked at them. 'We came all the way here for that? Result.'

'Your objection and sarcasm are noted.' Raven

climbed out of the car. 'As is, as always, your complete lack of understanding as to what is going on.'

'My sisters and I know what they're doing,' Annabelle and Raven had become snippy in the car, with each other and Adam. 'So shut up and watch.'

'Okay fine,' Adam scowled. 'But first tell me what this place is.'

'This is where a large number of my more gifted sisters live.' Her voice was cold and bored. 'I think they'll be willing to help us, though we aren't exactly on what you'd call the best of terms. But that's what family is right? The people who have to take you in no matter how much you hate each other?' She rolled her eyes and walked upstairs, the others following behind. 'Walk slowly, step lightly and don't step on anything.'

'Are you sure they're there?' Adam looked around. 'I mean if there were any people out there wouldn't we already know about it?' As he said that he reached the second-floor landing and he spotted the biggest spider he'd ever seen. It was black and white, oozing some kind of fluid out of its mouth and sitting not five feet away from his face in an intricate web. Adam lashed out at the web, hoping to scare the thing off. 'Spider!' He smacked at it but before he could make any kind of contact Annabelle hit him with a backhand, knocking him flying off his feet. He landed on his back and spiders started crawling out of the walls by the dozens. They were coming for him fast and he turned to crawl away.

'Apologise!' came the yell from above him.

'What?'

'Even one bite from any one of those spiders could kill you, now apologise, quickly!'

'Apologise to the–'

'Yes, say you're sorry, you idiot!'

'I'm sorry, I'm sorry, please don't bite me! I didn't mean to hurt anything, or anyone, or whatever. I'm sorry, please don't bite me!'

'It's okay,' Annabelle picked up the big spider in one hand, stroking it with the other one. 'It's okay, it's okay, he didn't know. He didn't understand. It's okay, you're okay, he's no threat to you.'

'What the hell is going on?' The spiders were now all over Annabelle, skittering around on her skin and Adam was the only one who seemed at all perturbed by it.

'It's all right, you absolute moron.' Her voice was soft and calm. 'These are my sisters, as in Spinning Sister, as I am theirs. Sisters this is Adam, he's one of us and we're wondering if we can use your way to get to the World Between Worlds. I know it's a little rich expecting you to help him after all of that, but he's very new and very stupid and he didn't know.'

'I'm not stupid,' Adam snapped. 'I just didn't know spiders had–'

'Shut up,' her voice was a soft singsong.

'So what, spiders are going to take us to another world?'

'That is about the size of it.' She nodded. 'I'm going

to help them build a web to take the rest of us out, and the rest of you are going to be very quiet and very still and not annoy my sisters to a greater extent than you already have. They're easily frightened and they don't want you here anymore than you want to be here. So the quieter and less obstructive you are, the quicker we'll be done. Leave them alone and let them do the same for you.'

She walked up a small flight of stairs into the attic and they followed her up, watching her helping the spiders weave. She sung softly to herself, webs draining out of her fingers as they did the spiders' abdomens. The rest of them went to the windows or back downstairs so they saw it when the white vans began to pull up and Blank Faced Legionnaires began to pile out. A couple of dozen of the creatures began making their way toward the house.

'Annabelle dear,' Xavier said softly and calmly, keeping his voice neutral. 'Are you thinking of perhaps being finished at some point soon? Because you have company.'

'A few minutes.' Her voice was distracted. 'If there is anything you can do to hold them off I would suggest you do it.'

Xavier pulled his sword from his sheath and straightened his hat on his head as he walked out of the house, Pan in hot pursuit, his tattoo already starting to glow on his head. Adam watched the offensive unfold, some of the creatures trying to get by the door's defenders, while the others tried to climb the walls and make it in the windows. The windows were blocked by Raven's roadies. The scarred man had barked a simple command and they had stripped their faces, with shreds of their old clothing remaining to mark their side.

Raven himself was aided by the spiders, using long thin strands of rope to pull himself from window to window and sticking the creatures as he climbed. Adam watched from his attic window position as the monsters fought on the walls, tendrils and tentacles meeting with spiked and bladed appendages. Legionnaires from both sides were torn from the walls and thrown down into the melees below, others released gouts of gore as appendages and heads were torn from bodies. Raven moved with perfect calm, driving single stabs and slits into the creatures and sending them down to their fellows.

On the ground Xavier and Pan went about their bloody work. The Red Gentleman moved like a bullfighter, his coat in one hand and his sword in the other. He twirled, swirled and snapped the garment, deflecting tentacles and blades as the bodies began to burn, and using the large, distracting movements to give him places to stick his sword. Whenever he thrusted, he aimed for the chest, head or some other visible weak point, not wasting a strike on anything but a killing blow. Now and again he would flick the coat onto his shoulder or around his neck so he could throw the hat in impossible arcs and twists that ripped and tore through creatures.

Pan just waded into the fight and began laying about himself in every direction; he didn't bother with anything fancy. He slammed heavy, glowing fists into the creatures, grabbing tentacles and limbs and ripping them clean out of sockets. He drove any hard place on his body into any soft part of anyone else's. He would sometimes lift creatures bodily up and use them as weapons against each other. He laughed as he waded through them, bobbing, weaving and throwing the beasts into each other's paths. The few of them that managed to hit him lashed into his arms and chest, and he appeared to ignore them completely.

As well as they were doing, Adam could tell they weren't winning. Even as Pan and Xavier carved out a zone for themselves away from the door, more and more of the tentacle creatures made their way to the walls. They made their way faster and faster, more and more, and soon more of the monsters were climbing up than down. Raven sighed and shook his head, jumping down out one of the windows and landing on some of the monsters to join the melee.

'I'm ready!' came Annabelle's call from the room. 'Get in here and we'll get moving. Come on, haul ass!'

Xavier ran at Pan and the big man launched his partner up in a cheerleader style throw, sending Xavier a story and a half into the air and allowing him to tumble through the window. Pan then lowered his head and charged like a rhino through the crowd of monsters, knocking them sprawling away from him as he made it toward the door. The creatures stopped falling and began to make ground toward the door as well as up the walls.

'You should go now,' Raven called up with a smile on his face. 'Farewell!'

'Are you gonna be okay?' He looked at the strange, tall, coated figure and saw a little laughter in his torn and scarred eyes.

'Probably not. But whether this works or doesn't, this has been a long time coming for me.' With that, he re-joined the fight, now alone. He started to laugh louder and louder as he struck at them and they quickly covered him. As Adam turned around to face the others no one commented, they hadn't heard a car, they knew what was going on. Annabelle had built a massive intricate swirling web leading to a half broken down wall.

'Everyone grab hold of the line. Don't be worried about breaking it, it's stronger than steel. Once you grab the line it should stick to you like glue, you can slide your hand across it, but pulling it loose is going to take some doing. Just walk ahead and follow the line, my sisters and I know the way.'

The four of them took handholds on the thin line and began to walk across the web, each one secured to it by one hand as they tight-roped across the lower strands. As they started to walk they headed toward the half-collapsed wall; the spiders swarmed around it and Annabelle calmly pushed the wall away. As they walked the scene changed underneath them and Adam froze completely at what he saw.

'There is no ground.' He had no idea how many times he said it and how many times he just thought it. Each of his feet was on a single thread of web just longer than it, and the nearest line straight down was five meters below. All around him were thousands upon thousands of threads as far as the eye could see, cascading into patterns that mixed and broke apart and formed smaller pieces of even bigger patterns. 'It's just, threads, and I'm gonna die.'

'And we haven't even reached the tests yet,' Annabelle grumbled. She turned and effortlessly swung her way back to him, placing her hands gently on the sides of his face. Her hands felt a little wet and sticky, but they were familiar and comforting enough that he didn't recoil.

'Relax, okay?' She kept her tone steady for his benefit. 'As long as you keep a good hold on the line you're not in any danger. There's no real risk of falling. I know it's a little scary, but you're not in any real danger as long as you keep walking and don't make too much noise.' She retreated from him and swung back to the front of the line.

'How big is the web?' he asked and for once Annabelle seemed cheerful.

'This particular one goes in a few directions, covers a few cities and bridges a few dimensions so it's very large indeed. The sum total of the web even I wouldn't know. We shouldn't need to traverse more than a couple of kilometres until we reach the exit. Provided none of the locals decides to stir up any trouble?'

'What locals?'

'Well given that we're inside a giant spider web I'm going to let you guess.' She turned her face to him and smiled, her voice soft and carrying. 'Just keep one foot in front of the other and don't yell or scream and we should be fine.'

'And what if one of the locals does decide it's interested in us?' He looked at her and she turned away, back to moving.

'Then I'll try to talk it into keeping calm and letting us leave.'

'And if you can't?'

'Well then, I take back all restrictions on running and screaming. Get as far through the web as you can and I'll do something desperate and insane, but that shouldn't be a problem.'

'Any chance the Legion will follow us through the spider web?'

'No, that's our advantage. Much like Raven they can't travel by spider web, the sisters won't take them out of loyalty to me. They'll have to wait for a thunderstorm, or take the long way,' Adam let that go. Asking any more questions would lead to answers that would just raise more questions. He took a few deep breaths and kept walking, his eyes fixed straight ahead. When he saw the first of the locals he started to shake, and his foot slipped off the thread. He held onto the line for dear life and tried to pull himself back up. He felt the world spinning underneath him and tasted blood in his mouth, he must have bitten down on his lip. He pulled up and kicked out until he felt his foot touch the rope he'd been standing on. Pan reached forward from behind him and steadied him on the rope. Adam was frozen, holding himself up but unable to look at anything other than the creature he'd just seen.

Crawling across a few lines not fifty meters away was a spider who whose bulbous abdomen was about as long as a man was tall, with spindling legs about that long again. The creature was as high off the ground as a small horse and it moved with a strange jerking crawl.

'Is that thing going to–'

'Not if you keep your rookie ass quiet and moving, she hasn't noticed us yet.' Annabelle's voice was tense under her breath. As he walked he saw a few more spiders crawling through the web. Some were black and the same size as the first one, some were brightly coloured and a little smaller, and a few were black with designs on their backs that were three or four times the size of the first one he'd seen. One of the biggest, almost the size of a large truck came close to them, crawling across the threads directly beside the group.

Annabelle slowly raised her hand, motioning that they needed to stop. Pan reached forward and pressed one hand tightly over Adam's mouth to stop the scream that may or may not have been coming at that very second. He hadn't realised just how quiet this dimension was until now. With his conversations with Annabelle and the sounds of the four of them walking together the sounds of skittering spiders had been muffled.

Now all he could hear was the chittering, twitching, rustling sound underneath him. Something that sounded halfway between someone raking leaves and knuckles being cracked rang out every time the giant creature stepped. It turned suddenly to face them and made a strange chittering noise.

Pan clenched his hand tightly around Adam's mouth. Adam closed his eyes and tried to breathe slowly through his nose trying to keep himself from panicking. The others, for their part, didn't even seem to be breathing. They were just frozen like statues on the line. As the creature began to crawl away Adam started breathing properly again, and so did the others. Pan removed his hand from Adam's mouth and patted him on the shoulder.

'Keep quiet,' Annabelle whispered. 'And keep moving, she might still be able to hear us.' They walked together, moving as quickly and calmly as they could. It was about an hour's tense walk later that a group of spiders moved around them. Annabelle looked around the crowd and shook her head, bending down and picking one up.

'She's spotted us,' she said softly. 'She's sent a few of her servants to apprehend us.'

'Who?'

'Whichever one of my aunts or sisters rules this area.' She ran her hand through her hair, now a stylish purple and red with a single streak of pink between them. 'If we're lucky it's trapdoor or the bird eater, just, still and quiet. I'll see if I can talk us out of an audience.'

'If she's your sister why are you trying to avoid talking to her?'

I can certainly get whoever it is not to eat me but the rest of you might end up snacks if you aren't careful.' She turned to the creatures and began to speak to them in a strange chittering language similar to the noises they were making. She leaned over and started to play with the creatures as they conversed. When the conversation ended and the group dispersed she clenched one fist tightly.

'Fuck. That couldn't have gone much worse.'

'Oh?' Xavier kept his tone mild and polite.

'This is the domain of the Black Widow. She built and maintains this web, allowing no one to pass without her consent. She has,' she paused and took a deep breath, looking at the spiders around her, 'she has graciously agreed to meet with us on the matter of our passage.' She looked at the guys. 'Don't look at her for too long, don't talk to her unless you have to and for the love of gods don't flirt or stare at her.'

'What do you mean don't flirt or stare?' Adam looked at her for a moment.

'I mean you're allowed to, I suppose.' Annabelle apparently misinterpreted his objection. 'But once you do you may not want to leave. You will be in very real danger once you get too close.'

'But aren't we talking to a black widow spider?'

'We're talking to the Black Widow for whom the spiders are named.' Annabelle was visibly twitching, bouncing one foot as she walked. 'Just, try not to fuck it up and whatever you do don't mention Raven.'

'All right.'

Now they moved with a lot less hesitation, no longer worried about being noticed. Still there was no sound of talking or chatting, the entire group trying not to consider their immediate future. Annabelle continued to chitter and chat with the creatures. The only words said in English was when Xavier stopped for a moment, leaning back to whisper softly enough that he was barely sure he heard the words.

'Watch what you say around spiders. They may not speak our tongue, but I assure you they understand it.' With a couple of breaths to steady himself Adam stepped forward into the chamber of the Black Widow.

CHAPTER FIVE

The room Legate made his home in was almost pure white, it was expansive and he needed time to think. The floors were nicely carpeted, the walls were tiled and the decoration was minimalist. Soft lighting shone through the room and the only signs of colour were the dozens upon dozens of books that filled the space. It was the kind of place that inspired soft voices and steps, where anything beyond a whisper seemed somehow profane. Nothing was out of place and nothing was anything less than perfectly ordered.

The creators would probably be insulted to hear the noise that was currently piercing the air. The ragged half laughing screams that came from the mouth of Raven the Slave Breaker. Blood splattered drop cloths and plastic sheets lay across the carpets and six hours of pain and torture had managed to yield only a single result. They now knew that the Slaver Breaker's first name was Raven.

The tall man was chained to a wall, his hands above his head, suspended form them high enough that he could take the weight off his hands by standing on his toes and take the weight off his legs by pulling himself up with his hands. He was never entirely comfortable in any position, he could never entirely escape pain in a single moment. There were spikes through his skin attached to pulling ropes and wire wrapped around his limbs, digging in tightly. For all that, he seemed to be in very little pain.

'Come on.' Raven looked at them. 'Can you just get to whatever you plan to do here? Because frankly I'm a little bored. Kill me, let me go, do whatever this is but it's not going to yield any positive results. Unless your plan somehow hinges on tedium.'

'I don't know.' Ursas looked up from the car battery he was holding. 'I'm havin' a good time.'

'Though admittedly with less positive results than he usually accomplishes.' The Legate was tired. 'I admit you have displayed impressive fortitude. Far more impressive than your intellect certainly. Did you not know your allies would leave without you?'

'On the contrary,' Raven smiled from his position, 'I knew full well that they'd leave. I also knew they wouldn't make it out without me, and I thought it may be a good chance to test out a theory I've been working on. If it worked, I'd be fine, if not,' he sighed and shook his head, 'well I suppose I've probably earned whatever punishment is in store for me.'

'It seems that your experiment has not gone as well as you had hoped.'

'Yes, it does.' Raven was still smiling. 'So it would seem indeed. I have apparently made some manner of error.' He seemed to feel some kind of detached disappointment. As if none of this were happening to him in anything but a scientific sense.

'Indeed you have,' Legate sighed. 'So you have no intention of revealing anything pressing?'

'My intention is one and one only.' Raven closed his eyes for a long moment. 'I intend to leave this place as soon as I can.'

'Well then,' Legate turned away, 'I shall be departing. I have preparations to conduct. We will see how resolute you are in twenty-four hours.'

They continued their work. Raven looked bored.

Spider webs were everywhere. Little ones dotted the corners and the walls, bigger ones sat strewn around almost haphazardly as if their spider occupants had simply made them wherever was convenient at that moment. Spiders crawled and moved everywhere as well as a few other creatures leaning indolently in most of the webs, though a few of them looked like they were struggling to get out. From all corners of the of the room came lines like the ones the Lost had been walking in on, and suspended in the centre of the room was a massive silk canopy. Laying in the very centre of that canopy, atop a mountain of cushions, sat the Black Widow.

She was dark skinned, as dark as the night itself with bright red hair that cascaded down her chest and back. Across part of her body was a draped cloth of what looked very much like the same silk she was laying on. The cloth was draped strategically and with its thin fabric did more to draw attention to her nakedness than conceal it. She left just enough to the imagination to make Adam want to see more. She lay lazily on the pile, with her eyes half closed and a smile on her face.

'So,' she said softly. 'What have we here?' She

scanned each of the men in turn through half lidded eyes, looking them up and down as if judging some factor before moving on to the next. When it came to Annabelle her face slipped into an easy grin. 'Hello there little princess.'

'Hello Auntie,' Annabelle approached her and hugged her tightly. The two held each other for a moment while the Black Widow stroked her niece's hair.

'How many times must I tell you to get this silliness out of your face?' She shook her head, holding one of Annabelle's pierced lips in her fingers. Annabelle slapped her hand away and took a step back.

'At least one more, just like last time and next time.' She gave her sweetest smile. 'So we were hoping to just make our way through your territory. I hope we didn't make any disturbances for you.'

'Not at all dear!' The voice was emphatically dismissive, as if the idea was preposterous. 'You've been the epitome of a gracious guest, as always. On the other hand, a lady does get a little curious when she hears about strangers making their way through her home without asking, especially around harvest time. She may want to meet these lovely new people; she may want to make some new friends. So why don't you introduce these people to your favourite aunt?'

'Certainly,' Annabelle's voice wavered a little. 'These are the Red Gentleman,' Xavier took off his hat and gave a flourishing bow, 'the Lost Soldier,' Pan nodded, raising one hand, 'and Adam.'

'A name, not a title?' The spider woman straightened herself up and her eyes were suddenly alight with attention. 'Could it be that you've brought a newly plucked flower into my little home?' she licked her lips, her eyes focusing like a laser on Adam. 'With no Presence or power to speak of yet? Well that is something indeed.' She placed one finger on her lip and smiled. 'I so rarely get to see anyone in that little spot between harvest and power.'

She beckoned him over to her and he made his way without questioning it. His breath caught in his throat, his heartbeat pounding in his ears and all blood leaving his brain bound south. 'It's very interesting.' She held out one hand and Adam kissed it, knowing instinctively that was what he was supposed to do.

'Auntie please.' Annabelle sounded strained.

'Oh don't worry little one,' the Widow locked her eyes on Adam, 'I'm just playing.' But her eyes told a different story as she stared at Adam. 'So you're still looking for your first Presence are you darling?'

'Yeah.' Adam's voice sounded far away to his own ears. It was still his voice but it was somehow different. 'I'm on a quest for it I guess.'

'A quest?' She laughed, a deep rich melodious laugh. 'How very exciting. Still it must be dangerous, not to mention tiring.' She ran her hand across his face with surprisingly tenderness. Her hands were soft and smooth as silk.

'It is,' he said blearily. 'A little scary too.' He chuckled a little as he admitted it. 'I mean I was a normal person a couple of days ago and now there are faceless freaks trying to kill me. I think we left someone to die back there and it's just, I mean…,' He sighed and lay down on the canopy without realising it.

'It's too much.' She moved aside to make room for him.

'Auntie.' Annabelle's voice was strained, but both Widow and Adam ignored her.

'It is,' Adam admitted. 'It's kinda wonderful as well though. There's some really cool stuff going on and I like the idea of having powers.' He expected her skin to feel strange but it didn't, it was soft and smooth and warm. 'But…'

'What if I told you,' she ran her fingers under his shirt and up his stomach, 'that I could give you these powers and let you walk into the world without risking yourself.'

'That'd be great.' He could hear Annabelle saying something now, something he couldn't quite understand. Oh well, it didn't matter.

'All you would have to do is agree to stay with me,' she said softly. 'To live with me and explore my world.'

'That'd be…' He smiled. 'That'd be amazing. I'd love to.' That was as far as he got before he was startled out of it by the sound of someone choking. To his surprise it was Widow whose breath deserted her courtesy of a black gloved hand around her throat.

'That's quite enough of that.' Pan's voice was soft and dangerous. 'I know full well what you're doing and I don't intend to stand for it.'

'You don't want to fight me.' Her voice was soft and sweet.

'Oh but I really do,' he disagreed. 'And that trick doesn't work on me.'

'Oh damn,' she sighed. 'You're homosexual, aren't you?'

'I am indeed,' he said coldly. 'And proud of it, now if you don't turn off this little piece of witchery of yours I am going to clench my fist and the fact that I'm holding your throat right now isn't going to slow me down, of this I can assure you.'

'My daughters will get to you before you can finish me.' She seemed perfectly calm.

'Through me?' Xavier's voice was soft. 'Because understand the stakes under which we are playing; any reinforcement you get will be coming through me. One of us was sensible enough not to look at you.'

'Annabelle,' she said in a silly singsong voice. 'Is there something you would like to say on the matter?'

'I won't protect Adam from his idiocy.' Annabelle's voice was cold. 'But I won't protect you from your appetites either.' Annabelle was leaning against a web of her own. 'I'm sorry auntie but I don't protect people from themselves.'

'Very well.' The voice was vaguely disappointed as Widow clicked her fingers. Afterward she was still beautiful, but her skin cold and rough, suddenly not an irresistible temptress. With a few awkward seconds Adam managed to pull himself out of the cushion pile and climb down from the canopy. Widow shook her head and sighed. 'It was a good offer you know, still,' she flipped one hand, 'you may pass through my territory. None of my family will stop you but I would advise that the rest of you pick a different spider to bother in future. Or find a very pleasant gift.'

'We shall.' Xavier nodded.

'And as for you,' Widow fixed her eyes on Adam, who was now as scared by the glance as he was intrigued, 'feel free to reconsider my offer whenever you like. There will be a place in my web for you.'

'Thank you.' He bowed clumsily and gave her a smile. 'I'd like to see you again just as soon as I'm done with all of this nonsense.' He was just saying the right words now. He had no idea how he felt.

'I shall look forward to it.' She waved him off and he retreated back to the others, trying not to look as embarrassed as he felt.

'So we just go now?' Annabelle confirmed.

'Yes dear,' Widow sighed. 'I'm a little annoyed with you and your little friends right now. So you just head on out, and make sure to show this darling boy back if he asks.' Annabelle looked at the others and headed off to the line, slowly and carefully, not taking her eyes off her aunt. Adam followed her closely, looking anywhere but. As soon as they were out of the immediate sight of the Black Widow's canopy

Annabelle broke into a run.

'So we don't have to worry anymore?' Adam moved as fast as he could.

'No, we have to worry more.' Annabelle dashed his hopes. 'I would say we have about five minutes before my dear Aunt Widow decides she's angry with us and sends one of the sisters to kill Xavier, kill Pan and capture the two of us. She's flighty when she gets angry, she doesn't think things through. Therefore we run like hell.'

'So wait,' Adam gasped. 'All of your family are spiders? How does that work?'

'I'm adopted!' Annabelle snapped. 'Now shut up and run!'

Adam would have really liked to tell her that wasn't a real answer, but if she was this worried he supposed it was time to run. Finally the group saw the end of the line, a light slowly getting brighter and brighter as they moved. He looked over his shoulder to see a few dozen giant spiders swarming in from every direction.

'Right on time!' Annabelle called out. 'I hope you're not tiring!'

He was and he knew it, his legs were burning and he could feel the air burning in his chest, his breath was coming hard and he was getting a little woozy. He could see a haze developing in front of him as he moved, but he took a deep breath and did his best to pick up the pace. He could feel himself starting to slow down. Pan was getting closer and closer behind him and Xavier and Annabelle had outpaced him easily by now. He could hear the spiders getting closer and closer and looked over his shoulder to check, but Pan just hauled him forward.

'Less looking,' Pan snapped. 'It won't make them slower, just you, now run!' Adam could feel his legs start to give out, they were turning to jelly and were starting to shake as he moved. He was breathing hard as he ran for the light.

Pan ran into his back and lifted him up, the big man letting go of the line to haul him up off his feet. He tossed Adam through the portal and he had to roll and take a deep breath to get up on his feet. By the time his head had cleared the others were already out, Xavier driving the creature back as Pan ducked under and threw it with all of his strength. Annabelle reached out with one hand and flicked the portal closed.

'Well,' Xavier smiled as spots appeared in front of Adam's eyes, 'that was bracing.'

'All right.' Annabelle clapped her hands, already walking away. 'Let's get moving. We're burning our lead and time is money. The Legion will find a way in soon enough.'

'I just,' Adam spoke between sucking wind, 'need a minute.'

'Oh come on!' Annabelle snapped. 'I knew you weren't going to be of any use, but I was at least hoping you weren't actively going to almost get yourself killed. Since you have, and before we even got started mind you, could you perhaps at least not waste our time as well?'

'Well,' he barely managed to pull himself to his feet. 'Excuse me all to hell, but I've gone from normal person to almost dying three times in a matter of days. You know what might have been helpful to keep me screwing up? You telling me, over the day we spent in a truck together about what we were going to have to deal with. Like, say for example that your sisters are spiders and one of them would try to brainwash me? Still, I suppose you didn't have to take me out with you, you could have just left me to die since apparently, that's not a problem for you. So yeah, sorry I didn't have "running for my life" on my resume. So next time you feel like dragging someone with you maybe get someone who's used to it.' He paused for a moment feeling the need to finish the sentence. 'Bitch.'

'If you had just done as you were told, dead weight, there wouldn't have been a problem!'

'Believe it or not I'm not all that inclined to blindly obey random people who don't tell me what's going on. So I'm going to catch my breath right here and, when I can walk again, we'll keep moving.' He sat back down.

'You've got five minutes.' She turned away from him.

'Or what?' he retorted. 'You'll leave without me? Because frankly I feel like I'd be safer without you in particular.'

'You'd be in the hands of the Legion right now if it

wasn't for me!'

'Just like the guy you left to die, or is my turn for that still coming?'

'How dare you!' She raised her fist and Pan neatly caught it in one of his own before she could land it.

'That's enough, the pair of you.' He stepped between the two of them. 'We could all have handled this better.' He thought about that for a moment. 'Well you three could have, I'm doing all right so far but I guess I could have done more than I did to defuse this. So here goes.' He turned to Annabelle first. 'Sister, Adam is confused, he's alone and scared. He's not ready for this and he's doing his best. You need to make allowances for that.'

'But he–' she interrupted.

'And Adam!' He cut her off with one raised hand. 'Annabelle is used to a certain level of ability and professionalism, we all are, and the fact you can't keep up is annoying to us. You have to try to understand that we need the best you have.'

'But she–'

'No!' He shook his head and raised his hand at Adam this time. 'You both need to make allowances for the other's shortcomings and chill. So, what we're going to do is take a few minutes to let Adam rest and he's going to get moving again as soon as he can. And we're all going to stop being total dicks about the whole affair.'

'Fine, I'll wait,' Annabelle sighed and slumped down onto the bed. Adam looked around.

'Are we in an apartment?' The walls around them were gold and cream frescoes, on their right was an ultra-modern kitchen and a hardwood floor was under their feet. Adam made his way up to a couch and relaxed.

'We are,' Xavier smiled. 'We left through an apartment building and we've come out the same way. We are in the upper word, where the Seraph call home.'

'So we're going to get Seraph power here?' He looked around like he was expecting it to come popping out of the walls.

'No. This is where we're going to find out where we can find the Presence. This is the next step on the path and where Pan pays his rent.' He patted the bigger man on the shoulder.

'As soon as we're ready to go.' Pan yawned and removed his gloves, cracked his knuckles and put them back on. 'When we get out of there just keep your heads down and your mouths shut. You shouldn't have to deal with any of the Legion here, but the Seraph run the show and they get a little weird. Don't pay them too much attention and try not to seem as confused and curious as I'm sure you will be. I know a guy who spends time up here, I'm sure he'll be able to show us the way.'

'All right.' Adam took a few more deep breaths and pulled himself upright. 'All right, let's go.'

The Seraph creatures were as strange as Pan had

said. As they climbed down onto the streets he marvelled at the mixture of strange wildlife. Creatures that looked like angels twirled and weaved and turned in the sky. Small faceless things ran through the street on all fours, chittering and chatting with each other in small groups. Tall gawky looking bipeds hobbled awkwardly around above them.

Among the crowd, watching their feet to not step on the things that ran between their legs were monsters that stood as tall as small buildings. They clomped as they walked, looking like statues of white and gold, with expressionless faces and giant weapons. There were tall distorted creatures in long white dresses who ran in wheels of flame wearing strangely serene features.

Pan looked at him and smiled as he took the lead, moving through like nothing was wrong. Adam remembered the simple instructions, keep your head down and your eyes off anything in particular as you walk. The creatures steered around them, not bothering to interact. A couple of the faceless creatures came close to them, running around them a couple of times before they wandered off apparently deciding there was no entertainment to be had. Annabelle's only reaction was to draw her garments out of their reach and Adam kept walking, keeping his head up. One of the big creatures bent down to stare at them.

'Hello,' the big creature said, its voice booming for probably a block.

'Hello.' Pan smiled up at it and it focused its giant eyes on him.

'Who are you?'

'My name is Pathfinder.' He motioned to the others to keep walking. 'These are my friends.'

'What are you doing here?' The expressionless face suddenly twisted into a smile.

'Just passing through,' he smiled. 'We're going to meet a friend here, and take him home.'

'Mkay.' The thing raised one fingertip about the size of Pan and pointed to him. 'Don't make any trouble. Or I'll stompy-stomp you flat.'

'We won't.' He nodded.

'Stompy-stomp.' The creature wandered off and they continued on their path.

The city was like an older version of the one he'd been in during the last hallucination. Where the one he'd hallucinated was ultra-modern skyscrapers and high rises, this area was all spires and cathedrals, white cresting spikes breaking the air and giving a kind of gothic feel to the whole thing.

'Come on.' Pan turned off at one of the cathedrals, climbing up to the main door and pushing it open. He stormed his way through the pews as the church was bathed by multiple stained-glass frescoes of light. Pan made his way through to a small door and pulled it open, hauling himself up a ladder.

'Are we following him?' Adam looked at the others and Xavier considered this a moment, then jumped up the ladder to follow. Adam followed behind, Annabelle after him. He hauled himself up the ladder as long and hard as he could.

'I do hope you're not tiring yourself out,' Annabelle noted from beneath him. 'Have a snack, take a nap.'

'Go,' he took a deep breath as he hauled himself up another rung, 'fuck–'

'Myself?' Annabelle smiled up. 'All right, keep up if you can.'

When they finally got to the top Adam looked out over the city and took a couple of breaths, leaning over to look at the world.

'It's pretty if nothing else.' He looked out at the strange creatures moving through the serene city. 'But are we up here for any kind of reason?'

'You are up here to see me.' The deep crackling voice sounded like rocks grating against each other. 'Or at least the Pathfinder is. I assume the rest of you are here with him.'

'Who the hell said that?' Adam looked around, there was nothing up there except the gargoyle statue, sitting hunched over on the roof.

'I did.' It was a few moments before he realised it was the gargoyle making the noise. 'Hello Pathfinder.' He raised one hand slowly and certainly. 'My dear friend.'

'Pathfinder?' Adam looked around.

'Me.' Pan embraced the stone creature and it wrapped its heavy arms around him. 'The Eldritch call me the Lost Soldier, and the Seraph call me the

Pathfinder. You'll know why soon enough.' He looked at the creature as he pulled back from the hug, moving at the same slow pace the gargoyle seemed to move. 'Have you seen anything?'

'I have seen many things,' it rumbled. 'I have seen birds and angels and births and deaths.' It slowly turned its head around, its neck cracking slowly as it fixed its eyes on them. 'I also see that it is harvest time, and I see someone without a Presence.' It laughed, a sound like rocks rolling down a hill. 'I see that there is one nearby and I see many ways to get there.' Its face twisted into a bizarre rictus that he could almost imagine to be something like a smile. 'And I see the shortest path.'

'The Legion are on our tail.' Pan's voice seemed just faster than completely calm. 'We don't have a lot of time Bell.'

'Then I shall abandon the formalities.' The thing raised both hands. 'Very well, we shall get down to business.' It crunched and cracked briefly as it dropped from its pedestal onto the ground with a sudden boom. It spread its wings wide, the movement obviously costing it a lot of effort. Pan removed his shirt and slowly, glacially slowly lowered himself to his knees. The Gargoyle's clawed hands pressed on either side of Pan's head.

'Oh I hate this part,' he grumbled. 'Fuckin'… hate… this… part.' Then he suddenly screamed in pain. He shook and shuddered as his bare back began to grow a strange design in his skin. He reached up and held onto the creature's arms with his own to keep himself up as his screaming grew less sane and more animal. The creature began to crunch and grind and its body seemed to shrink and fade as Pan wailed and shuddered. As the noises got louder and louder Pan's screams shifted from pain to agony.

As soon as the creature was gone Pan collapsed onto his face, letting out mewling pained noises. 'Hate, hate, hate, hate haaate that part,' he groaned. There was a small trail of drool and tears on the ground under his face. He struggled to his feet and the others stared at the strange picture on his back. It was a map of the city, with a symbol clearly marking the cathedral they were on.

Pan's voice was deeper and rumbling now. 'I have seen a Presence and I have seen no Legionnaires or monsters coming toward us. We shall need to pass through the diamond gates here,' a gate image appeared in one place. 'And then cross the Glass Knight's Bridge and go through to the Temple. From there things get a little hazy but that should get us a decent lead.'

'Do any of you have any idea what that means?' Adam looked at the entire group.

'We do,' Xavier nodded. 'Or at least close enough.'

'All right.' Adam looked at them. 'Hey, while I have to waste our time climbing down I might as well ask you what's the deal with all of the names?'

'We each have at least three names, including the one we were born with,' Pan began to explain, his voice calm and regular as he moved in spite of the effort of climbing. 'One human, one Seraph and one Eldritch. Some of us have more names based on certain things. It's an easy way for them to build legends around us, and tell stories. Also the occasional prophecies that crop up now and again tend to refer to us by one name or the other. They're also clues into our nature at times.'

'Sometimes it just questions our fashion choices,' Xavier said cheerfully.

'We both know that the name Red Gentleman does not refer to that stupid coat.' Pan glared at him. 'Be more of an idiot.'

'I'm not sure how to do that.' Xavier seemed to be seriously considering it.

'I'm not sure it'd be possible,' Annabelle chimed in.

'I thought he was just talking about the name Top Hat Man.' Adam looked at Pan. 'Isn't that his other name?'

'Well yeah,' Pan nodded. 'But that's because that's where his first Presence is. A lot of us have at least one name based on our power.' When they were down and walking the streets again Adam picked up the conversation.

'So wait.' He looked down at Pan and noticed the fact he had no tattoo on his head anymore. 'So the Pathfinder thing means you can turn gargoyles into maps?'

'No.' Pan looked up at him with a smile. 'I took

him into my tattoo for a while. He'll show me where you want to go and then I'll be expected to take him where he wants to be. It's useful for Lurkers or Gargoyles, the kind of creatures that see a lot but don't get to move around all that much.'

'So how does it feel?'

'At first it hurts.' Pan scowled. 'Like a lot, like, just a whole fuckin' bunch. Like, you have no idea how much it hurts. After a while it folds back to just painful, which is where I'm at now, then it just feels weird. I also have him in my head. He doesn't do or say much and he doesn't have any input into what I do but he exists and he can let me know he's here.' He leaned back and scratched his back.

'Belfry's an old friend of mine. I've lead him across a few rooftops now and again to get him better vantage points. Now, in the interests of preparing you when we get to the Glass Knight's bridge, don't do anything. Let me and Annabelle go first, then you go and Xavier will bring up the rear unless Xavier says otherwise. He should be softened up enough by then for you to get by him without too much trouble.' He took a moment to consider things then shook his head.

'I know I'm supposed to give you information in accordance with your earlier request but I can't tell you much. If you're too prepared for this it's going to fuck you up and you'll misstep. He'll explain the trial, so just show up, stare the dude down and as long as you're a decent person you should be okay.'

'Should be?' Adam gave him a look, gritting his

teeth a little. 'That's not exactly optimistic you know.'

'I know, and I'm sorry for that,' Pan tried to explain. 'But if you knew what was going on you'd be completely screwed. You'd try too hard to guess the right answer instead of just acting as one of the Lost would, on instinct and without too much thought.'

'That sounds insane.' He shook his head. 'I mean, you're telling me you don't want me to be prepared or aware of what I'm doing before I do it?'

'Some things you'll just have to take me at my word for.' Pan shrugged.

'Especially since after you take one more turn we'll be there,' Annabelle interrupted.

As they turned the corner they saw a giant glittering crystal bridge, with spires up and down the sides. It shone and glistened, glittering in the sun with light sparkling off in every direction. On the other side was a giant gate that went so high that Adam could barely see the top of it.

For a moment Adam confused the man who stood on the bridge for a statue. He wore what appeared to be armour made of some kind of glass, flashing mirror images of everything around him. The helmet turned slowly and certainly to the group and he raised the giant sword he had been leaning on into a ready position, but did nothing else.

'I'll go first,' Pan sighed and walked forward, seeming more bored by this task that daunted. The knight approached him and bowed, Pan bowed back and the two of them stared at each other, Pan's hands wrapping around the base of the sword. They held it there together for a long moment, then the knight lowered the sword, put it down beside it and raised its hands like a boxer.

Pan lunged at the knight and the two danced for a moment, trading blows and punches as they moved. The armour didn't seem to slow down Pan's blows all that much; he still made the knight stagger and falter as easily as the knight did to him. In the end he overcame it by brute force, slamming his entire body into the creature and tackling it onto the ground.

The two rolled on the ground and Pan ended up on top, his knees bracing the position and began laying down blows to the chest and face until the knight went limp. From there he got up and walked over its downed body, cracking his knuckles on the way to the other side. He leaned against the far wall and the knight climbed slowly to its feet, reeling a little as it made its way back to its sword. It slipped back into the ready position and faced them again.

'My turn.' Annabelle seemed to feel legitimately daunted as she advanced on the creature. She began to whirl and twist her fingers as she walked, long strands of white thread slipping out of her skin and winding around each other. By the time she got there her hand was trailing a long white whip made of that same web, though this one seemed less sticky and more, barbed. The knight approached her and the two bowed, then took hold of the sword and stared at each other. The knight spun his sword and it seemed to shrink, switching from a massive two-handed blade to a smaller short sword. The knight began to pull itself out of its armour, revealing what looked like a mirrored blank copy of a person. It dropped the armour around his feet as they faced off.

Annabelle began her offensive with sudden vicious whipping motions, lashing across his chest arms and face. The knight advanced on her in sudden jabbing bursts and she retreated just as quickly, bobbing, ducking and weaving to land painful strikes onto him. Some he ducked or weaved, some he blocked with his blade and some he tried to take on the less dangerous parts of his body but some of the strikes still struck home causing a strange silver sludge to leak from its skin. His return offensives resulted in some spectacular acrobatics on her part, rolling, handspringing backwards and twirling. On one occasion, she even turned her back and ran a short distance in outright flight before turning around and renewing her offensive.

The greatest point of tension in the fight approached as Annabelle slowly but surely ran out of retreating space, nearing their end of the bridge and somehow Adam knew that if she stepped off the back of the bridge she would somehow fail whatever test she was being subjected to.

As she hit the edge of the bridge her eyes narrowed like she was counting something, then flicked out the hand that wasn't holding the whip, a small glob of white mess struck out for his face and the sword cut the web ball in two. She lashed out with the whip toward his face and ran to the knight's side. She feinted right and as he began his return strike she lunged left. He swung the sword at her and only managed to cut open her back. She turned and swung the whip low, catching him in both knees, then spun down and lashed at the hand, a harsh crack ringing out as whip hit hand and the sword fell loose. She leaned forward and wrapped her whip around his neck, wrenching with all her strength. After a moment he went limp and she turned, staggering and bleeding off the bridge.

'You go next,' Xavier said softly. 'Trust me, he is currently injured and after our confrontation he will be,' he thought for a moment as if trying to find the right word, 'aggressive.'

'All right.' Adam nodded and took a step forward. 'Let's do this I guess.' He tried not to look as scared as he was as he advanced on the knight. He tried to stop his legs from shaking, tried to stop his hands from twitching. His breath was coming fast but he still didn't feel like he was getting enough air.

As he faced the knight, in all of its armour again, he looked into its visor.

'So what do we do?' he said to the figure in front of him, unsure it was going to respond.

'We test.' The voice was surprisingly soft and gentle. 'If you succeed I shall fight you on your terms, if you should fail I will fight you on mine.' He bowed deeply and Adam bowed back.

'All right.' He looked at the creature and it held up its sword. 'What am I supposed to do?'

'Just look into my face, and take the sword.' And he did, wrapping his hands around the blades hilt and staring at the reflecting face. He looked at the helmet and saw his own reflection.

'You are alone,' the reflection spoke without Adam talking.

'No I'm not.' He couldn't hear himself saying the words but he knew he'd said them and he knew it had heard.

'Them?' the reflection laughed. 'They do not care for you. They see you as a waste, an anchor dragging them down as they have told you. They see you as useless, no help to anyone. You are nothing but a burden hey must carry until you are something worth using and then something they can use until they end up getting you killed.'

He didn't have a response for that, he wished he had. This thing, this reflection seemed to know the truth of the situation. Hadn't Annabelle said the same thing? Pan seemed happy enough to have him around and he had no idea what Xavier was thinking but Annabelle had come right out and said it.

'And who else do you have?' the reflection asked. 'How many thoughts have you spared for them throughout the last few days? Your long missing parents, sister, your friends or job or life. As soon as you found something else worth the distraction you came into it and their supposed importance for you has so little wroth that you have not even dismissed them from your mind. They have never commanded enough attention to even be worth dismissing.'

'I've been busy,' he protested.

'Busy,' the voice mimicked mockingly. 'You have enjoyed the business, the activity. You have craved the lack of room for thought because it has freed you from the lonely, pathetic life in which you lived.'

'My life,' he clenched his jaw, 'was not pathetic. It was a little boring and yeah, maybe even a little lonely but it was not pathetic. I had a job, friends, a family, people that I love and just because I've let myself get carried away doesn't mean I don't. Even if I did,' he cracked a grin, 'it wouldn't fucking matter. When I need someone to be with, I'll go get someone. When I want a busier life, or more purpose I'll go looking but right now I am who I am and I'm okay with that. It's okay to be a little lonely sometimes. So don't tell me what to do.'

'You will always be alone,' it replied. 'You know it and fear it. No matter what you do you will never find another to love, to share your life with. There is no one who really cares about you. Your life is empty and you are alone.'

'Not as full as it could be maybe.' He shrugged, still smiling. 'But as full as I need it to be for now. I'm done here. I'm okay on my own for now, and who knows, I might end up liking these people.'

'And when you are not? If you do not?'

'I'll deal with that then.,' He smirked and pushed

the sword away. 'We're done, I passed.'

'How do you know?' The knight raised its sword.

'Because I said so and no one argued, so drop the sword and let's do this.' The knight stood still for a moment and for a second Adam thought his bravado would fail. Then the knight calmly let the sword drop and began to remove its armour, tossing it away piece by piece. The breastplate fell last, landing with an ominous thud. It raised its bare arms to fight. 'For all the good it does me you might as well have the sword. It's not like I'm any kind of fighter.'

'Do you know how to fight?' the knight asked.

'My dad taught me a few things,' he admitted.

'Then since you have no Presence I shall gift you with a piece of guidance. You cannot be faster than me, you cannot be stronger than me, you cannot be a better fighter than me. In this fight you are none of those things.'

'That's not advice,' he shook his head. 'That's just you being an arsehole.'

'You must remember that there are two things you can be.'

'What are they?'

'I do not know,' it shrugged. 'But I know that you remember.'

'No, I don't.'

'Then you should think quickly.' The knight came at him, swinging at his stomach. The fist landed in his gut, not hard enough to knock him off his feet, just hard enough to show him two things. One, this guy's punches could really knock the sense out of a man. And two, Adam could take a hit. Sure he was stumbling, it hurt, but it wasn't enough to take him out of the fight, or even knock him down. Just like that it came back to him, the lessons on how to fight his father had given him. He'd stood up for himself when he was twelve to two bigger kids and got beaten up. His mother had been mortified, but his father had taught him to fight, not so he could use it, just so he could be ready.

Adam faced off against the knight again and when he came in high Adam ducked, aiming a punch right at the solar plexus. He'd missed and his fist had landed in the meat of the chest. It didn't seem to trouble the knight but at least his hand hit flesh not metal. This was a person, a real person with the same organs and limbs and ability to be hurt as anyone else.

When the knight lashed down at him with his elbow Adam felt his head ache as he stumbled back, his vision blurring a little. The knight took a step back and let Adam get back to his feet.

'Never let him back up once you knock him down,' his dad had told him, laying on his back on the ground. 'Some people think it's fighting dirty, and it is, but it's also fighting to win. You were fighting bigger kids, right? Well you can't let them use that size, keep moving and keep him moving with you.' He ducked under the knight's hands and crashed into him, running his shoulder into the knight's chest. He knocked the knight backwards and the reflective man hit him in the face, sending him staggering back.

'But he's not just big, he's strong and fast too.'

'Remember this Adam.' His dad had put his hand on Adam's shoulder and looked him in the eyes. 'You could spend your life working out and you wouldn't be the strongest. You could run twenty kilometres a day and not be the fastest, but there's always two things you can be.'

'What's that?' he looked up at him and his dad had smiled.

'The toughest and the meanest.'

Adam fake stumbled, falling down onto one knee and the knight advanced on him. He struggled slowly to his feet and then suddenly "recovered" gaining speed. He ran toward the knight at full speed, running all out at it and throwing a knee into the stomach. It staggered for a moment and he rammed his forehead into the bridge of the creature's nose. It stumbled back and regathered its strength, landing a kick to his thigh but he ignored it, moving toward it, ignore the pain.

Once you have an advantage you have to exploit it. Tough'll win you a hundred fights strong would lose. He aimed a punch at its throat and it threw its hands up to block him, so he stepped in and gave a short punch to the solar plexus, exactly where he'd aimed the first shot. It gasped and coughed, but managed to punch him in the ribs. As he staggered it stepped around him and reached out to grapple him from behind, throw him down or choke him.

He grabbed the arm and bit down on it as hard as

he could, ignoring the foul taste that filled his mouth. The creature winced and he thrust elbows backwards, one, two, three before it started to stumble. He let it go and turned around, spitting the creatures own blood into its face. It raised its hand to wipe its face and he hit it again and again with everything he had, aiming for the ribs and kidneys.

The knight had some tough of its own though, it recovered faster than he could hurt it and slammed its fist into his cheek. He staggered backwards, his balance gone. It advanced on him, hands raised and he did the only thing he could think of to do, a move he had used a week later at school and few times since; he took a step in and raised his knee between its legs, landing the point of the kneecap right where the male sex least likes to be hit.

It turned out that the creature was male after all and as it staggered Adam hit it in the nose with his forehead, then struck again and again, finally bearing the thing to the ground. He put his forearm on its throat, pinned one hand against his own wrist and pushed down for all he was worth. The creature went limp and closed its eyes, completely still. Adam climbed off its prone body and walked the rest of the way across the bridge, holding his ribs with one hand and his head with the other. He spat again, the taste of metal in his mouth.

When he got to the edge of the bridge he looked around, sat down and leaned against the bridge to soothe his aching ribs and watch Xavier cross. As the

Top Hat Man made his way across the bridge he took his cane's sheath in one hand and the sword in the other, the knight already back in his armour and leaning on his massive sword again. Fully armed and armoured the two of them faced off. The knight began his bow and right at the deepest point Xavier stepped forward and slammed his sword through the neck joint in the armour.

'Come now.' Xavier struck again, his sword finding another crack and pushing deep into it. 'We both knew I would never pass your ridiculous test. Frankly I suspect bias.' The Knight let out a roar and launched itself into the fight.

The Glass Knight had been holding back in his last fights, that was pretty clear. Even in that giant armour he spun and twirled like an acrobat, turning aside Xavier's small probing blade with his plates. He whirled and slammed his giant sword in broad strokes that made Xavier jump twist and whirl to avoid it, but jump twist and whirl Xavier did.

He moved at speeds that became confusing to the eye in his long coat, dodging, ducking and turning the giant weapon just enough with his blade or cane that the mirror sword only grazed his garment. On one occasion, he even jumped over the blade, landed on it with one foot for a couple of seconds and leaped clean over the creature's head to stab it a few more times. This seemed to slow the knight down slightly, although a fast, unexpected elbow did slam into Xavier's jaw and knock him flying across the bridge.

He rolled in mid-air and landed on his feet, to leap back into a fight that now seemed more or less in his favour.

Xavier's blade probed and tracked the knight, but the big sword did manage to rip into him, tearing open the coat and slamming into his ribs, opening a free-flowing wound. Xavier rolled aside and attacked again, seemingly unperturbed.

With every wound, the Glass Knight began to slow more and more, relying more on its power than its speed. Xavier no longer needed to turn aside the blade, simply stepping weaving and dodging to avoid it. The knight went for one big overhead swing, missed completely and slammed it into the bridge. In that moment of distraction Xavier stepped around and rammed his blade right through the knight's face plate. The sword had no sooner left the knights body than the gentleman had turned around and sprinted off, moving at an almost blurring speed toward the end of the bridge. No sooner had the Knight of Mirrors finished falling than it was immediately back on its feet.

It moved like nothing had happened, travelling even faster than it had during their fight. It outpaced Xavier, gaining ground quickly. It almost reached him when he got to the end of the bridge, hurling himself forward into a roll just as the blade nicked the tail of his coat. He rolled and rose to his feet, ready to fight but no sooner had he left the bridge than the knight retook his earlier position as if nothing had happened.

'When killed outside of honourable combat,' Xavier straightened his ruined coat, 'he becomes enraged. It makes him strong, fast, superhumanly durable and heals all of his wounds instantly. It also fills him with an eternal hatred for whoever killed him. If I ever come back this way again I shall need to be at my best.' He removed his coat and gave a broad grin, straightening his hat. 'Still such sacrifices must be made.'

'Okay, putting aside how goddamn creepy Xavier is again,' Pan looked at them, 'are you all okay?'

'Bleeding a little,' Annabelle winced. 'But I patched it up already so I'm more or less okay.' Indeed the injury was already covered in that same white silk, and she was currently making ready to do the same to Xavier's injury.

'Still aching in the stomach and face,' Adam coughed. 'And badly in need of a breath mint, but other than that I'm all right.' He spat again and wiped his mouth. 'But honestly the breath mint is the biggest concern. Do not bite strangers, its foul.'

'Did I see things?' Annabelle looked at him. 'Or did you really knee him in the balls?'

'I really kneed him in the balls,' Adam nodded. 'I couldn't think of anything else to do!'

'You kneed the Immortal Knight of Mirrors in the balls.' Annabelle began to laugh, shaking her head at the absurdity of it all. Pan started to chuckle and Xavier joined in, soon the group was all chuckling as they sat at the gates. Annabelle bandaged Xavier's wounds with ease as she smiled. As the laughter ended Xavier reached into his hat and threw a brightly coloured candy to him. Adam shook his head and unwrapped the candy.

'Travel candy?' He looked at Xavier. 'You keep candy in your magic hat?'

'I do,' Xavier nodded. 'And a range of other things as well. Though not a rabbit. I tried to carry a rabbit in it once and then I ended up carrying the corpse of a rabbit. From there it became something of an issue.'

'All right.' Adam moved right along. 'So how do we get through the giant crystal gates?'

'We don't.' Annabelle looked at them. 'We go over them. It'll take a couple of hours, but these gates don't open unless the feel like it and they're a giant dickhead.'

'I heard that,' came a deep booming voice. It made the ground and the bridge shake. Adam looked back at the knight, but it seemed to be preoccupied with leaning and staring.

'I really don't like you very much.'

'Nor I you,' it replied.

'So wait.' He looked around. 'The gate doesn't let people through?'

'I will, if I have an order from a recognised authority. Or if anyone can give me a good reason why I should.'

'I need to get hold of a Presence that just developed in our world. If I don't get it someone who will abuse it will.'

'Ahhh,' it chuckled. 'We have a misunderstanding. See this is isn't a good reason to do it, it's a good reason for you to want me to do it. Not the same thing. I have less than no interest in the business of insects and irritants. One irritating, whining human having more power than another gives me no great joy or despair. I will be here, in my place, either way.'

'All right then,' he nodded. 'Seems fair, but if I'm going to give you what you want, you have to tell me what that is. What do you want?'

'Nothing in particular.' Its voice was bored. 'I have no great care for money as I require no sustenance or shelter. I have no investment in your wars. I want to be left alone to do what I do. If I have an order from a recognised authority I will open but there is little you can give me.'

'Then why did you tell us that you would move if someone gave you what you want?'

'I wanted to see how pathetic your scrambling would be. Fairly pathetic as it turns out.'

'I don't know.' He thought about it for a moment. 'Annabelle, how long would it take us to get over the wall?'

'Hours,' she shrugged. 'And it's a little risky but we can do it.'

'I have a plan.' He smiled. 'The gate told me it's weakness and I know what to do but I'm going to need Xavier's help.'

'What must I do?' Xavier shrugged and drew his weapon.

'Oh you don't need that.' His smile widened. 'Just chat with the door. Have a conversation with it. Tell it about things you like and don't like, stuff you want and ignore whatever it says.'

Xavier looked at the solid wall for a moment, walked up to it, removed his coat and hat and began to talk. He spoke in long rambling passages that allowed for no interjection or interruption. His chatter ranged from the intellectual to the whimsical to the insane ramblings of a madman. As he rambled Annabelle, Pan and Adam sat off to the side.

'Give it,' Adam thought about it, 'ten more minutes. He should be ready to let us through by then.'

'All right,' Annabelle smiled. 'Perhaps you aren't such a burden after all.'

'Thanks.' He scowled at her for a long moment. 'I know what you do with burdens.' Annabelle winced and looked at the ground for a moment.

'We didn't, you know,' her voice was soft and a little sad, 'leave him to die. At least not like you're implying we did.'

'Seems like it to me.'

'Yeah, I can see why it would.' She thought about it for a moment. 'Then let me try to explain. Raven knew full well what we were planning to do and how we were planning to do it. He chose to come with us knowing that. Besides, as far as survivors go, Raven is one of the greats. If anyone ever stood a chance of making it out of that place alive and intact its him.'

She shook her head. 'The point is you might not be able to understand it, but he made his choice and I don't think we've seen the last of him just yet. I can't say for sure but stranger things have happened.'

'All right.' He didn't believe her but there was no need to push her on it just yet. 'So was he the fourth? The fourth person I saw in the café?'

'Describe the fourth person you saw.'

'He was wearing a hooded coat, there wasn't really much to describe.'

'Do your best.' She leaned back and steepled her fingers.

'He was, about my size, sort of pale, wearing a hooded jacket. That's about it.'

'Okay.' Annabelle looked at him. 'Was Raven your size?'

'Around that,' he shrugged. 'A little taller I guess, so it wasn't him?'

'And more to the point,' she raised one finger, 'did Raven seem at all the type to cover his whole body in a hooded coat?'

'You've made your point.'

'Did I?' She quirked her eyebrow. 'I'm trying to teach you to look harder at the world around you. To study people, the ability to know who a person is can be the difference between a surprise attack and a meeting. It can mean you can identify one of theirs and one of ours. It will allow you to see through illusions and deceptions. Knowing who you and the people around you are might just be the most important skill you can learn. So, why doesn't Raven look like the kind of person who would cover himself in a hood.'

'He never stooped or hunched.' He thought about it. 'He stood straight up and always looked you in the eyes, always stood tall.'

'Was that all?'

'No,' he realised. 'No, some people with scars cover them up. They move to make sure you don't stare or look at them. Raven was different, the way he looked at everyone it was like he was daring us to stare. Like he was almost hoping I would say something about them. That kind of person doesn't hide themselves, and if they do it's not with a hood.'

'Very good,' she nodded. 'I guess you're learning after all.' She started weaving web in case Adam's plan failed and Adam took a look around. The sky was pure white, no cloud textures, no blue. It was like someone had been drawing the city and had just forgotten about the sky. The wall behind them was white pearlescent crystal but it looked like it was all made of the same single piece. It appeared to be one untarnished block with no damage or scars to it.

'How old is this place?'

'Old,' Annabelle shrugged. 'Older than me and my mother and her mother, older than the oldest webs and older than the spiders remember.'

'Then shouldn't there be some kind of damage in it?' He looked up at the rock.

'From what?' She looked around. 'The gate opens

itself if it opens at all, and most people who won't make it through don't bother risking the Knight of Mirrors for a path they know will be closed to them. The few of them who make it through but don't have permission from the gate beat on the stone a little but trust me when I say that you don't want to attack this thing. As for weather damage well, lick your finger and tell me where the wind is coming from.' He tried, licking his finger and holding it up to the air.

'There isn't any,' he realised.

'No,' she nodded. 'There isn't. The sun doesn't shine because the Seraph world has no sun. The wind doesn't blow unless one of them makes it blow and it doesn't rain for the air has no clouds. This world, for all of its beauty, is static and unchanging. Unless it is acted upon, nothing happens here that needs to be acted upon. Just like the Eldritch have no inherent order or logic and need it imposed upon them. That's why they need us.'

'All right.' He looked at her. 'Do you really think Raven's going to be okay?'

'I don't know,' she admitted. 'I hope so.'

CHAPTER SIX

Legate and Ursas strode ahead of their unit, a small Blank Faced Legion following them. They carried the Slave Breaker above their heads as they walked. They never slowed down, never stopped or raised any variety of complaint or objection. That was why he liked the Blank more than almost any other being. There was no argument, no objection because each of them understood their obligations. They understood the deal they had entered into and the rules by which they played. They made no attempt to fight their fate, even those who had entered into it unwillingly, or unknowingly.

'I know what you're doing.' Their captives voice was soft. There was a little pain in it in spite of his resilience, but there was also cold resolution running underneath. 'At first I thought you just weren't very good torturers. You're too slow, you take breaks in between that last too long. You feed me too well, let me sleep too often and say the wrong things,' he laughed. 'But you aren't inept. I figured out what you're doing.'

'Did you?' he questioned. 'Did you indeed? Well it matters not. You knowing my plan does nothing to dissuade it. You cannot change your situation, or your intentions. So, if you wish to tell me what I did, you may feel free.'

'You're trying to remove every path but one,' he declared. 'You know I won't talk, you know I won't

117

give up, you've eliminated every path to my existence except to get out of this in the only way I can.' He gave Legate a smirking little smile. 'You intend to use my own knife against me.' He coughed up a tiny amount of his own blood. 'That little bear of yours is going to drive that knife into me and you're going to see if I have only one path remaining.'

'Yer damn right I am.' And with that Ursas pushed Legate to one side and jumped past the Legion, drawing the knife from his belt and pouncing on Raven in one smooth motion. He drove the long black blade into his victim's neck even as Legate moved to stop him. The Blank Faces held their victim up to Ursas, given no command to stop the smaller man doing whatever he liked save attacking Legate himself. As the knife drove into him, Raven began to shake and shudder, letting out a strange hissing sigh of pain and relief. Legate had seen many men made Blank, and many Blank enslaved but he had never seen someone go completely from normality to slavery in seconds. Raven shuddered, convulsed twitched and shook and finally stopped. His breath became slow, level, steady and routine, just like another enslaved Blank.

'Let him up.' The Blank removed the chains holding Raven still and put him down on the ground, letting him climb to his feet.

Raven was gone, that much was immediately clear. He wore the same black trench coat and face, but as he moved his skin rippled and fell away to reveal pure black. The blank, formless, matte black of an Eldritch Blank, tall and lithe like all the others but without the sharp blockiness that were always that of the Blank. This one's limbs were defined, its stature as rigid and simple as any other man. There was one other difference, upon his face. Where all the others had nothing other than the blank formless mask that was the mark of a typical Blank this one had a pair of long marks upon his face. Where once had been real scars there were now defined marks on his mask, two formless slits like the eyes of a scarecrow. But he formed up with the Blanks like any other and took his place in the formation.

'That was perhaps unwise,' Legate said softly. 'Though I cannot entirely deny the validity and efficacy of the action it may have been smarter to be certain of the consequences before you undertook it. In the future, I would be obliged if you were to check with me before you took up a deed with such possibly titanic consequences. Please, be certain to keep yourself restrained whenever possible.'

'Aint one of yer damn Blanks Leggie.' Ursas spat again, that was becoming as persistent a habit as it was distasteful. 'I don't always do as I'm damn well told. Anyway, it worked out, didn't it? Move on.'

'Very well.' Legate looked at him, straightening himself up. 'I am forced to consider that perhaps you need another lesson in who is in charge of this operation!'

Ursas's stocky frame lost some of its swagger and

power, faltering for a brief moment and looking at the ground. 'I'll check in before the next big thing.' He scowled and looked away.

'See that you do.' Legate smiled under his mask. Perhaps the animal would learn to do what it was told after all. Any beast can be managed, given the right carrot and stick. This he believed above everything else. He heard a rumble of thunder above his head and saw a flash of lightning and he knew the path to the world of the Seraph would be open. He looked at his Blanks, and his last associates, a pair of small women who walked beside them, one dragging the other on a leash.

'It is time to go.' He looked at them. He could not show his face to his enemies, not without risking his life and his plans, but he could easily send those two.

In the end Adam was revealed to have been optimistic; it took just over half an hour of Xavier's conversation before the door agreed to open just to keep him silent, under the condition that he promise not to come back.

The heavy, white stone slowly forced itself open with a grinding shudder to reveal the monastery within. Adam had been expecting it to be the same white on white that he had seen throughout the world, but as he walked in he was quite surprised. This monastery seemed to contain every colour under the rainbow, a prismatic blur of shape and colour that gave Adam a headache within seconds of walking into it. It looked like the inside of a few dozen kaleidoscopes had splattered themselves over one another all over the temple. They pushed their way through the strangely coloured gates and things only got stranger.

The spaces that would be pews, were beds rather than benches, actual plush mattresses with people laying, relaxing, even cuddling with one another on them. The pulpit was black, the one thing that wasn't decorated in many colours, the single point of central sanity that governed the room. Even the monks that sat within the temple were decorated in every colour. Their robes were decorated in a spinning pinwheel of colours and their skin was painted in strange hypnotic patterns.

'What the hell is this place?' He looked around.

'This is a monastery of the chapter of monks devoted to the grandeur and mystery of the world, to its infinite strangeness and majesty,' came the voice from the pulpit. 'And I do not recall inviting you, which is a marvellous occurrence indeed. It is rare and strange that those not allowed beforehand are permitted entry.' The man at the front was covered in almost every colour under the sun. It looked like there wasn't an inch of his body that wasn't painted.

'We're here to find a Presence.' Pan turned and removed his vest, showing his bare back to the monks, the map that lay on his skin. 'The creature that gave me this map said that yours was the only way through he knew. My friend,' he gestured toward Adam, 'has no Presence and requires one to protect himself. I would like you to let us through, to attend that Presence, to gain it for someone who will respect it, someone who will understand and accept it with the reverence it is due.'

'Well that is wonderful,' the monk smiled. 'But you will forgive me if I take a moment of your time. I trust it will not be long, but if you are to pass through this place we must be sure you are willing and able to understand the beauty of the worlds in which we live.' He placed his hand against his head and bowed. 'We are a few of the entities allowed to live in a world other than our own. We see that as a high honour, but since we need to earn that we cannot allow just anyone to find his way through.'

'I understand.' Pan looked at him. 'But we do not have a lot of time. We will make our way through this place, we will stop for a brief moment if you need us to but we really must be on our way.'

'So be it then,' the monk nodded. 'Very well, a single conversation and a cup of tea and you may be on your way.' He walked across the room, motioning for them to follow him. They did so, all of them looking around suspiciously at the strange people around them. Some of the monks stared back at them openly, some seemed not to notice them at all, but Adam noticed there was no kind of middle ground. No one looked at them out of the corner of their eyes, no one glanced or noticed and forgot them.

The room they walked into was grey and brown. It

looked like a completely ordinary office tea room, with a kettle, some drawers and a table. The monk set himself slowly about making the tea with a small smile on his face.

'So, who are the four of you?' he looked at them. This time Adam decided to go first.

'My name is Adam.' He looked at the monk. 'I didn't know any of this was real until a few days ago, frankly I'm not entirely convinced I'm not dreaming.'

'Well if you are then this is a unique dream indeed.' The monk gave a broad smile. 'I feel as if I should resent the assertion that I am figment of your imagination, though I can't entirely dispute it so I will simply let it go.'

'Yeah, so, I'm a little lost,' he confessed. 'But it's not the worst thing in the world. I'm still kind of deciding what I think of all of this.' The monk looked over the rest of them and Annabelle raised her hand.

'The Seraph know me as the Carnival Queen,' Annabelle spoke up. 'I was adopted by the Spinning Circus and travelled with them since I was young. I have seen many of the terrifying and beautiful things of the world, though I do not fancy that I have seen all of them quite yet.'

'Indeed you have not my dear.' The monk began to pour them all tea and they drank politely. In spite of it all it actually tasted exactly how Adam liked his tea. He hadn't seen the monk add any sugar or anything, but he guessed it was part of the magic.

'I am the Pathfinder.' Pan offered no other

qualifications, folding his arms.

'And I the Red Gentleman.' Xavier bowed. 'I have seen things no other man has ever seen and done things you could not begin to imagine. I have waded through the darkest and brightest parts of this world and I have no need of your limited, little mysteries.'

'Then they will not be offered you,' the monk nodded. 'So the primary reason behind this journey is for you?' He looked at Adam.

'Yeah,' he shrugged. 'I mean I guess it is.'

'Very well,' the Monk nodded. 'I think I will watch this with great interest. I will gaze into your journey through this world.' The colours of his face seemed to twist faster and faster. 'I will be happy to show you to the exit whenever you would like.'

'It's that easy?' Pan looked at him.

'We are monks,' the monk shrugged. 'We are not confrontational or political. We are neither Legion nor Lost. Please, finish your tea and leave as you like.' Pan looked at Annabelle and she nodded calmly, so the group finished their tea and got up.

'The way out if you...' Pan paused and blinked, shaking his head to clear it. Adam felt himself becoming queasy and shook his head.

'What's going on?' He noticed the room was spinning all around him. 'Did they drug us?'

'No.' Annabelle shook her head. 'I would have felt it if it was. I know poisons and we weren't poisoned.'

'Then the room really is spinning,' Xavier said softly. Adam could hear the sound of metal rasping and he knew that Xavier had drawn his sword. The colourful room was spinning, slowly at first but now faster and faster, the colours blurring together as they watched. The monks were spinning around as well, standing beside their beds, their bright cloaks twirling in front of them. Adam felt a pressure behind his eyes and began to look around, looking for some kind of respite from the colours. He walked back toward the room, into the comforting grey, but the colours had obscured the exit and he couldn't remember where it was. Everything was moving so fast, everything was so blurry, everything was shaking.

Adam felt his legs give way before he realised that was what was happening. He stumbled, looking around for his allies.

Pan was already on the ground, his eyes firmly closed. Annabelle was holding onto her knees, stumbling toward where she guessed the door might be. Xavier was still on his feet, sword drawn. He was trying to walk straight, trying to find something to stab or cut, the monks moving away from him effortlessly. Adam felt his consciousness leaving him as he slumped onto the ground, and he was almost grateful to feel an end to the wooziness and pain in his head.

CHAPTER SEVEN

When Adam awakened he was in another world altogether, a world full of the same colours that had been around in the monastery. He looked around and something seemed strange. When he looked down he saw that his own clothes were colourful as well, and that his own hands were painted.

'What's going on?' He looked around.

'We are giving you a chance to see the world around you, to understand what you see, what sees you and more importantly why you see things. We require you to understand that this is not a world you can treat as a burden, as something you can be around without being part of. We need to be sure you have some concept of the majesty and magnificence in which you walk. If you wish to be involved with us, then you will have to be involved.'

'What about my friends?'

'They are safe,' the voice reassured him, and somehow he knew it was true. These people would never hurt anyone. He was uncomfortable, but not unsafe. 'If you are to understand and believe in a Presence, then I will need you to see it. I will need to watch you watch our world.' He started to walk and the world grew dark under his feet. It grew black and twisted, the floor writhing under his feet.

'This is the Eldritch world most see, but you will need to be able to see what lies beneath as they do.' He wiped his hand across his eyes and suddenly he could see through the darkness as if it was daylight. He could see the creatures that lay beneath it, some of them truly grotesque, with twisting tendrils and many eyes, but some of them moved with a strange kind of flowing grace. He saw a crawling, many legged creature with no eyes flowing up a wall, the curves of its body moving like a work of art. A long black snake reared up and extended its… fins? No, not fins, wings.

'That's a fucking dragon!' The words slipped out without thinking.

'Yes.' The voice was soft and comforting. 'The Eldritch plane is home to many strange and wonderful creatures.' There was a creature with a kind of light on its fins, like a manta ray swimming through the air, glowing softly as it flew. 'Some of them are strange to you I'm sure, but there is a great deal of beauty and value there.'

The architecture was a senseless, jagged mess, a random sequence of spires at odd angles and jutting twisted strangeness, like if MC Escher had decided to mess with everything rather than just stairs. As he watched he could suddenly see the earth as well, civilized and normal, with people wandering the world. Each one followed their own path without noticing the others. He looked up and he could see the angels flying through the Seraph world. They had always been beautiful, but now they were more than he could have imagined, trailing lights like comets as they flew. He looked onto the Seraph streets and saw the strange, faceless creatures, and another pocket world full of strange, elven people. He looked up and spotted the statue people again, but this time he looked closer. These creatures wore an entire ecosystem on their bodies. Creatures crawled across one's body, cleaning it, eating and sleeping on it, making their own lives on it. These gentle giants were these creatures' entire world, each one playing host to a world of their own. It was beautiful.

'Do you see now?' the voice asked. 'Do you see the stakes for which these people play? Whichever way things go, whichever path we take and direction we steer the world in we have no choice but to follow it. It will have an effect on each and every entity, both in these worlds and your own. You need to understand the incredible importance of the decisions you may be forced to make. The choices you make will help define the world for everyone. Will you choose to join this war or step aside? Will you allow yourself to change and be changed by a world of creatures and magic. Or will you simply walk away? Trust that the world will unfold as it should with or without you and simply go home? This is the choice you have to make.' And with that he was awake, looking into the eyes of a monk. He was in one of the colourful beds, without the headache.

'Are you okay?' Annabelle was sitting on a bed next to his, looking at him without facing him.

'I guess,' he nodded. 'I'm feeling a little sick but yeah I think I'm all right.' He ran his hands through his hair and took a deep breath to steady himself. 'Did you guys all trip out on this too?'

'I did,' Xavier shrugged. 'Though for myself it was more a token attempt to convince me to change my ways and then a polite request for me to at least not stab anyone when I woke up. They let me go when I agreed. That was hours ago.'

'I had some visions,' Pan shrugged and folded his arms, not saying another word, his face twisting into a scowl.

'I had them, but then I'm used to them.' Annabelle nodded and smiled. 'A large part of my training was delivered like that, visions and trips and things of that nature. I was the last one to wake up, and that was about an hour ago.'

'You have been unconscious almost three hours. We knew you would not stay to experience what we needed you to of your own accord.' This monk wasn't the same as the first one, he wasn't anywhere near as colourful. He was just two block colours, each one covering half of his body. 'We hope you do not seek retribution against us, but should you need to do so we will accept any and all violence without any resistance or protest.' He held his hands out in a gesture of peace and Xavier started forward, his sword already clearing his sheath. Pan moved quickly, grabbing him by one hand and pulling him in close.

'Don't.' His tone was cold as Xavier twisted in his grip.

'But he said I could!' Xavier's voice was high and

whining, but he was smiling broadly.

'And I'm telling you that you can't.' The two pushed at each other for a moment but it was pretty obvious Pan was stronger.

'You are not my superior!' Xavier snapped.

'I am, in every sense of the word,' he snarled. slack and when Pan let go he put the sword away.

'Very well,' he sighed. 'No monk murder.'

Adam stared at the two of them for a long moment. He was travelling with lunatics. One of them had to be physically stopped from murdering a monk, even with provocation that didn't seem like the kind of thing anyone with any marbles left did.

'Well then, now we've recovered.' Adam got to his feet and looked around. He needed to distract himself from what was going on around and inside him. Besides, physically he was okay, a little off perhaps but no more than he had been since this all started. His ribs and face even felt more or less okay. 'Shall we go?'

'I'd like to indulge my curiosity for a few seconds.' Pan looked at them. 'I mean no offence but, is this all? You have the knight, the wall, and then nothing more than some magic monks who teach a few little lessons? Is that all? I'm still looking for the blade in your sleeves.'

'That's not all,' the monk smiled. 'We are the third line of defence between the outside world and the city that lies beyond. You couldn't get out of this temple without learning from us or killing us. Even after killing us it would have taken you months of pain and discomfort to find your way out. The ability we just used on you would have trapped Xavier in his own mind for years had the rest of you not seemed good people. If you get through and kill us all then there is very little we can do about it. It has happened to us before, it will doubtless happen again.'

'You seem remarkably circumspect about being murdered,' Xavier said, seemingly intrigued by the concept, leaning on his cane.

'We are not incapable of defending ourselves,' he smiled. 'After long enough spent with us dodging and blocking attacks, and with a few small strikes, our enemies will almost certainly be rendered unconscious before they can kill us all.'

'Still,' Xavier smiled. 'You seem to care as little about being killed as I would about killing you.'

'Such is life,' the monk smiled. 'I have lived a long and happy life enjoying the world around me and trying to make a difference. I have seen a lot of what the world has to offer, and made a positive difference. If you kill me that would be awful but I would go to my end knowing I lived as good a life as any man.'

'See?' Xavier looked at Pan. 'He doesn't mind and I would really enjoy it.'

Pan's hand settled around the back of Xavier's neck and he started to drag him forward. 'Let's move on before Xavier completely fucking loses it.' The group walked out of the chapel, following the two-toned monk. Looking at the ground this time in order to avoid losing his lunch Adam filed out of the monastery

'So,' Adam looked at the monk, 'any idea what else we have to face before we get to the city?'

'Nothing,' the monk smiled. 'Once we have allowed you through, the guards should not attempt to kill you as you pass. Try to see the beauty and magnificence of the city, even while you go about your business.'

'All right,' Adam nodded. 'Let's go.' The group started to head off again, looking down into the city. 'Pan where to next?'

'Down into the city,' Pan smiled and rolled his shoulders. 'From there we follow the map until we need to go through to the next world. As we near the Presence the map should help us less, but we will know what to do.'

'So what is this city?'

'It's a holy place,' Pan said softly. 'A town made of artists and engineers, inventors and scientists out of time and space, plucked out of the world by a guardian angel right before they die. He keeps them here, keeps them safe, gives them a place to work. He can't do it himself but he built tests and guardians to keep out undesirables. The last of them would be the people who are trying to look like they aren't approaching us aggressively right now.'

The figures were men out of time, knights and warriors of various ages and ethnicities. There was a medieval knight holding a broadsword and a viking carrying a spear walking beside a guy in a SWAT vest and carrying an assault rifle. At their head was a

British Redcoat solider carrying a rifle with a smile on his face.

'Good evening ladies and gentlemen!' The British accent was strong and cheerful. 'Welcome to our humble little town. Since you've managed to make your way through you are of course welcome. However I would ask you to keep your visit brief. The citizens of this place encourage new minds, but we like to keep disturbances to a minimum.'

'Relax,' Pan smiled and raised his hands. 'We're not moving into the neighbourhood, we're just passing through. We don't want to hurt anyone or get in your way. You have work to do and we don't want to bother you or your master.'

As they walked Adam looked over at the others and discovered that Xavier was no longer wearing his coat.

'What's up?' he asked as he walked over to Xavier and for the first time he scowled rather than smiled.

'The Red Gentleman is known by his coat,' he replied. 'The Top Hat Man is seen by these people as something of a clown. An amusing creature who, while troublesome poses no real danger to them. The Red Gentleman is known as other things.'

'What kind of things?'

'That is not a story worth the telling at the moment.' The smile was back. 'Just leave it be and hope these men do not take us to their leader.' Pan and the Redcoat were chatting calmly with each other, but the conversation died down quickly when they reached the city.

'So where do you need to go?' The Redcoat looked at them. Pan shrugged his shoulders and turned his back, pulling off the vest to show the map.

'That black spot is where.' The Redcoat examined them for a moment and made a disappointed clicking sound and shook his head.

'Then I am afraid there is a certain barrier between you and the Presence you seek. For the location you are bound for is beneath the Angel's chamber.'

'The Angel? We're actually meeting an angel?'

'The Guardian Angel who makes this place.' The Redcoat gave him a beatific smile. 'He is much depleted, but he still guides and leads us and when he is strong enough he seeks out more like us. If you wish to make your way under his home, you will have to greet him. I hope he will have time to see you.'

'I hope so too,' Pan nodded. 'We really can't delay.'

'Then I shall see to it as soon as possible.' He picked up his pace and the rest of them followed. The city was so strange, suburban houses crossed paths with ancient farm houses. There were small tents set up in fields and ancient rockwork castles. There were cathedrals and art galleries all through the streets. There was even an empty lot that was completely empty for no logical reason, but for a single painting easel that sat in the middle. On either side of that were spired glass statues that appeared to have one man living in each of them.

'Weird place.' He shook his head.

'It isn't built practically,' said the person beside

him who was covered in tattoos and wore a tailored suit. As he looked at the man the only strange thing about him was that two of his fingers were missing joints. 'It's built according to the whims and desires of its occupants.' His eyes cast over to a bunker that was locked down with utmost security that was just there for no reason. He guessed that was probably SWAT guy's house. 'We don't consider things like conservation of space and resources. We only have to listen to what the artists and managers want to happen.'

'Managers?'

'Artists have trouble taking care of themselves sometimes.' Holy crap was this guy Yakuza? They had their fingers cut off and tattoos, right? 'And according to popular thought, limitation is the mother of invention. The managers decide what is best for the artists who need to be managed.'

'We're here,' the Red Coat cut through the conversation.

The chamber of an Angel wasn't exactly what he expected. The building was humble, a rundown cathedral only two stories tall, with none of the artistic flare or showing off that seemed to characterise the rest of the city. As they headed inside Adam looked around, again it was simply designed. It was a simple stone room without flare or ostentation. There was not even any furniture, beyond a few pews and a simple altar that sat in the centre of the room, with a winged figure sitting atop it. He looked more human than human. It was strange to think, but that was the first thing that came to mind. He looked somehow too vital, too full of life and energised to be a normal human being. His features were too generic to be well described. He was pale and wore no clothing, his wings covering the bottom half of his body. He would have been wholly unimpressive if not for his bearing, a strange intensity about his nature that pulled all eyes to him.

'Good evening,' he said softly. 'I am Mareul, the Guardian Angel of this town, and I am pleased to meet each and every one of you.' He bowed and bowed low. They all bowed back, and Adam couldn't help but notice that Xavier didn't rise from it to his usual height. He was standing with a slumping stance, like he was intent on hiding without looking like he was hiding, so Adam just let him.

'I'm sorry to bother you.' Pan looked up at it. 'We're just passing through and need to get from this world to the one beyond. Apparently the only correct entrance sits beneath your feet. We were wondering if we could pass you by and use it.'

'Well,' the Angel smiled. 'It is one of the easier portals to travel through, and without my particular abilities you could only have one destination and not use it for ill.' It thought about it for a long moment, its passive neutral face showing no expression. 'Very well I am certain I could allow you this usage and not regret it.' Its neutral face smiled and it was like rocks splitting. 'Go then, feel free and with my blessing.'

The group looked at each other and filed past the angel as it graciously stepped aside, moving toward the stairs that it revealed. It was dark stone and their footsteps echoed as they moved. The door closed behind them with a resounding boom.

'Is it just me or did that all seem,' Pan rounded the last turn of the stairs and slapped himself in the face, 'too easy, fuck!'

'Hi there, kids!' came the voice of a young woman, who waved at them through a procession of Blank Faced Legionnaires who filled the room. She was small and white haired, and in her off hand there was lightning glowing and crackling. She wore a long white dress that swirled around her feet and a sapphire choker around her throat. She had rings on her fingers and looked at them like they were old friends she was truly happy to see. 'Hey Red, did you know just how much that angel up there hates you? I mean honestly, he out and out refused to help us, wanted nothing to do with us at all until I mentioned that you were coming. What on earth did you do to it?'

'I honestly do not remember.' Xavier thought about it for a moment and shrugged, pulling his coat out of his hat and pulling it on. 'I think it was probably one of those things that's very important to the other person, but doesn't mean a great deal to me. I get a lot of those, more and more every year so it seems. And who is your companion?'

'I don't know its name.' She gestured with one

hand to a young woman, who was curled up on the floor. She was completely naked and with long black hair, though she showed none of her body, obscured by the curled posture. She twisted and twitched on the ground like she was in pain, but her face had a freaky grin on it.

'But honestly, you really thought showing up without that stupid coat of yours would disguise your identity? Wearing a top hat and carrying a sword is not, even in our circles, a common description of a man. All we had to do is mention that you were coming and he offered to help. I mean he wouldn't risk his own people but he was happy to help risk ours.' She flashed them a bright grin and her other fist lit up.

'Well then.' Pan reached into his pocket and held a small black knife out to Adam, which he took. He had no idea whatsoever what he was going to do with it, as he'd never been in a knife fight in his life, but it was a little reassuring in his hand. 'I suppose we'd best get to it!' He shoved Adam backwards and launched himself across the room.

The naked girl suddenly sprang to life, launching herself through the air to meet him. As she moved she turned into a white furred dog with a black streak across its head. It tackled Pan out of mid-air and the two of them started to roll across the ground together. He grunted and lashed out at her with fists knees and elbows, it snarled and growled, biting and clawing at him. Its teeth were massive and jagged, no trace of her former humanity remaining.

Adam crawled back as the rest of them joined the fight, hitting the deck and getting away from the Blank Faces, hoping to whichever gods cared that they didn't notice him. He held the black knife out in front of him but, luckily, they seemed focused on Xavier and Annabelle, the people who were actually fighting back.

Xavier moved with his usual terrifying speed, flashing through the strange figures around him, jumping and dodging their strikes, whirling away from them and making them look clumsy. As Adam watched he ran up the wall, vaulted off it, landed on his feet behind one of the creatures and rammed his sword through its head, then he kicked the creature into the path of a lightning bolt shooting at his face. He used the creature as a shield and stuck another one through something in its chest that looked a lot like an eye.

The girl with the lightning in her hands raised them up and fired at Xavier and Annabelle, short sharp bursts of electricity. Xavier rolled turned and stepped out of their way and the lightning bolts hit more of her own people than even got close to Xavier.

'Incredible,' Xavier laughed, whipping off his hat and hurling it at her, which she dodged by throwing herself to the ground. 'You simply and absolutely cannot aim, can you? You are terrible!'

'I only need to hit you once.' She sounded more or less calm, but spoke through gritted teeth. She aimed her hand at Annabelle, shooting off a blast of lightning at the whip wielding woman. She hit the deck, rolled away and lashed out at one of the Blank Faces with her whip. She moved like she was dancing, turning and swirling, her only focus on not getting hurt. It was only when he had a few moments to watch her that he saw that there were spiders crawling out of her sleeves and the bottom of her flowing skirt. She danced through the crowd of Blanks with equal parts flair and desperation, trying to keep them between her and the lightning lady. She gave up on her dignity and shame as things got desperate, crawling and scrambling to get away from them. She turned and sprinted away at the last moment, diving into a corner and heading toward the wall.

Adam looked for something, anything he could do to help his allies. Xavier was rather neatly taking care of himself, with a band of Blank Faces laying in a pile of goo and guts around him and a dozen more approaching from every side. Adam didn't feel like getting in the middle of that, or the rolling mass of fur, flesh and blood that was the ground pounding, gutter brawl that Pan and the wolf girl had going on so he moved over toward Annabelle, and tried to figure out what she was doing and how he could help. She whipped at the creatures, trying to hold them at bay as they advanced on her.

One of their tendrils whipped out and caught her around the neck, beginning to choke her as she gripped the limb. Adam picked up the knife and started to run toward them, hoping to do something about it only to see the creature beginning to crack and break on its own. Its grip seemed to weaken out of nowhere and it dropped Annabelle, the limb cracking and falling. As it fell apart spiders began to crawl out of its decomposing corpse, scattering in every direction. A few more began to break, flaking and collapsing around her feet and spilling bugs in every direction.

As she celebrated in the chaos, one of the big black ones slammed a clublike arm into her back, sending her tumbling across the ground even as one of its own legs cracked off. He jumped onto the creature and stabbed it with everything he had. It swung itself like a bull and sent him pitching off into the wall, his head ringing. He blinked the fuzz out of his eyes and watched Annabelle crack the creatures head in two with the whip, spiders flying out in every direction.

He got up and lunged at her, tackling her to the ground as the lightning girl sent a blast that flew over her head. After the crackle of lightning subsided Annabelle got to her feet and Adam froze up. He wanted to do something, wanted to help but his body wouldn't do what he told it to. He literally couldn't move. He didn't know what the others could do, what they could take, but he knew one simple fact from his spot on the ground. If he got clipped by one of those lightning bolts or got hit by one of those monsters, he was going to die. He was going to fry or break or pop like a ripe fruit. Panic made his guts churn and it was all he could do not to throw up.

'Everyone okay?' Pan spoke as he headbutted the creature, ramming his forehead into its snout while he pulled on a Blank's tendril that was wrapped around his hand.

'Fine.' Xavier artfully slipped his burning coat onto his latest adversary and it caught flame, its tentacle no longer holding Pan's hand at bay. He shrugged the tentacle off and drew back from the wolf, beating it about the head with one fist. Xavier was favouring one leg, and had the look of someone recently electrocuted but he seemed nimble as ever as he ran another Blank through, leaving them with only a few of the strange creatures left. The lightning thrower had been distracted by a wave of spiders, which she was currently frying where they crawled, short range wide bursts were killing them by the handful. It wasn't really scaring her off but it was keeping her busy.

As he passed, Xavier landed a sudden and ferocious kick to the side of the wolf's head, making his way to the place where Annabelle was surrounded by Blanks. It jumped, distracted for a moment and Pan got his knees under it. He pushed it up with his legs and wrapped a hand over its snout, holding the mouth closed.

'There we are!' His voice was triumphant, as he slammed his fist a few times into the side of the creature's head. It fell beside him in an unconscious heap, a woman once more, and he got to his feet. He looked at the lightning thrower for a moment and began to advance on her with slow measured steps. In response, she, to no one's surprise, threw a bolt of lightning at him. Pan stumbled for a moment as the bolt struck him but he advanced with slow steps. She shot him again, this time with both hands and he fell to one knee. He sat there for a moment, then spat, growled and got to his feet again. He started to walk and she shot him again and again, ending up with a single sustained burst that rocked his body even as he moved. His teeth were gritted and animal sounds escaped as he walked toward her, one hand extended.

'Anytime Top Hat!' he barked with the last of his voice and made a sudden dash for the girl, managing to get a hand to her skin even as she shocked him, his fist starting to clench around her throat. She started to shake and shudder with him as electricity ran through them both but she kept up the shocking. It was the only thing stopping him from choking her to death.

Xavier looked at Annabelle and she nodded, lashing about herself at the last two blanks. The creatures were moving slower than they had, but she was no longer releasing spiders by the horde. She was moving slower than she had been before and Adam decided that now was his chance to actually help. He got to his feet and started to move as quickly and quietly as he could toward them on shaking feet. He wondered if he was going to puke when this was over. Probably.

The electric woman screamed suddenly as Xavier's sword pierced her side and the creatures turned to face her. Adam got to his feet and ran toward the creature, more holding his knife out and running into the creature with it than actually stabbing it. The blood was black as it leaked out, slow, globby and barely any warmer than the room around it. It slowly covered his hand as he breathed shallowly and softly, then he left the knife in the creature as he turned and threw up on the floor. He knew the creature wasn't quite a person, it didn't think or feel, but it was still breathing, and it had still been a person at one point. He held his knees and squatted over the pile of vomit as Annabelle came over to him, tossing the last of the creature's bodies away from her.

'Well.' The sound of meat hitting meat hinted to the fact that Pan had punched the girl in the face, and the sudden appearance of a big man entering his field of vision hinted to the fact he no longer had the energy to stand. 'That hurt.'

'Well then, if I may make a suggestion,' Xavier piped up cheerfully. 'During your next combat, you may consider an alternate strategy to charging headlong at the opponent whilst they are wielding a ranged weapon and simply hoping they run out of desire to shoot you before you die.'

'I was angry,' Pan grunted drowsily from his prone position. 'And punch drunk.'

'An excuse the reaper will gladly accept and allow you to return from the pits for I am certain,' he chuckled. 'Perhaps next time we think before we attack the Lady Raiden with our bare fists? Provided she survives of course, which I sincerely hope she does not, but assume she probably will.' Xavier raised his sword and looked at her, then at them. 'May I put her out of my misery?'

'No,' Annabelle shook her head and sighed. 'As nice as it would be to be rid of her I have standards to uphold. I won't treat her, but you won't kill her either. We'll leave it to destiny.' Strangely Xavier seemed pleased with the idea and wiped the blood from his sword and slipped it away.

'What about the other one?' Pan looked at the wolf that had once been a young woman.

'Are you mad?' Xavier scowled. 'I would no sooner extinguish the life of a good wardog than I would slash a Van Gough or blow up a church.' He considered it for a moment. 'Well, I absolutely would blow up a church, and depending on the Van Gough, but you get my meaning. This one is young, and while it hasn't been trained much it has significant power to stand up to our loyal soldier in a fight.' He reached into his hat and pulled out a business card, placing it calmly beside the woman's unconscious form. 'I shall give her the number of a trainer I know, good man, capable soul.'

'What's a...' Adam started to ask. 'Right, a trainer is someone who trains wardogs. What's a wardog?'

'Essentially that.' He pointed to the woman who was twitching and snarling in her sleep on the ground. 'Someone who does the things it did and looks the way it looks. It is a young specimen and has a great deal more natural ability than I have seen in a long time. I am worried for its wellbeing if it is left untrained for too much longer. This much power and so little control.' He clucked his tongue.

'Why are you calling her an it?' He stood up, ready to stand up to the weird sexism.

'Because it is an it,' Xavier glared at him. 'It is a wardog, a grand combatant of the highest order. Am I to prioritise the fact that it is female over that trait? Over the fact that this wonderful creature made a choice which will define its life. It chose to make its life about the sacred art of combat, becoming better, more powerful, mastering that which it holds dear. It would be disrespectful for me to choose the fact that it was born female as a priority.' He shook his head.

'Now, it is unconscious and the Lady will likely survive and recover, for all that I wish otherwise. So I would suggest we collect our belongings and be on our way, because being knocked out too many times in a row is bad for even our kind of people's health. Besides, I haven't ruled out the possibility that that angel upstairs will decide to take their failure to kill me personally.'

'All right, all right.' Pan pulled himself to his feet and took a deep breath, trying to shake off the pale, shadowed weariness that was plain on his face. He cracked his knuckles and began to draw a circle in the ground with his foot. 'But be aware that after this I'm not exactly gonna be combat capable for a good long while.' He began to intone some words Adam didn't recognise.

146

'What's he doing?' Adam looked at Annabelle and she pulled him away from Pan and Xavier, who were working on the circle.

'They're opening the portal, between the two of them.' Annabelle gave him a smile. 'Pan's our magical expert, and Xavier knows exactly two things, one of them being portals.'

'What's the...' he stopped short. 'It's killing people, isn't it?'

'Killing things, indeed.' She sat down and he took a seat beside her, leaning against the bare stone wall. 'I know a bit of magic too, but it's not the kind that helps me here.'

'Look,' the thought finally popped into his head to ask the important question, 'can you give me some kind of idea of what I'm working with here? Not the world, just the powers around me. I'm not sure if we were in trouble during that fight or if we had the whole thing handled. Was Xavier playing with them? Could Pan have stood up to ten more minutes of that or ten more seconds?'

'Well, as far as combat goes,' she thought about it for a moment, 'it'd be you, the Blanks, me, the wardog and Pan at about a tie, the Lady Ray and Xavier. That's just raw combat power though, only counts how we are in a fight. When it comes to all round magical ability and power? We can all do a number of things, but it'd be you, the Blanks, me, the wardog, Xavier, Lady Ray and Pan at the top. Pan's the most powerful by far but as you can see,' she looked at the burn holes in the big man's vest, 'he gets a little too stupid to be much of a fighter. When he doesn't have any time to think he reverts to fight or flight and he doesn't have a piece of flight in him.' She was smiling broadly now.

'You used to have a thing for him, didn't you?'

'Yes indeed.' She shook her head. 'It feels stupid now, and it was forever and a day ago. I figured out intellectually that he was gay, but it took my emotions time to catch up.'

'So what do they do, magic wise?'

'Can't tell you that,' Annabelle sighed. 'I would if I could but there are some things you have to learn directly from a person. When they like you, when they trust you, if those things come to pass, then you get to know those kinds of things about someone. Or you can spy, get someone else to tell you because you need to know badly. You can pay someone off or convince and scare words out, but it won't be me.'

'So you won't tell me what you do?'

'I can control arachnids, insects and some vermin,' she shrugged. 'I can make traps and webs, and go to the other world whenever my sisters congregate. I'm venomous, and poisonous, I have some healing and mending.'

'You like me?' He was surprised.

'A little,' she shrugged. 'You're not a complete waste of humanity and you're too scared of me to trouble me.'

'All right.' He considered things. 'But I have to ask one more thing because it's killing me. Why did that angel hate Xavier so much?'

'That one I can tell you,' she nodded and pointed to Xavier. 'Because that man, with a couple of small exceptions, is the most hated person in the world. Even his own side can't stand him.'

'Then why do you have him around?'

'Because there are things in this world we need that he can get us, people we need to talk to that he knows and things we need done that he can do. He's a member of a very secretive and very dangerous society we don't want to upset. Those things are so much more valuable than the enemies he makes. Which is saying a lot because he's made a lot of enemies. He doesn't care who he upsets if it gets in the way of what he needs, whatever he needs. In our lifestyle you run into a lot of guys with old grudges and even if you try to keep your head down if you're going to stand for something then you're probably going to make a lot of people very angry before you're done. It's just a part of the high intensity world we live in.'

She pointed up. 'For something he did at some point, that angel up there hates our little Red Gentleman with the devil's own passion. I really hope Pan gets this done fast. We need to get out of here before it decides it wants to call on its own people to finish us off. I don't think either of those two are at their best right now and you and I aren't going to be able to pick up after ourselves.'

'Is someone telling tales outside of school?' Xavier

had apparently taken a break to pop one of his knee into place. He smiled over at the two of them.

'Just general stories,' she shrugged. 'Nothing in particular. Just that he needs to be willing to accept that sometimes we make people angry, that it's something he'll have to get used to.'

'No tales of the Red folk?' he smiled. 'That's a shame, they're interesting tales to hear.'

'Maybe,' she shrugged. 'But they're not mine to tell.'

'True enough,' he nodded. 'True enough indeed. Well then if you should ever require or desire to hear tales of the Red folk, who we are and what we do I would be happy to share them with you.' He flashed Adam a bright smile that seemed genuinely affectionate. 'They are gory, bloody, happy and ever so amusing and I do so love to share them.'

'Some other time, I think.' He looked at the strange man for a moment and turned back to Annabelle. 'I'm not gonna lie, I'm not kind of sure I want to be a part of this. I mean I thought you were the good guys but,' he paused, 'I mean an angel hates you. It's hard not to ask a few questions after that. I mean, seriously an honest to god angel just tried to get us killed and no one has argued it wasn't deserved.'

'That's not the least valid criticism I've ever heard.' She looked down at her hands while she was thinking, then wiped some of the black muck off them with webs. Her outfit, once in even black and red stripes now bore a lot more spots and patches of the two colours all over. 'Honestly, I never had that choice, but if I could make it I'd choose to be here a thousand times over but I think a lot of our number would make that other choice. They'd just lay low and let it all blow over.' She patted his shoulder. 'Once you can keep yourself safe that's a choice you get to make too, though you might have to throw down a few times before days end.'

'Yeah,' he nodded, guilt and a white masked face churning up his stomach to his head. 'Hey, Pan, are we ready to go?' Anything to distract.

'We are.' His voice was straining. 'And I'm out,' They looked over and Adam saw the man lying on his face. Above him sat a portal, a large black hole in the empty air in front of him. The colours swirled through the shades of purple, going from pinkish white on the outside to black in the very centre.'

'Is he unconscious?' Adam moved over to the guy and gently slapped him on the face.

'That is the conventional meaning of the word out.' Xavier handed Adam his cane and lifted the bigger man without any visible effort. He turned and carried Pan through the portal. There was no sign of effort or indeed any emotion at all as he went through.

'He'll be okay.' Annabelle squeezed Adam's hand once before she let it go. 'Sorry I was hard on you before, maybe you're not completely gutless.'

'Actually, I might be.' He looked at the portal. 'I'm pants shittingly terrified right now and I kind of froze up during that fight.'

'That's not being gutless,' she smiled. 'That's a realistic estimation of your relative power to everyone else in the room. It's being something other than stupid, and you pulled your weight better than I expected you to.' She looked at him for a few long moments and then took his hand. 'Here, hold my hand and I'll lead you through. Nothing bad's gonna happen, I promise.'

'Thanks.' Her hand was warm and comforting, and he didn't feel any spidery-ness in it; she felt like a normal girl. 'That's a far cry from punching me in the face. I thought that was more your encouragement strategy.'

'Yeah well,' she shrugged. 'I was provoked back there, but I'm willing to accept that I may not have been entirely without fault. So how about it? Clean slate?' It was the first time he noticed that she was pretty. He thought of her as strange, then scary, then he hated her but now? Her features were strong, her skin pale and smooth, her smile was, dare he say it, cute?

'Clean slate.' His smile mirrored hers and they walked together through the strange glowing portal in front of him. From there, everything went dark for a while.

CHAPTER EIGHT

'It seems our associates failed us,' the Legate said as he ran his hand across the Lady Raiden's wounds. They began to knit together slowly but surely. The young noblewoman blinked her eyes and then scurried away on weak legs, wanting to put distance between herself as her master's wrath. 'Just as you warned me they would.' He gestured toward Ursas. 'I must bow to your expertise and apologise.'

'Ya shoulda let me go,' Ursas growled. 'I wouda finished 'em off!'

'Perhaps,' he looked at his associate, 'but already the young man is feeling the doubt. Feeling that perhaps this is not the best place for him, that his life is now too dangerous and that perhaps his associates are not people he should be around. That they are not the "good guys" after all.' He chuckled at the foolish concept. 'He is beginning to think that perhaps it is not worth risking his life for people he is not even sure he likes, much less truly cares for. I am thinking it may perhaps be time to call in the King's Man and his kin.' 'Those filthy fuckin' Russians,' Ursas snarled and spat on the ground. 'You don't need 'em. I can do this. I can handle this.'

'That is not your decision,' Legate snapped, but he allowed his stance to soften and gave no hint of the broad smile under his mask. 'But I shall allow you one more opportunity to get the job done if you believe so completely in yourself. Kill the Lost Soldier, kill the

Spinning Sister, drive them out of this world and place this young man in a position to consider both the worth of his associates and the danger to his own life. Left with no one but the Red Gentleman he will be afraid. If you can put him in that position then perhaps the King's Man is not needed to serve his will this time'

The Legate looked over at Lady Raiden, who was berating the wardog loudly and with several prohibitive shocks. The Legate sighed and took a deep breath, taking a valuable moment to think. He looked around the room at the meagre associates that had been foisted upon him. He had been given so little, asked to work with so little and to do so much.

The Lady was a thunder thrower who could not even perform the most basic assassination with an entire squad and a wardog. She too had assured him that she could get this job done, that she could perform this task, that she didn't need Ursas's help and could handle this herself. She could plan and execute this little ambush and she had failed him. If he could afford to lose numbers he would have her Blanked in an instant. Would Ursas do the same? Would the bear disappoint as all the others had? 'Take a squad of Blanks with you and assemble them in the best position for the job. Strike at them where they are weak.'

'Right,' the bear snarled at him and Legate raised his hand.

'Do not fail me,' he growled.

'I'll get it done,' he nodded, knowing the risks if he failed. 'I'll kill the Soldier and the damn spider girl and this'll all be over. He'll give up his Presence, we'll be done and we can move on to the real plan.'

'Very well,' he nodded. 'Now get out of my sight, I have planning to do and I need space to think.'

The world around Adam was white, absolutely, pure white. He couldn't see for a few long moments. He blinked a few times and tried to clear his head, taking a step forward. As he walked things started to fade a little into focus. The world in front of him became less pure white and started to fade into a pattern of green and grey. As he kept moving things started to become clearer and clearer, blobs of colour solidifying into objects.

He was sitting in the middle of a peaceful green glade, the sky above him a pristine white, with steel and white painted buildings all around him. The building right in front of him was a clock tower, white with no handles to indicate the time. In the middle of the glade was a simple wooden bench, brown and held together with simple black metal. A few trees decorated the horizon, pristine foliage that looked like they had been put there by an artist.

Among the branches sat a small, tanned, young woman in a white dress. Her head turned toward him like she was looking at him, but she obviously wasn't, the black blindfold covering her eyes making that an impossibility. Apparently it didn't slow her down much, since she could still wave at him just fine.

'Hello,' she smiled at him

'Hey.' He waved back and sat down on the bench. She jumped out of the tree. He got up and moved to catch her, but she landed with no difficulty on her feet, bending her knees as she did, then walked over to him. They sat down on the bench together. 'Who are you?'

'Call me Kate,' she grinned. 'I thought you could use some time, some relaxation, some peace. Even if it's just a few moments worth.'

'You're not wrong.' He leaned back; it was peaceful here, he wasn't in pain, he'd been in a little pain since the first fight, and now he was calm. 'But how did you get me here?'

'I didn't,' she shrugged. 'Not really. I mean once you wake up you'll be in the exact same place as you were, in the exact same time and state as you left. This is just,' she thought about it for a few seconds, 'a moment between moments. A place you can hide in for a while, for a few seconds at least.'

'So you're one of them too.' He tried not to sound disappointed, but he was.

'Well, I'm not certain anyone you just met could be classified as 'one of them,'' she scolded. 'Especially with your limited understanding of "us" and "them" but as an old friend of mine would say I am near enough as makes no difference. But I'm not here as a representative of any group, this is my place, my little kingdom of stolen moments that I offer to whoever needs comfort, or safety, or a moment to think. I believe you are all three.' He chuckled at that.

'What do you suggest I think about?'

'Well,' she considered it, 'cats are nice, and dogs are fuzzy, which is an oddly comforting thing to think about,' she chuckled. 'But honestly who am I to tell you what to think about? Or what to think? Just, consider your situation. Take some time to think about your situation, or think about nothing.' Her expression turned pensive. 'There's a lot to recommend thinking about nothing, or thinking about the little things for that matter. There's a surprising amount to love about the normal world. Take it from someone who knows.'

'All right.' So he did. He took some time and he thought. He thought about friends and family, new things and old. He thought about nothing and then about everything. He had some ideas, made some plans and mused on a few subjects.

After a few, short moments Kate tapped him gently on the shoulder. He looked up and saw her smile.

'I'm sorry,' she smiled. 'You looked peaceful, but this is as much time as I can give you. This moment is over and if you don't leave now you'll be stuck here till the next moment and things won't happen the way they're supposed to.'

'All right,' he nodded, though he was a little disappointed. 'So how do I leave?'

'Just close your eyes again,' she smiled and waved. 'Goodbye.'

'Wait,' he called out quickly. 'I'm Adam, just, by the way.'

'Nice to meet you Adam.' He closed his eyes looking at her face, and the world wasn't white anymore.

'Hey.' Annabelle clicked her fingers beside his head and he woke up looking into her eyes, they were red and black, just like her skirt. They should have been disconcerting, strange, odd, but on her it worked. 'Please don't tell me you're unconscious too. Xavier's already carrying Pan and that's all he can do. I'll have to carry you myself.'

'Ah of course,' he nodded as he got to his feet. 'Because the worst thing about my being knocked unconscious is your inconvenience.'

'Of course,' she laughed and checked him over, then ruffled his hair. 'Welcome back dude, where'd you go?'

'The land of the unconscious I guess,' he lied. He didn't feel like sharing the details of his moment. 'What do we do next?'

'Well this is where things get weird.'

Adam scoffed, now was when things got weird? This was going to be difficult.

'We don't have a map so we just do whatever it is we do and what'll happen will happen.'

'Well what I do isn't much,' he shrugged. 'But for some reason I think we should go this way.'

'Then this way we go.' Xavier smiled and hefted

Pan on his shoulders then followed the direction Adam had indicated. They walked for a few minutes, Adam started to feel a little stupid. He'd just picked a direction and they started walking. There was no logic here, no thought or plan of any kind, he was just wandering around. Then he turned around and realised Pan and Xavier weren't following him anymore. Annabelle looked at him for a moment, then waved with one hand and disappeared from sight. He started to walk through the darkness, keeping his eyes peeled. For some reason, he didn't feel scared, he was okay.

In the distance, he could see a single green light, swirling and jumping and pivoting in every direction. He reached out and tried to catch it, but it jumped out of his hand. He followed it, breaking into a run and laughter slipped out of his mouth. He snatched at it and it swirled away to one side. He turned to catch it and it flew behind him.

This time he moved slowly, turning little by little, not spooking it until he was close. He reached out to it and just before his hand closed it split into three dots. A line spread to join then, then another, and it turned into a bright green smile, hanging in mid-air. It fell to around his stomach height and pulled away from him again. He moved to follow it and now it was moving in a way that made sense. It was moving past him at a steady pace. Two dots joined the smile and the black started to ripple, still black, but textured darkness It was rippling muscle and hair with the green in the front.

Suddenly there was some kind of panther, prowling in front of him, moving in a swishing motion around him. Its lights changed and switched around until they made eyes and a mouth in bright green.

'What are you?' He looked at it.

'He goes straight to the what?' The voice was wry, quietly amused. 'Not a who, but a what. Perhaps you're more perceptive than the rest, or perhaps just ruder than they are.' Its mouth opened and some kind of strange broken panting laugh slipped out. 'Either way you may be worth a little more than those who came before. You may even be amusing in your own limited way.' It brushed against him, its fur was warm and he could feel muscle and power rippling underneath it. He slipped out one hand and ran it over the comfortable fuzz. 'Still I suppose at the end of the day it doesn't really matter. You're my way out which means you're the right one. You may as well be the grandest of heroes in my eyes. You and Hercules.'

'What?' His eyes narrowed and this time the laugh sounded more human.

'Not a lot of comprehension,' it smiled. Its mouth wasn't capable of a smile, but that was the sense it gave off. 'But needs must and you can't possibly be any more boring than this place.' The creature turned sharply and jumped onto him, tackling him onto his back. He pushed against the creature and it pushed its head into his face. He felt cold to his bones, then a flash of pain, then he was back with the others again, standing in an empty space, like someone had loaded the characters of a game without the background.

'Well, well, well.' Xavier was supporting Pan now, rather than carrying him. 'That is wonderful, gorgeous, I love it!' He began to applaud, slapping his free hand against Pan's shoulder. 'Well, what do we think?'

'Very nice,' Pan nodded through the pained look on his face.

'Not bad.' Annabelle was grinning like the sunrise.

'Could one of you maybe explain all of this to me?' He jumped at the voice that came out of his mouth. It was like his, but it was as if someone had run his voice through one of those identity obscuring voice synthesisers. He raised his hand and touched his own face, he couldn't feel anything on it from the inside, but his fingers touched cold metal not flesh. 'What the hell is going on?'

'You've got yourself a Presence all of your very own.' Xavier seemed truly delighted. 'I hope you get to see it soon, but I do not carry a mirror in my hat. So I suppose I will have to get you out of here so you can see what you've become.' He raised his sword and the tip began to glow white. He held it out, his face screwed up in concentration and he pushed it against nothing, like he was probing. Then he suddenly slashed down and the world split open, the blank walls suddenly allowing colour. After a few seconds of careful cutting he opened a hole in the wall, exposing an alley on the other side.

'Let's go,' he smiled and took up his burden again, and the group made their way into the real world.

CHAPTER NINE

They landed in the city, an actual real city. Adam didn't know how but he knew as soon as his feet hit the ground that this was a real place. His boots hit the ground and everything just seemed more solid. Somehow less wondrous and more secure than the world he'd been walking through. He looked around the alley and smelled familiar garbage and car fumes, saw the familiar bright lights and architecture. As well as one less familiar sight, one he'd only seen once before.

'Evenin'.' The man was grubby and small, in a brown suit that looked like he'd worn it for decades straight. He had long, crooked, yellow teeth. Behind him stood three Blanks, two whites and a black. As Adam turned to run he saw three more, one with black slits across its eyes.

'Well,' Xavier sighed. 'I thought the thing that eventually killed me would be a little less hideous.' He pushed Pan off him and the big man staggered, landing against the wall with a pained breath. 'An old bear that has been all but forgotten, if he was ever worthwhile, is going to end the legacy of the Red Gentleman. This is, frankly, rather hurtful.'

'What are you talking about?' the man in the ugly suit asked the question Adam was thinking. He looked around and saw Pan trying to ready himself, saw Annabelle standing very still but for her twitching, twirling fingers.

'You and me.' Xavier shook his head with a sad little smile. 'I mean really, it's just sad that I fell into such a pedestrian trap. Such an ugly, basic technique from such an unevolved dolt of a being.' He really did sound upset with himself. 'Me, ending up like this because of the three of them.' He sighed and motioned toward Pan, Annabelle and Adam. 'It hurts me.'

'You'd best watch your damn mouth,' the squat man growled.

'Or what? You'll kill me even more?' Xavier drew his sword and looked around. 'Honestly you lack even wordplay. There's not a single aspect of what we could be that you manage to achieve.' He shook his head. 'Sorry all but I cannot stand this idea. If you want to kill me Little Bear you're going to have to catch me.' He turned, struck out with the sword before one of the Blanks could transform and struck it through the head, then vaulted off another one and headed out of the alley. Ursas let out a guttural roar and chased after him, barrelling through his own creatures to follow his enemy out into the world.

'Does that Presence of yours know how to fight yet?' Annabelle said softly, the whips falling from her sleeves where she'd been building them.

'I have no idea how to use it, or what it does,' he replied.

'Well I suggest you learn fast!' She lashed out with the whips as the creatures started to transform, dozens upon dozens of spiders scattering off her skirts. In Adam's head, he heard a strange sound, like someone was rifling through the pages of a book.

'I hope you've got a good idea,' he mumbled to the panther in his head.

'Shut up a minute I'm looking for something,' came a voice in his head. 'Something I have a use for.'

He started looking for a chance, started looking at the Blanks for some kind of gap or weak point he could stick his knife into. It wasn't much of a weapon, but if he could get a couple of lucky hits, he and Annabelle might be able to get away.

'Well now,' the voice sounded pleased. 'Opportunism, spite, ruthlessness and a little desperation. Stay alive for a few moments and I may have something.' He hit the deck and a massive black blade passed over his head, then rolled to the side as the blade slammed into the pavement. He lunged up with the knife and stuck the white creature, wrenching at it with the blade. It ignored the wound and smacked him in the face with the pommel of the sword and he staggered back. Annabelle was holding four off with her whip, and she already had a number of bruises and scratches on her body. A few of the creatures were struggling and falling. He guessed they might have been full of spiders.

Pan had one tendril wrapped around his arm several times, pulling it closer and closer to him. As the Blank Legionnaire lashed at him, barbs and blades cut into his skin as he pulled it closer and closer. Once it got within his reach he pulled it over to him and slammed his face repeatedly into its Blank mask. He seemed like he was faltering but he was doing a decent job of fighting considering he had one working arm and had to lean on a wall to stand.

'If you have a plan,' he muttered to the thing in his head.

'Now is the time,' it finished the thought with triumph in its voice. He heard a soft hum and a hot feeling ran down his elbows to his hands. Heavy black gloves had formed on his arms and from the knuckles slipped a set of long shining bright green claws. That wasn't the strangest thing. The strangest thing occurred as he looked at the creatures. As he studied them he could see the trails their movements were leaving in the air. He could see how far they could reach, how fast they swung, the patterns they swirled in. He moved forward and one of the Blanks advanced on him a hulking black monstrosity that drew back its arm to punch him, but he knew full well where and how it'd swing and stepped around it almost effortlessly.

The creature whirled to throw an overhead strike and he ducked to the side. He saw a long, green line under the deformed creature's shoulder and struck the claws of both hands into it, pulling the torso apart across the line. It was like pulling the exact right thread to make a tapestry fall apart. The strike went all the way through the creature's side and it just collapsed in on itself, fading into a pile of nothing important on the floor. He turned and jumped onto another one, this one armed with a pair of whip-like tendrils. He tolerated the blows it was landing about his chest and stomach and tackled it onto the ground. He knew the thing was dangerous but not terribly strong. They struggled for a moment and slammed his claws into the side of its head. He twisted his hands, ripping the face apart with a growl of effort. Another one kicked him off the creature and pitched him into the wall. As he tumbled head over heels through the air he suddenly had all the time in the world. Suddenly he could turn in mid-air and had enough room to land on his hands and knees before he pulled himself to his feet in a ready stance, sliding back until his back only landed with a small bump on the wall that would have cracked his skull if not for the Presence.

'All right.' His voice wasn't his voice, not even the synthesised version. It was an insane high-pitched giggling noise, something that made him think of things strapped to tables and screaming in the middle of the night. 'That… wasn't… very… nice… now, was it?' He launched himself back off the wall with one foot and lashed out at the monster, only to realise that the creature was aiming its strike almost perfectly, two long horizontal bladed cuts that would slice him up no matter what he did. No jumping or twirling would work. He had no choice but to just let himself fall and land on his face, feeling the tendril hack into the meat of his back.

He rolled to his feet and came up with a long uppercut that gashed deep into the creature's chest. It lashed out with its blades and he reached up with his claws, ripping into the arm and wrenching it off. He felt the pain as the other tendril ripped into his face. He knew it hurt, he could taste the blood and feel the break in his own cheekbone, but it simply didn't matter. His own shattered bone somehow wasn't relevant. He twisted his clawed arm and drove it up through the creature's stomach until he felt the resistance against his arm end. The flesh tore and sprayed over his arm, face and chest. He let out a cackling laugh without even thinking.

'Come on!' Annabelle shoved Pan at Adam and he caught the bigger man, the weight meaning surprisingly little to him. She turned to run through the gap in Blanks, throwing fistfuls of spiders at the monsters. The creatures lashed out at them, but with how they were moving they wouldn't hit him. He set off at a sprint, looking over at Annabelle.

'Have you got a plan?' he panted, his voice mashed and garbled as he spoke, between the broken mouth and the mask. He was dimly aware that the mask was the only thing holding his face together.

'There's a doctor!' she called out. 'And besides, those things can't walk into public without risking exposure, and they won't dare risk exposure!'

'Why not?'

'You're asking questions now?' She looked at him, her eyes wide.

'Right!' he nodded. 'Shutting up and running!' He did so. After about five minutes and a lot of very confused looks from passers-by he ran into an abandoned cinema. Annabelle fell against the wall and took a couple of deep breaths.

'Hey there Sister girl.' The old cinema was white and red, and the floor was black. The paint was chipped and peeling and the walls were covered in old movie posters. Cheesy, tacky, old B movies that went back to before Adam was born. The curtains were moth eaten and faded. Sitting in a worn leather seat was a stoned guy with long hair and a green shirt that looked like it had seen better days. His hair was long, matted and greasy. In one hand was a cigarette dangling from his fingers. His eyes were bleary and red and he smelled like weed smoke.

'Hey Sage,' she smiled and waved at him. 'We're here to see the doctor.'

'You're all injured?' A bored looking girl behind the ticket counter seemed suddenly less bored. She tucked her dirty blond hair behind one ear and slipped one hand rather deliberately under the counter. Adam looked at her and reached up with one finger to lower his mask a little and her eyes widened. 'Well shit dude, I'm convinced. Doc's in theatre four.'

'Why are we in a movie theatre?' he mumbled as he started to walk past the box office.

'Because that's where the doctor is.' Sure enough as they walked through the door with the four on it and sure enough there really was a movie theatre. There were seats and there as even a movie playing, some bad comedy he didn't recognise exchanged clichéd lines in eerily quiet voices. About a dozen chairs had been taken out of the middle of the theatre and replaced with a bunch of medical equipment and a bed.

'Hey.' The woman who looked over at him was wearing very little. That was the first thing Adam noticed because he was after all still male. She wore an open lab coat and only underwear beneath it as she sat in a cushioned chair. She wore no shoes and her hair and makeup were done in a strange fifties style. 'Wow,' she grinned, looking over at them. 'You went and done got yourself fucked up honeypies. You two put the Soldier on the bed and the two of you sit yourselves down. What the heck happened?'

'We got ambushed,' Pan's voice was groggy. 'And I was already like this.' Adam put him down on the bed where he smiled a little and then passed out immediately.

'Is he okay?'

'He's just drained,' the woman smiled. 'So, hi there stranger. I'm Doctor Mercy. Why don't you take that scary old mask off and I'll fix that pretty face of yours?' He lowered his mask and spat the half of a tooth that had been knocked off. As he started to undo the fastening he felt his jawbone start to fall away and Mercy moved up to him, holding the jaw in her hand. As he finally got it off the pain began to rock through his body and he screamed, or tried to through a shattered cheekbone and half removed jaw. Mercy put one hand on his face and the pain began to trickle away. Mercy held his face for a few long seconds and her own suddenly flashed, her flesh ripping, her jawbone separating and her cheek shattering in front of him. It just sat there for a second before it vanished. She didn't wince or flinch, but the wounds had been very real for a moment. After she was done with him she sat down between him and Annabelle.

'Give me a minute,' she told them. 'I can only take so much of that. I might have to settle the rest of it with my lesser gifts.' She yawned and took a swig from a cup in the nearby hand rest. 'I can only do that now and again, it takes a lot out of me.'

'What did you do?'

'I showed you mercy,' she smiled at him. 'I showed you my pain, and in doing so took yours away. Don't worry, it doesn't have any permanent effects on little old me that haven't already happened.' She coughed once and then got up, rolling her neck and cracking her knuckles. 'All right spider girl,' she lifted a few of the hand rests and pointed at the space left there. Annabelle took off her shirt and Adam looked away, but judging by the sound of the squeaking and pained groaning Annabelle had laid down on the chairs.

He put the mask back on, and the gauntlets appeared in his hands, but didn't light up to claws.

'Hey, are you there?' he whispered.

'Yes Adam,' the voice was in his head, the synthesiser copy of his own. 'And there's no need to speak out loud, I hear anything you want to communicate to me.'

'All right, that's handy,' he nodded. 'So, what the hell are you?'

'I am the Presence bound to you,' it explained. 'The thing that appeared to you as a panther and previously as a light. I am in a very real way now a part of you. Get up, go to the bathroom and you can see what I look like.' He headed into the surprisingly pristine bathroom and took a look at the mirror. He stared into it for a long moment, across the bottom of his face, from the nose down was a mask. On the front of the mesh metal mask was a bright green smile that went far past his lips, giving him a slightly creepy appearance. It made his eyes seem somehow darker and his face kind of intense. He raised his hands and he could see thick gloves with what looked like metal plates attached to them. Inside the plating were three slits on each hand and as he clenched his fists and focused the claws materialised, turning the rooms white tile green.

'So, what is this green stuff?' He looked at them. 'I see it on the other people as well.'

'It is,' the reply had a small pause for the creature to think, 'focused opportunism. It, even more than your claws, is my gift to you. You can see the weak places, the cracks in the armour, the faults in the strikes laid against you. I hope it serves you well.' He got up and walked out of the bathroom, heading back into the theatre and sitting down. Annabelle was dressed again and Mercy had Pan hooked up to some machines Adam didn't recognise.

'Hey,' Anabelle looked at him. 'How are you?'

'I'm doing well,' he smiled. 'Been looking at this thing.' He raised his hands and pointed to the mask. 'I think I like it.'

'Well its validity as a fashion accessory should of course be your first priority,' she grinned. 'But I'm glad you can fight with it as well.'

'Well I hate to butt into this adorable moment,' came a voice from the doorway. 'And I don't mean to imply that it's not heart-warming because I assure you it is. If you wouldn't mind clearing that table I think I have a more urgent need for it than our resident Lost Boy.' Xavier was leaning heavily on his cane; his red coat was in tatters and his shirt was stuck to his chest with a liquid that Adam guessed was his own blood. His hat was on his head at a strange angle and he bore a massive claw mark down his face. It took Adam a couple of minutes before he noticed the fact that one of the sleeves of his shirt was hanging empty. As Annabelle pulled Pan off the gurney with Mercy's help, Adam took Xavier's weight and helped him stagger his way down to the bed and lay on it. With as much care as possible he pulled the Top Hat Man's shirt off and Xavier winced, letting out a soft grunt of pain. Adam paused and looked at him, feeling bile rise in his throat.

'I'm sorry.'

'Stop talking and pull.' Xavier grit his teeth. 'Faster is better and I promise not to stab you.' All at once Adam ripped as hard as possible on the garment to

172

reveal the blood coating his entire chest and arms. He bore several claw marks all over his chest and stomach. The blood flow seemed to have stopped but dry and wet blood were mingling down his entire torso. Adam lifted Xavier gently as he could and cut the shirt away, laying him down on the gurney. Xavier let out a sick wavering groan but he didn't thrash or scream and more importantly, he didn't stab Adam.

'We should leave.' Pan's voice was weak, but he was standing and holding his own machine. 'Mercy's going to need to concentrate if she's gonna keep him alive and away from any more permanent harm.' He looked at where Xavier's arm had been, a roughhewn, bloody stump now oozing in its place. Pan started to drag himself out of the theatre and the other two propped him up, helping him out of the room and into the front office. Adam tested his jaw to be sure it still worked and it seemed to. Adam put the machine down and set him down on a chair.

'So, what's going on?' He looked at them. 'Can you tell me anything about my Presence?'

'No planning.' The stoner looked up at him and Annabelle raised her hands.

'We're not planning war.' Anabelle looked at him. 'Just trying to figure out what's going on with him. He has a new Presence and we're trying to orient him.'

'All right.' Sage narrowed his eyes at them. 'But if I hear one word I don't like.'

'What is his deal?' Adam looked at him.

'The Sage is this place's guardian,' Anabelle looked

at him. 'Start a fight here, he kills you. You come in looking to chase someone, or wait outside for them to come out and he kills you. You start making plans to fight later...'

'And he kills you?' Adam guessed.

'No dude,' she scoffed. 'He just throws you out. It's just talking, don't get all crazy.' She thought about it for a moment. 'About a block away from this place and he's got about as much power as a puppy, but if you cross a line here, well.'

'He kills you,' Pan grunted.

'But back to you,' Annabelle nodded.

'Yeah so,' he raised his gloves, 'what do Presences do exactly?'

'Well of course there's a few different things,' Pan nodded. 'As far as your first couple, there's the blunt uses,' he raised his own fists, 'like my gloves or Anna and her webs. As far as that goes yours appears to be pretty weak.'

'I hacked through the blanks well enough,' he pointed out.

'Which was kinda surprising to me,' Pan replied. 'I can see a few things and I mean they're not very strong. I could take those claws in my hands and shatter them, but they went through Blanks just fine. Presences also boost your strength, or your speed, sometimes they stop you feeling pain or discomfort. They'll let you keep going long past human endurance.'

'I noticed.' He put his hand on his own cheek. 'I

barely noticed that I was carrying one of my own teeth in my mouth the whole run over.'

'It can also do several deeper things, some of which you may take years to discover, or never discover at all. You've seen the Map, Anabelle's sisters. Every Presence can form into a weapon to be wielded and has several far more important other uses. What yours can do may not be fully apparent to you for a while, but I have faith you'll figure it out.'

'I already kinda have.' He held out his hands. 'I can spot weak points.'

'What do you mean?'

Adam focused and looked at Pan for a long second, then reached out and tapped him between the second and third ribs. 'Your left glove hardens your skin. It makes it almost impossible to cut into but that hardening gives out for a small section there.' He poked it. 'Someone hits you exactly there and it'll be like hitting anyone else.'

'Good to know.' Pan's hand drifted over the spot Adam had pointed out.

'And thus, a nervous tic was born,' Annabelle smirked. 'Don't tell me mine it'll just make me panic. Unless I can fix it.'

'All right,' Adam shrugged. 'So, as I get more Presences I get more stuff?'

'Yep,' Pan smiled and raised both hands. 'My third one's a little weird, so I'm not gonna show it off.'

'So, that's why Xavier throws his hat at people?'

'Oh, you have absolutely no idea what that stupid

hat of his can do,' Pan laughed.

'But wait, he said he only had two. His coat sets things on fire.'

'That's a different thing,' Pan nodded. 'I'm not even going to pretend I can understand how he makes those coats.'

'So,' he looked at his gloves, 'these are weak if I don't hit the exact right point. All right, good to know I'll keep it in mind.' He tapped the glove. 'I hope I can figure out what the rest of it does.' And without knowing he realised he'd started to enjoy the idea.

'I hope you get the chance,' Pan grunted and detached the machine, smiling to himself. 'Best of luck man really, I hope this works out for you.'

'Yeah,' he looked down, 'me too,' and thought about things for a moment, hoping to move onto the next thing. 'So why won't the Blank Legion risk exposure?'

'May I?' The generic looking girl was no longer behind the counter, she'd sat down beside them.

'Be my guest,' Annabelle shrugged. 'Sage can't punch you.'

'I'm Adam.' He reached out.

'Isabelle,' she smiled. 'I'm the nurse I guess. I keep Mercy from any particularly dangerous lunacies she might be considering.' She shook his hand. 'Or I try anyway.'

'The reason the Blank Legion won't risk exposure, why none of you should risk exposure, is the fact that people, like everything else in this universe, have an analogue in both the world above and the world below. Some of them are just beings, like imps or gargoyles but some of them are building sized monsters or creatures that can pop your skull just by glaring at you. When you show your power to normal people it alerts the things above and below and might even drag them into full manifestation. Which means if you show your power too loud you might end up dealing with a person's other half, which might be huge powerful and very angry that you just dragged it into a world it doesn't belong in. Which means you and everyone nearby is all kinds of dead.' Suddenly her eyes were sharper, her hair was darker, she was taller and stronger and more intimidating and not just because she was talking about a monster murdering a person's entire family. 'So yes, keep your magic tame.'

'Does that mean no claws?'

'It means claws probably aren't a great idea,' she shrugged. 'But hey, if the other guy pulls a knife take your chances and go to fucking town.'

'Shifter,' Sage spoke in a singsong voice.

'Don't be shitty,' she snapped at him, her body swelling further and her face growing more aggressive. 'I'm alerting him to the world around him, not arming him for the war.'

'All right,' he folded his arms. 'But your toe's on the line.'

'You can't throw me out.' She was back to looking normal. 'I'm under the same rules and obligations that you are.' The two of them locked eyes with each other for a few long seconds and then the Sage leaned back, lighting another cigarette. 'But yeah, that's about the score. Keep any magic you use discrete and if anyone rushes you with magic you can't beat go out in public, they might not chase you.' She thought about it. 'Or they might shoot you in the back. The fuck do I know? I don't know whoever's shooting at you.'

'Neither do I,' he admitted. 'I really don't like the idea of being shot at.'

'Yeah, it's not something I recommend,' she nodded. 'So, you know, try not to piss anyone off.' Her face slipped into a smile. 'By doing something stupid like existing on one side of a war.'

'Did I forget to warn you that she's a total bitch?' Sage noted. 'My bad.'

'Well I'm glad you're up to speed, after all I am rather fond of you and I'd hate to think I lost my arm for nothing.' Xavier wasn't in his jacket or shirt, only his hat and pants. He still only had one arm, the other sewn up at the shoulder as if he'd had it amputated weeks ago. He unsheathed his sword, letting the cane drop and brought it up to Adam's throat, quivering. 'Which reminds me, you have exactly thirty seconds to explain what deal you made with the man known as the Legate before I slit your throat.'

'Red,' the voice rang and echoed around the room, and the stoned man now looked a lot more imposing, with glowing red eyes and a long knife in each hand.

'Don't try it,' Xavier said softly. 'Even you are not that fast. Twenty-five.'

'What the fuck is going on X?' Pan growled.

'Twenty.' A tiny prick of pain ran through Adam's neck.

'All right,' Adam raised his hands. 'He came up to me and told me that when I got a Presence that if I gave it over to him instead of you he'd keep the Legion off my back forever. That I'd get to go back to a normal life and forget about all of this.' He looked around at the group. 'I mean I would have told you but I was afraid you'd,' he pointed to the weapon, 'act pretty much exactly like this. I mean seriously why would I tell you?'

'Well your estimation of my manner is accurate, however, may I ask that you look at this from my perspective. Imagine for a second that I just risked my life repeatedly, went through violence, fought the Knight of Mirrors, burned a route through the world of the Seraph and confronted a very powerful Guardian Angel who, despite my earlier statements, I do completely remember and who bears a deep, abiding and entirely legitimate grudge against me. Oh, and I actually, quite literally and with no exaggeration lost a fucking arm so you could survive and thrive!' His face twisted with disgust and he spat the words.

'I find out that you plan to sell the divine gift that I actually crippled myself securing for you to one of my greatest enemies and the employer of the man who just removed my second favourite limb in exchange for,' he paused and spoke through gritted teeth, 'you having, what did you say? A normal, uninterrupted life? A boring, average, every day existence? Do you have any idea how much that absolutely sickens me?' He was yelling now, the ever smiling, ever jovial Xavier screaming in his face.

'Put it down Gent.' Sage's focus was now laser tight, his stance crouched and deadly. 'Before I take my chances and put you down.'

'He won't do anything to him.' Pan's voice was soft. 'He wouldn't dare. He knows exactly what'll happen if he kills someone he's not allowed to.'

'The problem with blackmail,' Xavier switched his focus to Pan, withdrawing the sword a little, 'is that eventually the person being blackmailed decides a life where he has to live under blackmail's restrictions is worse than the life he will have after the blackmail takes effect.'

'Maybe.' Pan didn't even bother looking at him. 'But that day is not this day.'

'No.' Xavier was smiling again. 'No, it is not.' He shook his head and kicked the cane up with his foot, sliding the sword away. 'But do you understand what we may be giving up?' He spoke even as Sage lunged suddenly, tackling him to the ground and beginning to drag him outside. The others followed him while Pan spoke.

'I'm Lost,' Pan shrugged, a smile on his face. 'Part of that means I have to let people make their own choices. If he wants to leave then he can, if he wants to be one of us then he's welcome.' He shrugged. 'Will I be pissed if he bails on us? Hell yeah, I might even kick his ass, but we can't kill him before we get started. We have to give him that chance.'

'I,' Xavier enunciated each word clearly, pausing between each one as his limp body was dragged out the side door, 'really and truly despise you.'

'Yeah, I love you too Red,' Pan sighed. 'But I'm still right.'

Xavier pulled himself to his feet and walked off into the world, seemingly unbothered by the fact he was strangely dressed had no shoes and had lost an arm less than an hour ago. He appeared to be singing some kind of song Adam didn't recognise.

'Now,' Pan put a hand on his shoulder. 'Why don't you go home for a while, go to bed and rest up for a few days. No one should be willing to attack you.' He shook his head. 'Annabelle will see you home, I hope you make the right choice but I'll respect it either way.' He turned away and walked back into the operating theatre.

'Operating theatre,' Adam smirked. 'I just got that joke.' He looked at Annabelle. 'So, how do you feel about all of this?'

'I'm,' Annabelle waved her hand from side to side 'reserving judgment until I have all the facts. If I had ever had that choice maybe I wouldn't have wanted to be one of us either I mean I think I would but I can't say for sure.' She shrugged. 'I'm a person who became not human by adoption. My take on how loyalty and appreciation work are a little twisted conceptually.

Now come on.' She patted him on the back. 'Let's go out for a drink before we get you home. Something to eat too, I know you're hungry.' He hadn't realised that even though they'd spent entire days in those other worlds he'd been walking through he hadn't felt the need to eat once. Now she'd mentioned it his stomach let out a growl that probably could have been heard a couple of blocks away. She smiled and gestured toward a car on the street, which he climbed into as a small man in bright clothes stepped out of it. In five minutes, they were in a pub he'd never seen before with a beer in his hand. It was quiet and the music had decent atmosphere to it but there weren't many people. Annabelle sat down and motioned to one of the waiters, who nodded but didn't come over.

'What's going on?'

'He knows me,' Annabelle smiled. 'And he knows right now that fast is better than good and fast and good is better than picky. You're not vegan, are you?'

'No, I eat meat,' he nodded.

'Capital, then you'll have steak and we'll like it.' She smiled, the rings on her lips glinting as she did. 'Now, tell me what you think of our little fantastic voyage to another world?'

'Did you just use the word capital?'

'I did,' she smiled, puffing herself up a little. 'It happens when I spend time with Xavier, I get steadily more and more loquacious. Now answer my question Sir Stalls-a-lot.'

'It was,' he thought about it, 'weird and scary

mostly. I mean people tried to kill me, I mean, things tried to kill me, people tried to kill other people and as a side effect almost killed me. Which is probably the scariest part.' He looked at her for a long moment. 'The lightning woman almost killed me. She threw a bolt of lightning at my head to get me out of the way. Not to beat me, not to kill me, just because she didn't want me to distract her from the people she actually felt like fighting.' He shuddered, he'd be seeing that girls face in his nightmares for a few years. 'I think I could go my whole life without ever feeling like someone was going to kill me as an afterthought again and not ever miss that feeling.'

'Yeah,' she nodded. 'I get that.'

'And, I mean, I don't wanna fight you about it again but,' he shrugged, 'you left a guy behind and even if you didn't, someone literally volunteered to die in a fight in front of me. He got mobbed, probably killed and you tell me he knew about it beforehand and did it anyway.'

'Which is intense,' she nodded. 'I mean you don't understand what's really going on and I think half the time neither do I. I just trust that things will work out as they should, and they will because they always do.'

'All the same, Xavier lost an arm and I mean, he was the guy who, weird as he was, seemed more or less invincible and he got his ass kicked.'

'He did at that,' Annabelle nodded.

'But,' he chuckled. 'The world is really cool here. I mean,' he looked down at the gloves, 'a panther who talks to me in my head has given me claws and let me see the entire world in a completely different way. I've met some weird and wonderful people in this world and even though most of them have threatened to kill me so far,' she had the decency to wince and look a little embarrassed,

'I've actually gotten to walk through other worlds. That was so amazing. A lot of it scared me but I got to meet the Black Widow, a person I didn't know existed, who is apparently the physical epitome of spiders and is also, for some reason, a really hot black woman. Which I'm just letting go by the way because it still makes a negative amount of sense. I met a girl adopted by spiders, I flew two stories on a hat. I've done some weird things and I don't see how I can just go back to a normal world where nothing strange is happening. I just don't know if I can just be a normal person anymore.' He shook his head and laughed. 'It's so weird.'

'It is.' She smiled and patted him on the shoulder. 'It's scary and amazing and a truly wild ride and I hope you don't give it up.' Their food arrived and the two of them ate without further conversation. The steak was, in a word, excellent but honestly, he would have eaten and enjoyed it uncooked at the moment, he was so hungry.

'So,' he spoke between steak and whatever came next. 'Why didn't I need to eat?'

'Things work different there,' she shrugged, seeming to think that was a satisfactory answer.

'You know you keep giving me few word answers that aren't really answers and acting like you've just told me something of value, don't you?'

'Yeah,' she chuckled. 'It's one of my favourite things in the world to do.' She tucked her hair behind her ear and the smile faded. 'But this time I'm doing it as my nice-ish way of telling people that it's something I can't explain to them because I'm not allowed to. It's not my right, I don't trust you with the information or I simply don't know myself. It's just easier and more fun to give a roundabout answer than provide complicated explanations, hurt someone's feelings or admit I don't know something. Honestly, I just couldn't be bothered this time so here goes. Biological rules, and most of the rules of physics and general existence, tend to be local standing only. Sometimes in other worlds you'll need to eat and sleep like a normal person and at other time things like inertia, gravity momentum, force, they might mean a good deal less or more there.' She leaned over. 'For instance, did you notice you didn't breathe once the entire time you were in the other world unless you gasped, or took a moment to take a deep breath? There was no air, no oxygen in that Seraph world and we didn't' need it.'

'Really?' he raised an eyebrow and she grinned and nodded.

'Cross my heart and hope to die, stick a needle in my eye.'

'You sure you wouldn't enjoy that?'

'I didn't enjoy most of these.' She poked her pierced tongue out at him. 'Did you know how annoying it was to eat soup and not talk for a week?'

'So why get 'em?'

'I like how they look,' she shrugged. 'Besides I grew up in a family where they literally build traps in which to keep people they eat. I mean you met Aunt Widow and she's not the worst of them. The one thing my family hold sacred is purity of form. You never alter yourself, you never interfere with your pattern. We are, by our nature, incredibly vain and altering my form in some strange manner was the only real rebellion I could pull off. The more of them I got the more I liked them and now…' She turned a little and showed him her side, a picture of a gaudily dressed man throwing a large deck of cards down her shoulder winking at him.

'So, you're completely covered in things like that?'

'Completely,' she winked at him and smiled for a few seconds. 'First few were rebellion, some more were aesthetic and most of 'em I just liked. So, no, to answer your question I'm not interested in doing anything with my eyes.'

'So, any other rebellions I should know about?' Oh dear god was he flirting?

'I picked a side,' she answered him seriously. 'It's not a complete and total thing. I'm not absolutely lost. My first loyalty is still to my family and to the webs, but if there's ever a chance to support your side then that's the chance I'm taking. Some members of my family don't like that very much. I've mentioned the Funnel Webs as one we don't ever want to go through and that's partly because Uncle Funnel Web doesn't approve of my choices. He's one of the few males in my family with any power and he's as dangerous as he is clever. I'd only ever go through his web alone. He won't hurt me but he might kill whoever I'm with out of spite.'

'One hell of a family,' he noted.

'Our values aren't yours and they aren't yours to judge.' Her tone was cold for a second, then she softened a little. 'Sorry, that sounded like an accusation and I don't like being put on the defensive.'

'No, you're right,' he nodded. 'There's a lot about this place I don't understand. I guess I should probably reserve judgment until I know something about something.'

'That'll serve you well,' she nodded. 'Judgment in our world is a dangerous vice very few people can afford. If I judged others we would have made this journey without Xavier and the Lady Ray would have fried us while Pan and the dog were grappling on the floor. We're a strange bunch who have a lot of conflicting values.' She thought for a few long moments. 'I remember from somewhere, someone once said do not judge others with your yardstick for they may be using an entirely different measure.' She finished her drink in a long swig. 'If there's one lesson I can teach you, that'd be it.'

'Then I have some advice for you too.' He shrugged and

took his own drink. 'Don't judge, but always question.'

'What do you mean?'

'Don't judge other people if you don't have to. Don't try to make them live your way, or tell them to do things how you want them to but you should at least try to understand the reason they do what they do.'

'I'll take it under advisement,' she nodded. 'Maybe you're a little more worthwhile than I gave you credit for.'

'In your world that's actually a compliment, isn't it?' He smirked and she nodded.

'Spiders aren't very loud with our affection. We kind of just expect people to understand how we feel when we talk rather than paying too much attention to what we say.'

'Well I'm going to guess that was a statement of your new-found respect for me and my contributions to this weird little army you're building.'

'I wouldn't be uncomfortable with you believing that,' she nodded. 'Now I'll settle up the bill and then we should get you home. Mercy wasn't lying, you really do need to rest.'

'Which I assume you're going to do?' He looked at her and she sighed, tucking one hair behind her ear. 'Probably not but I will take your concern as understood,' she smiled. 'I have the ability to give good advice, and not so much the ability take it.'

'All right.' She settled the bill and they headed for the car.

He was a little nervous about heading home. He'd have to prepare a good lie for his friends and he wasn't sure they'd listen to it whatever it was.

'Allow me,' came the smug tone in his ear. He was more or less used to it by now. 'Let me speak for you and I will provide them with an explanation they will accept.'

'All right,' he nodded and headed home, the nerves in his stomach settled for now. It was weird but he was actually starting to trust this thing.

CHAPTER TEN

'Holy shit Adam.' Looking at Bethany it was clear she wasn't sure whether to be happy, worried or angry. 'Where the hell have you been?'

'A whole group of people got caught up in it, the police came in and turned into kind of a, well, a riot I guess. Anyway, everyone got arrested and when people got rowdy the police decided they were going to keep us all for a few days.' He heard the anger in his voice growing and felt none of it. It was a good lie though. 'I didn't get to call anyone. I didn't get to go anywhere, we were stuck there so if no one minds I'm gonna go take a shower without anyone watching. I've spent a week in prison clothes and it was gross.'

'Wait a minute.' She reached out and grabbed his arm. 'Shouldn't you, I don't know, talk to someone or call someone or fucking sue someone for that matter? I don't know!'

The voice sighed and his hand rose to run through his hair. 'Look I might do something about it at some point. Right now I can't think about any of that. I just want to put this behind me. I met a couple of other people on the way and they're talking about meeting up and organising a class action something or something like that. I'm not sure if it'll go anywhere but I'll talk to them.'

'So, what's with the mask and the gloves?' Bethany's boyfriend Nick spoke from the doorway. Adam hadn't known he was there but something told him the Presence had. His friend's ability to appear suddenly was no match for the Presence's hyper awareness.

'Well between the red coat and these,' he took the gloves off, 'I've started a new thing where I'm gonna pick up any weird cool things I find and build weird cool outfits out of them.'

'All right,' Nick shrugged, apparently deciding he didn't care anymore.

'So yeah, I bought these to cheer myself up.' He tapped the mask. 'What do you think?'

'The smile's a little creepy,' Bethany pointed out. 'But you know, it's not so bad. I could see you building some pretty cool stuff based on this.'

'That's the plan,' he nodded and raised one hand. 'Now as I said I'm gonna go take a shower on my own. Seriously the lack of privacy was the worst part by far.'

Bethany looked like she wanted to keep talking, but Nick put his hand on her shoulder and she nodded, waving Adam off. He went up to the shower and washed, removing the mask and putting it away.

The next few days passed more or less without incident. He rested, recuperated and followed the advice of the strange doctor. He chatted with old friends and let the world catch him up a little. He found out two days in that he'd lost his job, not that it particularly mattered as he'd only been a faceless office drone anyway. As hard as it was to find jobs these days Adam had always been pretty good at it.

He didn't go looking, he'd had savings but they were more because he didn't have much to spend money on rather than any good sense. Still he had a few weeks before things got dire. If he decided to stick around he'd have to ask other members of the Lost how they made money.

He watched the people around him with a little tension as he went around, not sure if he was looking at normal people just living their lives or if they were secret agents of the Legion, or even the Lost, keeping eyes on him. He wasn't sure why but it seemed like he was important. Two people had sacrificed life and limb, in one case each, for him after all. Still with nothing else to do he went back to his normal life, strange as that now seemed. The only difference was a noteworthy precaution, he kept the mask with him at all times. He carried it in a pocket of his jacket, or the messenger bag he carried his stuff in. Every night he fell asleep wearing it. It actually made sleep easier. For whatever reason, as soon as he decided he wanted to sleep while he was wearing the mask he seemed to fall asleep almost instantly. It took him longer than he would have liked to admit to realise that was probably not a coincidence.

The mask saved him a few nights into his time back in the world. He woke up to a strange humming sound and rolled out of bed, keeping himself low by some instinct he didn't understand. Then the window shattered above him with a sudden high-pitched hum.

'What was that?'

'Stay low and give me a moment.' The voice was soft, and after a few seconds there was a grunt of grim satisfaction. 'Is there anything within your reach that you wouldn't mind losing?'

'A pillow I guess,' he shrugged.

'Grab it and throw it into the air.' He did and he heard the hum again. The pillow exploded.

'Well that tells me two things. One, our opponent is using a ranged weapon, likely some form of sonic cannon. Two, our opponent is young and inexperienced. He has not been fighting long.'

'How do you know that?'

'Because an experienced sniper would have fired a shot half a foot below that pillow in the hopes of killing the man holding it. This one is new; his reflexes may be sharp but he does not have a clear head. I would recommend you stay low and get out of the room.'

'Wait, you told me to do that knowing if he was any good he'd kill me?'

'I had faith in you.'

Adam rolled his eyes and started crawling slowly and steadily toward the front door. He reached up, twisted the handle and felt another hum as the door opened. A hole appeared in the wall beside him.

'Oh shit.' He set off running as fast as he could through the door, another shot following him. He ran over to the side of the house and jumped out, catching hold of a tree branch and then swinging and dropping down onto the trunk, and then the ground. He had no idea how he knew to do that, or how he knew how to do it for that matter. He stayed low as he looked across the house. 'Any idea where he was shooting from?' he asked the Presence.

'One of those two houses.' The two houses across the street started to glow green. 'Get across the road, stay low and alter your movement patterns. I believe the term is serpentine. I will attempt to isolate the point of attack as you move.' He stayed low and ran across the street, swerving back and forward and hearing the humming sounds of the sniper's fire. He bobbed and weaved, zigzagging as he ran and soon green beams began to accompany the humming sounds. Soon only one of the houses was glowing as he ran around the side of the other one. He hid behind a wall and let himself breathe.

'Is that thing gonna kill me?' he asked.

'It seems likely,' the Presence replied. 'Judging by the impact to the pillow it seems likely that any body part that beam hits will be severely damaged. At the same time, the longer we spend in this position the more time he can take to consider his position and regain his calm. I believe we should attempt to take him by surprise.'

'Back window.'

'Seems sensible.' He snuck around to the back of the first house to the house his assailant was lying in wait in and climbed up a few wooden slats that were running on the side of the house. The window was closed, so he took out his claws and cut out the bottom of the window, smashing it in and climbing inside. 'A contest of assassination then,' the Presence spoke only to him, seeming a little amused by the whole idea. 'How very entertaining, I believe in this setting you have the advantage, but he does have experience on you.' Adam was running through the house, getting clear of the room he didn't doubt the sniper was already aiming at.

'Come now,' the voice was hard to place. He couldn't figure out where the weird mismatching accent came from. 'Do you really think I can be lured out of my entrenched position by a window smashing?' There was the sound of someone clicking his tongue. 'This is the best vantage point in the house, there's no way you can reach me from there.'

He kept his mouth shut. Even he could tell that this guy was trying to pick up his position through conversation. He kept low and moved quickly as he ran toward the voice, suspecting his Presence was quietening his steps. As he rounded the corridor he realised why the sniper had been so reluctant to leave the room he was in. He walked around it and he could see there was only one entrance, which was the main door. There was one window, which the sniper was already looking out of and as Adam poked his head out of the next room's window he saw that there was no getting in through the window without getting hit. All right then, he'd have to shake things up and see what happened.

He got as close as he could to where he guessed the

sniper was and slammed his claws through the wall. The sniper let out a gasp of surprise as he turned and fired, and Adam ran as the sonic beam ripped through the wall. He slammed the claw in again a few steps later and set off at a run. The Presence kicked in and he saw the invisible blasts as green lines punching through the wall. He ran for the door and busted through shoulder first. He hit the deck and rolled as his enemy let go of another shot and sprang to his feet, then launched himself at the gunman.

'Weak point on the gun,' he spoke in his mind as he moved, the gun coming up to face him.

'There,' a small second of the gun lit up green and Adam lunged for it with everything he had. He could hear the humming sound of the gun powering up as the claws slammed into it.

The result was enough to blow Adam backwards and slam him into the wall. The gun rang out with a sudden high-pitched scream as the discharging energy detonated. He looked down at his gloves and saw that they were damaged, the claws gone and metal ripped. He looked up at the sniper and saw him struggling to his feet, looking at the remains of his gun with mortified confusion. As he began to approach he tossed the pieces aside and raised his hands, flashing Adam a grin.

Squaring off was like looking at an anatomic diagram of a person, he could see various parts laid out in green. Muscle and bone that would be weaker to impact, a falter in one knee, a lapse of focus in the eyes. Adam lunged at the sniper, no claws; they couldn't turn on with the gloves damaged, but the other guy didn't have a weapon at all. He hit him in the solar plexus and the sniper buckled, then hit him with an elbow to the nose that sent him down. He grabbed the slim, pale man by the hair and held the space the claws would have come out if they could to his throat.

'I hope you understand the implications of all of this.' His voice came out much colder than it had ever sounded before. 'Because I'm not by my nature a killer.' He let out a chuckle he didn't feel. 'But you know what they say, there's nothing like a new skill set.'

'I assumed when you broke my gun that I was already dead.' The strange accent was completely calm. 'I prepared myself before I came. If there was anything you would like to know I assure you I have only one thing to tell you.'

'Which is?' He looked down at him, sounding a lot calmer than he felt.

'That this will not stop.' He glared up at Adam with hate in his eyes. 'That for my failure there will be two more, and four more and ten. Better plans, better armies, better powers. Gifted assassins. I was not all we could muster, just the first they could find. You will not be allowed to stand, you will not be allowed to continue to your miserable existence. You will not be allowed to insult us with your–' Adam hit him in the temple and he went quiet.

'You could kill him.' The Presence's voice was soft in his ear. 'It would definitely be the wisest course of action. You could finish him now, send a message, cut off an enemy before he truly forms and gain yourself another Presence in the bargain.' The voice was low and pleased, excited by the idea of such power. 'Can you imagine operating that rifle? With my ability to see vital points and key positions I could calculate the range, wound points and vital areas and we could cut a swathe through any who would dare oppose us.' Adam stayed quiet at that and the voice started up again. 'Perhaps I went too far with that suggestion, but it would end your concerns. You would not need to be afraid anymore.'

'Sorry.' He picked up what was left of the rifle and smashed it into pieces, grabbing the snipers coat and wrapping the pieces up in it. 'But I'm not a killer.' He hauled himself out the front door and started to walk back towards home. 'Even if it's not smart, I'm not a killer.'

'All right.' The voice was, surprisingly, not disappointed. 'Then I hope this does not come back to haunt you.' He got up, dressed out of his pyjama pants and into actual street clothes, put on some shoes and loaded the gun parts into the bag.

'Hey, Adam.' Sage looked up at him through bleary eyes. 'I didn't expect to see you so soon.'

'I need someone's help and you were the only people I thought might be around this late.' He looked at him. 'Are any of the people I know here?'

'The Gentleman is, entertaining Mercy, and I may be able to contact the Lost Soldier just this once.' He tipped a wink and smiled. 'Don't tell anyone, since I'm technically not supposed to but just between you and me, because you're little and I'm in a good mood.' He didn't understand why this guy was helping him, or why he was in a good mood but he didn't look the gift horse in the mouth. An hour or so later Pan arrived, looking fazed and with his Lost tattoo back on his head. 'What can I do for you kid?'

'First of all,' he looked at him, 'I need you to give me a phone number I can reach you on so I don't have to come out here every time I need to talk to one of you guys. Apparently, Sage wasn't supposed to do that for me. Second, do you have any way to repair a couple of houses in,' he checked his phone, 'three hours? Because an assassin almost killed me earlier tonight. Oh, and there's an unconscious Legion assassin in the house across from mine. You know, because it seems like that's the kind of thing you're interested in.'

Pan looked at him for a long moment, then nodded as if this was all in a day's work. He took Adam's number and sent him a message to give his own back. 'Give me your address and then go into my phone. There's a number in it under the name Omega Brotherhood, call that number and tell them you need a patch up at your address before sun-up, then cooperate with the guy in the black Stormtrooper looking armour who shows up there. His, her or their name is Omega, be polite, be discrete, do whatever they say and they should have the place back to normal before those who live with you get up. I assume that's why you need this.'

'It is.' He picked up the phone, dialled the number they gave him and put the parts of the rifle down in front of Pan. The Solider collected them and Adam looked at Sage to see if the guy would do anything, but he just raised one hand and smiled. Adam hit the button that said Omega.

'Omega Brotherhood.' The voice was generic, female, pleasant and professional. Like the stereotype of a receptionist from the fifties. 'What is your request?'

He gave his address.

'Minor, Moderate or Major?'

'Minor I think,' he shrugged. 'It's walls and a couple of doors. I mean I'm not sure but–'

'Origin?' the voice cut him off.

'I think it's a sonic cannon.' He paused. 'I'm not sure, sorry.'

'Minor sonic cannon damage. Witnesses?'

'No.' He shook his head, then realised he was on a phone. 'But there are sleeping people in the house and I need it fixed before they wake up.'

'Confirmed.' The phone hung up.

'Well, that was, abrupt.' He tossed the phone back to Pan. 'Weird bunch.'

'Aren't we all?' Sage smiled. 'Judge not lest ye be

judged my friend.'

'Some say understanding is wisdom,' he retorted.

'Then you should understand a few things.' Sage smiled and waved a hand. 'You should get back immediately. Omegas don't like to be kept waiting or stood up. That is information I will furnish you with to aid your understanding. They're punctual, efficient and they don't take sides. They have a job to do and they do it, so don't get in their way.'

By the time Adam arrived, there was a small woman in black armour standing exactly still by his front door. She had a black face plate and heavy, black, tactical armour that didn't include her midriff for some strange reason. There was an omega symbol on the face plate and a series of tattoos, in brightly coloured spirals, swirled around her belly button.

'I am Omega.' Her voice was soft. 'You called.'

'I did,' he nodded.

'You are late.'

'I did my best to make it, sorry.'

'Which room?' Her voice was generic and emotionless. He pointed it out and she scaled the tree the same way he had, slipping inside with no difficulty. He climbed after her and her face plate turned to him for the briefest moment before she started patching the wall with a substance Adam didn't recognise. It was a strange, black gel that changed colour and became part of the wall in seconds.

'Is there anything I can do to help?' She turned to

him, her blank face plate facing him.

'Stay quiet and out of the way.' The pleasantness was gone from her voice, leaving only a flat monotone. He sat down on the bed. He'd been told to be discrete and listen to her. He relaxed and watched her clean up. He thought about at least gathering the feathers but as he reached out to them she lifted the black mask for half a second and the dark eyed woman looked at him for a long moment. As she went back to what he was doing he lay back on the bed. After a couple of moments he looked at her.

'Mind if I sleep?'

'I encourage it,' Omega replied. 'Sleep is essential for proper function. I shall depart when my work is done.'

'There's some damage to the road as well, and the house across the street. But no one lives there so you're good for a day or so before anyone might notice.'

'Understood.' He thought he caught the vaguest tone of annoyance from the figure, but he didn't let it stop him from laying down and going back to sleep. Sure enough, when he woke up everything was fixed. He even had his destroyed pillow back. The only difference, the only sign that the last night's events had even occurred was the Greek symbol for Omega on his pillow.

'At least they have a sense of humour.' He smiled and got up to face the day.

CHAPTER ELEVEN

'I feel as though I must ask you if there was any part of the rather simple assignment I gave you that you found somehow unclear.' More than angry, more than upset, irritated or confused he was disappointed. Of course he was all of those other things as well.

'I asked you rather simply to do your job. To kill off some of the less objectionable members of the Lost to allow for a skewing of his personality. To allow for us to show how distasteful the world we have built for ourselves is. We wish to show them how violent, aggressive, monstrous both our own side, represented in this case by yourself, and the other side, represented by the Red Gentleman, can be. I was clear that if you failed in this task you would be replaced and the Russians would be called. I told you to get rid of the Lost Soldier and the Carnival Queen and isolate him. So what do you do? Rather than attacking the largely noncombative Queen and the crippled Lost Soldier you start a fight with a Red Gentleman. A fight which, may I add, you took up outside our target's view. You chase the one man who, should you kill, would actual hinder our cause!' Without meaning to his voice had actually broken into a yell. He cleared his throat and calmed himself. He should not have yelled, men like him did not yell.

'Please, explain your actions to me.'

'I don't have to explain a fuckin' thing to you.' Ursas glared at him. 'I don't answer to you. All you do is tell me what to do. You don't get to choose how I do it. The Gent pushed me to my limit and I tried to kill him because that's what fucking happens!' Ursas had a massive scar across his face and a few stab wounds in his chest but it didn't seem to be bothering him.

'I lost my temper. If you wanted someone to calmly and dispassionately assassinate someone you should have sent a dispassionate fucking assassin!' He slammed his fists down on the table. 'Now you know as well as I do I'm just here to play a little part in a much bigger plan. If we convince him to give up the Presence, great! If not, fine! Let's not act like any of this shite matters!'

'All of it matters.' Legate fought to keep from raising his voice too much. He had always prided himself on his composure and he could not afford to lose it. 'We must always strive for the correct answer. We must strive for the right answer, the best way, not just any way that works. This failure to do so on your part, your willingness to simply accept the easy answer rather than finding the right one, is why you will never succeed among the Legion. You will never be truly accepted among our number and now I have been given no choice other than to allow the Donjeviks to do their work. I require that you understand that it is your failure that caused your demotion.' He turned away, allowing his disappointment to fill his voice. 'Be somewhere else, anywhere else, and consider the implications of your "good enough" attitude carefully.'

'You motherfu–,' Ursas growled and started toward him for the briefest second. Legate raised his mask and looked the Bear in the eye. Ursas growled again then turned and walked from the room. The King's Man was a formidable foe and a useful ally, and his family were as gifted a pair as one could hope for, but they were also competition, rivals to his status among the Legion. Still a shared victory was far better than no victory at all. Failure was not an option, not as far as they had come.

If the new one chose to give up his Presence then he would die, the Presence would find its use and the world would be a better place. If he chose not to, well, then that was why he'd brought in the King's Man. He provided contingencies.

'Are you all right?' Adam was back in the park, looking at the bound eyes of Kate. As he looked around he noticed that the panther that was his Presence was there as well. This time Kate was already sitting on the bench, stroking the head of her ibis like it was a pet.

'Yeah.' He looked at her. 'Is that your Presence?'

'He is.' She stroked the bird's head and cooed gently to him.

'Do you know what happened somehow?'

'I do,' she nodded. 'From within the moments between moments I see all manner of things. You can stay here as long as you like this time; you're asleep so you have an entire night, as well as all the moments in between to have this conversation. This is, in part to give us time to talk, in part for you to think and in part for you to have a conversation with your little associate.' She smiled and reached out one hand to the panther, who gently placed his head against it for a moment. 'Does he have a name yet?'

'I have always had a name,' the Presence said. 'Though I do not think the man himself has earned the right to the title.' There was a soft rumble of amusement. 'I am the Laughing One, which, if he chooses to accept it and earns it makes him the Laughing Man.'

'And what earns me the right to the name?' Adam asked, looking at it.

'Understanding the joke,' it replied. 'Now focus on the girl, she has something to say to you.'

'I need you to understand the people you walk with.' She raised her hands and suddenly Pan was in front of her. 'This is the man they call the Lost Soldier, one of the finest among your people on his best day. He appears to have a level of honour, a level of ability to understand and believe in the world around him. He wishes for a world of peace but he knows only war. He earned the title Lost Soldier and I would encourage you not to underestimate his potential for violence and brutality.' Suddenly the pictures of him standing normally flickered into images of him wading through strange battlefields, surrounded by a palpable aura that seemed to drink in light. He broke people without even thinking as they faced off against him, wandering through crowds that became corpse piles.

'He may or may not be a good man, that is not for me to say, but he is definitely a man of war. Do not expect him to hesitate to sacrifice if it means victory. Do not forget that he was as willing to see the Scarred Man dead as everyone else.'

'He seems like he's trying to do the right thing though.' The Scarred Man was Raven. He knew that without even thinking.

'If trying is good enough then yes, perhaps he is.' She flicked one hand and dismissed the image. 'But this one is not.' The image of Pan was replaced with one of Xavier. 'I know this man only as the Red Gentleman and I assure you he is not called such for that ridiculous coat. For all of his jokes and buffoonery and all that he fancies himself some kind of courtier he is a disciple of the Red Lady and he does his order proud. There is nothing he will hesitate to do, nothing he will not stoop to, in order to complete his quest.'

'What's his quest?'

'No one knows.' She shook her head. 'There is no way to understand and I have done all I can. Everyone I know has attempted to figure out what his goal might be, what his court's goal might be, but it does exist and if you get in its path he will cut your throat with a smile on his face.'

Adam felt like he'd been kicked in the gut. He'd known Xavier was questionable at best, but he didn't have any idea what she was talking about. Was he some kind of monster? Some kind of cultist? What was he?

'Which brings you the last of your number.' It was Annabelle, standing tall and straight, the spiders crawling out from beneath her and her whip trailing from her hands.

'What do you have to say about her?' He raised his eyebrow and she looked down.

'I know you have a level of fondness for her and I accept that. There might even be a good reason but you cannot trust that spider. She may be human but she was raised by the spiders ever since she was so young it makes no difference. She is clever, she is opportunistic and her emotions are liquid. She may have feelings of friendship toward you and they may be genuine but once she has something to gain, any friendship you think you have will fall by the wayside. She has had dozens of friends and partners who she allowed to die. She has accepted their sacrifices and watched them fall away in front of her. Just because someone volunteers to die for you doesn't mean you actually let them die. The only loyalty she has is to her own sisters, her own family and you see how she turns away from them as well.'

He saw waves of spiders swarming toward the Lady Raiden, burned to death in charring waves. 'She sacrifices people for her own ends and I don't want her doing the same to you.'

'Well I am, of course, touched by your concern for our safety,' the panther chuckled from his position by Adam's feet. 'But I cannot help but detect a disingenuous note to it, what with you being a complete stranger with no good reason to care about us at all.'

'My interest is in keeping this idiotic war as small as possible,' she stated calmly. 'I don't care of you pick the Legion or the Lost; both are horrible places full of terrible people and I cannot say enough how much better it would be for you if you left.' She turned and walked away. 'Please talk it over together, think it over and be clever about it. I would prefer not to watch you die painfully.' She sighed and held her hand over her face, then got to her feet and walked away, slipping out of the garden.

He waited for her to leave before he started talking. 'So what do you think?' He reached down and petted the creature. 'Are you capable of having feelings? Do you have opinions of your own? Are you just a part of me or are you a separate thing?'

'I would really prefer not to be torn into a dozen pieces and thrown into boring people to follow orders the rest of my existence. So yes, I definitely have opinions on the matter, but I will not fight you on any decision that you make. I can advise, I can argue but my ability to disobey is limited at best.'

'But you don't think I should do it?'

'You can.' It jumped onto the bench. 'I won't stop you, I can't stop you, but I think the world will be a much less interesting place for you if you should choose to take that path. You will spend the rest of your life wondering what could be, what might have been, if you hadn't made the choice you did. It is hard to live with regrets, or so I hear. Also if you go away or die I won't be there to watch you fail and laugh at your stupidity, which is also a loss for me.'

'Well that's what really matters,' he scowled. 'All right I'll think about it.'

'Here?' it asked.

'No,' he shook his head. 'When we get home. I don't know enough about this place to be sure I can trust it.'

'Very well.' It smiled an oddly human smile and turned back into a mask. He put it back on his face and felt everything power back up, returning to a state of calm. He had so many questions, so many things he wasn't sure about, so many things he didn't understand and so few people he could ask about things. He wasn't sure if he could trust his friends, he wasn't sure if they were his friends. He had no idea if he could even trust his own Presence. The biggest question mark hung over the head of the girl in the blindfold. Who was she? What was her goal? What was she thinking? What did she want? He understood so little and he needed to understand so much.

'Then you have two choices,' the panther spoke in his ear. 'Go and find all the information you need or just ignore everything you've been told by both sides and go with whatever seems like a good idea to you right now.'

'You really think that's a good idea?' He looked down at the creature and it let out a snorting laugh.

'Of course I don't,' it laughed. 'But I think it's an entertaining idea and that makes me happy to think of. So I think you should absolutely do it.'

'You are not a good advisor.'

'I never claimed to be,' it chuckled. 'But I can guarantee you that I will absolutely never be boring.'

'That's…' He considered what it was exactly. 'It's not what I expected but it's a lot.'

The more he thought about it the more sense it seemed to make, strange as it was. He was never going to understand all of this, he was never going to realise what was going on in its totality. There were too many weird things going on, too much strangeness, too many agendas and tricks. More than anything else, there was too much weirdness.

'All right,' he grinned. 'Screw it I'm gonna do what feels right.'

'What will that be?'

'You'll find out the same time everyone else does. Any idea how I can get into contact with the Legate?'

'Call the Lost Soldier and tell him you've decided to tell the Legate to shove his offer up his ass. He'll find out where he is soon enough.'

He did, and he did, and soon he was on his way.

The Legate's building looked exactly like he expected the corporate headquarters of an evil corporation that relied on complicity in order to thrive to look like. The walls were glass and the floor and furniture was white and polished steel. Against the wall was a series of lights radiating various colours, bathing the room with floods and flashes of colour that lasted exactly to the count of five before they faded through the colour pattern to the next one. He noticed it as he walked across, heading for the front desk. The receptionist came over and pointed him toward the elevator. An elevator attendant looked at him for a moment and buzzed him up, pressing the button to take him to the top level.

'You're seriously not going to tell me?' the Presence's voice was frustrated.

'I am seriously not going to tell you.'

'That is not a good feeling.'

'Yeah well, call it a bitter sense of humour.' The door opened, and he walked out of the elevator and entered the main office. The place was pure white. White walls, white carpet, broad windows across the back gazing out into the city. Legate sat behind the one thing that wasn't white, a table made of some dark hardwood. His white mask was blank and he settled his hands on the desk.

'How do you get around in that mask?' Adam chuckled, taking a seat at the table.

'I am wealthy,' the man said simply. 'People are so rarely willing to point out the flaws in others in polite society, especially not their social betters. Money and standing makes one a social better and thus no one dares comment upon the steps I take to conceal my unfortunate injury.' He leaned back in his chair. 'Have you made up your mind?'

'I have.' He smiled and took out the mask, slipping it over his face. 'It took a lot of thinking, a lot of ideas, a lot of work. I tried to figure out every detail, every piece of the puzzle, every player in the game and I realised that I don't know the board and I can't know the details.' He felt his face splitting into a grin. 'So I decided to go back to something my old man once told me.'

'Enlighten me.' It was the tone of someone humouring a stupid child.

'Don't let anyone take anything from you you're not sure you can part with. No matter who they are,' he chuckled. 'Sorry but my answer is go fuck yourself. You're not taking him away from me. You're not taking anything from me.'

'Very well.' Adam could feel a headache coming on, a buzzing sound in the back of his head. 'I am disappointed but I will not question your right to make that choice. We all make our own and we all accept the consequences. Goodbye Adam, we will not see each other again.' As Adam turned around to leave he waved to the man in the hooded cloak sitting in the corner. He hadn't seen a hooded man standing in the corner before. The door hadn't opened either. Of course he'd seen him, he just hadn't been paying attention. How do you miss a giant in a massive hooded cloak in the corner of a room as you walk in? Why hadn't he been paying attention to a seven-foot beast in a cloak in the room?

He blinked and put his hand on the door, and as he

pushed he felt a simple tap on the back of his head. Then he saw nothing.

When he woke up he was in a hotel room. A pretty nice one that that. There was a decent sized TV, a queen-sized bed, a sink, a kitchen. It was furnished with a generic pleasantness. There was only one strange thing about the room. The giant hooded man leaning against the door. He wore a cloak that fell down to his feet and a hood over his head. The only parts of the hooded man he could see were the hands, black and white patterns painted locking around each other on his fingers.

'Do you know the name of the King?' He could hear a strange whispering around him, as if there were people standing all around him, muttering things he couldn't quite hear.

'Don't even know which King you're talking about,' he shrugged. 'Wasn't even aware there was a King. The Queen's name is Elizabeth if that helps.' He stroked his head. 'Do you have any painkillers?'

'Sad for you,' the big man said, and his tone did sound sad. 'Not to worry, by the time you leave this place you will.'

'Wait until he moves,' he could barely hear the sound of the Panther, the thing that had called itself the Laughing One. 'When he looks away, when he shifts, that will be your moment to strike. Wound him and use his recovery time to escape. We cannot fight him today.'

'The Blank Legate tells me that your name is Adam, and that your other part is the Laughing One.' His voice was calm, almost too calm, like this was something he did every day. 'My name is Alexi Donjevik. They call me the King's Man, and I serve the King whose name is...' He heard a strange static sound a person's mouth shouldn't make. He couldn't hear a clear word. 'Do you know it?'

'What the hell was–' He looked at him.

'That noise?' An empty emotionless laugh came out of his mouth. 'I did not make the noise you heard. I simply said my King's name and your inability to understand it converted it to white noise.' The man got up and took a couple of steps toward Adam, his head turning to look out the window. Adam popped his claws and lunged at the man, feeling faster stronger and more alive than he ever had before as he flew in, waiting for the green place to indicate where he should strike.

Where was the green? He couldn't see any green. The Presence's vision scanned his body, ran over it then over it again and couldn't pick out a single detail. The green light scanned as he lunged and found absolutely nothing. So Adam picked the first thought and went for the neck. At first he thought he'd done well. He'd been smart enough, skilled enough that this guy hadn't had time to react or get ready. The man didn't so much as raise an arm to fight back. The claws hit home perfectly, slamming into the neck of the man named the King's Man.

The claws bounced off like he'd flicked him with a rubber band. The claws cut through the cloth and hit the skin, only to skid off, slip, and do nothing at all. He withdrew the claws and ducked right to slip around him. That was the only time the King's Man moved to fight, his tattooed hand snapping out to grab Adam's wrist in an iron grasp. He pulled him back and tossed him onto the bed.

'Please do not attempt that again,' the empty voice said. 'I did my best not to harm you and in this instance, I succeeded. However, as the number of attacks increases, the probability of you being critically injured eventually reaches one hundred percent.' He pulled down his hood and for a brief moment he actually looked disapproving. His face was covered in tattoos as well, and when he dropped his coat he saw that the rest of his skin was the same, one massive swirling tapestry that it made Adam dizzy to try to follow. Strange black and white designs that spun around each other in patterns that confused him.

'Understand that statistically it is only slightly less than impossible that you will defeat me. Your Presence has power, perhaps more than any one of mine but where you possess only one I have five. The statistically important question is whether you manage to escape before I cripple you. This is not a bet I advise you to take. Instead I advise you to take your time, spend a few days here. We will provide you with food and beverages, as well as media with which to alleviate your boredom. You may not leave but there will be ample opportunities for you to attempt escape when I am not present, or when my guard is lower than it currently is.'

'What do you want?' He wasn't just sore, it wasn't that his head was hurting, everything was just so fuzzy. He just couldn't think.

'I would like for you to know the name of the King,' the King's Man shrugged, his face impassive. 'But my task is to keep you here until the Legate decides you may leave.' His lips quirked a little, giving the slightest sign of disapproval. 'Until I receive that order you may not leave and your only company will be me. I advise you to become accustomed to this reality as quickly as possible.'

'Doesn't seem likely.' He looked up at him. Well that was a stupid thing to say. He still hadn't moved off the bed.

The man turned and walked toward the door. 'But at least wait for an opportunity.' The door closed and Adam was left on his own.

Over the next days? Weeks? Months? Adam had no idea how long he was kept in that room. There was food and a bathroom, every request he made through the intercom for food, entertainment or anything else was met within the hour. Even when he got stupid and detailed about them. For a couple of days he experimented with gastronomic adventures, ordering strange dishes he'd always wanted to try to amuse himself, sure enough a Blank would deliver whatever he wanted. They never hurt him or messed with him, beyond the conversations conducted with the King's Man and the whispering that seemed to be going on in the back of his head most of the time. He checked the room for speakers and listened for some sign of where the noise was coming from. He didn't find anything.

He wanted to know what he was doing here, what they wanted from him, what was going on but the only person he got to speak to was the King's Man and he didn't talk about anything he didn't want to. When he didn't want to answer a question, the big Russian just didn't answer. When he wanted Adam to answer a question he didn't force him, he didn't hurt him or even raise his voice. He would either ask the question over and over again or simply let the conversation drop.

Whenever Adam said anything or a few seconds went by without comment he would ask a question. Sometimes he asked about the other people, about Xavier, about Annabelle or Pan. Sometimes he asked about nothing except Adam, details and minutia into his life and that would usually lead back around to one of the questions he'd refused to answer earlier. Sometimes the conversations were even almost pleasant: the two of them discussing Adam's past, talking philosophy and arguing about various issues. Sometimes they even made small talk, though the King's Man didn't seem to have many opinions on the little things.

Adam only refused to answer two questions, both

of which were about his new allies. Both times the King's Man tried multiple tactics and eventually just left the room which Adam took as the closest the guy got to losing his temper. Sometimes things became more and more detailed until Adam wasn't remotely sure what kind of purpose they could possibly have. Sometimes they'd even sit together and watch TV and drink as they chatted. Sometimes they would find one of the King's Man's few topics of interest and he would go off on rants about random pop culture things he enjoyed, was obsessed with or hated. He'd lose himself in his opinions and often ask Adam his opinions in his usual insanely minute detail. When Adam asked him to give him a moment he would wait patiently as Adam assembled his thoughts and gave his answer. The King's Man never judged the opinions given. Sometimes he would debate them or even argue with them. He gave his own opinions and expected Adam to either have an opinion or think of one. Whatever Adam said he just paid attention, with that strange kind of focus that seemed to be typical of him.

He tried to escape five times. The first was when the King's Man was on the other side of the room and wasn't paying attention, or at least didn't look like he was. Adam made for the door and the King's Man somehow blurred through the air, striking him once in the chest and knocking him sprawling across the floor. Again he was warned that every time he tried to escape it made it more and more likely he would be seriously harmed. Adam's head rang for hours afterwards from where his head bounced off the floor. He did all of this without a change of expression or any indication he was even trying. He wasn't allowed painkillers for that one, the impact serving as an object lesson.

The second third and fourth times Adam waited until he was long gone and then made his way out of the room. To his surprise he found out that the door wasn't even locked, though he supposed he could have cut through it in less than a minute so there was no point. He turned and sprinted out of the hotel room and made his way out. The second time he used the elevator, the third and fourth the stairs. Every time he tried the King's Man appeared seemingly out of nowhere and less and less gently forced him back into the room. He wasn't unnecessarily rough, but every time he got a little closer. The fourth time one of Adam's fingers broke. The King's Man set and bandaged it and had things brought up for the pain, he apologised with what seemed like sincerity and stated again that the amount of times he could recapture Adam without seriously hurting him was limited at best.

The fifth time he actually made it out of the building. This time he ran and hid rather than trying to leave. He made his way to a closet and hid there for a couple of minutes and then moved a few floors down the stairs. Again he hid in various places, walking down corridors and finding out of the way places to duck into. Eventually he found a service elevator and went down the last few floors, slipping out the back door and making a run for it. He made it a couple of streets before the King's Man made his way out of the alley and grabbed him by the throat, wrapping him up in a choke hold until he passed out. When he woke up in the hotel room he found it hard to breathe and even harder to swallow. Again the King's Man warned him that there was a limit to the amount of times he could recapture him without seriously harming him. He didn't try to escape again after that. He waited and planned, trying to think of a new thing he could do, something that would allow him to injure or escape the enemy and every day the whispering got louder and louder in his ears.

No that was wrong, at first he thought it was getting louder but it wasn't, it was still only the softest whisper in the back of his head but it was getting clearer and clearer. Sometimes he managed to get letters and even whole syllables of sound out of the words he heard and started to track them, listening to them with more and more detail.

He tried to find the words that repeated themselves in the whisper. He could hear the sounds, he could hear them repeating themselves. He could hear them with more and more detail as he listened to them. They weren't words he could recognise, they weren't even particularly clear now he thought about it but they became the most interesting thing in the room. It became maddening that he couldn't figure out what the words were, that he couldn't quite place the syllables and the sounds. When the King's Man arrived to have another conversation, the big guy seemed agitated. The gaps between the questions were smaller and smaller, he demanded more answers with more and more depth.

Where was his mask? He'd lost his mask. He hadn't noticed that he wasn't wearing it. Had he been wearing it the fifth time he'd tried to escape? The Fourth? Third, second, first? He'd had it the first time he'd woken up, he'd had it when he'd been captured but he couldn't place it. Had he lost it when he passed out? When he'd been in a fight? When the King's Man broke his finger or beat him down? He knew he'd had it. When had he had it?

The King's Man suddenly stopped talking, stopping asking questions and sat there, his almost pleasant demeanour disappearing while Adam lost himself in his own speculation. He sat there like he had all the time in the world, like he could wait forever. His posture honestly reminded Adam of the monks in pictures, of the people who could sit in one place for days under a waterfall without moving a muscle and suddenly the Laughing Man knew suddenly and incontrovertibly that this man had done exactly that. That this strange tattooed figure had sat alone in an empty room or on a mountain for hours, days, weeks. He'd eaten nothing, drank nothing and just breathing in the air in the hope of finding some level of revelation.

'Did you find it?' He looked up at the King's Man and for the first time the hooded man showed real emotion on his face. He'd heard it in his voice many a time but he'd never seen it on a face before. He looked honestly confused.

'What was I supposed to find?' He cocked his head slightly.

He looked at him. 'When you sat on the mountaintop, or in the room, did you find some level of revelation?'

'I did,' he nodded. 'That was when I first truly understood the nature of the King.'

'When you heard his name?'

'No.' He shook his head. 'I knew his name long before that. I knew his name the first time I met him.' He tipped his head and stared at the Laughing Man for a few very long moments, his muscles flexing and bulging, while his face was neutral his eyes showed pure terror. 'When you meet him you too will already know his name.'

He said more things, but Adam's ability to pay attention left him, he was listening to the words in the back of his head. He was hearing things in more and more detail. Things were repeating themselves and he was finally starting to pick them. He was starting to pick words; the whispering noise was gone and it wasn't words being whispered. It was the same word, being repeated over and over, over and under itself until it became clear.

'I would like you to depart.' He got to his feet and smiled, holding out one hand for his mask. 'I have something I must do.'

'Very well.' The big man nodded and pulled up his heavy hood, getting to his feet and making his way outside. 'Do you know the name of the King?'

'Yes.' And the Laughing Man began to laugh. 'I do believe I do.'

CHAPTER TWELVE

The Laughing Man returned home, a smile on his face and his claws undrawn and returned washed and with a new outfit, ready to face the world. As he headed into the café where he became lost back when he was Adam he couldn't help but let out a chuckle. He had found it to be sparse, empty, almost abandoned at the time. He hadn't taken the time to look around, busy being intimidated. As he looked around now, with the King's name in his head, he looked around and saw the quiet, empty, squalid little hole it was. The people there had some power certainly, but nowhere near as much as they seemed to think. They were disorganised, they were lazy and they weren't paying attention. He smiled and nodded to the barista, holding up his mask.

'So you found yourself something did you?' the barista laughed. 'Well done you. When's the party?'
'Yeah.' He looked around to make sure no one was watching before he brought the claws to life, holding them up and ready to use them if doubt began to show in this fool's eyes. He could get the item and make his way out before they had realised what he'd done. 'What do we think?'

'All right I guess,' the fool shrugged. 'I'm glad you're on our side man. Welcome.'

'Me too,' he nodded. 'Anyway, the Lost Soldier, Pan, he told me to head out and bring something back, something important.'

'Aye aye, Sir.' He gave a mocking salute. 'Should I let him know you're getting it?'

'No,' he said quickly and moved to cover himself. 'He already knows that there's some weird shit going on. If he had enough time to be bothered with my little problems he'd have enough time to come get it himself.'

'All right man,' he shrugged. 'Fair enough, go on through.' The Laughing Man brushed by him and walked through the back into where he knew the real storage room would be. *Was it really so simple to get by the Lost? All you needed was the face of one of them?* They should have taught one of he Lost the name of the King a long time ago. They could have ripped the secrets out of the rabble and been done. Still there was time now and there would never be a shortage, until the plan was complete and, well, then it wouldn't matter.

He moved to the shelves. There were so many things piled up everywhere without a scrap of organisation or any kind of system. Ancient relics were piled aside glowing technomystic inventions. Patterned, magical accoutrements of various form, function and power lay all around. No safes, no bunkers, no guards, no filing! After a few minutes of rummaging through the disorganised nonsense he managed to find what he was looking for. He held it up to catch the light and studied it carefully. Like most items of great power it was slightly underwhelming to examine. He could feel the power running up his arm but until he knew what he was doing there was no way to... No, he would never know what he was doing, he remembered that now.

The entirely of his task was to bring the item back to the Legate and the King's Man. It was not for him to use the item himself, neither his honour nor his duty. Still, for all the power he knew it had, it seemed to simply be a sceptre, no more powerful or magical than any other item in this dusty little shit box. It was gold, with a crystal head that looked like there was a roaring flame flickering within the blue stone. There was no oxygen within the stone but, even were he in the vacuum of space, the fire inside the stone would burn. This was the sceptre made by the King of the Eternal Flame whose name none could know without falling under his will. He twirled the sceptre in his hand and closed his eyes, breathing in deep, enjoying this moment, then slipped it into his coat.

He rummaged through the possessions to secure one of the other items, something powerful enough that it would be an errand but not so powerful that his exit would be questioned. He picked up a red crackling bauble and tossed it from hand to hand as he walked out, holding it up to the barista. The man shrugged and nodded, examining it for only the barest moment before letting it go, finding no good reason to stop him. He flashed a smile and walked out, heading toward the building, heading back to his new master. The man who had ruled his life ever since he had first heard the name of the King. He returned calmly to the building in which the Legate resided. He would be able to give to his new commander the weapon that would allow for the King to take his natural place in the order of the world. Everything would be as it should, the end would come to the unworthy and all would be right in the world.

The Legate sighed and allowed himself a reluctant smile behind his mask. This was not what he wanted, this was not optimal at all. With Ursas's failure he had needed to call in the King's Man and his family. Whether he liked it or not this was too important, though he would have preferred to do this the right way, the way that did not involve foolishness and complications and violence. Still, he leaned back, took a long moment to himself and accepted that into every life a little rain must fall. He would find a way to work things out, to turn this new resource into something he could use. Perhaps he could achieve even more than he had anticipated. When the Laughing Man emerged from the elevator, far more upright and straight backed than once he had been, none of his sardonic slouching and messy hair, he'd actually presented himself like a professional for once. With an appropriately dramatic flourish he reached into his coat and pulled out the sceptre, bowing low to offer it to its rightful owner. The Legate held it in his hands with awe. The Lost had stolen this from him so long ago it almost seemed like ancient times

'They kept it in a café.' The Laughing Man seemed

amused by this. Well not all of his personality could be taken away by the Name he supposed. 'After all these years and all this work it was in the stockroom of a bloody café.'

'Do not judge what was there by what seemed to be there,' the Legate scolded his newest servant gently. 'Anyone who had entered without permission would have found much stauncher resistance. Once you have shown yourself to be on their side of the war no one could imagine that you would betray them. You are not capable of becoming one of the Legion and thus treason would make absolutely no sense. People very rarely act against their own interest.'

'All right then.' The Laughing Man did not seem to mind being called a traitor any more than he minded being called unworthy. It seemed odd, was this man without any self-respect at all? The King's Man was good at his work indeed. Legate let the moment pass without addressing it, simply watching the eager young man. 'So what's next? I wanna get this done!'

The Legate held the sceptre in his hand and felt the power run up his arm to his mind, connecting him to his King. He knew he could not truly use it, not until the King himself awakened and took it up, but this was the next best thing. 'I require the corpse of one of your former associates,' he ordered. The young man responded to the order with no more emotion than being asked to take out trash. 'It does not matter which one, my purposes simply require that one of your number is killed and their corpse is brought to me.'

The Laughing Man thought about this for a long moment, and for an instant the Legate though he may raise some kind of issue. The silence became awkward and the Legate readied himself to speak, only to be cut off by sudden speculation. 'Can't kill the Red Gentleman.' Ah the King's name was potent indeed. 'Because, well, I can't kill the Red Gentleman. Even with one arm he'd stick me. The Lost Soldier trusts me but I think he's almost indestructible so I suppose the answer is the Spinning Sister.' He thought this over and came to the resolution. 'She seems to have a level of affection for me, in spite of everything.' He shrugged and left the room, whistling to himself. At the door he stopped, looking around confused. The Legate nodded, allowing the young man to depart and go about his work. He turned to the King's Man, who was, as usual, sitting hooded and robed in the corner of the room.

'This could be even better than I expected.' He allowed himself to be cheerful. 'I doubt he will succeed but if he does this could be wonderful. Even if he does fail he has more than returned upon the investment we made in him,' he chuckled to himself, allowing himself to indulge in just a little pride. The King's Man of course refused to be any kind of impressed.

'I believe you should have allowed him to provide the corpse.' The King's Man folded his arms. 'If he dies before he returns with another corpse then I will be obliged to go out and acquire one myself. A duty that I do not relish.' What did the kids call them these days? A buzz kill?

'Do not worry.' The Legate shook his head. 'It seems even now you underestimate me. I have a corpse already provided. I would prefer not to lose it while I still have a use for it, so I have asked him to get me another.' He freely smirked under his mask. He was doing so well. 'No matter the outcome we will have what we need for the ritual. Believe it or not you are not the only capable man who serves our King. Now I suggest you begin your own preparation. If you feel the need to be here anyway you had best pull your weight. I am allowing you to be a part of my plan. Do not forget it.'

'I shall not.' The most infuriating thing about the King's Man was that he could not be insulted. Legate's supreme self-control would ordinarily allow him to trade barbs with anyone he liked without risking losing his control before his opponent did. The one exception was this; Alexi had never reacted with anything beyond vague annoyance or amusement. 'Understand that failure in this enterprise will end in your death.'

'Of course I know this,' Legate nodded back. What the King's Man could do naturally the Legate used his mask for. It hid the expression of blind fury that was currently decorating his face. 'I shall summon the King of Eternal Flame and you shall serve.'

'Of course,' Alexi nodded. 'As shall we all.'

The Legate looked around. He required no company, not when he heard the words of the King echoing through his ears and mind, but in spite of himself he wished there had been someone there he could have shared his moment of triumph with. Everything was finally starting to go right.

The Laughing Man headed to Adam's home again. It was not his, he no longer had a home. Everything was too messy, too disorganised. After multiple days of him being away all that was required was a couple of small excuses and all of a sudden, his disappearance was acceptable. If this had been the first or only time that had happened it would have been one thing, but this was the second in as many months After a night of preparing and allowing his body to repair itself he called the Lost Soldier.

'Hey,' he spoke through the mask, letting his voice distort so he would not have to worry about his tone and voice. 'I need to talk to Annabelle.'

'Oh? What's up?' the Soldier asked. 'You doing okay?'

'It's just something personal. I need help with some of the side effects of my ability.'

'I'd know it better than she would.' The Soldier wasn't suspicious, he was honestly trying to help. He would have made a good convert.

'Yeah, I know you would.' He felt a small laugh slip from his lips. 'But I like her more than I like you. No offence, we just get along better. If I need any special stuff I'll give you a call.'

'Don't chase crazy man,' the Soldier advised.

'My decision.'

'Good point.' He could hear the nod on the big man's tone. 'Well sadly she's not anywhere I can reach her. You could go ask Mercy and Sage. She could have left where she could be reached for purposes of her recovery.'

'Really?' he sighed. 'They might be helpful but they give me the fucking creeps.' That and they might have the magic to catch what was happening to him.

'Yeah well, they're the ones who know where she is, so I suggest you either go that way or start thinking with something other than your dick.' His tone was getting frustrated. Time to end the conversation.

'Sorry dude, thanks for your help.' He hung up and slipped his mask back into his coat, making his way to the cinema. When he entered the Sage's eyes widened, the Shifter's face showed vague surprise and as he reached Mercy, the doctor actually applauded. He jumped and made ready to defend himself. He didn't like these reactions.

'Wow,' she grinned. 'Well done, I mean you actually did it!' Did these people secretly support the King? That would explain their enthusiasm.

'What did I do?' He looked around.

'You actually took the time out to heal!' she grinned. 'I mean I don't think anyone actually done it before. I've heard stories of Lost members actually taking time off to heal themselves, but I don't think it's ever happened to me. Please, I must check your jaw.' She did and then shook her head. 'This is going in my diary. A fully healed wound without a new one.'

'I did that once.' Xavier scowled and made to fold his arms then realised he only had the one, at which point he looked almost scoldingly at his stump and smiled. Mercy had been treating him apparently.

'Going to another doctor is not the same as allowing yourself time to heal,' she snapped at him and then turned back to the Laughing Man. 'What do you need my dear boy?'

'I need to find the Spinning Sister,' he smirked. 'You know, Annabelle? I need to get hold of her.'

'Yes, I know her,' the sweet Doctor Mercy nodded. 'She's with the Omegas right now. I can quite easily bring you to the location, but wouldn't it be easier to find someone else to help you? I mean you have Pan's phone number.'

'Also I am right here.' Xavier raised his existent hand. 'Any questions you need to ask I can almost certainly answer. I am surprisingly knowledgeable about most of the side effects of a Presence. I should also probably mention to you that since you are here and you still have your Presence I no longer want you dead. How did you manage to keep it by the way? When last we saw you, you were wondering what your choice was going to be and then you disappeared for days. I honestly expected you were dead. Was planning my rampage of revenge and everything.'

'I told the Legate to shove it up his ass and then I

went away and hid for a while.' He shrugged but when Xavier gave him a sceptical expression he gathered up a better answer. 'Annabelle set me up in a spot where I could be alone for a while and get my head right. Figure out what I'm doing and how I intend to do it. It's hard to figure out your own point of existing. I still have no idea but I'm more comfortable about it now. I hope you understand I needed some time. Plus it gave me some time to get fighting fit, for the inevitable revenge.'

'That is often the wisest course of action,' Mercy nodded. Adam had found her mode of dress and physical attributes most attractive, but the Laughing Man didn't see the point. 'It helps you learn what you can do and what you shouldn't be doing. Both are about as important as the other.'

'Yeah well I'm back now.' He clapped his gauntlets together and motioned toward them. 'And having said that I'm going to go see the brotherhood and go for a walk with Annabelle. Mercy? Address?'

'Certainly.' She flashed him a bright grin and wrote an address down, passing it over to him. He moved to the address and as he entered he was promptly surrounded by a giant number of Omega Brotherhood Members. All of the troops were, in theory at least, dressed exactly the same. They all had the template of the black body armour with an omega symbol on the face plate. However, in practice each member had made their own alterations and none of them were wearing the entire uniform to specifications. Some had things drawn on them, others had removed plates or pieces of armour. Some of the face plates had the Omega symbol removed or altered, one even had an explosion instead of the letter. One man had a full set of the Omega Brotherhood armour that would have been entirely perfect if not for the fact that it was neon pink.

'What are these people?' he said to himself, unable to resist the swelling of amusement at the ridiculous spectacle in front of him.

'These people are the Omega Brotherhood,' said one of them. 'By the way these people can hear every word you are saying. They are people, like any other people and they have simply surrendered their own individual identity and personality to the greater cause of keeping the world safe.'

'Then how are you offended?'

'I am not.' The Omega in question only had a third of its full-face plate, enough to cover one eye and a little of his cheek. The rest of his face was twisted into a cheerful little smile. 'I am simply informing you of the facts of your situation. It's a matter of politeness. Now I will invite you to enter. Please do not touch anything without asking permission beforehand.' He stepped back and gestured to invite the Laughing Man to enter with one hand. He entered and sought out the Spinning Sister immediately.

'Hey,' she smiled and waved. She actually smiled when she saw him now. That was a sign of, if not trust, then at least affection. Affection would quite easily serve the same purpose in this case.

'Hey,' he smiled and waved back. 'I need to talk to you.'

'All right,' she nodded. 'What's up?' She looked so sloppy. Currently in green and silver, her hair was wild and her face punched with metal for no functional reason. Could Adam truly have been attracted to her? At the same time he knew he had been. Strange.

'In private, please.' He flashed a smile. 'I've been busy for the last few days and I'd like to talk to someone I trust. At the moment that entire list is you.' She climbed off the bunk. Together the two of them turned and walked out. She hadn't built a whip, brought out her spiders or even looked back as she left.

'So what's been up?' She walked down the riverside. The Brisbane river was disgusting at the best of times and now it filled the Laughing Man with a measure of contempt. These fools had simply dumped and thrown their trash into the river with no thought of what would come of it. With no thought of the order in which things had to be done. They hadn't thought of the inevitable ending and it made him absolutely sick.

'I was gone for a few days, getting accustomed to what I can do.' He looked down at the ground and made a show of his embarrassment. 'It all scares me a little and I'm not sure what to do with it all so I just took a few days off. I got to know what I can do and tried to figure out why I should do it. The mask makes me so cold. My emotions die out and I'm left just feeling cruel, cold and opportunistic.' His eyes scanned the area as he held out his hand and she took it. He saw no one around and lead her away. 'Come see. I'll show you want I can do.' He moved with her underneath a nearby bridge, away from the view of streets. He knew the local indigent population slept there, but given that it was the middle of the day everything should be secluded.

'So what am I looking at?'

'I refused the Legate's offer,' he reassured her. She looked relieved but then of course she did. How else was she going to look? 'So I spent the next few days in a quiet room practicing and trying to figure out what I'm doing. Meditation, talking to whatever it is lives in my mask, failing to meditate giving up and going drinking.' He laughed and put his hands over his face as he leaned against the wall under the bridge, feeling the hard plastic of the gauntlets against his face and watching her through his fingers. 'But I feel so lost Annabelle, so goddamn lost.' His voice was shaking as he pulled the mask down from under his mouth, his hands shaking a little.

'Suddenly I've got some kind of beast in my head who wants me to cheat steal and kill. I've got the world around me tilting on its axis and I have less than no idea what I'm supposed to do next.' He spread his fingers to look her in the eyes, pulling the mask gently up so she wouldn't see him smile. 'Help me. You're the only person I can talk to. Pan's a hardass and Xavier's a psycho and you seem like you know what you're doing. But me? I feel like a scared, stupid kid.'

He watched her approach him, sympathy in her bright eyes. She reached out one hand and placed it gently on his shoulder. He slowly powered up the claws and as she moved in to hug him he struck, swinging at the area the focused opportunism told him was vital. The claws slipped up her chest toward her lung, only to slam into something harder than steel, turning on their edges and ripping through her clothes, taking only a few tiny shreds of white spider web with him as she jumped back. She looked him in the eyes and flicked her hands, her whips slipping out of her wrists as she watched him, taking up a combat stance.

'What the fuck Adam?'

He lunged at her and she danced to the side, slamming her whip into the side of his head. As he struggled to his feet he lashed out at the green spot on the whip, only to have the spot, a thick and white section stick itself to the blades on one of his hands. He drew back his free arm and lashed out at her throat this time, she couldn't be protected there. She twirled and kicked him in the stomach and he fell backwards. As he got up he felt a prickling under his skin. She squared off with him again and as he tried to mount an offence he staggered again, once again catching a whip strike to the side of the head. He slumped off his feet and suddenly the world was spinning in every direction. It wasn't as hard as the Legionnaire had hit him in the jaw when it had sheared his face, academically he knew this to be fact, but for some reason this hurt a good deal more. He remembered the perfectly aimed green strikes that had somehow been wrong and the pieces clicked into place.

'You miserable, rat bastard.' He let his amusement show as he spoke to the mask, his head swimming as he lunged at her throat.

'I have to help you,' came the cheerful voice. 'I never said I had to do whatever you say, or that I couldn't choose the extent to which I do it. Sorry puppet, but I'm not stupid.'

The prickling on his skin grew more and more pronounced and he looked down at himself. He'd been in pain, why had he been in pain and now he was shaking, why was he shaking? Why were his knees giving out? Why was his strength draining out of him? He could see them now, the answer to the question. Dozens and dozens of spiders ran up and down his body, spreading hundreds upon hundreds of red bites up and down his skin. He pulled the mask down and threw up all over the floor, weaving and shaking with the disgusting, burning, twisting itch. Then Annabelle hit him in the side of the head and he felt nothing at all. By that time it had almost been a relief.

When he awoke he was tied to a chair by steel hard spider webs. The Pathfinder, the Spinning Sister and the Red Gentleman all stood around him, looking down at his supine form.

'So what are we going to do with him?' The Soldier lifted his chin and looked into his eyes. 'I'm not entirely sure what's going on with him. Did he switch to the Legion? Is he on the other side now?'

'Entirely impossible.' The Gentleman smiled and didn't bother to examine him. 'He has no Legion potential at all. So the question becomes,' he moved one of the bare wooden chairs that were in the room so he could sit in front of his captive, 'what did happen to you?'

'I have learned the name of the King of the Eternal Flame whose name is…' He spoke the name of the king and everyone flinched but the Gentleman. 'I obey his will as all who know his name do and follow the will of his instruments upon this earth. I will free myself of these mere bonds of flesh and magic and I shall–' he fell silent when the spider web slapped down over his mouth, holding him to his silence.

'Why did he tell us that?' The Soldier looked over at the other two.

'I don't pretend I'm an expert on arrogance but I think he figured it didn't matter much at this point,' the Spinning Sister scowled. 'I mean however we were going to treat him for being caught trying to stab me in the neck it's probably not going to matter what his motive was at the time. Though he did give away the fact he's working for the King, which is strange.'

'Yes, indeed more fool him.' The Red Gentleman pushed the others away and swept his hat down off his head, then perched it gently on top of the Laughing Man's, placing his hand with almost tenderness on the side of his face. 'Is there anything left of you in there Adam?'

'I am all here.' His voice was soft, malicious and flat and it made Xavier smile wide.

'I think you may be.' He moved his hand down to the shoulder. 'I think that underneath the ridiculous creature speaking with your tongue you may indeed be all here and that is wonderful. Give it time and we will free you.' And then his voice grew cold. 'Now I speak directly to the King of Eternal Flame who rules above and whose name is…' and he spoke the name. He spoke it without shame or hesitation, not even a breath at the awe-inspiring name of the King. 'And to the piece of him that is pivoting around inside that precious little head. This piece of you inside my ally is not long for this world, and when I wring answers from it, and when I find the rest of your pieces and rest assured I shall find them!' His voice rose to a yell and then fell again. 'I will cut them to pieces one by one until I finally find your heart, your soul, whatever it is that makes you function.' He was serious. How was he serious? The Laughing Man had only seen him serious once before. He was almost impossibly enraged. 'Then I will remove it from this world and all others and destroy them. This I swear and until that day well,' suddenly the smile was back on his face, sweeping his hair from his eyes and giving an understated little chuckle that slipped the tension from the room and made him question for a moment that the previous outburst had happened at all, 'you get to try on my thinking cap. Congratulations.' He pulled the top hat down on the Laughing Man's head until his eyes were covered.

Adam found himself standing on a giant chess board. Or, well, there were white and back checkerboard pieces all over the board but it looked as though a crowd of freaks and oddities were occupying it. There were a couple of dozen giant figures standing around the edges of the board, waving their hands and making the people move in ways that probably made perfect sense to them. As he looked around himself he saw a giant spider with a woman's head and a living statue swinging a massive axe in every direction. There was some kind of strange red imp jumping on someone and ripping pieces off them with tooth and claw. Adam was standing on a white piece and that felt profoundly wrong to him right now. He looked around himself, looking down at his feet, or paws or whatever they were. His feet were dark and clawed, but he was standing on two legs so he wasn't entirely a beast. That was good he supposed.

He was surrounded on all four sides by strange beings, one of whom was a tall creature in a red coat leaning gently on a beautifully made sword. He faced away from Adam.

'Evening,' the figure spoke softly, chuckling a little. 'Are you in there?'

'Who the hell are you?' A face appeared in the back of the tall man's head when he was addressed.

'You saw me as a top hat once, that the young man was wearing,' it flashed a smile. 'And I do not mind you doing so in general but right now I need you to understand why you're here.' Behind the two-faced man the statue tossed side its axe and began to strike at something that looked like a genuine angel wreathed in fire with its bare fists.

'So why is that?' He barely managed to keep his eyes on the two face who he realised now was Xavier. 'Because you're a pussy.' All of a sudden he didn't have beast legs, he was just a person, standing beside the panther he knew was his Presence.

'What?' He looked at it.

'Well, isn't it?' The panther looked up at him with its bright green eyes that saw into his soul. 'I mean that's it, isn't it? You lack any vestige of individuality. You cannot act for yourself and this is what makes you weak. This is what has broken you and put you in the place where the King can hold over you.'

'I don't know what the hell you're talking about who do you think you...' But he could feel a churning in his gut.

'That's enough,' the hat said softly.

'No, it is damn well not,' the creature shook its head. 'This isn't funny. I worked with him because of who he is and who I am. I thought all of this was going to be interesting. I didn't ask to be the passenger in the eyes of a damn slave!'

'Stop it!' the face snapped.

'No.' The creature didn't move its eyes from Adam. 'I am absolutely sick of you Adam. I mean at what point are you actually going to make a decision for yourself. Just one, rather than just doing whatever anyone tells you to do? I mean gods above and below, you get attacked, someone saves you, you get a quest and you don't even ask a single question before you do it. You find a being you have less than no reason to trust and you take him with you anyway.'

'I decided to keep you, didn't I? Despite what people were telling me.' He could feel some kind of pressure, a burning feeling in his hands and behind his eyes. As he looked down at himself he saw white flames burning on his hands.

'Yeah, but did you though?' The creature's voice was soft and cruel, dark and vicious. 'Or did you just take the option that best held onto the status quo? You had the option to give up as someone told you, and the option to keep going forward as everyone told you,' it scoffed at him. 'And now, this has got to be a dream come true, doesn't it? You can just sit back, relax and let someone else make every little decision for you. When to fight, when to talk, when to scratch your...' He stopped then. He had very little voice as Adam had grabbed him by the head and slammed his knee into the base of its panther jaw. The creature fell back and Adam wheeled around, attacking everything within reach in a blind rage. He lashed out at the panther, the two-faced man, the spider and the statue, the imp and the angel. He struck out at everything. He didn't really do any damage and he got his ass kicked but he didn't care. He lashed out at everyone. Eventually the statue grabbed him and slammed him onto the ground, pinning him down with one hand and one knee.

'Thank you.' The man with the face in the back of his head grabbed Adam and turned him over, holding him down. The statue, having moved away as soon as two face grabbed him, returned to its earlier fight. 'You see, Adam, you can make your own choices. They may be violent and ill informed, but at least they're yours. You need to understand that you can make them yourself. You are strong enough, you are good enough, you can and should go in whatever direction you decide is best. You should take the counsel on board, but act only in as far as it meets with your own wisdom.'

The second face, suddenly in the other one's hat, sitting above its head spoke. 'You have the strength, you have the rage and hate and violence in your soul. You have the determination to see your goal, the loyalty and care for those around you who trust you. I see all the potential in your brain right now and you have done nothing because you have simply had no chance to use them. You must take your options, you must make your own decisions. Don't just lash out and don't just do as anyone tells you. Don't be stupid, but don't be weak either. Do you understand?'

'What if I like doing what I'm told?' He stared up

insolently. 'What if I like lashing out?'

'Excellent.' The man let him go and flung his hands wide. 'Wonderful, so much the better. Do those things, all of those things, but know what you are doing when you make that choice. Do not make it blindly. Do not make stupid choices.'

'Unless of course you really want to,' the panther that was his Presence laughed from beside him, completely unharmed. He placed his head against Adam's hand and, without realising it, he was stroking the creature's head. 'Now are you ready to dispense with this stupidity and be you again?'

'So what, it's that easy?'

'Oh gods no,' it laughed at him. 'This is going to hurt like hell.'

'You seem more pleased about that than any ally of mine should be.'

'Well you did just knee me in the face.' It made what he understood to be its approximation of a shrug.

'I really don't like you.'

'You really aren't required to.' It glared at him. 'You are required to dispense with this silliness and take your identity back. Then we can sit down and figure out what the fuck we're going to do next. Because this? This is not funny anymore.'

'Well you're right about that,' he nodded. 'This isn't funny anymore. All right, let's get this done.'

'Set your feet Adam. Hold your hands out and try to find all of this amusing.' He did and the panther set his teeth just past where the white fire was burning one of his arms. He winced as the teeth sunk into his skin. He heard a rustling sound and discovered that the man with the face now once again in the back of his head was taking out a knife. With a quick, surgical detachment he cut a ring at the white point of the other arm. It levered up the white point of his skin and he screamed, the noise of pain slipping out of his mouth unbidden as the fire ran up his arm. The panther and the two faced man pulled back together, wrenching back on the white points. Adam stopped screaming, he was in too much pain now, and focused everything he had on not collapsing as the burning skin was torn off his hand. Over the next, he had no idea how long, he probably begged, screamed, shouted and demanded that they stopped what they were doing. He probably cried and whimpered and breathed hard as they tore the skin off his wrist and up his hand. Eventually he lost the ability to make noise, just gasping and doing everything he could to suck air and stay upright.

The panther was groaning and whimpering and he heard a strange rustling, hissing sound. He looked down at the creature and saw smoke slipping out of its mouth. He realised exactly what it was in a few seconds. Inside its mouth the white fire was scorching it. As the two faced man pulled back his burning hand he could see that the strange man's hands were bleeding slightly, as if needles or razors were cutting open his skin. The face on the back of the head was screaming, he could hear it and the front face was biting its lip to keep from joining in.

Adam's legs had given out by the time the fire was gone. His knees had buckled and he had fallen to them, crying and breathing hard as he held out his arms. When, what he realised were gloves, were gone he fell on his face, shaking with pain as if someone had dunked both of his arms in a vat of acid and it slowly ate his flesh.

After a moment he felt a rough tongue against this face and the pain faded a little. He looked up and spied the slightly scorched face of the creature that was his Presence, who somehow, in spite of its facial features and its burning, appeared to be smiling. Then between the two of them they managed to get him to his feet.

As soon as foot hit ground Adam was back in the normal world.

'Do you know the name of the King of Eternal Flame?' Annabelle was the one in front of him. In as much as he could tell behind her now silver and green eyes she looked concerned.

'I do,' he smiled and nodded. 'But that doesn't mean much anymore. It's just a name.'

'Good,' she smiled and patted him on the shoulder.

'Do we know he's telling the truth?' Pan asked. Xavier gathered up his hat and flipped it back onto his head. He kicked up his cane and caught it, spinning it in his fingers. He thought about it for a second.

'If he's not he has somehow managed to confound my magic hat,' Xavier smiled. 'Adam, is there anything you can say that will prove you are who you say you are?'

'Yeah,' he nodded groggily, the idea coming into his head. All he had to do was come clean. 'I took a couple of things from the café.'

'I expected something personal or revelatory.' Xavier appeared to be thinking about it. He smiled and shrugged. 'But a confession of guilt will do just as well for me. What did you take?'

'A glass bauble crackling with energy, I've still got that though, but I don't know what it does and some kind of staff or something.' He shook his head, trying to clear it as the pain and poison worked its way out of his system. 'Sceptre, it was sceptre, that was what the King called it. It had a blue gem at the head of it and it was like there was a fire inside it. Somehow I knew that the fire would never go out no matter what I did.'

Xavier and Annabelle moved as quickly as they could, each of them grabbing Pan and hauling him back as he moved toward Adam, who felt the better part of valour was going back to trying to cut himself loose. Pan stopped and closed his eyes, placing his hands against the sides of his head and breathing deeply in and out. He appeared to be counting, clenching and unclenching his fists on his head, like he was trying to meditate or something. After a couple of long moments he stepped back and Annabelle moved away, letting Adam up from his bonds with a flick of her wrist.

'That thing that you took,' he spoke softly, his teeth gritted, 'is the Sceptre of the True Flame. One of the items owned, created and used by the King of The Eternal Flame. One of the items that, with enough knowledge and a complicated enough ritual, can be used to summon him. Knowledge which the Legate has and a ritual which the King's Man can do I may add. It can summon him into this world, completely.' Everything about him was held tight and rigid, violence barely contained by every last piece of a human being's self-restraint. He was practically shaking with rage.

'He wasn't in control of himself.' Annabelle's tone was gentle, reassuring. 'Any of us would have fallen into the same trap as he did. I mean, it would have taken us a little longer but in the end we all would have given up. We all would have done exactly what he did.' Pan looked from Annabelle to Adam and then turned and tossed her across the room. She landed in a perfect three-point landing, completely unharmed and he threw his hands up and stormed out.

'Well.' Xavier pulled a flask out of his hat and took a swig, the hat now moving of its own accord. 'I think literally everyone you've met since the first time you met me has wanted to murder you at least once.' He tossed Adam the flask, who took it and swigged. 'Honestly I can't help but be impressed.'

'I don't think Raven did.' Adam forced himself to

stay calm, hoping his mask would help him a little. 'But he's not going to lose it right? He's not going to come back and just rip my head off or something?' He could literally do that Adam realised, with a cold feeling in his gut.

'We'd stop him,' Annabelle tried and failed to reassure him. 'Don't worry, logically he knows you couldn't have done anything other than what you did. Mind control is pretty formidable and this really was going to happen anyway. He's just, taking a few minutes to let his emotions catch up to his thoughts.' She pulled the chair across and sat down beside him.

'Sorry if I hurt you.' He looked over at her. 'You know, while I was crazy.' She snorted with laughter, shaking her head.

'Dude, I truly and completely kicked your ass. I mean I've seen you fight and you were only kind of worthwhile there, and this time you were half-assed at best. You don't have the heart of an assassin in you.'

'Maybe not,' he liked that idea, 'but I'm not sure that was what it was. I remember something went weird when I took a shot at you. The wrong spot went green.' He made the connections all over again. 'I couldn't see your weak points, I couldn't hold back pain, I wasn't as fast or as strong as I had been. The fucking mask screwed me.'

'Your Presence is a dick,' she laughed. 'You wouldn't be the first person who didn't get along with their other half. He suckered you into getting beat up, but I guess he knew what he was doing in the end.'

'Yeah, I guess so.' He shrugged and pulled off the mask and gauntlets. 'Man, I really don't like him.'

'You'll figure out how to work with him. We always figure out our balance with our Presences, no matter the personality clash.'

He looked around the room but it was bare concrete other than two chairs and a table. It looked like a police interrogation room from an old movie. 'We sometimes get a little vitriolic but I don't think anyone gets completely impossible. You just have to figure out your balance. How much of him you can stand and how much he can stand you.'

'All right. Points for the correct use of vitriolic by the way,' he nodded. 'So, do you actually have one? A Presence I mean? Or do you just have some kind of crazy spider magic?'

'Crazy spider magic,' she laughed again, a small snort coming out. 'Yes and no. I do have,' she stared at him, deliberately making it awkward and drawing each word out, 'crazy, spider, magic, and it does help me. It allows me to pass through dimensions and keep my sisters with me and I use my Presence to power those abilities. They also extend to making the webs. My Presence is allowing my personality to dictate terms, she's obliging like that. I had the magic beforehand, the Presence just kicks it from a one to a ten.'

'Is that–'

'How most of them work?' she finished for him, shaking her head slightly. 'When are you going to get this straight Adam? There is no 'how most of them work.' I got mine because I was adopted by spiders and they gave me power. Pan was born with one. Xavier…'

'I wouldn't,' Xavier said in a singsong voice from where he sat on the table.

'Did something I can't tell you about and earned his and you just sort of stumbled into the situation, that ended in you earning it.' She shrugged. 'There is no one way things are done. There are some kind of nebulous, half-made rules but nothing real.' She thought about it. 'But yeah, now that I think about it, if someone is an animal chances are their Presence is helpful rather than essential to get the job done.'

'So after that big ass lecture about how there are no answers you're telling me the answer is yes?'

'No, it's…' she sighed. 'Fine, the answer is effectively yes, while at the same time being no, in about a dozen different ways and a maybe in a few more.'

'Effectively is all I need.' Adam smirked and she held her head like she was actually in pain.

'Fine, you jackass,' she spoke through gritted teeth. 'Yeah, the way the powers manifest is the person not the Presence, except when it's not. If you got rid of yours and switched it for another one you'd probably still have claws and altered perception, unless the Presence was particularly wilful or notable and you didn't. On top of that, what exactly that perception shows and the nature of the claws would be different.

On top of that, of course, the more power you get the further the range of your gifts expands. Pan has three and he can do a couple of dozen things you don't know about.'

'So if I get more I can do more?'

'In a nutshell, probably.'

'All right people, listen up!' Pan came back in, suddenly with energy to burn, the previous anger more or less forgotten and ignoring what everyone else had going on. 'What we have here is the Sceptre of the Eternal Flame. As I said, if you have the knowledge of the ritual, which the Legate has and the skill to perform it, which the King's Man has then you can summon a direct and complete manifestation of the King of the Eternal Flame into our world. The King in question is about the size of a large building, is almost impossible to kill and can burn most things out of existence by glaring at them hard enough. He's a giant lunatic with a backwards ass mentality and he wants to impose pure order onto everything and burn everything he can't. He's pretty clear about his motives and for servants he usually picks the big, old, holy fire types. Guys who never back down, never rest and won't stop. Plus, to know his name is to be subject to his will, which is not great for our side. Now, to perform the summoning the Legate needs a few things. I'm not sure what exactly but I do know he can't perform the ritual until the exact full moon. Which means we've got...'

'Three weeks.' Somehow no one wondered how

Annabelle knew that. 'So I guess we've got time to prepare, so that's worth something.'

'Yes,' Xavier scoffed. 'And we've only to face down the King's Man, the Legate and his Legion, Ursas, and possibly the Wardog and the Lady Raiden. Any one of whom could horribly kill our two weakest links in a fight and one of whom could probably take on all of you at once and have a decent hope of victory. If I had both arms I may have been able to fight the King's Man to a standstill, or even to our mutual death, which I would do and be proud.' He fixed a glare on Adam. 'However, I do not have two working arms now, do I? So we are going to need a bigger bag of tricks ladies and gentlemen or we shall be all too quick to die.' He looked around. 'Since I am, of course, assuming that we shall engage in this little suicide mission.'

'Don't ask obvious questions.' Pan was smiling.

'Wait a second.' Adam threw up his hands and climbed to his feet. 'Why are we doing this?'

'Did you miss the part about the bad guys summoning a building tall monster that can set things on fire by looking at them real hard?'

'Okay, but why us? I mean think about it. You people have got to have like an army or something. That brotherhood of yours, people who have some experience with that kind of thing. Actual soldiers for fuck's sake.'

'Yeah there are.' Annabelle shrugged. 'But they have their own stuff to do. Their own creatures to summon and plans to plan. So listen up, this is pretty much how things work in our world. We've got dozens of things in this world cropping up at any given time. The ones who can actually help us might not. Some people can't, some people won't and some people would only make it worse if they showed up. I mean of course I'll run through my contact list and see what I can see. If we can get any help so much the better but some of these things we at least have to try to do on our own.' She gave an all-encompassing gesture to the group. 'The boards been set and, as much as we're going to try to cheat, we might have to play with the pieces we have.'

'All right.' He nodded and his brain started to work in overdrive. 'So what can we do if we can't do that? Any advantages we can get in the mean time?'

'A few,' Pan nodded. 'I have something I have to get to build my own power, Xavier needs to keep recovering and work on whatever evil he may have in mind.'

'He does indeed have evil in mind.' He smiled and spun his cane. 'A trap I cannot yet inform you of, if you know about it, well, you will probably fuck it up for me.'

'And I have to go visit my family.' Annabelle shrugged and got to her feet. 'I have to go refill. I lost quite a few spiders in my time in your world. I'll have to spend some time in mine.'

'We needed to know that,' Pan sighed sarcastically.

257

'I'm a spider, I'll say what I like.'

'Which leaves Adam here to secure another potential advantage involving the players currently on the board.' Pan gave him his most reassuring smile. 'I'll get you a little intel and then tell you the details of what you need to do.'

'And in broad strokes what do I have to do?'

'Well you remember that wardog who almost killed me that one time and might contribute to killing us all?' he smiled. 'I want you to poach her for me'

'Well, that sounds… interesting.'

CHAPTER THIRTEEN

'Well I won't pretend not to be disappointed,' Kate said from above him. He opened his eyes and this time expected to see that same park, with the same skyscrapers and the same tree in which sat the same blind woman kicking her feet in the air. 'I tried to warn you that a normal life wasn't possible if you took this title. That hostility and pain were your fate after this and there was no avoiding it.'

'So what is this?' He looked up at her. 'This is an 'I told you so'?'

'Would you blame me if it was?' She petted her Ibis and smiled serenely.

'Not really,' he admitted. 'I might be a little pissed that you think you could make my choice for me but I don't think I'd actually hold it against you. I mean you did tell me so, and I did get kidnapped and brainwashed. Far as I'm concerned you did your level best to warn me what would happen. It's not your fault that I didn't listen and ended up in the shit.' He shrugged and stroked the panther as it jumped up beside him on the bench. 'Are you one of the Legion or the Lost?'

'I am one of those things,' she admitted. 'Though frankly I resent the fact I am characterised by something I didn't want. I am technically a member of the Legion and in response they do not involve me in any of their hostilities. They let me live and enjoy the moments between the moments. I get to live in the world beyond your world. They do not trouble me with little things and nonsense. In my place I guide people on the paths that they are supposed to walk. I encourage people, I dissuade them and I show them the truth as I see it.' She held her bird gently. 'And I get to share my time with him of course.'

'Then how am I supposed to trust you were trying to help me? I mean if you're one of the Legion?' She looked at him for a moment, jumping off the tree and standing with her hands on her hips in front of him.

'I want you to know that I would be rolling my eyes at you if you could see them. Have I given you any bad advice? Said anything that was untrue? Given anything but advice that served you well?' She folded her arms and scowled at him. 'Or would have served you well if you had decided to listen to me?'

'No,' he admitted.

'Exactly.' She flopped down onto the bench with exaggerated frustration. 'What I tried to show you, what I've been trying to show you since the first moment you arrived here, is the fact that there's no real difference between the Legion and the Lost. They might have different values but they have the same methods. They have the same practices, they're all dangerous and most of them are disgusting.' She raised one hand as he tried to speak. 'Don't. I know I can't convince you of that yet and that's okay. I just need you to understand that you're going to have to work it out on your own and keep your wits about you. Just, when the time comes remember that there is no in it too deep, there is no come too far to turn back. There is always a way out and no one who tries to convince you there isn't is your friend.'

'Why do I get the feeling this isn't just a party line for you?' He looked her up and down for a moment. 'You've really experienced all of this, haven't you?'

'I can't tell you about that yet.' She shook her head with a smile on her face. 'Well I can, but I shouldn't, so I won't.' She gave a disappointed sigh. 'Just protect yourself okay? I put a lot of interest into you and something tells me that you're going to get in very deep very quickly. Try not to die and don't be afraid to run if you need to.' She was talking as quickly as she could now. 'I'm really sorry to do this to you but.'

'Our moment's over?'

'Our moment's over. Sorry.' She waved to him and he woke up in bed again.

'Her name is Wraither.' There was a picture on the board and Pan was standing in front of it with a pointer in a mockery of military discipline. The picture was of a young, pale skinned woman with flirty eyes and a vicious smile. She had long hair tied into a ponytail and about a half dozen piercings in each ear. She wore a simple white dress and a black necklace with a ruby in the middle of it. In this picture she was in the middle of some insane dance, her arms above her head and her hips in mid swing. 'She's a Wardog, and their business works like this. Someone hires them, sometimes with money and sometimes with something else they want. It doesn't much matter what they want as long as you can give it to them. They work a single job and they're free agents again, they don't do long term contracts. For the length of that job they're entirely loyal. You're their only priority and the second it's over you're pretty much nothing to them unless you hire them again. If we're really lucky her contract is up and she's looking to negotiate, which means we might have a chance to get her on our side.'

'And if her contract isn't over?'

'Then she'll probably attack you if you're not in public and you'll have to flee.' He thought about that for a moment. 'So do try to meet her in public. She's been running up and down all of the clubs in the area so you should be able to find her. She's usually got a giant entourage following her around because she apparently has something of a magnetic personality. Go there, get her on side and see if you can get her help busting up the ritual.'

'And if I can't?'

'Then I'll take a run at it once I'm done with the other thing,' he smiled. 'Don't worry, this is you making things easier but if at first we don't succeed we try, try again.'

'So you're giving me this job because you're pretty sure you can cover for me if I fail.'

'I never said that.'

'You're planning for my failure.' He folded his arms. 'Aren't you?'

'I didn't say that.' Pan raised his hand. 'You may have heard it, I may have thought it and it may be true, but I didn't say it and that's what's important.' But he gave a smile that authentically seemed like he was kidding.

'All right you dick.' Adam glared at him. 'I'll head out to find her tonight.' He'd figure something out, just to spite the bastard.

So head out that night he did. He wasn't really all that much of a clubbing person at the best of times but he felt a little more secure knowing that he had his mask in his jacket. It wasn't just that he had the ability to defend himself, though that helped. The most important thing was that the panther had the ability to do social things without screwing them up, which Adam kind of lacked. He walked through a few clubs, wincing at every entrance fee he had to pay and drink he had to buy. It was all draining his already limited resources as he searched for his target. He slipped his hands into the jacket and willed the gloves on so he could see in better detail in the dark and confusion.

It was in the fifth place where he finally encountered her, already in a crowd of admirers and glowing green with power in the green eyes of the Laughing Man's sight. He slipped the gloves off and made his way into the crowd, trying as hard as he could to look more comfortable than he was. A few of the crowd objected to him passing them by, but since they didn't do anything about it he swallowed his anxiety and kept walking.

'Hey.' She recognised him instantly and waved to him. She broke from the crowd and hugged him with a strange and sudden affection. She seemed to be legitimately excited to see him. 'How are you doing? Last time I saw you, you were hiding in a corner!'

'And you were unconscious on the floor.' He shrugged and smiled. 'Wanna go again? We can see who repeats.'

'Oh.' She flashed her teeth at him. 'You got one? Let me see it!' She ignored the crowd as he reached into the jacket, taking out his grinning green mask.

'Pretty smile.' She put her hands on it.

'It is, isn't it?' he looked at her for a few seconds and she shook her head and laughed, putting one hand on the side of his face.

'Wasn't talking about the mask.' She looked into his eyes. 'What do I call you?'

'My name's Adam.' She shook her head.

'I didn't ask what your name was, I asked what I could call you.' He leaned in close to her so her gaggle of admirers couldn't hear.

'The Laughing Man.' And in spite of the fact he wasn't wearing the mask the distortion came out. She shuddered a little and bit her lip.

'I like it.' For a woman who turned into a dog, she purred like a cat when she ran her hand across his chest. 'How you doing?'

'Yeah,' he smiled. 'I'm all right. Got beat up a few times but I'm feeling a little more ready for the world.'

'You think you can take me now?' She crooked an eyebrow at him.

'No, probably not,' he admitted. 'I figured there was no other way to shut you up for ten seconds and take me seriously. So if you take me up on it I guess I'm just gonna have to take the beat down. Faint heart never won fair lady after all.'

The crowd was full of questions, basically along the lines of "what the hell are you talking about" and "who the hell is this guy". They suggested places and clubs they could go and complained that they were bored but Wraither was ignoring them so Adam did too.

'So how'd you bounce back after Pan?' The two of them headed into a bar and she grabbed them a pair of drinks with no regard for the money, handing one to him. They walked away and he looked back for half a second before he decided to play along.

'Hey, I gave as good as I got, right up until the part where I got stabbed and beaten into unconsciousness.' She laughed and downed her drink. 'I backed up all right. My people can take a lot of punishment and keep going without a problem. I heal quick. How about you?'

'I got beat up a few times after that,' he admitted. 'But Mercy ended up putting me to rights.'

'Okay.' She stepped away from him. 'Does that settle the necessities of small talk?' She looked at him. 'Because I'm kinda shitty at it and the reason I became a Wardog was so I never had to do anything I didn't care about ever again.'

'Really?'

'It didn't quite work out that way but yeah,' she admitted. 'I minimise the amount of meaningless shit, boring shit and shit I'm no good at that I have to do. Now, what are you here for?'

'Negotiation,' he admitted. 'Though I was hoping for more chatting and drinking and getting to know you first so I could sort of effortlessly slip it in.'

'Looking to slip it in with me huh?' She winked and grinned, then returned to serious. 'Well my contract is up and I don't exactly like the idea of signing on with the Legion again. I don't like the way they do things or their attitude. Plus they do some really weird shit I have some issues with, but at the same time I'm not entirely sure what you have to offer me, if anything.' She finished her second drink and grabbed his hand. 'All right, come out onto the dance floor with me. My contract isn't technically up until midnight anyway. Once that's done I'm a free agent and I'd be at least willing to be taken to your leader. Why didn't he come by the way? I would have thought the guy who beat me would be the first guy they'd send to start a fight.'

'That's not how I do things. I'm not coming here to start a fight.' He looked around.

'Then start a dance.' The two of them joined hands and slipped into dancing together. After a few minutes of losing themselves in a crowd, Adam slipped the mask onto his face. Adam had never been much of a dancer, no real rhythm or idea of how to move, but apparently the Laughing One was. He danced with her and the two of them both started to lose themselves as they drank. As soon as one of them got bored or uncomfortable they agreed and made their way to the next place. They lost and gained followers as they moved, not really minding how the numbers worked out. They drank more and more and lost themselves further and further in the fun of the night. Whether they liked it or not the two of them steadily picked up a bigger and bigger crowd. He'd never been one of the cool people in his teenage years, and it was an amazing feeling to get what he'd been denied his whole life.

Wraither seemed to show very little regard for anything but her own good time and tangentially his. She didn't bother attempting to learn the names of their various followers and ignored the fact that people were probably fairly angry about the fact she hadn't paid for a single drink the entire night, or the ones she picked up to give Adam. He mostly paid for the ones he ordered for himself but when Wraither appeared out of nowhere and pressed another drink into his hand he couldn't exactly tell her no.

When they were asked to leave the occasional club Wraither would shrug her shoulders and drag him with her to the next place. At the beginning of the night Adam kind of admired and envied her and it only got worse as the time went on. This woman took everything so easily, she didn't seem to be worried about anything and as he drank more and more and hung out with her for longer and longer or maybe some mixture of both he started to care less about the problems of the world around him. His own priorities filled his head and he stopped worrying about unimportant things.

'How you doing?' she asked at around midnight, heading out into the open air yet again.

'Great.' He said it quite a bit louder than he had intended to. 'I actually think I kinda needed this a lot.' He looked at her. 'I mean seriously, you have no idea how much I've had to put up with lately. Did you know the world might end? Cause the world might end.'

'Oh the world won't end, don't be dumb,' she laughed.

'No no but seriously, it might, like we might all die or be slaves or whatever like next week.'

'You worry too much.' Her hand was around his shoulders. When did that happen? Nice anyway. 'You're not gonna die okay? Just chill and it'll all sort itself out in the end. Besides that,' she tapped him on the nose, 'is a future problem. The current problem is the fact that I have to go renegotiate my contract, and since that means cancelling my contract people are gonna get mad. You wanna come with?'

'Sure,' he shrugged, not getting that this might be an issue. They made their way out to the meeting place, only to spot two familiar faces. One was the top hatted, red coated, one armed form of Xavier, holding his undrawn cane in one hand and the other was the greasy brown suited Ursas. He was too drunk to be scared right now.

'Evening.' Wraither seemed perfectly sober again, cracking her knuckles and looking at the two men as if they were just normal people.

'I'll sober you up if something kicks off,' the voice came softly into Adam's ear. 'Other than that, just relax and don't say anything stupid. Better yet don't say anything at all.' Adam leaned against the wall and stayed silent as the three participants stared at each other. They exchanged paper with one another, each of them reading over what seemed to be a contract. Wraither looked it over and signed it, as did Ursas. From there it got a lot more intense, the group beginning to snap, yell and bark at each other. They steadily got louder and louder.

'If you don't shut your fuckin' mouth, fancy boy, I'm gonna take the other arm,' Ursas bellowed. Xavier wasn't daunted in the slightest.

'And if you do?' he responded. 'Unless I'm much mistaken you've been chewed out for everything you've done so far. Are you sure you're supposed to kill me?' He dropped his cane on his foot and balanced it there as he reached out with one hand to pat Ursas insultingly on the face. 'Or should you perhaps take that contract you're going to fail to renew and get yourself out of my city.'

'Get out of your city?' he snarled, his face getting uglier and hairier, and his teeth getting longer and longer. 'If it was ever yours it won't be for long. This whole place is comin' the fuck down in days.' He turned to the Wardog. 'Last chance to be part of the solution rather than the problem little puppy.'

'Not interested.' She shook her head. 'Sorry, but you creep me out and I really hate the Lady Ray. Did she die by the way? I truly hope she died.'

'Why would I tell you that?' He reached out and gripped her neck with one claw-like hand, beginning to squeeze even as the claws started to extend from her fingers. She readied herself to strike as he strangled her.

'Are you sure you should be doing that?' Xavier asked, leaning against the wall, obviously a little tired. 'Perhaps you shouldn't risk the reprimand. Go home little bear.' He waved the sword at him and gave a derisive little chuckle.

Ursas snarled and tightened his grip just a little further, then tossed Wraither across the alley. He spat on the ground, turned and got into his brown sedan and drove off, his car letting out a loud backfire as he pulled out.

'You okay?' Adam moved over to her and she spat blood on the ground.

'Arse licking, miserable, old, shit eating bear!' She spat again and he pulled her to her feet, holding her up.

'Makes for a good reason to join us don't you think?' She smiled at that one.

'Dude, a plus for timing and opportunism.' She gave him a thumbs up. 'But nowhere near good enough. You've got a fucking spider and that's no better than a bear.' She patted him on the shoulder with the arm he was holding her up with. 'I'm not sold sweetie, so throw out your pitch.'

'Mind if I do that in the morning?' He shook his head. 'I mean I am truly and amazingly drunk right now.'

'You gonna be with me in the morning?' She quirked an eyebrow at him as Xavier slipped quietly out of the alley, apparently deciding that Adam was doing well enough. 'What are you offering me now?'

'Oh damn it.' He put his hand over his mouth. 'Sorry, I mean shit, I mean sorry.'

'Awww honey,' she giggled. 'He gets awkward, that's so adorable.' She ran her hand through his hair. 'What? You aren't interested in me?'

'Oh I'm interested.' The words slipped out of his mouth without him ever meaning them to.

'It's okay Laughing Man,' she smiled. 'You need to blow off some steam, find some of that laughter of yours. I can give you something to smile about.' She took his hand. 'Come on kid.'

'Wait seriously?' He looked at her and she shrugged again. 'I mean you don't have to do that for me.'

'Wardog dude. Fuck you, I do what I want.' She grinned. 'Wait a minute, rearrange that and it works. So, do you wanna go?'

'All right let's go!' He shook his head. He couldn't really believe this. This was insane, was this really happening?

'Really?' The panther's voice was soft and a little mocking. 'You've been mind controlled, developed superpowers, picked fights with blank faced, form changing monsters and been tortured by the high priest of some kind of elder god. None of these things surprise you but, what, the fact that you might once find it easy to get laid does? There is something desperately wrong with your ego kid. Go, have fun.' He took her hand and she lead him to a taxi. Her place wasn't nice, the paint was peeling and the walls were scratched. Other than a perfectly maintained kitchen the entire floor of the house was covered in mattresses, rugs and cushions. This was so strange. Why would she have that? Then he asked himself why he was worrying about her furnishings when there was a beautiful woman in front of him and came up with no good answer. She pulled him down onto a particularly large pile of pillows and blankets, pulling the mask off his face to kiss him.

The rest of the night was a blur, an enjoyable, passionate, massively pleasurable, drunken, slightly painful blur. He couldn't remember the details of the situation but he remembered the taste of her skin. He remembered what it was like to be between her legs, her holding onto his back and raking her nails down as he drove himself in and out of her, his head reeling with the mixture of pleasure and pain. He remembered her moaning and growling in his ear, and the beautiful expression on her face. When he eventually passed out, a few hours later he woke up with a half dozen different aches on the same pile of cushions with a pair of comfortable old blankets strewn carelessly over him.

'Hey there pretty.' She wasn't wearing anything, and sat calmly on a different pile of cushions, in front of a TV which was sitting on the floor. 'There's leftover food in the kitchen and coffee sitting in the maker. None of it's too cold yet.'

He made his way into the kitchen, his stomach doing donuts and writhing as he saw a plate. It really did seem to be a collection of whatever she hadn't eaten, but there was an egg, some bacon and a sausage on a plate which suited him just fine. There was a box on the bench that said "breakfast" and a wolf's head underneath it. 'Hey, have you seen my mask?'

'It's on your pants.'

'Where are my pants?'

'Against that wall I think,' She pointed and he stumbled over to it. He picked up his mask and pulled it on, sending it a message with his mind. 'Please tell there is something you can do for this damn hangover.'

The panther gave a smug chuckle and Adam felt the weakness and sickness draining out of his body to be replaced with a ravenous hunger. 'Now we're even for letting the spider venom almost kill you.'

'Wait a minute,' he snapped at it. 'You almost let the spider venom–'

'Even!' the panther said loudly. 'Now go eat.' He pulled the mask down so it didn't cover his mouth and started in on his food as he put the coffee on.

'So that was fun.' He looked at her and she cracked a smile before turning back to the TV.

'It was. I had a great time. If I'm still in town after this job ends I might give you a call.' When he reached for his pants she waved one hand. 'Don't worry about giving me your number. I already took it off your phone while you were sleeping.' That was a little weird, but hey, she was cute and it was early. It wasn't too worth thinking about.

'Sure, if you like,' he shrugged. 'You seem cool.'

'I am cool!' she agreed. She seemed genuinely and childishly pleased that he'd realised that about her. 'So, are we gonna do business?'

He thought about it, shaking his head a little to clear it. He couldn't switch gears that fast.

'Can you give me time to finish my coffee?'

'I can indeed.' She relaxed cheerfully back into her cushion pile. He calmly finished his drink, formulating various thoughts, plans and ideas as he went. Finishing his drink, he got dressed and sat down beside her. She turned off the TV and turned to face him. She was a little older than him he realised; she was young looking, but she wasn't so young.

'All right.' He took a deep breath and tried to think of things to offer. 'Well, I guarantee you that we can pay you whatever they did. More if you like.' He had no idea if that was true. If it was, there was no way he'd be doing the paying. He was absolutely broke by this point.

'Keep me in my lifestyle.' She nodded and yawned. 'Pretty much a given.'

'You can keep any Presences from people you can take them off.' Was that standard? That seemed like it would be standard but her eyes widened with what looked like surprise.

'All right pretty boy, now you have my attention.' She grinned brightly. 'How long's the job for.'

'Just the one mission all in all but,' he looked at her for a long moment, 'it's probably gonna be a dangerous one. It's probably going to get people hurt, it might even get us killed. We're coming in without a huge chance of success here.'

'Most of my missions involve going in as underdog. That's not a big deal for me.' She shrugged and smiled. 'What's on our side?'

'Me, you, the spider girl, the guy who whupped you and the Gentleman who was with you last night when you cancelled the contract. Why was he there by the way?'

'Upon every negotiation of a wardog's contract at least one representative from both the Legion and the Lost must attend in order to be sure of a healthy market and to allow both sides the opportunity to make their case.' He thought about it for a moment.

'Doesn't that mean one of them should be here now? Isn't that important?'

'No.' She shook her head. 'I chose not to join their side which means I'm going to go over to yours. That means either I go with what you want or I bail out. I got to another city and find myself some new work.'

'Those are all of your options in life?' She thought about it.

'I mean, not really but kind of?' She shrugged. 'I could go into training like red coat suggested or find some other group of Lost in the city to work for. Look, do you want to hear the minutia of my meaningless existence or do you want to ask for my help? Come on, tell me what I'm going to be up against.'

'A guy called the King's Man. Big Russian guy covered in tattoos. He wears a giant white hood most of the time. I don't know much about him other than the fact he says he has five Presences and he's badass enough that I believe him. There's also Ursas, the guy you met tonight, the Legate, don't know what he does other than command a Blank Faced Legion.' He thought about it for a moment. 'Also that lightning bolt girl if she's alive. Which I'm not sure, but the way my luck's going she probably is.'

'So wait,' her eyes were suddenly alight, her teeth pointing in her mouth, 'if the Lady Ray's alive she's gonna be there?'

'Yeah.' He shrugged. 'I mean she will if I'm right. But that seems to be how that kind of thing works out.'

'All right.' She folded her arms. She sounded somewhere between angry and aroused. 'I'll sign up on one condition. If Lady Ray's there she's my issue and I get to handle her without all of you getting in the way.'

'As long as she doesn't make herself our problem

she's your problem. If you screw up she becomes ours.'

'Okay, deal,' she nodded. 'Have your guy draw up the contract and we'll settle it.' Adam walked over to the kitchen and she turned back to her TV as he made the call.

'Hello.' Pan picked up. 'What's up Adam?'

'I'm done with the recruitment thing. Met the Wardog.'

'Really? Already?' The tone was suspicious, like he was preparing for disappointment. 'How did it go?'

'Couldn't have possibly gone any better.' He smiled. 'I'm at her place now, waiting for my guy to draw up the contract and get over here. I don't have a guy, or at least I don't think I do. If I have a guy I guess you're my guy.'

'You do and I am.' Pan sounded as surprised as he did pleased. 'Seriously, you got this done alone?'

'I did,' he nodded. 'I'm at her place now. Hey Wraither!' he called into the next room. 'What's your address?' She gave it to him and within minutes Pan was at the door, holding a blank piece of paper in one hand. Wraither took Adam's hand and pressed it onto the piece of paper, she muttered something in low growling tones and words filled the page, the type getting smaller and smaller as the page filled up. Pan and Wraither both read it over, the latter pulling a pair of glasses out from behind her TV to read through it. Each of them pressed one finger against the signature line, then Pan took Adam's hand and did the same.

'Okay, cool, so now that I'm on your side.' She leaned in close to him and pressed her face into his neck, nuzzling at him a little.

'Not that I'm not up for another round,' he stepped backwards as she nuzzled him, 'but there's someone else here and I really don't want to make it awkward.'

'If you're up to go again I'm totally in,' she mumbled into his skin. 'But in this particular instance this isn't part of the foreplay. I'm this close for an entirely different reason.' She sniffed the air and moved around behind him, then sniffed the air one more time, smelling his skin. 'Here we go.' She pressed one long thin claw against his neck and suddenly felt a shift of pressure on his skin, like the popping of a pimple. She withdrew the claw and held it out, a small white creature squirmed on its razor point impaled like a worm on a hook.

'What the fuck is that thing?' He jumped back, his eyes wide.

'I knew I smelled something weird on you.' Her voice was quiet and dangerous. 'It's a monitor. Blanks, particularly powerful ones anyway, can sometimes make them. They're recording units who steal your senses. They take note of everything you see, hear, smell and feel and I'd wager this little one in particular has been tracking you since the first time you met with a Legion member.'

'Which was,' he realised and almost smacked himself in the head, 'all the way back before any of this happened. Way back that first night outside the bar, where I met Raven and Annabelle, he put his hand on my shoulder.'

'Which means they've been spying on us since day one.' Pan's voice was cold and angry. 'Well I suppose we know why they were always one step ahead of us. Why they got to the angel before us, why they knew where we would come out after you left the world where you got your Presence. Is the little bastard dead?'

'It is indeed.' Wraither shrugged and walked away. After a moment he heard the sound of running water and she returned. 'And washed down the sink. Aren't you ever so lucky to have me?'

'No kind of luck, it'll all thanks to the kid.' He smiled and patted Adam on the back. As Adam looked at the big guy he noticed that the Lost tattoo on his head was now gone, presumably replaced by some other tattoo on some other part of his body, probably for the sake of the fight. 'I'll let you know when we need you. You'll be busting up a ritual but we'll be messing with some fairly major players. So be ready.'

'Let me know when the official briefing is.' She smiled. 'Anything I can do in the meantime?'

'Relax and get ready I guess.' Maybe it was a front, but he sounded confident. 'If there's anything you can do to get right before the big fight do it now because it's coming up fast.' He looked over at Adam. 'And as for you we don't have long to go, or much left to do. Any loose ends you've got, it's time to clean them up.

We can't have you coming in distracted.'

'How do I talk to Annabelle?' he asked. 'I tried to call her but her phone wasn't working. Is she out of service or something?'

'She's at home.' Pan looked at Wraither out of the corner of his eye, raising one eyebrow to show he was hinting at something. 'With her family?'

'Oh, dude, it's fine,' Wraither chuckled. 'It's so not like that with me and him. It was less emotional connection and more itch scratching. If he has some kind of history with some girl or they have something going for them don't spare my feelings, I don't have all that many. Besides I know she's a spider and I'm not okay with it but I'm under contract so I'll deal.'

'All right,' he shrugged. 'Yeah, just find any of her sisters and ask her where to find the carnival. There's a decent chance you'll get someone who knows.'

'What carnival?'

'The carnival she's queen of? Like in the title that's her title that you've called her like five times?'

'All right.' Adam nodded. 'Sure, go visit the spider carnival I guess, why not? I guess I'll head off then.' He looked at Wraither. He wasn't sure exactly how he was supposed to handle one night stands with magical beings who didn't seem to have any ability for long term emotions and had the ability to turn into a throat ripping wolf monster. 'It was fun.'

'It was.' She smiled and stepped in close to him. 'If you do it again and your girl's okay with it, I'm up for it,' she gave him a kiss and then pushed him backwards. 'Now go on, get.'

'Any idea where I can find a spider?'

'I don't fucking know dude, literally any attic I guess.' She scowled at him and went back to her TV. He nodded and figured that was fair enough before heading out. Pan followed him, unlocking his car.

'Need a lift?'

'I do.' The two of them pulled themselves in and the powerful engine rumbled to life. The two of them drove in silence for a while.

'Do you have any idea what you're getting into?' Pan asked softly.

'No idea,' Adam replied. It wasn't a pleasant reality to face, but it was as close to a complete truth as he could muster. 'I haven't had any idea since all of this started and it's more or less worked fine for me so far, hasn't it?'

'Oh god.' Pan put one hand over his face as he pulled up to a red light. 'I was hoping you'd at least make it a couple of weeks before you flew into the typical lost, clueless bastard attitude,' he snorted and took off again. 'A little naive I suppose.'

'Yeah, a little bit.' They drove back to Adam's and after yet another short conversation, yet another boring explanation with his friends who couldn't begin to understand what was going on in his life, he made his way up to the attic.

He could see the webs as he walked into the attic. Like everything else important in his life, they started to glow green. It certainly was a handy little trick.

'One of these days someone's going to shine a green floodlight around whatever room I'm in and I'm gonna piss myself.' The voice in his head laughed as he searched through the webs with delicate hands. He crouched in front of them, not wearing the gauntlets the mask could form for him. He kept his hands gentle against the web, careful not to damage or break it. The last thing he wanted was to piss off the spiders he was going to ask for help. After a few seconds, a spider came out of the webs, small, delicate and glossy black with none of the hairs or grossness. Across her back was a small patch of red. The creature slowly crawled down the web, moving slowly and carefully without any kind of jumping or stumbling. She slipped down the web and finally, gently touched down on the back of his hand. He wanted to jump back, every part of him wanted to jump back, pull his hand away or go do something else. He wanted to wait for Annabelle to come into the real world. Spiders were already a little creepy at the best of times and he was pretty sure this one was venomous.

'I am,' came the voice, deep, dark and female with sultry undertones to it. 'And while that's probably a healthy attitude, all things considered, I still find it a little insulting.'

'Well if you don't like my thoughts don't read my mind,' he scolded her.

'Well that's a good point.' He got a feeling of assent from her. 'Well my name is not anything you would recognise, lacking a spiders' sensibilities as you do. So why don't you just call me Redback?'

'Isn't Redback just a colloquial name for a Black Widow?'

'I suppose it is.' She turned over on his hand and he imagined it was some kind of shrug. 'But I wouldn't call myself by her name now would?'

'I don't know.' He thought about it. 'Still calling you by some classification doesn't seem right.'

'Then call me Scarlett.' She seemed quite pleased by the whole idea. 'I like that any better anyway. So why don't you tell me why I'm here. Why are we talking, dear?'

'We're talking because I need your help.' He held her up to his face. 'I need to visit the woman whose title is the Spinning Sister, the Carnival Queen. Which means I have to go to see the carnival.'

'Annie!' She heard the sound of applause in the back of her mind. 'I love the carnival! I've met her a few times before. I haven't known her for long but she's nice. Still, as well as I wish her and all the same I can't just take you there for free.'

'All right.' He shrugged, that seemed simple enough. 'I don't have much, but whatever you want I'll do my best to give it to you.'

'A secret.' She crawled closer to him, placing one leg against his face. 'One you've never told anyone. Something strange and a little dark.' He stared at her for a few long moments and then brought her in close to his mouth, whispering to her.

'I can't honestly remember most of the details of who I used to be. I can't remember anything about my old life that means anything to me anymore. I know I had a life, and it mattered but it just… doesn't feel at all important anymore.'

'That will most definitely do.' Her tone was pleased. 'All right, let's take you to the carnival my darling.' She scuttled off his hand and jumped back onto the web without a second thought. 'You'll have to trust me though, more than you did just then.'

'You knew?'

'I mean I was reading your mind,' she reminded him, significant amusement in her voice. 'You were wondering how fast you could swat me if I looked like I was going to bite you. You asked your other self whether or not the resistance supplied by your Presence would protect you from my venom long enough for you to get to a hospital.' She laughed, an empty hollow sound. 'It's all right. I'm not mad. I know full well that humans don't trust spiders. Did you know that's not a two-way street at all? We trust you almost completely. Although that is mostly because we have some very low opinions of your intellect and guile. We trust you simply because we're better at lying, cheating and stealing than you are.' She spun between her webs, threading and threading. 'Every trick and plan you think of, we've already tried.' With that she finished the web and pulled out a string on one tiny leg. Adam reached over and grabbed it.

'Now I do believe you know how this works. Hold onto the thread, keep your hands and feet inside the ride at all times and please, try not to scream.' Suddenly in front of him was a dark-skinned woman with a long black dress and a distinctive red birthmark on her shoulder. She lead him down the line, down that same strange, long, interconnected web. She transferred strings a few times, which caused a bit of a churning in his gut as he moved, but eventually the darkness began to clear and lights started twinkling in the distance. In the centre of the web this time there were lights, there was music, there was an honest to gods carnival. He let out a laugh without even thinking about it.

'What the hell?' He turned to Scarlett.

'Spiders occasionally speak in riddles and metaphors my darling but this is not one of them. We really do have a carnival and there really is a queen.'

'I thought it was ants and bees that had queens?'

'Ants, bees and this particular carnival. She's not the Queen of spiders or anything. She just runs one carnival.'

'So wait, I'm curious. Is every spider I see one of you?'

'Yes and no.' She walked with him, the carnival getting closer and closer. As he walked toward it he saw that it had all the typical markings of a carnival, except without any attraction names. Even the carnival itself never actually showed its name on the sign, the gaudy lettering simply said 'the carnival'. 'That doesn't help does it? Very well, just except that we can be if we need to be but we aren't all the time. There are a certain number of mental beings that can jump in and out of spiders. All the same you should be very careful before you decide to swat a spider, it might just be someone's sister. On the other hand, if you're referring to the ones that some of our fighters use as weapons, then the answer is no. they are no more sensible, coherent or sentient than you thought spiders were before all of this came along.'

'All right,' he nodded. 'So what exactly is this place for?'

'Money,' she shrugged. 'Ever wonder how we always seem to have money for food, cover identities, transport and clothes? A lot of things like this.' She patted his head and gave him a slightly condescending smile. 'Don't worry sweet boy we don't actually seriously harm or kill anyone. Well, no more than an average carnival does anyway. Accidents do happen after all.'

After a few minutes they headed inside and Scarlett began nodding to people, the bored ticket taker just smiling and waving them through. The place was tacky, but with a deliberate self-aware tackiness that was all people came here for. People wanted silliness and nonsense, and the smiling clown faces and bright lights gave them that. Sawdust billowed around their feet and people called out various wares. He could smell sweat and cotton candy and popcorn and paint.

'So wait, there are normal people here?'

'Most of the people here are normal,' she nodded.

'They're normal people out there in various places in the world. They think that this place is just one of any dozen travelling shows, circuses or carnivals around the world. They walk through the same ticket gate to get in and suddenly they're here and they all get their first taste of real magic. They have no idea that's what's going on but it is.' She looked around. 'It also helps that some of the supernatural community come, as the energy they give off with emotions and natural power makes us stronger.' She kept talking but his attention was stolen by the exhibits.

He saw a man breathing fire with no visible gasoline or fire stick with which to pull off the trick. They passed a group of acrobats who were flying around with just a little too much ease for it to be entirely biological.

'Even now they're seeing the fifty or sixty of our hundreds of shows and exhibits that we think they're most interested in, and when they leave and talk about it to their friends they attribute any difference in experiences from their friends to not seeing every part of the park.'

They walked past jugglers and magicians, a man being stabbed with swords by the crowd. As they passed they saw one of the spectators push against the blade and cut themselves a little to make sure that it wasn't sliding back in before he drove it into the man's stomach. The man bled, but didn't turn, slump or show any sign of pain. There were spinning rides and rollercoasters and sideshows they could play. Finally they pushed their way through the crowds and made their way to a small pavilion, somewhere quiet and out of the way. There was no gaudy sign on it like there was on the others, only a single silver tiara decorating the entrance.

Inside was a red, purple and black room with whirling lights throwing shadows in every direction, built for natural creepiness. There was a simple, deep red carpet leading up to the only piece of furniture in the room. A throne on which she sat, leaning against one of the armrests in a long purple dress and covered with spiders. They slid from her skin, falling out of her hair and crawling from her clothes.

'Usually I just entertain myself or do paperwork here,' she smiled. 'But sometimes people who come looking for adventure find me. I offer a prize to anyone who has the courage to keep their hands on me for more than a minute. I get a couple of winners every so often, but I don't think I've ever had more than a couple in a day.' She spread her arms. 'Would you like to try?'

'Yeah, sure,' he nodded, holding out his hand.

'I'll let you have your first try for free, just this once.' The spiders began to spread wider and wider, more and more of them spreading to cover her body. 'I assure you you're in no danger. They won't hurt you.' She smirked suddenly. 'Unless of course I tell them to.'

'All right.' He advanced toward her slowly, focusing on her face and trying not to count the spiders. There were dozens, maybe even a hundred of them swarming all over her body. A few of them even dropped from her feet and crawled across the carpet. Adam approached Annabelle and reached out one hand, closing it around her arm. In a sudden burst of courage he moved forward quickly, wrapping his arms around her in a hug.

He closed his eyes and he could feel the spiders that were a part of her swarming all over her, then across her onto him. After a moment he realised the simple facts of their situation. They weren't any danger to him at all. They were a part of her and if he liked her there was no reason not to like them. They were strange, dark and a little creepy and whether it was logical or not, he didn't think he'd have any kind of affection for them in his life. If the alternative was not being a part of her life, not being her friend, no chance of being with her, then he had no problem with the spiders.

'Minute's up,' she said softly.

'Okay then.' He pulled back and looked at her for a long moment, then flashed her a grin and sat down beside her on her throne. 'So, what do I get?'

'What do you want?' He kissed her. He took a long moment in doing it and savoured the feeling of her soft, perfect lips against his.

'That.'

'All right then,' the spiders scattered in every direction as she got to her feet. 'I guess we need to talk, huh?' She took his hand and lead him outside. As she moved outside Scarlett switched places with her, reclining on the throne. As the two of them walked together he smiled.

'I should probably warn you,' he informed her. 'This was an entirely spontaneous decision. I didn't really make it thinking ahead or considering the repercussions. I kinda just did what I wanted.'

'Sometimes those are the best kind of decision.' She smiled and squeezed his hand, looking to all the world like a slightly strange couple walking through the carnival. 'So you've decided the spider thing doesn't bother you anymore?'

'Not too much,' he shrugged. 'I mean it's a little creepy but I wouldn't call it a deal breaker for me.' The best he could give her was that honest answer. She nodded, deciding that, on balance, this was pretty much good enough.

'Well I'm glad you told me, gave me the truth and nothing more. Though I have to say I don't exactly think much of your timing.' She tousled his hair and smirked at him. 'You're about to watch the world fade away, watch fire roam through our city and turn everyone into slaves or corpses and you decide that now is the proper time to kiss the girl?' She shook her head and chuckled.

'Oh, you don't know the half of it,' he admitted. Best to get all the bullshit out of the way now.

'Oh?' she sighed.

'I just had a one night stand,' he admitted. 'Like it finished a couple of hours ago. I'm sorry if I'd been planning to do this I wouldn't have, well, you know.' He paused for a long moment and she dragged the moment out.

'That,' she chuckled and shook her head, 'is truly fucking terrible timing.' She slapped him on the back and let out a bitter little chuckle. 'I mean gods below dude, you had to know this was going to piss me off so why tell me at all?'

'Spiders are better at guile than humans are, Scarlett told me that,' he shrugged. 'Figured it'd come out sooner or later, better than drop it now than have it come out at some shitty time and raise tension.'

'Spiders are better at guile than humans are, that's true,' she nodded. 'As proved by the fact that you, my sweet boy,' she poked him in the chest, 'cannot lie to me. You weren't afraid you'd get caught. You didn't even consider the possibility until a few seconds ago.'

'Meaning?'

'Meaning I know you had another motive.' She leaned in closer and stared at him. He was reminded of Wraither sniffing the creature on his neck out. 'Come on, I have to know now. What was the real issue?'

'I didn't want things to start out with lies,' he admitted, shaking his head with embarrassment. 'I mean I could have. I doubt it would have even come up until we'd been at a point where you wouldn't care or it wouldn't work out anyway. If I could hold out a while we could get to the point where it wouldn't matter what I did or didn't do. I either would be in trouble already or I wouldn't get to it, but I figure if you start something on an imperfect foundation there's no way to end up with a perfect result.'

'So our relationship or whatever it is, budding and uncertain as it may be cannot be allowed to be compromised before it really begins.'

'Yeah, I guess.' He closed his eyes for a long moment and tried not to let his embarrassment show. 'I'm kinda getting ahead of myself, aren't I?'

'You're only human I guess,' she shrugged. 'Everyone has their things and issues. Some people get ahead of themselves, some people have to test people and get a result in order to really trust them.' She pointed toward the pavilion behind them. 'I knew you were coming and I set up the spider thing. I wanted to make sure you'd accept me for me rather than the front I put up for you people. I needed you to see me at my most, me.'

'You people?' He raised an eyebrow at her and she smirked.

'Yeah, I just "you people'd" you and you can't do a damn thing about it, because one of us is a spider and the other isn't.' She shoved him a little and he shrugged.

'So yeah.' He ran his hands through his hair again. 'I hope you aren't, you know, mad or anything.'

'Honestly? I am a little,' she decided. 'But in short term, logically I know it's not a terrible thing but it makes me feel bad right now kind of way. The kind where I know that pretty soon I'm going to get over it and I don't even particularly blame you.'

'Well of all the kinds of mad someone could be at me that's one of the better ones I guess.' He looked at her for a long moment. 'So does that mean I should take a hike or?'

'No I don't and even if I did it wouldn't matter. Which brings me to the second and possibly more important part of this conversation, meaning the terrible timing. This.' She leaned in and kissed him gently and tenderly. 'The mad, the kissing, any affections we may or may not have toward each other and other people and any problems I may or may not have with you, have to be put on total hold. Complete and absolute. It's not that it's not important, it is, and that's why we have to delay it.' She moved away from him a little. 'None of us can be allowed to fuck ourselves up getting personal while everything's getting serious. We are in for the fight of our lives, maybe the only big fight you'll ever be in. A fight where I'm going to lose plenty of my spiders, which does hurt me emotionally and a fight that might kill us both, and will probably kill you.' That one hurt like a kick in the gut. 'I'm sorry but that's the hard truth of the situation. You're the least experienced, you have no more power than the rest of us and the Legate has a personal problem with you. The person who least needs to be distracted, who is least allowed to lose his temper or become compromised, is you. So please don't fuck this up trying to take care of me because I do not need to be taken care of understand?'

'Good to know.' He nodded and looked her up and down. For all the weirdness, she really was a special kind of beautiful. 'But I do have some kind of feelings for you and I'm pretty sure you have them for me too. I'm not sure I can just turn them off.'

'Too bad.' She pushed him a little. 'Because you have to, because that's the only way you survive. But don't worry, you have a few days. Figure it out.' She walked away, this time stopping only when she was a couple of metres away from him. Well, anything was better than nothing he supposed as he made his way with her out of the carnival. She stayed a couple of metres away from him. He was going to have to work out how to ignore his feelings until this was over. She clicked her fingers and he realised she'd been talking and he hadn't heard.

'So, as I asked while you were zoned out, who was it?'

'What do you mean?'

'Who'd you fuck?' She stared at him, standing still with her hands on her hips.

'Really? You really wanna know that?' He studied her for a long moment. 'Cause that's almost certainly not going to make anything better.'

'Yeah but I feel like I should probably know.' She nodded and smiled. 'Get it all out into the world before we put it on hold.'

'I can't help but feel like this is a really bad–' She raised one finger to cut him off.

'Dude, it was your fuckup which means I get to handle it however I like. So, you're going to tell me now.'

'Her name is Wraither, and yes, that's an actual name apparently.' He shook his head. 'She's the Wardog that Pan beat down, remember that?'

'You nailed a Wardog?' She snorted a little. 'You were wrong darling, that actually does make me feel a little less bad.'

'Why?'

'Well one, most Wardogs are smokin' so I'm pretty impressed with the kind of girls who are my competition. They're kind of hard to resist and I don't want a guy I might consider sleeping with to be the kind of guy who'll just nail anyone. Two, Wardogs don't take sexual or romantic connection all that seriously. It's not really their kind of thing. Their lives are transitory so they don't get attached and they're sure not to put more importance on one night together than they really have or make big things out of small things. I don't have any kind of competition or jealousy to deal with.' She cracked a smile. Wow, she wasn't kidding when she said she was putting her emotions on hold. She was dealing with the situation by pushing it to the side and tackling things logically. It was pretty impressive. 'So, is there anything else we need to talk about?'

'Nothing non-feelings related I guess,' he nodded, looking at the ground and trying not to feel silly.

'It's all right.' She approached him this time and patted him on the shoulder. 'You're allowed to have feelings but I'd just prefer you didn't beat me around the head with them or anything.'

'I'm scared,' he admitted. 'It's been pretty heavily drilled into me that we don't have much of a chance here. I don't wanna die. I don't want people I know to die and I don't want to have to kill anyone. I'm pretty sure one of those three things is going to happen and I feel really shitty about it.'

'I can't say for sure what's going to happen, but I need you to know something important. You can run right now.' When he looked her in the eyes she looked absolutely sincere. 'You can absolutely run. I'll get one of the girls to take you out of town and get you as far away as possible.' Her eyes became more sad and serious as she spoke. 'But if you're going to do that you have to understand what it means. At that moment, you're walking out on us, you're walking out on this city and you give up whatever stake you had in us. You're walking out on things that matter, but we wouldn't ever blame you. No one could blame you. Ninety percent of humanity would do the exact same thing in your situation. So, there it is. If you need permission to run you have it. I officially permit you.' 'I'm not going anywhere.' His voice was harder and more intense than he thought it could ever be. He spoke without thinking, which was probably good since if he'd thought about it he'd probably be a country away by now. 'For better or worse I'm in this now. No matter what it means I started this and that means I have to finish it. I need to be free and I know I can do it. This is what I want.' He took a long deep breath. 'So I'll find a way.'

'Welcome to the Lost.' She embraced him and gave him a quick kiss on the cheek. 'Seriously, this is what we do. We yell 'fuck it', throw up our hands and do whatever it is we do. Then we find a way to win.'

'What do you mean?'

'I was adopted at seven years old by literal spiders and then I was raised by figurative representations of spiders. I mean you met Aunt Widow and like I said, she's not the worst. Far from the best but not the worst. Don't get me wrong, my family is awesome and I love the carnival. I mean I really and truly love this place. I basically get to run it how I want, when I want, but think about how that started for me. I'm seven years old, my parents just died and I follow a trail of spiders into a magical world because apparently spiders are a thing I was crazy enough to follow at seven years old. I just made shit up, I improvised and I kept doing the things that worked and abandoned the ones that didn't. That's what I do. It's what most of the Lost do and you know what? Most of the time it works.' She kissed him again, deeply and passionately, and it took him completely by surprise. 'See that? I promised myself I wouldn't do that again until we were done with this but I did it again anyway because it felt like a good idea. Plus, Xavier has a plan and that's a scary idea I'm looking forward to. It's gotta be some table turning shit.'

'I certainly hope so.' But he was smiling in spite of himself.

'Trust me,' she held him close, 'it's our curse and

our gift. We're almost always losing but we rarely lose and they're almost always winning but they rarely win. I mean sometimes they do but they won't. I know it.'

'You realise that you make very little sense.'

'Yeah, it's a spider thing.' She smiled. 'The more you get to know us the more you'll understand. Just do what feels right and don't fuck everything up.'

'Don't fuck everything up. Well that's an excellent critique thank you very much.'

'Happy to help, asshole,' she snorted. 'Go back to my pavilion and have Scarlett escort you home, okay? I'll be here a couple more days and it needs to be with my people. I've gotta be at my very best.'

'All right.' He looked at her for a few long moments. 'You're strange, but I like you a lot.'

'I like you too. Now go. Get ready and remember, if all else fails, trust the Laughing One. He's a malicious little shit but I'm pretty sure he knows what he's doing and he's got your back.'

'All right, I can do this.' He took her hand again and she stared at him for a moment.

'I thought we agreed to–'

'We did,' he nodded. 'But that felt wrong so I'm not doing it. Maybe protecting each other is what we're supposed to do this time.'

'That sounds… pointlessly sentimental.'

'Well we've already got the reasonless, cold-hearted lunatic and the dedicated soldier. So maybe a little bit of the sentimental is what our side needs right now.' She shook her head and scowled, but kissed him again anyway.

'All right, we'll do it your way.' And the two of them set off back to the carnival.

CHAPTER FOURTEEN

'This will not do.' The King's Man looked down at the Blank with the scars over its eyes. 'This is not the body of one of the Lost. It is unacceptable.'

'Yes, it is.' The Legate's brow furrowed under his mask. 'That is the body of Raven the Scarred. He was run through with his own dagger and turned Blank, but he was one of the Lost.'

'Was.' The King's Man's voice was slightly clipped and cold, but any discernible change in voice was a sign of remarkable emotion for him. 'That man who was one of the Lost was run through and became a member of the Blank Legion, and thus he became a member of the Legion proper. Were he to be killed now as you are suggesting he would, for every intent and purpose, be that of one of the Legion. As you can probably discern that is not exactly the result we were looking for!' One sharply raised word. That was all and he had never heard it before. 'And since you sent the target we spent so long converting on a mission from which he did not return, rather than simply sacrificing him for the ritual as I suggested to you, this would not be a problem.'

'Hindsight is as it has ever been, the finest of all men's sight.' The Legate allowed a little irritation to pervade his own tone. 'I sought to use him for my own purposes. It did not go well. I take responsibility for this but it is not the end of the road for us. After all, they will attack us sooner or later anyway. Why not simply kill them and use their bodies there?'

'That seems risky but potentially promising.' The big Russian looked at him for a moment.

'Only if we should fail to defeat them. We have seen their forces. Do you honestly think they could form any offensive force powerful enough to remove you, the Lady Raiden, Ursas and my entire Legion? And all this without losing a single one of their own? I admit it is far from the perfect plan, but I see no reason it should not work.' He smiled beneath his mask. 'We kill the Lost, use one's body to summon the King and unleash the King upon the city.'

'Hardly a masterstroke of strategic genius.'

'But it will work,' he insisted.

'And how do you suggest we deliver the information, the time and place of this ritual?'

'It doesn't really matter I suppose, all things considered.' The Legate returned to his neutrality. 'Any method will do. Even if I walked up to one of them and told them directly to their face they would come. They need not believe me, they need not suspect us of anything but the most obvious of traps and they would still need to come to that place at that time just in case. I see no reason to bother further with any measure of subtlety. We shall simply surround them completely and kill them.'

He was upset, truly disappointed. This was not at all how he liked to do things. He would prefer to handle this with the absolute minimum of violence. He would have liked not to hurt anyone he didn't have to. A body count of one would have been perfectly optimal. He should have let the poor lad die peacefully. If only he had just given up the Presence. It would have been a simple Lost body and it would all be done, and now they all had to die. He opened up a communication channel to Ursas. 'Have one of our people caught with the information by the Lost, and make sure it gets back to them. If that doesn't work feel free to call the Wardog and insist that she'll be there. Then give her the time and place of the ritual and inform her of what this is for. They will walk into the trap and this will be over.'

'Are you going to be all right?' Kate looked at him again, sitting in her tree with her Presence on her lap. He'd come to really enjoy showing up in this place.
'Yeah sure,' he nodded. 'Unless I die or kill people which is absolutely going to happen and other people are absolutely going to die if I don't. So I pick the lesser of the two evils.' He gave her a wry smile. 'I guess that's pretty much what I've been doing the whole time since we met, huh?' He didn't want to make a joke out of it, but he didn't know how to approach it. 'I think that might be the best way to handle this whole new world of mine.'

'You could have–' she interjected and he raised one hand and looked at her for a long moment.

'Can you just, not, please?' He didn't want to sound rude, but he didn't want to hear it. 'There's no room in my brain for second guessing and contradictions right now. I don't want to look back at some vital moment. If after this you want to convince me again to bail out and leave all of this behind I will be one hundred percent open to any and all arguments you may care to make. Right now, I need to be thinking about what I'm doing next not whether or not I should be doing it.'

'Fine.' She smiled at him but there was something that flashed across her face. 'I'm just worried about you.'

'I understand.' He reached out one hand and she took it from her tree. 'I really do.'

'But I think if anyone can do it you can.' He almost smiled for a second there.

'Why would you ever think that?'

'You seem like the type.' The response was quick and simple. 'You're quick, clever and you have an eye for opportunities. I can't guarantee you'll win, or even survive, but I've seen more of the world than most people ever do from my moments between moments and I truly believe that you'll know what to do. You'll be able to do the right thing when the right time comes. Things really will unfold as they should.' she placed her hands on the sides of his head, her eyes seeming to burn into his even behind the blindfold. 'Which is not to say we don't give our level best. We take action, we have to take action, but at the end of the day if it's meant to be it will be.' She released him and the intensity faded from her manner.

'I've heard that a lot,' he admitted. 'About almost

every facet of my life but talking to you I actually think you believe it. Which is pretty significant. I never heard anyone say that with any real intent behind it. Any real,' he shrugged and shook his head, 'faith, I guess? Is that the word?'

'I suppose you could call it faith, yes,' she nodded. 'True faith. True belief, the likes of which is short and limited in this world.'

'And where did you get this faith of yours?'

'From watching the world.' She smiled. 'From my moments between moments.'

'Doesn't that mean the Legion's going to beat us? I mean you joined them. You must think they should, or at least want them to.'

'That is a big assumption to make,' she noted. 'I may not want them to lose, but I certainly don't want them to win.'

'I'm not sure what that means.' She took a moment to collect herself before she responded.

'Well, I know that there are a number of things you don't see or understand yet.' She could see him rise a little. 'That's not a criticism, or at least if it is, it wasn't meant as one. Even if you were the smartest person on Earth you still wouldn't be able to understand because you haven't been in this world long enough. So, suffice to say, there are more things in this world than the Legion and the Lost. Those are the distinctions we put upon ourselves, or that the creatures from beyond have put upon us. Right or wrong these are the limits we have to abide by.' She shrugged. 'But if a limit can be imposed, it can be broken and I see no reason not to at least attempt to break this one.' She shook her head and waved her hand at him. 'But you don't have the time or the attention to put up with my preaching so I'll give you the details as to the bigger picture some other time.' She jumped down and gave him a quick hug. 'Suffice to say, if it matters at all, I absolutely believe you can do this.'

'Thanks.' He hugged her back. He found it meant more than it probably should. It wasn't like he'd known her long. Still, she seemed to know so much, know things most people didn't, so it really might matter how much she believed.

'And now our moment is over.' She kissed his cheek. 'Goodbye.'

It was a few days later and the entire group, such as it was, were positioned around a table. Around them were members of the armoured Omega Brotherhood who were allowing them to use one of their safe houses for preparation. Wraither was the centre of attention, recounting her recent call and appointment with Ursas. As soon as she finished Adam looked around the room.

'So.' Xavier looked around, nodding at each of his allies individually. 'So, who thinks it's a trap? Trap, trap, trap, trap?'

'Trap,' Pan nodded. 'There's no doubt that this is a trap but the question is can we afford not to spring it? I mean if the ritual's not taking place that's one thing but if it's taking place and they're just ready for us then we still have to go in there.'

'It makes sense that it would be.' Adam was looking at his hands, memories had started coming back from his time with the enemy. 'They talked about needing the body of the one of the Lost. I was in the room while they were running their mouths. They have to kill one of us for the ritual to go off.'

'Shit.' Pan looked at Xavier. 'That means we can't even lose one of us without risking the King coming out.'

'We can't think about that.' Xavier's voice was a cheerful singsong. 'We can't weight ourselves down with any more problems. If one of us dies, one of us dies. We just have to break their toys badly enough before that happens.'

'All right.' Adam raised his hands. 'Let's focus on what matters. We know where we are and where we have to be. Take your time, get all the power you can. We've got a few days so if any of you have any last-minute plans, tricks or edges get them ready. I'll go check out the site, do a stakeout or whatever. Let me know when Annabelle gets back.'

'Why would you go? How is this your job?'

'Expendability.' He shrugged like it didn't matter. 'Unless any of you have any particular abilities in stealth, none of us are better than any of the others and if you can afford to walk into the fight without one of us it's me.'

'That's,' Xavier looked at him, 'something I would say.'

'And I'm going to take a moment to be both frightened and traumatised by the fact you said that when we're done here. For now though, this works.'

'It does,' Wraither nodded. 'And I'll head with you. I'll wait a couple of blocks away and if you decide to go in I'll come with you for tracking reasons. Besides, you'll need someone to pull your pretty ass out of the fire if you screw up.'

'All right,' he nodded. 'We'll go tomorrow morning.'

'And in the meantime?'

'I need to sleep.' He got up. 'It does me no good to be tired doing something risky.'

The two spent the day performing a pretty basic stakeout, hanging out in a café across the street and occasionally doing laps of the block to be sure they weren't missing anything. Wraither had traded out her white dress for a grey hoodie and pants and the two of them wasted an entire day watching the area. At first the two took care not to be seen together but eventually Wraither got bored and sat down with him. The two of them chatted the day away and Adam found out some interesting things about the young woman, her issues and her lifestyle. Watching a condemned set of storefronts was about as boring as it was easy. Very few people went into the area, a few local teenagers spent an hour or so in the burned-out parking lot drinking beer and smoking weed but they didn't exactly fit the Legion aesthetic. Adam didn't want to go inside yet, just in case someone was watching it other than them.

Eventually the two of them gave up and went home, only to come back a little over an hour later with Adam all in black, his bright neon smile turning a dull blackish green. With a few quiet steps, he reached out and gently cut open the padlock that was the only thing on the door before he shoved it open. He kept himself low, Wraither moving in behind him and securing the area. The walls between the stores had been knocked out, leaving space for the ritual to take place. It was a big area.

'Any idea what I'm looking for?' he questioned Wraither, though he knew it wasn't much more experienced than he was.

'Any sign of preparation you can discretely screw with,' it responded. 'Anything you can break or ruin, anyone you can take out of the equation early. Even just mapping out the lay of the land for where an actual fight will take place.'

The place looked open and abandoned but he kept his claws out just in case. There were a few vantage points, construction equipment that had been left behind but if there was going to be magic done here it was a good place for quiet action. As the green overtook his eyes he saw the environment proper.

The feature that dominated the floor was a series of dozens of interconnected symbols and circles. Each circle intersected with at least one other and every circle was full of strange geometric symbols he couldn't begin to understand. There were a series of windows running around the top of the walls and what looked a lot like industrial equipment from a nightmare held a bunch of strange items. Some were stones that glowed softly and malevolently, some were just junk and others honestly looked like body parts floating in jars. Adam lashed out at the equipment, trying to find something to break but as the eyes focused he saw a strange hovering shied covering every piece of the gear. He struck at it a few times, looking for a weak point, trying to cut a hole in the wall and when he eventually gave up on the easier stuff he used his claws to chip away pieces of the floor, scarring them deeply and messing with the patterns where the ground fractured. They would be fixed, Adam knew that. This guy wasn't the type to let the details go uncounted but it might slow them down a little. It might be just enough that one death wouldn't stop everything, one death wouldn't bring out the King. That was grim he realised, planning for one of his people to die.

From there he mapped out the space as best he could, noting down the terrain and anything that could be used to his advantage. He pointed out cover spots and hidden places, potential hazards in the ground someone could trip or fall over, or might slow down one of the others during the fight. He looked around, mapped everything out in his mind, took a video just to be certain and was just about to leave when Wraither spoke up from the doorway.

'We could always get them out of the way you know,' she said softly. She stood behind him, her feet bare and her face mostly covered in the hood. Her hands had long claws hanging from them.

'What do you mean?'

'Well it would be simple enough. I could track back the last person who came here and we could show up, rip a few throats out and offset the odds for the day.'

'And if he's in that fortress of his? That thirty-storey building with an army between us and him?'

'Then we'll abort it,' she shrugged. 'It's worth a try anyway. Might as well go for the hunt. It's an hour of your life, what do you have to lose?'

'Nothing unless it's an ambush.' His voice was more confident than he really felt. 'Unless it's a trap to knock two of us off before we even get started. They know we have you so they've probably planned for you.' It wasn't true. He knew it even as he said it. As much as he talked about making his peace, as much as he talked about being rid of this and doing what he had to do, he wasn't ready to kill anyone. Part of him was still hoping he didn't have to. 'Unless he's more prepared for an ambush than we thought or–'

'All right!' she cut him off, her voice ruined by her slightly extended teeth. 'Fine, you've made your point. We won't go for the hunt, I'll bide my time and get myself killed on your schedule like a good dog.' She stormed off with a foul expression. Adam took a deep breath, shook his head and headed back home. He spent a good day with his friends, took a couple of drinks and tried to make his peace.

In a couple of days, he was probably going to die.

CHAPTER FIFTEEN

'So, are you ready?' Xavier and Pan were facing each other in the café storeroom at the night of the ritual. They watched each other, they had been for the last ten minutes, silent and still, ignoring the world around them. Adam had been there too, waiting for the others. Xavier was in his usual outfit, the red coat, the top hat and crisp black pants. He was barefoot and had his blade drawn, the cane which hid it apparently discarded. Pan was shirtless, wearing ripped jeans combat boots and those hardy gloves that contained the monsters that gave him his power. He sported a brand-new tattoo, his Lost mark gone again. This one was a dragon filling his back where he had once had the map. Its massive black wings flared and a jet of flame streamed from its mouth as it roared. They stood at the centre of the room, though the space had been cleared out for the meeting and there were more than enough chairs for everyone.

'We have one last thing to do.' Pan looked at Xavier. 'If you're still up for it.'

'Always.'

Wraither had been the last to arrive, barefoot and wearing only a formless white dress that hung loosely off her. Adam guessed that this was probably her concession to modesty, remembering that she'd been naked the first time he'd seen her fight. Her body language was strange and a little disturbing. Her hands curled and uncurled, the muscles tensing and relaxing sporadically. She paced throughout the room, her feet never touching the floor for more than a couple of short seconds. Any trace of "pretty" or "cute" he'd assigned to her face was lost in the snarling, twitching expressions that chased each other across her visage. She greeted everyone with a nod, but would not speak no matter how she was engaged.

'Let's do it then.' And suddenly the two of them moved, Pan's hand snapping out and clenching around his throat even as the point of Xavier's sword quivered under the larger man's throat, a single drop of blood running down the blade. Pan started to speak, loud and clearly, his deep voice filling the room. 'Here lies Xavier, known as the Top Hat Man.' Pan looked down at him, malice sliding across his face as he tightened his grip a little. 'He died because he wasn't fast enough, wasn't skilled enough, wasn't ruthless or violent or clever enough. He died at the hands of the unworthy and because he failed the city burned at the hands of the King of the Eternal Flame. He lost to his great enemy and for his failure his order disowned him. His body was thrown in a ditch and he was not mourned because,' he smirked, 'who could possibly have ever loved him? He died alone, in shame, without dignity or grace. We will not remember him. '

'Here lies Peter Kincaid, who calls himself Pan. Known to the rest of us as the Pathfinder.' Xavier's tone was mocking, amused, but the levity didn't reach his eyes. 'Who failed his other half and died because he wasn't strong enough, wasn't powerful enough, couldn't take the heat. He couldn't take the pain and hold on to stop the death around him. He was the last to die and was forced to watch, helpless while all of those he was charged to protect fell around him. They begged him for help he could not grant. He was not mourned, because none of those who lived could accept the disappointment. They could not accept the shame of knowing that he failed them. He died in shame and helpless. He let down his friends and his sister.'

'Without the two of them the Legion was victorious.'

'And the world ended.'

With that the two of them lowered their arms and turned away from each other, walking out of the room. Pan's hand snapped out and he caught Wraither by the arm. He didn't drag her as such, he lead her gently but firmly by the arm and she followed him. As she moved she twitched even more, her teeth extending and cutting open one of her lips.

'When this starts,' Pan's voice was soft. 'Find the bitch throwing the lightning and don't stop ripping till the screaming stops.'

The noise Wraither made in response was half growl and half laugh and it would have haunted Adam for the rest of his nights if so many more disturbing things weren't about to ruin his personal trauma meter.

Adam turned to Annabelle once everyone else had

left. He couldn't help but feel like he was underdressed. All of them had come loaded for bear, even Pan, barely dressed as he was, seemed like he had come in a kind of uniform for the task, but Adam was just in his borrowed red jacket, jeans and his mask. Annabelle looked, well, for lack of a better word, colourful. In addition to her purple, red, blue, white and black hair, she was also wearing a dress that fell down to the floor. It was a hundred different colours, looking like the amazing technicolour dreamcoat as she turned. Her piercings had all been replaced with colourful ones to match the dress.

'What was that?' he asked her.

'They were killing themselves.' Annabelle's voice was serious and quiet. 'They kill themselves in their own minds before a big fight. Pan does it to remember the stakes of what he's fighting for. He can remember what he's fighting for and fight harder, do better because of it. It helps him to know that everything relies on this and the symbolic act of "dying" beforehand means he's comfortable taking the world upon his back and won't be thinking of himself. You can't be selfish if all you're protecting is your own dead body.'

'And Xavier?'

'Almost exactly the opposite,' she replied. 'If he dies before the fight begins he doesn't have to care about the world. Doesn't have to care about you or me or even himself. He focuses himself to the single pursuit of doing as much damage as possible before his body realises he's dead. He's going to kill everyone he can before he has to stop or there's no one left to kill.'

'So they do that every time?'

'Every big one,' she confirmed. 'Everyone has their own way to prepare for this kind of thing. For going into a fight with long odds of survival much less victory. Where you know it's going to be a challenge to make it out and that your own life won't and can't be your priority. It's a shitty thing to have to do and an impossible thing to be ready for but after the second or third time you start thinking of ways to adjust. Those two,' she shuddered, 'they've done it a lot, comparatively so they have their own entire routine.'

'So they're friends?' She actually laughed at that one.

'Fuck no.' She shook her head. 'Those two hate each other like poison. I think at the very least Xavier might be one of Pan's least favourite people and Xavier resents Pan more than you'll ever understand for blackmailing him with, well, whatever it is he has over him. He's been doing it for a whole decade now. You don't have to like someone to want to work with them and those two work better together than they do with anyone else, so they're stuck together. It's that or go with someone they like more and can't save the world with.'

'That's,' he shook his head, 'actually kind of sad.'

'It is a little.' Annabelle took his hand and they walked out together. 'But they have their routine worked out. They have a pattern and they know how to make the sacrifices they need to. So they make them, and honestly, at times like these they enjoy each other's company more than anyone else's. Hatred and all.' They walked out together and got into a car that looked like a dog catcher's van, in which Wraither sat in a cage.

'So how do you prepare?'

'That's one of the things about me you should ask someone else, weird as it sounds.'

Pan drove and Xavier sat in the front seat, with Annabelle and Adam sharing the back. 'It's kinda awkward to ask a person about their own coping mechanisms. Pretty soon you'll work out yours and you'll understand why.'

'I think for now I'll just trust the panther and you guys.'

'Not a bad starter as strategies go,' she admitted.

Adam kept his hand on Annabelle's for the stability she gave him. He was shaking a little and she was almost deathly still. She made chitchat and he tried to keep up but halfway through she informed him that he didn't have to respond if he didn't want to, that she just needed to be talking. Honestly, he felt like he kind of needed it too. It was good, some kind of distraction, even for only a little of his mind. Wraither sat in her little spot at the back and Adam kept his eyes firmly on the front as he heard the growling, whimpering and snapping coming from behind him. He could hear the sound of wood scratching and cloth ripping and a couple of times even the sound of something scraping against metal.

At one point Pan turned suddenly and Wraither leaped at the separating compartment, trying to claw him through the bars. He looked at her and saw a twisted face, her eyes bright red, her teeth long, pointed and jagged.

'Is she okay?'

'It's a Wardog thing.' Annabelle seemed almost grateful for the new topic. 'Before she fights, the rage and hate build up inside her. Layer by layer, piece by piece it gets more and more powerful and she puts more and more effort into holding it back until she has to let it go. Soon she won't be able to make words or understand human speech beyond simple instructions. Soon after that she'll lose the ability to walk upright, or move in anything but strange, crouching lunges, stumbling as she tries to move in a body she is no longer comfortable in. Eventually someone will unleash her on a target. She'll transform and rip whatever she's fighting to pieces, pick off enemy by enemy until she has no more enemies left. Then the rage will fade from her body and she'll pass out. She'll sleep it off for a couple of days and she'll be herself again.'

He heard the sound of screeching metal twisting this time, and a rasping, breathless attempt at a scream.

'Are you sure?'

'Yeah.' Annabelle gritted her teeth. 'You know, theoretically.'

'So, Xavier.' He leaned over to distract himself and

get his head away from Wraither's hands. 'How did those preparations you were making go?'

'Couldn't have possibly gone any better.' Xavier flashed him his usual sparkling grin. 'Trust me, this will be absolutely beautiful.'

'What do you mean?'

'Planning a perfect trap is an art as beautiful as any other. They have made a beautiful one here, they made their trap obvious and dangerous but gave us no choice to walk into it. However, to see a perfect trap and walk into it with a counter trap of your own, a method to counter and cut down the attack. That is even more beautiful still. Trust me, watch my show and be amazed.'

The condemned buildings hadn't changed all that much since Adam had come to scout it out. The strange machines were on, the ones with the blood in them were bubbling, the ones with the strange items were glowing and the Sceptre of the King was blazing at the very centre of all of the circles. The lights on the ground were glowing, filling the mundane space with an almost unearthly glow. It was all evident to human eyes now, where it had been hidden before. The strange blue light illuminated the room and everything was almost too quiet. It looked like a Western style showdown, if instead of the Wild West and their cowboys, there was all kinds of strangeness. To an observer this would have been almost funny.

On one side stood a one-armed man in a bright red

jacket, wearing a top hat with a red ribbon and carrying a long thin rapier. The cane hilt of his sword had a face on it, and it appeared to be laughing. Likewise, the man himself was shaking a little with barely held back laughter. Beside him was a young man in the exact same jacket, wearing heavy clawed gauntlets with a massive, psychotic, neon green grin shining off his face mask, his long, black hair falling loosely around his face. He almost seemed to be laughing as well, his shoulders shaking as if he were in on an aspect of the joke the man in red was struggling not to laugh at. On his other side was a large bare-chested man covered in tattoos. He had a large black and green mohawk haircut and the black gloves he wore seemed to be glowing a soft purple. Standing to his far side was a woman in a brightly coloured dress with multi-coloured hair, who spun her hands quickly and steadily in a pattern.

At the bare-chested man's feet, crouched a naked woman, shaking and shuddering, her hair now half black and half white, the white quickly swallowing the black.

Standing across from them stood a much larger group, illuminated by the blue, flickering light. In its front line was a man in a white suit that cost more than most families made in years. A neutral face mask was in his hand, leaving his horrifically burned face exposed. On his left was a man in a shabby brown suit, his greasy hair hanging on his face. His yellowed fingernails were claw long and he leaned forward as if aching to run at the other group. On the other side was a young, pale skinned woman with shining white hair, wearing what looked like a wedding dress. Surrounding both of her hands were balls of blue and white lightning. Standing a few steps away from them was a massive hulk of humanity concealed entirely by a giant, hooded cloak.

Behind the group were dozens of faceless black and white creatures, their limbs twisting and deforming in the wind.

'You came.' The Legate's voice was toneless and flat with no emotion or expression. It sounded almost dull. 'As I knew you would, as I knew you had to no matter how unwise it is.' He stepped out ahead of the group, spreading his hands wide. 'You cannot begin to imagine how far beyond hope you are. How little chance you have for survival.' He turned to his enforcers. 'You are all going to die.'

'Nah, I don't know,' Pan shrugged, seeming casual. 'Thundercunt over there isn't much in the way of a fighter, we learned that last time, and I always heard you were a pussy.'

'Pacifist,' the bored voice replied.

'I know what I said, pussy.'

'Even were those things exactly as you said them that leaves us with half a Blank Faced Legion, Ursas and the King's Man, one of whom successfully killed each and every one of you and cost your finest warrior an arm. An arm I see he has thus far not recovered. No two of you can defeat even one of my men. Even without my Legion and the Lady Raiden you would have no hope. We have such things prepared for you, things that will drive your bloodied and broken bodies screaming and begging before my King. Why are you laughing?' His monotone finally broke, a snapping bark of sudden rage directed at Xavier and Adam, who was now the Laughing Man in more than just name.

'Well I don't know about him,' Xavier shook and shuddered, leaning hard on his sword and barely managing to keep his balance. 'But I'm laughing because I have something up my sleeve that amuses me.'

'And I'm mostly laughing because he is,' Adam admitted. 'He's assured me that I get to see your face as the rug slips out from under you and I'm really looking forward to that.'

'What do you mean, you ridiculous children?' the Legate's twisted face scowled.

'Little Bear?' came the Top Hat Man's voice, gentle, like he was talking to a sleeping child. 'It's time to wake up now.' And then he stepped back, his laughter starting up again.

They waited for a moment and nothing happened.

'What on Earth are you–'

'Shhhhhhh.' The Top Hat man raised one hand.

'Whatever this plan of yours was, it has obviously not–'

'Hey,' the Laughing man gave him a joking scolding. 'The man said shhh, that's not shushing, that's talking. Talking is the opposite of shushing.'

'How dare you address me with such–'

'Shhh.' The Top Hat Man's smile was as wide as the one on his compatriot's mask. 'I'm trying to hear something.'

'And what,' his composure was thoroughly broken, his face a mask of rage, his voice raising to a scream, 'are you listening for?'

'The sound of the other shoe dropping,' he grinned. 'It should be coming any minute now.'

Sure enough a couple of moments later Ursas started to scream.

The group's attention was suddenly drawn to the same place, friend and foe alike, as the brown suited man started to shake and shudder. His hands went to his throat and he began to convulse, screaming in pain and horror as his body began to twist. He staggered into a few of the Blank Legionnaires and started ripping them apart with his claws. He lashed out without even noticing he was doing it. For a long moment he lay completely still and then he shook one more time and his body ripped apart. His skin cracked open and fell apart like the discarded chrysalis of a bug. There was no blood, no gore, just the pieces of Ursas falling to the ground to show what lay inside.

'That's...' Adam's laughter came harder than ever. 'That's the guy from my vision! The one in the hoodie!'

'Yes indeed.' Xavier patted him on the shoulder.

'You were told he would arrive when he was needed. And now seems like the moment. Now, Soldier.' He turned to Pan. 'Shall we?'

'We shall Gent.' Pan cracked his neck and began to glow with black fire. His muscles doubled and tripled in size as he walked. 'We shall indeed.' The two of them advanced on the man in the hood. The man tossed off the coat and revealed the King's Man Adam knew far better than he would have liked to, his tattoos dancing on his skin.

The man in the hoodie launched himself immediately into the lines of Blanks, slicing a few of them deeply before the rest could even begin to realise what was going on. He vanished into the crowd of limbs and weapons, emerging occasionally in a coat of sludge or blood before running off again.

'Wraither,' Adam looked at the Wardog who was crouched on the floor staring at her own hands. 'Ummm, guys, how do we make her do things? Do I just yell attack or go or–'

Before he had even finished the word attack Wraither let out a roar and leaped across no man's land, shifting her shape from twitching naked woman to giant, white wolf in mid-air and hurling herself at her chosen opponent.

'Okay.' He nodded and engaged his eyes to pick where he'd be some use. 'That did the job.'

Xavier and Pan were squaring off with the King's Man. Pan was covering Xavier's bad side and the strategy wasn't bad. Xavier kept the King's Man at bay with his sword and gave Pan the chance to rush in and hit the big Russian hard enough to rock him back. While he was rocked Xavier would alternate between pressing the attack and slipping out to cut down a Blank or two They worked together; they bobbed and weaved, duck and dove. They were fast, they were talented and they were cohesive, but they were, for all of their magic and power, just people and the King's Man was a monster. They struck him ten times for every one he landed but every idle swipe spent Xavier sprawling, every grazing punch drove Pan to his knees. They struck him, even hurt him but they didn't wound him.

Wraither jumped and danced around the Lady Raiden, who lashed out with lightning bolts to strike or manoeuvre her. Wraither was always a couple of steps ahead of the blasts but she was being held a few paces at bay. Lady Ray held a small ring around herself in safety.

The Laughing One tightened Adam's view and he began to wade into the crowd of Legionnaires. They lashed out with long ranging limbs and fast seemingly random movements, clubs and blades and lashing whips. But they weren't attacking him at random, not really. These creatures were inherently orderly, they were moving in a pattern and once he could comprehend it the world became all too simple.

'It's all about timing,' he realised.

'Well, yes,' the creature commented. 'Without the right timing, your jokes will fall flat.' Adam began to move, breaking into a sprint. He didn't break his stride, didn't stop moving or shift his stance as he drove his claws through a crack in one's thick head. As a tendril lashed for his head he ducked a few inches and didn't slow his advance. He sliced at the limb's base and watched as it separated, then turned to swipe another one in two. He rolled to the side and tagged two more in the legs, avoiding the massive sledge-like blows.

He pulled himself clear for a second and looked around, noticing a black spiked one rumbling toward him. He ran at it, jumped off its arm, then its head and then into a crowd of creatures who had surrounded Annabelle. He landed on one and crushed it with his weight, slamming the claws down to make sure, then lunged into the group. He lost himself for a moment in the middle of the fight, his consciousness dissolving into a flurry of limbs and fluid and pain and movement, in the dance dictated by the rhythm of combat and war. He could hear laughter, high pitched and maniacal, ringing in his ears. It took him a minute of wondering to realise that it was coming from his own mouth. He was covered in fluids of varying colours and foul odours and struggling for breath, pain running across his back from a source he didn't remember and in spite of himself he was laughing.

'You think you have won?' the Legate roared, tears running down his battered face. He was holding the sceptre in one hand, raising it above his head. 'You think your petty tricks can defeat me? You have no idea who I am! You have no idea what I can do! Now you shall witness my true power!' Adam looked at him for a moment as he raved. The twenty or so Blanks that were still alive had all pulled back from the three Lost they had been fighting. The hooded man was bleeding from his side, one hand holding the wound closed. In the other there was a long, evil looking, black knife. He looked up at Adam and smiled shyly, nodding to indicate that he was all right.

Annabelle had one arm wrapped in spider webs and was standing in one place with her eyes closed and both hands facing the ground. Dozens upon dozens of spiders were running in torrents out of her body, as well as out of the bodies of the dead Blanks around her. She was wavering a little, shaking, a head wound the mask told him but the creatures seemed to be backing off. Good, that would give her a few seconds to regain her focus.

Then Adam saw what they were doing. The creatures had piled themselves around the Legate and were stacking themselves on top of each other. The empty black and white creatures dropped themselves onto a pile, all seeming to collapse and deflate as soon as they landed.

'Stop them!' Annabelle yelled and Adam turned to run toward the creatures. Something crunched and he stumbled a little, then looked down. Was that his leg? Legs weren't usually shaped like that.

'I need you to stop thinking,' the Laughing One's voice danced in his head. 'I need you to be calm, focus and try to see the funny side or I can't work with you.'

'What the fuck is funny about any of this?' he screamed. 'There is a bone sticking out of my leg!'

'A month ago you were living a normal life and wishing something interesting would happen to you. Now you're probably going to die beside a spider clown and a man you've never met, at the hands of a monster made of enchanted corpses. Oh, and you have a crush on the spider clown.'

'Okay then,' he muttered. 'That is a little funny, and he could feel laughter starting to build in his chest again. They were too late, but that was okay, of course they were too late. If they didn't get to see the monster, then there wouldn't be any real stakes to the joke. That wouldn't be funny at all.

The Laughing Man heard a bolt of lightning behind him and he ducked, turned sharply on the leg that was now leg shaped again and away from the pile of creatures to see the Lady Ray in her silly wedding dress throwing lightning at him. Wraither lay at her feet, he realised with a little rage bubbling in his chest. She had been pleasant to him and now she was hurt. That wasn't funny at all, he'd have to do something about that. The creature threw a lightning bolt at him and he ducked out of its path, walking toward the Lady with indefatigable purpose. He couldn't dodge lightning, the idea was nonsense, but the Lady moved with flourishes that she no doubt thought where elegant. Paired with that absurd dress of hers she might as well have been calling in advance to tell him where the next bolt was coming from. She went low and he swerved around it, she struck for the face and he heard his hair crackle as he barely moved his head. She drew back and swung a wide arc of lightning at him and he rolled beneath it.

It would have been so easy if that had been reality, but she suddenly ditched the showmanship and varied up her routine, striking a sharp low underhand shot with no flourish at all. She hit him square in the belly and pushed her lightning into him, holding a solid beam. He was not the Soldier, he did not have that endurance. What barely slowed that man down drove this one to his hands and knees. She raised her other hand, a bright ball of lightning forming in a grand gesture he was far too busy being a shaking paralysed wreck to dodge. In spite of all of that, something was still funny.

'Any last words,' she asked him, pure malicious proud hatred upon her face.

'Don't look down,' he replied, his eyes wide open. She scoffed at him, she knew that trick, of course she knew that trick, everyone knew that trick.

What happened next wasn't a new joke, the "there really is someone behind you like I said" trick was kind of a classic. But the Laughing Man liked to think that perhaps the fact that the "thing behind you" was an angry, magic wolf lent some fresh flavour to it. Also, it was technically beneath not behind, though admittedly that was less significant. Wraither ripped at the Lady Ray's legs, launching up with tooth and claw at her groin and the girl screamed, trying to shoot the Wardog and rendered unable. She couldn't shoot straight down, she was limited by her ridiculous outfit. When the screaming stopped the Laughing Man took a moment to adjust to the shock of his situation. The pain leeched quickly out of his body as he recovered and climbed to his feet, smelling even worse now the rotting foulness was cooked on his skin. He took a moment to breathe and then turned back to Annabelle.

'Wow,' he said to no one in particular and the world in general. 'You people are not giving me a minute to breathe today, are you?'

The creature had to be summoned outside because it's head would go through the roof rather than under it. It had a strange, swirling, black and white pattern on its skin and its arms twisted and bent at odd angles. Its arms were massive, each hand big enough to wrap around a full-grown man. Its eyes were badly drawn diamonds and its mouth was a strange, gaping tear in its face. It had long fingers and was suspended from the ground by four lanky legs, with four arms that looked more or less like a human thrashing around.

All four of its legs were already covered in spiders, hundreds of the crawling creatures making their way up the abomination, biting and biting and biting. Black veins of corruption were spreading up its body but Adam quickly saw they were not crawling nearly fast enough. One of its hands was wrapped around

Annabelle, and the only thing keeping it from crushing her was the giant monster's confusion about what the little things were that were biting it and why there was a strange thing with a grey hood hanging off its face and stabbing it with a knife over and over. It was trying to brush the creatures off itself, frustrated by the fact that they were now on its hands.

'Xavier, I need your help!' He looked at the creature. He couldn't climb it, there were too many spiders on its legs and without even knowing how, he'd figured out exactly how he was going to get up there.

'I am just slightly busy right now!' the voice called out. Adam looked over at the Gentleman. The two of them had the King's Man on the back foot and retreating. Xavier was probing him with long vicious strikes, slamming them into him over and over and finally managing to make him bleed. He was defending himself from Pan's fists but had to let Xavier through. 'Perhaps if I had, say for example, two arms I could see to your needs!'

'If you don't do the hat trick right now Annabelle is going to die! So help me!'

'Get it done!' Pan slammed into the King's Man and bore him to the ground. Xavier turned away, tossed his sword into the air, grabbed his hat and threw it across the room to Adam. He caught the sword at the same time Adam caught the hat. Pan thudded into the wall as Xavier re-joined the fight.

'That's the best I have for you!' he snapped. 'Don't

throw the hat, let the hat throw you!'

Adam held the hat in front of him for a long moment, staring at the garment intently. He had no idea how to work this thing, no way of even guessing what the hell Xavier meant by don't throw it. He looked at the hat. How was it supposed to throw him? It was a fucking hat, hats didn't have arms. He took a tight hold of it, closed his eyes and decided to just go with his instincts. He didn't have any idea of what he was going to do so he drew himself back, spun in a circle and swung the hat, hurling it but not letting it go. Sure enough, the hat worked as advertised, launching him through the air toward the giant beast. Adam felt himself fly and his eyes tightened on the creature. The world around him seemed to slow down and he laughed that maniac laugh again as he realised he'd put all his thought into flying with the hat and none of it into what he was going to do once he landed.

'What the fuck do I do?' he asked the Laughing One. 'What do I do?'

'You can do this,' the voice was soft and reassuring. 'Come on, you know this joke, you've seen how it happens and how it plays out if you do it right. All we have to do is connect to the punchline.' He didn't give in to the Presence. He felt like he should have, like he needed to give up and just let it take control but that wasn't how to get this done. He understood after a couple of seconds that this wasn't the kind of thing you gave up and let someone else handle. The world began to speed up again and he let out that maniac laugh one more time. Of course he knew how to do this. All he had to do was wait until it felt just a little bit too late. Just as he swore he'd overshot it he dropped off the hat. The green began to zone in but he didn't need it this time. He knew what he had to do now.

He felt himself slamming into the arm and pinned his claws into the creature's flesh, letting them keep him attached even as the wind drove out of his belly. He didn't have time to lose control, it would only be a few seconds before the creature got its hands up to hit him.

He crawled across the arm as fast as he could toward the hand. It was like a dissection, it was bloody and brutal but sometimes good comedy had to get a little dark. He needed to get Annabelle clear before it decided to give up and just crush her. He got up, took the claws out and ran as he felt the giant hand begin to come down on top of him.

He threw himself forward and felt the shockwave run up his body from the impact. He tumbled to the side and almost fell off, clawing at the arm to be able to hold on. He dug them as deep as he could into the creature's wrist as he crawled along it, swinging from hand to hand. Dig in, jump, dig in, release, jump, dig in, release, just keep going. The creature was shaking its arm trying to get rid of him and it got close to succeeding a good, half dozen times but he managed to barely hold on. He felt one of his claws slip out to hang loose and swung his arm once, twice, three times and finally managed to dig the other hand back in. He returned to his pattern, keeping his focus tight and swinging from spot to spot. Just gotta keep him busy until he made it to the hand.

Finally he was there, hanging off the creature's finger, looking up at Annabelle held prisoner in the gigantic hand. He saw one weak point and one only, the base of the creature's thumb. He struck out at it, twisting his arm to land perfectly and hack through the joint. A few quick cuts and the digit, which was about the width of his torso, finally slipped and fell from the hand. He saw Annabelle unfurl her spider web whips and begin to rappel her way to the ground. While she fell, he climbed.

He hacked at the creature's tendons, ripping off fingers as he made his way across the palm. He couldn't have the thing grabbing him again. He climbed up the wrist and started to run again, a sprawling, twisting, stumbling run. Sometimes he was laying down and crawling claw by claw, others he was on a flat plane sprinting up the monster and he felt like things were taking a lot longer than they should have, but he had his target. Go for the throat. Anything living has a neck and a groin.

Apparently the creature had finally started thinking strategically, as it put one of its other hands on its arm and quickly brushed down, like it was knocking off a bug. He tried to jump over it but it turned its hand and swatted him from its body. He tumbled through the air and landed on a pile of debris, coughing and hacking as all the air was driven out of his lungs. He pressed his hands against his ribs as he choked and tried to breathe through lungs that could no longer take in air. He struggled, tried to be calm and took shallow breaths as he attempted to focus. As he felt himself heal he started to breathe deeper and deeper until he could actually move again. He had to get to his feet again, had to get moving again. His body screamed at him that it couldn't move but it had to, he had to. He couldn't feel any pain in his midsection, but he could guess it was probably the Presence covering for him.

'How am I?' he asked the creature in its head as he tried to square off again, looking up at the creature as the man with the knife and Annabelle kept it busy.

'A couple of your ribs are shattered,' it informed him. 'A few breaks and I think everything in your entire body is bruised but I can hold you together until this is over. We don't have time to focus on your injuries. We need opportunities.'

'All right.' He looked around and checked the area, clearing his head. The Lady Raiden was struggling to put up her final resistance but it was plain to see she was dying. Lightning was flying past Wraither's head but where she was once holding her area she was now slowly but steadily being killed. No time to worry about that. The Gentleman and the Soldier were losing, not losing badly but losing. They were forced back, hurt and damaged. No side was fine, every combatant was suffering and this fight would not last much longer.

Last and not least he saw what was left, the one giant creature and the three of the Lost who remained. They had fallen or climbed down onto the ground. The hooded man was no longer wearing his hood and his face and clothes were matted with blood. As Adam watched he brushed the blood from his face with one sleeve and threw himself back into the fight. The creature's legs were faltering and stumbling as thousands upon thousands of spider bites ran up it. The Carnival Queen, Annabelle her name was Annabelle. Her colourful clothing was shredded and ripped and her body was failing her but she didn't hesitate to re-join the fight. She apparently had no more spiders within her but her long whips were wrapped time and again around her arms. What was she planning to do, he could not be sure.

The hooded man was spinning his knife in his hand again, stepping around the creature's massive swipe and raising one hand to his throat. He jumped back and faced the creature, Annabelle moving beside him.

'Laughing Man.' The voice was soft, ringing in his ear although the man was apparently only mouthing the words. 'The two of us are going to distract the creature. While it is focused on us, go for the legs, hack them open and take away the thing's mobility. The less it moves the more damage we can do.'

The hooded man who had seemed so quiet and

reserved let out a massive roar and charged the creature. It struck down with the stump of a hand it had left on one arm but missed by the smallest margin. He jumped to the side and stabbed the thing, the knife multiplying itself in his hand. It lashed out at him and as he ducked low. To keep its focus the Carnival Queen tossed what was left of her colourful dress. The garment was weighted by some heavy object placed in its sides and attached to the long webs she had assembled. The webs stuck to the creature's face and the dress slipped over its eyes, the colours blocking its sight perfectly. It reached up to clear the blockage and Adam couldn't help but laugh as he moved in. Using a dress as a weapon, now that had ridiculousness, slapstick and nudity. That was good comedy.

He sped in toward the legs and his eyes zeroed in on the weakest points, striking for them with one slash of each set of his claws. No sooner was he between the legs than he turned again and began striking. Each time he threaded through the legs, striking the weak points. Strike and run, strike and run, strike and run, never stay in one place, never focus on one limb.

It wasn't a clever creature but even a stupid animal knows when it's being attacked. He varied and changed up his patterns, never striking in the same way twice. Even after it cleared its eyes its sheer size meant it couldn't see beneath it so it was reduced to striking down blindly with its legs. It slammed and stomped at him with no hope of hitting, even for all of its size it was slow and stupid. The diseased and damaged legs began to crack and weaken from the slashes and stomping. It leaked black slime and arachnids from the limbs as he struck at them. Finally, he squared off with it one more time, taking a couple of deep breaths and a moment to think behind the creature.

'Is it hurt enough?' he asked the panther.

'Not a fucking clue,' it admitted. 'I say we give it a try!' He moved between the legs and waited until one of them struck down at him, then he stuck. He slashed and stabbed with the claws, burrowing into the joint before it could rise. He danced around the limb and next time it slammed down the joint buckled and shattered under the creature's weight. It began to stumble and fall, teetering to regain its footing.

As he moved for the next leg the creature revealed that it was smarter than he thought it was, or at least willing to hurt itself to kill him. The Blank Faced monster leaped, landing hard on the ground and shattering its own legs, collapsing with the intent of landing on him as he ran. He felt the body begin to collapse and sprinted for his life to get out from under it. He leaped with all of his strength and tried to slide his way out from under the falling body but it was too little too late. The creature's weight fell down upon his legs and he screamed with a pain the mask couldn't block out for him.

The other two scrambled to grab him, their arms wrapped around each of his, pulling at him as best they could. They yanked until he felt pain running up his arms to his shoulders but he could feel the creature's bulk giving way. The giant fist came down just where the Laughing Man would have been had he not come free at the last moment, which just happened to clip where the Spinning Sister was as she was dragging him away. She was pitched back and lay worryingly, terrifyingly still. As he watched her he felt an impact on the back of his head, his unnamed ally had stuck him.

'No time to worry.' The voice was soft and cold. 'We can help her once we've killed the monster.' The two of them rushed in, each going to one side. As the creature lashed out at the Laughing Man he dove to the side and the hooded man slammed the knife into the hand, He half climbed onto the limb and as it tried to lift it the small man held it down with a surprising strength. The Laughing Man started to move to his objective as the giant creature reached down with its other arms to fight the hooded man, who bobbed and weaved between digits far bigger than his entire size, leaving wicked gashes across the skin. They weren't deep wounds, but it was enough until he was struck in the back with a bolt of lightning. The last desperate death curse of the dying Lady Raiden. He pitched and rolled and then he too lay still.

These were all things the Laughing Man noticed out of the corner of his eye as he ran up the shoulder to the creature's head. He slammed one claw just below the creature's ear, sticking it deep into the hollow then jumped down. He rode it by the claws of his hand as he slashed down, riding through the flesh like he was swinging from a rope. He swung with his whole body, using the momentum to bring himself around until he was most of the way through the neck. He couldn't make it all the way to the other shoulder, so he just let himself fall.

The creature reached up with all four hands, locking them over its throat, trying to hold the blood in. It was a surprisingly human gesture for such a strange thing. He couldn't stop now, that might kill it but it might not. He didn't have much strength left, but he had enough, he ran to the creature's back and began pulling his way up its back, climbing it hand over hand like a man scaling a rock wall.

By the time he made it to the top his arms were aching through the mask's dulling effect and his legs were numb and hanging limp below him, but he made it to the back of the creature's neck. He pulled himself up to lay between the shoulders and began to slash the creature.

'Not like that.' The voice was gentle, guiding. 'Like this.' And with the creature's help he began to burrow, digging down through flesh with his clawed hands at an almost frenzied pace. He ripped through it, that twisted laughter coming again. This time he knew nothing about it was funny. This was laughing to keep from crying, from throwing up, from being sick and scared and angry and a thousand other things too primal to have names for. Now he knew one of the last truths of the Laughing One: sometimes you laughed because that was all there was left to do. He ripped and tore until he felt something that felt like bone, and then further again, until the body collapsed. By the end of it he was laying flat on the ground through this creature's throat. Apparently nothing could survive a hole that goes through the spine and out the other side.

As the creature fell, the Laughing Man withdrew himself, climbed out of it and looked around for the Legate. The humour was gone, no more laughter, not even the desperate one. The cowardly, little fuck was running, ducking out of the back in the hopes his King would make his own way out. Suddenly there was no Laughing Man, just Adam again and nothing about this was funny. He pitched himself forward on damaged legs, moving with fast jerking motions as he ran at the burned man. When it became plain the Legate would make it away Adam did the one thing he could do. He reached out and grasped the sceptre of Eternal Flame. Pain like nothing he had ever felt ripped up his arm but he pressed the claws against the jewel.

'Don't ask me how I know this,' he bellowed. 'But if you leave, I'll be able to destroy this. So,' he tossed it on the ground in front of him, 'come get it you Michael Myer's looking motherfucker.' Mockery, it wasn't much but it was all he had left. A shitty cheap joke, but it worked.

The Legate descended on him, the mask now a white, blazing sword in his hands as he lunged for the sceptre. He'd never been in a fight before Adam realised. He knew how to make the sword, but not how to use it. Even with one working leg and pain running up every part of his body Adam could take him. He caught the blade between the claws of one gauntlet and heard it crack and break, but not before he twisted his hand and ripped the sword clear of his damaged glove. He tossed it behind him and tackled the Legate, bearing the suited man down. He stuck him, once, twice, three times and threw the sceptre back away from them all.

'Where the fuck do you think you're going?' Pan's voice was ragged and rasping and Adam held the claws at the one-time authority figure's throat as he looked over his shoulder. He saw the King's Man turning from them, one fist raised. 'You runnin' out on our little rumble?'

'This is over.' The Kings Man didn't even sound upset. More bored than anything, like something he had vaguely hoped would happen had failed to coalesce rather than losing his entire reason for being. He bent and picked up his coat. 'You have won. You will kill the Legate and you have already killed the Lady Raiden. The ritual is partially dispersed but not completely. If one of you dies in this combat there is still a chance you will summon my King. I do not believe this would be the case. In order for me to summon the King I will have to defeat you all, which I believe I would fail at. You may fight me, you may even attempt to kill me if you wish, but at least two of you will die in that attempt and if I can summon my King even at the cost of my own life I will have no choice but to try.' He pulled the hood up over his head. 'Or you can allow me to leave and I, in my turn, will leave.'

'Option one!' Pan took a step forward and Xavier put the tip of his sword to the back of his ally's neck.

'That's enough.' The voice was casual and cheerful as ever. 'This is done, this is over and I will not risk raising the King of the Eternal Flame because you can't handle a loss. Especially since you didn't actually lose anywhere but in your own ape mind.'

'What are you talking about. Get off me.'

'That line we were talking about before?' Xavier's jacket was shredded, he was bleeding from the chest and face, but his hat was once again balanced perfectly. 'The one where the blackmail is no longer worth it? Where even losing everything your blackmailer can take from you isn't worth listening and following orders anymore? This is it. You just hit it.'

'Get out of here.' Pan's voice was hollow and the hooded man turned and walked out, not even picking up his pace. The three of them who were still upright looked at one another for a long moment.

'Now,' Xavier cleared his throat. 'Peter, pick up the Sister. Laughing Man, finish killing the Legate and we can all go home happy.'

Adam was holding the man, looking at him, the burned and damaged face in front of him twisted with hatred. He hadn't heard the whimpering, the rambling, the complete loss of any kind of composure that had occurred but frankly that didn't interest him all that much. Crying, screaming, those were normal things people did when their life ambition was screwed and they were about to die. Adam raised his claws up to kill the guy, to end his first actual, human life, to kill his first person. He was a terrible human being, he'd tried to doom the world and all Adam had to do was land a punch, swing his fist and it would all be fine. He slammed his hand forward, closed his eyes and felt a crunch like cracking bone. The gauntlet had retracted his claws. He'd just punched him in the face.

'I can't do it.' He shuddered. 'I can't kill him. I'm sorry.'

'It's all right.' Xavier's voice was comforting as his arm wrapped around Adam's shoulders and pulled him up, almost hugging him. 'It's all right, you don't have to do anything. You don't have to take a life if you aren't comfortable with it.'

He was a couple of steps away when he heard a dull spluttering gurgling sound and turned around to see it. The hooded man had lifted the Legate up and was messily cutting his throat with the long, hooked, black knife. Adam stared at him for a few moments and he looked up. He was plain faced Adam realised. There was nothing strange about him except for the yellow eyes. Adam glared at him and he looked up, shrugging his shoulders as the body rolled off him and fell to the ground.

'What?' He seemed almost indignant. 'He had to die. Congrats. Your hands are clean. You didn't kill him. That meant I had to, but it's okay, I've done it before. You can still have his mask if you like.'

'That's not what I…' He took a few deep breaths and leaned on Xavier. 'I didn't want you to. I mean I… I didn't…'

'Annabelle's hurt,' Xavier reminded him. 'So is our other friend, and so are you for that matter. You need to go see Mercy. Actually now I think about it I could use a visit myself. We can discuss our actions and the ramifications of same when we are all well again. This isn't over, just get in the car and we'll get her patched up.'

He stumbled to the car. He didn't remember the drive, he didn't care to.

Chapter Sixteen

'Well that was a lot closer to what I expected out of you!'

Mercy had just finished healing Adam's injuries as only she could. His entire body was wrapped in one kind of bandage or another, patches over cuts, scrapes and abrasions, wraps around broken ribs and internal injuries. He'd been fed four or five different tonics and on both of his legs had been applied something that looked like a futuristic leg brace. She tipped him back in his chair and finished examining him.

'I must say though I'm a little impressed. You went entire weeks almost a full month between your first crippling injury and your second. Usually people only make it a matter of days. Very well done.' She smiled and glared out over the group with a judgmental look. Adam had been the second to last of all those who had been treated. Pan looked like just about everything in him had been cracked, broken or bruised but he assured them he had the endurance to hold out better than Adam could.

'Welcome to the Brisbane Lost, where you aren't a real member until the Sweet Lady Mercy is thoroughly tired of your stupid face.'

'Thanks,' Adam grunted. Mercy began to wrap Pan's arms and hands the same way she'd wrapped Adam's legs before the brace. 'So, this is a common thing?'

'Among these idiots?' Mercy extended her hand

346

to the rest of them. 'It happens now and again. They usually stumble in in ones and twos rather than the full moron combo meal. They have a knack for running headlong into trouble and getting themselves beaten bloody. Although I do credit you with bringing another new face to these hallowed halls. Now tell me, who is the latest fool?'

'Wraither.' The Wardog was speaking with a soft, wavering voice, like she was frightened to talk too loudly lest she rupture something. Her insides had been fried and shocked to hell and back during the fight and, while she had no external injuries, she had been throwing up blood in the car on the way over. Mercy had poured a dozen chemicals down her throat, but she had used all of her best healing on Annabelle. Wraither was currently occupying the bed, laying still to ensure her traumatised organs weren't agitated during the process. 'Nice to meet you.'

'I sincerely hope not to see you again.' Mercy blew her a kiss.

'Can't say likewise.' She looked Mercy over, managing to make her eyes flirty in spite of the half-broken posture. 'Got to be worth getting hurt for a view like that.'

'Please, don't.' Mercy shook her head and shuddered a little. 'I assure you I find the human body only interesting in an academic sense and you being only partly human doesn't help.' Wraither nodded a little and chuckled, then winced.

Adam turned his head and looked at the others.

Xavier was without his red coat and his body was a mess of freshly healed wounds, scratches and cuts running in every direction. His face was bandaged from where it had been shattered by the King's Man's fist but they could still see the grand smile. Annabelle wore 'hospital clothes': a pair of slacks and a shirt designed for a movie usher. She looked unhurt now, Mercy's gift healing her completely. The hooded man was in another jacket he'd borrowed from the Sage. His wounds, if he still had them, had been completely covered by his clothing. He sat hunched over himself, his face down, not looking at anyone.

'So.' Adam looked at the three other men in the room, certain Annabelle knew about as much of this as he did. 'Would one of you like to explain what the hell is going on right now?' He looked across the three of them.

'Don't ask me.' Pan looked like a boxer, albeit one who'd gone the full nine with a gorilla. His hands and arms were now taped up as was most of the rest of him. His fists had been pulp when he walked in. The consequences of repeatedly punching something a great deal harder than his own fists. 'I'm as in the dark as you are. The Gent told me that he had a plan and that he'd have to keep it secret just in case someone tried to stop him or gave the game away.'

'The phrase we're all searching for to describe the events of the day is brainwashing,' Xavier smiled. 'Using my faithful and beloved thinking cap I managed to convince our bear that he was a different bear.'

'What?'

'I suppose I should introduce myself now.' The voice was soft, mumbling, like the words had to be said but he didn't really want anyone to hear him. Throughout the day the jacket had come off a few times to reveal a young, dark skinned man with a close-cropped beard and short hair.

'I am known to most as Ursa Minor, or the Little Bear. Yes, like the constellation, it's a joke though not a particularly good one.' He smiled for about half a second before he went back to explaining.

'I am one of three bear spirits currently alive within this area. None of us are native and we're all known to pick and choose our own times to go places or hibernate. The man you know as Ursas is the Dread Bear, easily the most powerful and destructive of the three of us and one known for working with the Legion. He's also currently hibernating. Has been for a month or so but since he has hundreds of enemies he's not able to tell anyone when he intends to go underground. I have the ability to assume other people's appearance and some of their power and the more like me they are, the better my disguise is. By mixing my own magic with the stuff inside Xavier's wonderful thinking cap, I managed to convince everyone, including myself that I was the Dread Bear. Any lesser deception would have failed, for the Legate is a master in matters of the mind and the King's Man even more so. Frankly I was not entirely certain even this would fool him.'

'Yeah.' Xavier gritted his teeth and ran his hand through his hair, wincing a little. 'I am reliably informed of that particular gift. So what? You spent this entire time thinking you were someone else?'

'Every moment of it bar a few,' the Young Bear nodded. 'Except when I was called some variation of my real name. As soon as it happened I was reminded of who I was and obeyed the command I was given.'

'What do you...' he realised it at the last moment. 'Little Bear.'

'Little Bear, it's time to wake up,' Xavier joked. 'Every time anyone called him Little Bear he was forced to do whatever we told him to do afterwards. He would then rationalise it to himself as actions of the Dread Bear. Everything he did was manipulated by me, including when I woke him up.'

'Which reminds me,' the Young Bear reached into his clothes and pulled out another dagger as black as the one he used for a weapon. He muttered something and a Blank Faced Legionnaire wandered into the room. This one was a little different to the others, bearing a pair of lines on its face where the eyes should be. With a smile, the Young Bear gently inserted the knife in the eye holes and cut them open, then handed over the knife to the creature who cut itself free of the skin.

'Raven, holy shit!' Annabelle looked like she wasn't sure whether to be happy or frightened but she shot to her feet and approached him. She looked like she wanted to hug him, then retreated slowly and awkwardly back to her seat. 'Sorry, I just… thought you were dead. I mean, I thought I left you to die.'

'I took a risk and it paid off.' He spun the blade in his hand, looking at it like it was his dearest friend. 'Though it could have worked out rather badly, I admit.' He tossed it in the air and caught it. 'The Legate should have known that a Presence can only be transferred when you die or when it is willingly given up, and that the slaver's blade makes you only obey its own. If you have only one destiny when you get cut you fall to blind obedience. When I was stabbed by the blade I was both the ideal victim and the blade's owner. One of two things was going to happen, which either meant I was no longer capable of doing anything or I would only ever have to do whatever I want me to do for the rest of my life.' He slipped the blade up his sleeve. 'I think it worked out rather nicely for everyone.'

'Well a few people anyway,' Adam noted, then raised his hand to hold the conversation. 'Let's see if I got this right. You three formed a plan where you,' he pointed to Xavier, 'hypnotised you,' he pointed to the Young Bear, 'into being a sleeper agent who then enslaved you,' he pointed to Raven, 'to earn the Legate's trust and then hunt us until the moment of betrayal.'

'Yes.' They nodded as one.

'Okay, convoluted though that was, I guess I only have one question left.'

'Which is?'

'Your arm.' He pointed to Xavier's severed stump. 'You lost your arm in a fight with Ursas, which means you lost your arm in a fight with–'

'Me.' The Young Bear nodded. 'Yes. I was being observed just as you were.'

'I knew that if I were not injured, then I would not be convincing. I chose to give up my arm to win this fight.' He was smiling. How the hell was he still smiling? 'I can fight one handed well enough. It wasn't my favourite hand and perhaps, with time and luck, the other arm will be restored. And if not, well,' he shrugged again, 'there have been many one-armed warriors in the world.'

'So you just gave up one of your arms for the chance to screw over this King?'

'Should it truly give me a chance to win this fight, to hinder, injure or otherwise ruin the existence of the King of the Eternal Flame I would give a good deal more than my one limb.' His reply was like a bird chirping. 'Sorry about blaming you for the missing arm by the way.'

'Forgiven.' His voice was shaky. 'So you guys pulled a fast one on all of us?'

'I suppose a fast one was definitely pulled,' Xavier nodded. 'Though I say more that we pulled a fast one on him and we pulled it for all of you.'

'You're done.' Mercy patted Pan on the side of the head. 'Everyone get some rest here for a couple of hours, take in a couple of movies and you'll be good to go.'

'All right,' the Young Bear nodded. 'Next order of business.' The grey hooded man pulled something else out of his jacket and threw it to Adam who caught it out of mid-air. 'I mean technically we killed the guy but since you're the one who got the monster we figured you were the one who deserved the prize.'

'Except me,' Wraither raised her hand. 'I kinda wanted to keep it but I guess you can have it if everyone insists.'

'You already got one!' Pan snapped.

'I mean,' he held it, 'I already have a mask so shouldn't one of you…' He looked around them.

'No, it's only fair,' Pan nodded. 'You should take it, and it'll change shape to fit you as soon as you put it on. It's yours by right.'

'I'm totally willing to.'

'No.' Pan scowled at Wraither and she shut up.

'No.' Adam shook his head. 'I'm not okay with this. I'm not willing to accept this.' He held up the two masks, then pointed at the Young Bear. 'You killed a guy!'

'Technically as a collective we killed two guys. I mean none of us did it alone.' The Young Bear looked at Wraither. 'You did kill the Lady Ray, didn't you?'

'She is, as the French say, le dead.' Wraither nodded. 'When the inside bits were on the outside, that was the clue.'

'We killed two beings.' Xavier got up close and looked Adam in the eye. 'We killed two people who could think and feel and believed things. The things they believed were wrong and they wanted to kill a city full of people. They thought that was a sound idea. So we killed them. I'm sorry but that was necessary. There was no other way to resolve this. Now, let me pose you a question my young friend. A baby is destined to grow up to destroy the world. You know this, there is no doubt, no ambiguity, no room for change or alteration or negotiation. This baby will cause the world's end and the only chance to kill it is right now. Would you do it?'

'I...' he paused for a second, trying to figure out his answer.

'Too late.' Xavier tipped him a wink. 'While you were thinking, I just did it.'

'What?'

'In this metaphor of ours,' Xavier said. 'I already killed him while you were thinking.'

'But I'm not sure I even wanted you to.'

'Too late,' Xavier repeated. 'I did it, and now you get to hate me, blame me, dislike what I do and who I am as a person and that's fine because that's what I'm here for.' He twirled and bowed. 'And that is why I am needed. So yes, we killed a person, two people, and if the Bear hadn't I would have. We killed one in the heat of battle and one in cold blood and we would do it again in a heartbeat because frankly we need his power as much as he does and we'll abuse it.'

He thought about it for a longer moment. 'Yes, I think I can safely say we'll abuse it for better reasons though my candour compels me to admit we shall probably abuse it at least as much. Or I suppose you will, since it was you who beat him.'

'I don't want this.' He held it out. 'You take it. Someone take it!'

'Oh, just trade him for it you dim bulbs.' Annabelle spoke from her spot on her side of the room. 'I mean seriously kids, this isn't complicated. Anyone who wants it, trade him one of your own for it. It won't have any blood on it and everyone'll be happy. It's only fair.' It had been terrifying for him watching her on the way home. Apparently being hit straight on by a giant monster had broken her just about everything.

'Fair enough,' the hooded man agreed, taking off the grey coat and throwing it to Adam. He put on the white mask and at that exact second it turned into another hooded jacket. This one was nicer, white, a little mottled and as he settled it around him it became as ruined and patchy as the other one was it front of his eyes. 'Here, I make my Presence a gift to you. Put it on and you will gain its power.'

'Really? I'm supposed to just be okay with this?' He looked around at them again, feeling like the only sane man in the room. 'Be okay with watching a throat get slit?'

'You're supposed to accept that this is the reality of your situation.' Xavier's tone was bored and angry. 'Peter, I'm bored, handle this.'

'He's right,' Pan rumbled form his seat. 'Life in our world may be hard, frustrating painful and even just objectionable. For all of the amazing adventures we get there's also a lot of danger. We did the best we could today. We kept an abomination out of our city. To do that we had to kill a person. I'm sorry that makes you uncomfortable and I get that, I honestly do and I'm really glad to have the kind of person who's like that with me. If after this you want to pack up and hide from the Legion we can do that, I can help. If you don't want to be a part of this world you don't have to but that,' he pointed to the coat, 'will protect you for if things go wrong, so put it on.'

He took a deep breath and put on the jacket, pulling the hood up over his head which made it all the more confusing when the hood didn't go over his head. He felt the cloth around his feet and looked around. He wasn't wearing a hood he wasn't wearing a jumper at all. He looked down at the leather overcoat he was now wearing. 'I'll have to give you back your magic red coat,' he smiled at Xavier.

'Keep it for a backup,' Xavier shrugged. 'I would need to retailor it for the arm and I quite enjoy making new ones anyway. If things get too strange you can always put it under the other coat. It may look quite odd but it could help.'

'Thanks.' He nodded and looked at his hands. 'I can't believe we killed a–'

'Yeah, we killed a guy,' Wrather sighed and rose tenderly from her bed. 'It was war. That happens.'

'Okay,' he nodded. 'But I'm still going to need some time to be okay with this.'

'Take all you need,' Pan shrugged. 'But don't tell me you're ready until you are. I can't have you half arsing this.'

'And in the meantime,' Mercy raised one hand, 'shut up, stay still and heal.' She glared at the crowd. 'Talk amongst yourselves about anything but the war. Or better yet, watch a movie.' She left the room.

'Are you all right?' He looked around the crowd.

'Who you asking?' Wraither tried to make it to her feet then looked at the others. 'Could one of you go ask for food?'

'Start with you.'

'I got beat up and fried, but hey it only hurts when I breathe or move.' She chuckled a little and held her stomach. 'Also, I'm hungry and I would really like to take a nap, and by nap, I mean cocaine.'

'You want to take a cocaine?'

'It's an imperfect metaphor,' she scowled. 'As for my mental health, this is good for me. Another day in the life and I think I've really proved myself. It'll be good for my career.'

'I'm doing okay,' Pan shrugged. 'Third time this has happened, which doesn't exactly make it normal but I think I'm dealing,' he chuckled. 'Man that fucker turned my arms to pulp. It was a close call, but I'll recover. I'll need to talk to some people.'

'I am feeling quite triumphant,' Xavier nodded. 'Though a little disconcerted. He grew claws at one point. Peter's skin turned them aside whereas mine did not. I will have to step up my training if I hope to defeat such a formidable foe.'

'So he's coming back?'

'Undoubtedly.'

Adam chose to move on from this conversation.

'So why do you call him Peter?'

'His name is Peter,' Xavier smiled. 'I knew him when he was only a pup, small and stupid as a child rather than big and stupid as a child as he is now. His name is Peter and he thinks it's funny to call himself Pan.' Adam stopped listening while Xavier kept talking and moved to the real reason he'd asked the question.

'Just you left.' He looked at her and she got up, sauntering over to him and sitting down. Looking at her now, she looked like a normal person, maybe one of the artistic girls from the university working in a cinema to make ends meet.

'Just me left,' she smiled. 'I'm all right physically since I was the one Mercy gifted, but it gets to you, being slammed into the wall, concussed, broken. I had a broken arm, shattered face, cracked skull, broken ribs. I'll be out for a while on a mental health day. I think I need to go home, back to the carnival where my sisters can fix me up.'

'Do you need anything?'

'What could you get me at this point?' She smirked. 'No, just the company my pretty boy, just the company.' She reached out and wrapped an arm around him.

'As for me,' Raven raised one hand, 'I'm going to

go fuck off for a while and enjoy my freedom. Maybe have a drink or nine.' He started to whistle as he walked out of the room.

Xavier and the Young Bear were the first to leave, making light conversation amongst themselves as they walked out. Actually, Xavier made conversation while the Bear occasionally grunted or made some stuttering response. Xavier smiled at the rest of the group as he stood on the doorstep.

'I think this was a job well done,' he decided, stating it to the crowd in general.

'I still can't believe he thinks losing an arm makes for a job well done.' Adam looked at Pan for a long moment. 'You know him better than I do. Is he all right?'

'Would you care if he wasn't?' Pan smiled. 'Yeah, he's as close as ever he was. Look, I can't tell you why he feels how he feels but, do you remember what Xavier said to you while you were being controlled?'

'Yeah.'

'Xavier would give anything to stop the King. To him an arm is something that might be restored one day, and in exchange for stopping the King from getting his way that's more than a fair trade. He's...'

'Insane?'

Pan shook his head. 'Different. Insane doesn't do it any kind of justice. He's not just impeded. He's not just mad or unstable. He thinks on an entirely different level to the way you and I do. That's why half the time he's crazy and the other half he seems… silly.'

'That's kind of hard to understand.'

'Give it time.'

Wraither was the next one out and she said goodbye to Adam with a genuinely affectionate hug, walking slowly as she went.

'Give me a call if you have any work for me.' Wraither patted him on the shoulder. 'I think I'm gonna put you on my preferred client list, which makes you the first. Grats!'

'Where are you going to go?'

'I'm gonna go get some training,' she smiled. 'I need to refine my talents. I have plenty of power but nowhere near enough control over myself. As you've seen the only command I can really obey is 'kill that guy' and I don't have a lot of use for that if I can't do important things. No one wants a mad dog.'

'All right.' He patted her on the shoulder. 'Give me a call if you want to hang out, but, not that way.'

'Will do.' She walked out into the world again.

Pan was next, Annabelle seemed to be waiting for something despite her health. He embraced both of them, wrapping them into massive bear hugs.

'Let me know if you need anything okay?' Pan smiled. 'I know things aren't easy for you right now so if you feel like you're in trouble or if you just need to talk or hang out, I'm around. If you do decide you want to be one of us for real, let me know and I'll hook you up with the basics of how to survive in our world.'

'Sure.' And with that Pan was gone and Adam and Annabelle were alone.

'Hey,' she smiled at him and he sat down beside her. She pulled up the arm rest and hugged him. The two lay there for a while in each other's arms. 'I was wondering if you'd like to come home with me.' Adam let out a snort of laughter and she punched him in the arm. 'Not like that. Okay, maybe like that too, but I want you to come see the carnival with me. My sisters are putting on a show soon. It'll be fun and I could use the time to relax.'

'Yeah, sounds good,' he smiled. 'It'll be good for my recovery too. So, where do we go?'

'Sage,' Annabelle looked at him. 'Can we borrow your car? We won't be going far.'

'Yeah, it's fine,' Sage nodded. 'As long as it's within a few blocks I could probably use the walk.' He tossed her the keys and the two of them walked outside. The car in question had been mistaken for a broken down wreck in the front of the cinema. It smelled like weed and oil fumes and as it spluttered to life Adam wondered if his estimation of it being broken down wasn't too far off. The vehicle puttered a few blocks and up to what looked like some kind of museum. The two of them broke in with very little effort and made their way to the storage area. She stitched together the path to the other world in a few short minutes and together they made the walk into the spider world toward the carnival.

'Don't worry, we're safe here. These are my

spiders and they won't bother you.' It was less frightening now, though not much. He trusted her to protect him if things got strange and together they made their way toward the bright lights of the carnival.

They were delighted to see her. A string of brightly dressed acrobats and massive strong men, jolly looking clowns and various curiosities met her in a procession of hugs, handshakes and cuddles. The carnival shined in every direction and music bombarded them. Dozens of people lead her in every direction, looking for every exhibit. 'You have to see this watch me do this, watch, come see, it'll be great!' Annabelle lost herself in the atmosphere, insisting to Adam that they go see all the attractions and games and rides that anyone invited her too. He fought her on a few. The lady who couldn't feel pain was a little too close to home for one. She told him a few carnival stories and told them what happened to her, which earned Adam a few hateful glares. As she spoke to them her hair began to glow and when a woman with bright patterns glowing on her skin found her, she urged her into a tent. When she emerged she was wearing orange and blue, twirling to test out the garment and looked at them.

'Feels good to be home!' she told him.

'I still can't believe this is where you grew up.' He shook his head.

'I got to go to Earth a lot,' she confessed. 'I got a

few classes from various sources. It's how I learned all the basic stuff and I got to explore your world as well as mine.' She hugged a sword swallower tenderly and he pushed her away so he could go back to his show. 'But yeah, when you hear the word home you think of your suburbs or the city, when I hear home I think,' she gestured around herself. 'Popcorn and grease paint and bright lights and pretty colours. Now come on, we're about to put on the big show! We can watch it all from my owner's box!' She took off toward the main tent with an excited run and he had to sprint to catch up on worn out legs. He could have yelled at her to slow down but she seemed so happy.

The performers were spectacular, and what was even better was the fact that the Laughing One augmented his sight so he could see just how perfectly the two of them mixed with one another. The trick, he discovered quickly, was to throw in just enough real magic that no one would notice there was any at all. A bearded giant lifted a massive steel frame on which stood the entire rest of the performing cast and all of a sudden it collapsed, dropping into a mess. When the dust cleared only the strong man stood there, looking a little confused. The crowd was disappointed, which made them only much more delighted when they began to fall from the sky. As the excitement and wonder of the crowd rose, Adam noticed a steady trickle of some kind of light running from the crowd up to the VIP box, slipping into the VIP box, specifically into Annabelle.

'What are you doing with that?' He looked at her.

'We're draining a little of the excess magic from the civilians. That's how some of our number empower ourselves. This show is partly for me, to restore some of my power and energy. My body may have healed but my spirit is drained,' she said softly, shaking her head and smiling. 'They're so kind.'

'Really?'

'They take enough power to make it worth their while of course. They're not stupid, but they're sending most of it to me.' She looked genuinely moved. 'We've done it before for each other.' By the end of the show Adam saw that most of his time with Annabelle she'd been looking drawn, haggard, tired. She'd been working hard and it had taken its toll. He hadn't noticed because that was how she looked from the first time he met her. Now she glowed from the inside, her eyes bright and her face smiling. Her skin was healthier, her movements more active, the bags under her eyes were gone. She seemed so vital. As the final bows were taken, she rose and whistled, applauding as loudly as she could. He joined in, clapping and letting out a shrill whistle. He'd never been able to whistle until now.

'So they drained some of the energy out of people. Is that bad for them?'

'They'll sleep well tonight,' she shrugged. 'At worst, they might get the sniffles, but there's no chance of any real harm. I don't want anyone hurt. I want everyone coming back to the carnival. Pleasant experiences are the name of the game. Now come, I want a hot dog.'

Anywhere else they would have looked so strange. Him in an overcoat, gauntlets and his mask, her in swirling bright colours, but among the performers it would have been strange not to look strange. They spent the day like that, like children at a carnival, trying everything. He hadn't done a few of the rides and sideshows before and while he knew she'd done every part of this place at least a dozen times, she seemed almost childishly enthused about doing them all again. They talked about everything except the Legion, except the war.

'This place is great,' he decided and she shook her head.

'You haven't even seen the good parts yet. There are places in the other worlds out there that aren't like anything you ever imagined.'

'Will you show me?'

'Sure,' she nodded. 'Come on. I know just where to start.'

They took a walk through the carnival and climbed onto one of the cars of the ferris wheel. It was just like every carnival wheel. It was big, bright, colourful, spinning and a little less intact that any reasonable person would be comfortable with. The wheel creaked a little if you listened for it and he only got into the car because Annabelle had already climbed in. The two of them sat with his arm around her shoulders as they rode up to the top. When the car started to rock a little, he jumped and she laughed at him.

'You're afraid of heights?'

'No.' He shook his head. 'I have a fear of poorly maintained equipment that may cause me to fall to my death. The difference is subtle but meaningful.'

'The good news is this is magnificently maintained equipment. It rocks and creaks because it's supposed to. Places like this are supposed to be a little busted up. You're supposed to wonder, just a little, how safe you really are. That way you're a little happier when your feet hit the ground. Besides, even if the whole thing fell apart, I'd just web us to the frame and we'd climb down.' When the wheel stopped with them on the top she forced up the safety bar and threw out one hand, the web extending from it, to hit a piece of the spider web above. 'Take my hand.' He did and she started to lift, rise up into the air slowly but surely, the web retreating under Annabelle's skin as they rose up to the web.

'Where are you taking me?'

'I can show you a world.' She kissed him gently. 'Don't worry I've got you.' And surprisingly, he didn't worry. She lifted him higher and higher until they encountered fewer and fewer strands of web. Higher still until they finally came to the highest point, until they came to a single small spider web big enough for four or five people to lay on comfortably.

'This is mine,' she smiled. 'I made it myself, so I could look over my carnival and the world I live in. Now you can too.'

And he did. It looked like a strange quilting pattern, hundreds upon hundreds of white strands made out in designs he didn't recognise. Each one had its own internal order and fitted nicely into the scheme of everything around it in a way that seemed odd but somehow right. Some of the webs glowed with magic and others shined various colours. Every colour of the rainbow was mixed in with the white at one point or another. Where the stands grew thick there were places and things upon them, the carnival, suburban homes, a mansion, a barracks and if he looked very hard he could even see the curtained pavilion that he thought was where he had embarrassed himself and almost died with the Black Widow. He could only just make out the natives, most of them spiders, making their way around.

'It's actually kind of beautiful,' he realised. 'It's really scary, but yeah, kind of beautiful.'

'The whole world is like that I think,' she theorised. 'Our whole world anyway. It's fucked up and it's scary and it's beautiful. There's so much more to it than we can imagine and you could live a thousand years and still see new things.' She leaned over and kissed him. 'And that's why I can't ever leave it. I can't ever stop trying to make our weird and wonderful world better, more interesting. I hope you'll be there beside me while I do.'

'I'd like to,' he decided. 'And I do realise you just completely manipulated me into joining the war.'

'Oh I did not.' She shoved him. 'I want you there,

and I told you I wanted you there. That hardly counts as manipulation. '

'You're right,' he nodded. 'I just wanted to be there and it's easier for me if it seems like it's someone else's idea.'

'That's not a luxury I intend to give you,' she confronted him. 'If you want to make a choice you have to make the choice. That's on you.'

'You're right,' he nodded and looked out over the webs for a few full minutes. 'I'm staying because I want to,' he decided.

'Excellent.' She wrapped her arms around him and pressed her head to his shoulder. 'Well done. Now I want you to know that I would have done this whether you'd said yes, no or refused to answer.'

'Done what?'

'This.' She kissed him and pulled him down into the web.